FINDING ANNE *de* BOURGH

FINDING ANNE *de* BOURGH

a Regency romance by

RONDA GIBB HINRICHSEN

Covenant Communications, Inc.

Cover image: *Historical Girl in White Lacy Dress* © Magdalena Russocka / Trevillion Images
Steep White Chalk Cliffs at Birling Gap © GAPS / istockphoto.com
Cover design by Hannah Bischoff

Cover design copyright © 2019 by Covenant Communications, Inc.

Published by Covenant Communications, Inc.
American Fork, Utah

Printed in the United States of America
First Printing: May 2019

26 25 24 23 22 21 20 19   10 9 8 7 6 5 4 3 2 1

ISBN:978-1-52440-833-6

To Dawson and Madilyn. You bring joy to my life.

ACKNOWLEDGMENTS

FIRST AND FOREMOST, I MUST acknowledge Lizzie Huff. While her life has not been easy, she continues to inspire others through her goodness and her beyond-her-years understanding of what is truly important in life. I am one of those she has inspired, and Lizzie's words now live in this book through Gracie Bolton's last words to her father. Thank you, Lizzie. You are amazing.

Second, a tremendous, ongoing thank-you to my fellow Golden Pens: Josi Kilpack, Nancy Allen, Jennifer Moore, Becki Clayson, and Jodi Durfee. While our group continually changes, your help, wisdom, and encouragement never do.

Third, to Nancy at regencyresearcher.com. She doesn't even know me, and yet she promptly answered every Regency-era question I've put to her. She is a jewel.

Fourth, to my editor, Kami Hancock, whose expertise has been invaluable, and to all the kind and supportive people who work at Covenant Communications. Not only have they leant their talents and skills to make this book the best it can be, but they always have my back.

Last but definitely not least, to my dear husband and my wonderful family. Your love and support have made this book—and me—better. Thank you.

CHAPTER ONE

Hunsford parsonage near Rosings Park, 1813

Miss Anne de Bourgh set her kerchief in her lap and took the cup of tea Mrs. Collins, the clergyman's wife, held out to her. Anne lifted it to her lips, but as it was much too hot at present, she set it on the low table in front of her and took a finger-sized chocolate-topped biscuit from the serving plate. The pastry was sweeter than she had hoped it would be but still quite agreeable.

Mrs. Collins sat in the cushioned chair directly opposite Anne. "Mr. Collins tells me you and your mother are to leave us for Brighton in a month."

Anne offered a slight smile and a tiny nod.

"I hope Brighton will please you," Mrs. Collins continued. "I understand it to be a very fashionable resort where many of the *ton* retreat for the summer."

It is also famed for its debaucheries, overindulgences, and murders. Anne lowered her eyelids. It was the best way to hide her thoughts. "Mother considered Bath at first, but Dr. Crawford insisted sea-bathing in Brighton combined with its curative tonic would best heal my allergic rhinitis."

"Indeed." Mrs. Collins sipped her tea. "At any rate, you should not want for company. The society pages report Brighton has balls and soirees almost every night, which would indicate the presence of a number of eligible bachelors."

The two women looked at one another. Anne could not be certain, and she knew Mrs. Collins would never speak of it, but it seemed to Anne the names Miss Lydia Bennet and Mr. Wickham floated between them like a sour scent. Anne sniffed, coughed a little, touched her kerchief to her nose, and once again set it in her lap. "Mother deems Brighton will prepare me for London's Little Season in the fall."

"Where you will make an excellent match."

Again the two women looked at one another but said nothing. After all, what could either of them say that the other did not already know? Anne's mother was quite set on Anne making a match with a man of such good fortune and consequence that Mr. Darcy would at last recognize his great foolishness in choosing another over his cousin.

"Do you mind?" Mrs. Collins's voice was almost a whisper.

"My mother wants what is best for me."

For the smallest moment, Anne knew she had answered the wrong question, but Mrs. Collins, ever solicitous of Anne's feelings, quickly said, "To be sure."

Each glanced about the room. Several seconds passed.

"I must say again how very pleased I am you agreed to join me for tea this afternoon," Mrs. Collins said. "I so enjoy spending time with a friend."

A friend. Anne held the woman's gaze. The two met often, for Anne almost always stopped to visit Mrs. Collins when she went out in her phaeton, but there was certainly a loneliness in the woman's expression that reminded Anne of her own aching.

Anne bit the inside of her lower lip and swallowed. "I do not mind, you know."

Mrs. Collins lifted an eyebrow, and Anne winced inwardly. Had she misinterpreted their sudden camaraderie? Hoping she had not, she leaned slightly toward Mrs. Collins and added, "About Mr. Darcy. I-I know Miss Elizabeth Bennet—Mrs. Darcy now—is your friend too."

"She is. The best of friends."

"And I know my mother has been—offensive. It has been seven months since their marriage, and still she insists we not correspond with them. But the truth . . ."

Mrs. Collins tipped her head slightly to the side. "Yes?"

Anne touched her kerchief to her nose. "The truth is I am not unhappy with the Darcys' marriage. Mr. Darcy, though always a gentleman, never showed a particular fondness for me. Or for Rosings."

"And you?"

"I-I was only humiliated by the rejection. He did not break my heart."

"I am very glad to hear it. I do hope Lady Catherine will also come to accept the event one day."

Anne nodded. "It is not easy for her. She is a strong woman and . . . hard-minded. I daresay she has learned to be so, l-living on her own in a world so controlled by men."

"Of course."

"She truly believes her way is the best way."

Mrs. Collins, lowering her teacup, smiled. "And feels it her duty to bless others with her wisdom."

"Indeed." Anne picked up her teacup. As she had hoped, her tea had cooled to the perfect temperature, and she took a sip. It had a slightly fruity undertone. Very nice.

"Tell me," Mrs. Collins said. "If you do not think me impertinent in asking, I often wonder to where you drive your fine phaeton on so many afternoons."

"It is no great secret. I take it round the perimeter of Rosings Park."

"I believe I envy you. There are several pretty wildernesses out there. Mr. Collins quite dotes on Mr. Soulden's gardening prowess."

Anne smiled slightly and nodded. In truth, the de Bourgh's aged head gardener was fully responsible for Anne's favored spot in all of Rosings Park: a secluded, shady, pine- and floral-scented alcove surrounded by yards and yards of daylilies. Anne would drive there again just as soon as she finished her tea with Mrs. Collins.

A man's voice yelled from somewhere outside.

Anne froze.

Mrs. Collins set her teacup on the sofa table and hurried to the window. "It is one of the undergardeners. I wonder what could be the matter." She glanced back at Anne, should have curtsied her leave but did not, and rushed from the room to the front door.

By then Anne had regained enough of her wits to set down her teacup and hurry after Mrs. Collins. One of the young undergardeners, splattered with more dirt than Anne was used to seeing on any of the Rosings servants, filled the doorway.

"Fire!" the man yelled. "Where's Mr. Collins?"

"Fire? Where?" Mrs. Collins said.

"At the edge of the park." Anne stood on her tiptoes, trying to see over and beyond the man's shoulder, but he was much too tall. "We need Mr. Collins," he said urgently.

Almost immediately Mr. Collins appeared at the top of the staircase behind them. "What is it?"

"Fire. And Mr. Soulden." The undergardener glanced at Anne. "Ring the church bell, if you please, sir. We need all hands."

"Yes, yes, of course." Mr. Collins patted his pockets for what Anne assumed was the church key and ran down the staircase. He nodded to Anne and, passing her and Mrs. Collins, raced out the door behind the now-retreating under-gardener.

Anne and Mrs. Collins hurried after them, and Anne searched the distance. A thick ribbon of black smoke billowed above the trees and into the sky in the vicinity of Mr. Soulden's cottage. Mrs. Collins gasped. Anne coughed, pressing her hand against her chest. Was Mr. Soulden all right?

Mrs. Collins whirled to face Anne. "Here, let us go back inside and"— the church bells rang—"wait there for news."

"No. Forgive me," Anne said. "I do not wish to be rude, but Mr. Soulden—" *is my friend.* "I must first see that he is well."

Mrs. Collins's jaw dropped. Her eyes widened. "I must advise against that. Your health is not strong."

Anne brushed past her. She rushed out to her horse and phaeton, which were waiting for her at the end of the drive.

"Miss de Bourgh, please. Stay here," Mrs. Collins called. "I am certain Mr. Soulden is safe."

How certain could she be with so much fire scorching the trees and so much black smoke blowing into the sky? Anne coughed, climbed up onto her phaeton's high-perched seat, and coughed again as she pulled into the lane. She coughed several more times, slowing only twice to recapture her breath on her race out to Mr. Soulden's cottage, where there seemed to be more smoke than air.

Fire blared through the nearby wilderness. It consumed Anne's beloved alcove and flowers, but so far the pond that divided the main gardens from the woodland kept it away from the estate's main grounds, and the rocky lane and wet grasses kept it from spreading farther into Hunsford. The dozens of Rosings menservants who bustled back and forth between the fire and Mr. Soulden's white two-story cottage, throwing water and beating out flames with whatever they could get their hands on, kept it away from the vegetable garden.

Anne climbed out of her carriage. "Where is the gardener?"

Plowman, the undergardener that often tended this section of Rosings, ran toward her. Soot streaked his face and clothing. "You best get yerself back to the house, miss."

"Not until I speak with Mr. Soulden." She took a step toward the cottage, but all at once her knees buckled, and she grabbed a carriage wheel for support. She closed her eyes, summoning the determination she had felt only a moment before, but rather than feeling strength, her stomach roiled and she broke out into a full-out coughing fit.

Plowman wrapped his arm around her waist, supporting her. "Please, miss. Let me take you back. We have everything under control here."

Cough. "I suppose I must." Cough. "Mr. Soulden—is he all right?"

Plowman frowned.

Anne's core turned cold. "What is it?"

He shrugged. His voice softened. "He is gone, miss."

"What do you mean, he is gone?" She scanned the grounds. "He would never leave. Especially not now."

"No. He is here. It is only . . ." The church bells gonged over the fire's crackles. "It appears his heart gave out. One of the other men said it happened the moment he saw that flower garden of his catch fire."

The flower plot he called *Anne's Garden*. Smoke filled her lungs, stung her eyes. She slumped, teetered. "He is dead?"

"Yes, miss."

She doubled over, her coughing intensifying.

Plowman caught her. "Please, miss. We must get you home." He moved to help her into the carriage.

Dead? Anne inhaled and coughed again.

Plowman lifted her into the carriage, squeezed into the single seat next to her, and flicked the horse's reigns.

Less than ten minutes later, Plowman lifted Anne from the carriage and hurried her to the house. As all the menservants were at the fire, Anne's mother and two of the housemaids met them in the entry.

"What has happened?" Lady Catherine said. "Is Anne all right?"

"I believe she has had quite a shock, my lady."

"Of course she has. This is all very distressing. And the grounds? Is the fire contained?"

"I believe it is. We are doing our best." Plowman set Anne in the corner chair.

"Mr. Soulden—" Anne coughed. Would she ever again take a full breath?

Her mother flicked her hand, indicating for the housemaids Burk and Hale to tend to Anne, and turned back to Harris. "What does Mr. Soulden have to say about all of this? Does he know what started the fire?"

Plowman removed his cap and looked at the floor.

"I demand you tell me what has happened. Is Mr. Soulden's cottage ruined?"

"The cottage still stands, my lady, but Mr. Soulden . . ." Plowman twisted his cap and glanced at Anne then back to her mother as if afraid. "He is dead."

Anne's mother stared at him, and Burk and Hale gaped at one another. Moments passed.

"If it does not inconvenience you, my lady, I believe I am needed back at the fire."

"Yes, yes. You may go."

Plowman nodded, put his cap back on his head, and left.

"How odd," Anne's mother said when the door clicked closed behind him.

Odd? Anne thought. *It is horrible. Mr. Soulden is—was—my friend.*

"To be sure, your ladyship." Burk brushed ashes from the fur collar of Anne's cloak. "To think Mr. Soulden would die the very day—"

"Perhaps even the very moment—" Hale cut in.

"—that Mrs. Jenkinson died."

Anne coughed yet again. Her heart thundered against her chest. "How can Mrs. Jenkinson be dead? She was well this morning."

"'Twas a sudden fit, miss," Burk said.

"'Twas as if all of our guessings were right." Hale's voice rang like the inside of a hollow canister. "That she and Mr. Soulden truly did have another-worldly love for one another."

Burk pressed her hand against her chest and closed her eyes. "A love they could not have in life yet still bound them in death."

Anne's mother scanned the length of her daughter then turned back to the maids. "I will not have such fanciful gossip in this house. You will now take Anne to her room. And send her lady's maid to tend to her."

On that score Anne fully agreed with her mother. Mr. Soulden and Mrs. Jenkinson could not have had hidden feelings for one another. Mr. Soulden never entered the house, and Mrs. Jenkinson only ever left it when she was with Anne. In truth, they, in all likelihood, had never even been officially introduced.

None of this makes any sense, Anne thought. How could both Mr. Soulden and Mrs. Jenkinson be dead? On the same day? *What is going on here?*

CHAPTER TWO

Lees village, East Sussex

AT LEAST TWENTY FAMILIES HAD attended that morning's church service.

"There were fewer than I had hoped there would be," Mr. Brummell, the real curate, whispered to Kenneth Bolton as they stood side by side at the door bidding farewell to the congregants. "But it was a good showing nonetheless."

"I am grateful for whatever they can give." Kenneth wiped the sweat from the back of his neck beneath the black, wide-brimmed hat and white collar he had filched from his own local curate and brushed the dirt from the front of the black suit. He took a deep breath. All this getup had to do was get him through a few more hours of separating these pigeons, these people, from money he needed more than they did. He could manage the discomfort for that long. And since Mr. Brummel had expected a larger congregation, there were very likely more good souls in town willing to add to his purse.

One by one, the male parishioners dropped coins into Kenneth's collection purse. He grinned. Lady Luck had definitely smiled upon Kenneth the moment he'd come over the hill and seen this village spread out before him like a goose waiting to be plucked on Christmas morning—a goose Kenneth had no qualms about plucking until Mrs. Sweet, the aged woman who shared her home with the Brummells, stepped out the church door and handed him two shillings. It was much more than Mr. Brummell had suggested she could afford to donate, and guilt momentarily scratched the back of Kenneth's throat. He, an able-bodied man, was taking means from a feeble-bodied woman.

Kenneth gritted his teeth and lifted his chin. He might be able-bodied, but after his ability to feed and care for his daughter had been taken from him, what else could he do? He adjusted his too-tight collar.

A man holding a shabby brown hat and wearing dirtied farm clothes came up the path from the direction of the village center and stopped at the end of the lane. He nodded to Kenneth, who turned his attention back to the parishioners leaving the church.

Mr. Brummell, on the other hand, motioned to the man at the end of the lane. "It seems news of your cause has already spread through the parish."

"I hope you are right." Kenneth added an optimistic lilt to his voice, but he felt none of it.

The disheveled man, with his slight frame, smattering of blond hair, and especially his slackened stance could only be George Seymour in disguise. Seymour—the neighborhood lad Kenneth had grown up with. The friend—another confidence man—who had later joined Kenneth and his other accomplices in their travelling town-to-town shams. How Seymour had found him Kenneth could only guess, though he was certain it was no real trouble for Seymour. The man had always had a nose for locating people. That was his specialty.

The last gentleman to leave the church handed Kenneth a crown. "This is not much, but I do hope it will help the unfortunate souls of Youngston who lost so much to that fire."

"Thank you for your generosity, sir."

After the man left, Kenneth thanked Mr. Brummel for his help as profusely as he felt appropriate then walked straight to Seymour. Seymour tipped his hat to him.

"Since you are here," Kenneth said under his breath, "I take it the marks are finally where we want them."

Seymour glanced over his shoulder. No one was around, as far as Kenneth could see, but still Seymour made a grand show of taking a few coins from his pocket and dropping them into Kenneth's purse. "They are. Lady Catherine de Bourgh and her daughter have just arrived in Brighton."

"Took weeks longer than I expected."

"Leon had many arrangements to make. There must be nothing out of the ordinary. Nothing suspicious."

Two young women came up the path from behind Seymour. Seymour stepped to the side, pulled a not-quite-clean handkerchief from his vest pocket, and patted his forehead while the young ladies handed Kenneth a few coins. Kenneth, thanking them, tipped his hat to them.

When they were out of hearing range, Seymour said, "I will meet with the de Bourghs the day after next. You are to meet Evans at the Old Bamber Cottage in five days."

The two men stared at one another. While the gang had met last year to plan this scheme, it had been ten years since they had actually played one out. Were the four of them still up for the challenges ahead of them?

Finally, Kenneth and Seymour tipped their hats to one another and walked in opposite directions. Kenneth exhaled, but still guilt tightened his chest. He had promised his wife, Bridget, his old associations were in the past and he would never again fall in with his former ways, but with Bridget having passed and his daughter ill—Kenneth kicked a rock off the path—what other choice did he have? Besides, if Bridget still lived, if she knew what he owed Leon, she would understand. He hoped.

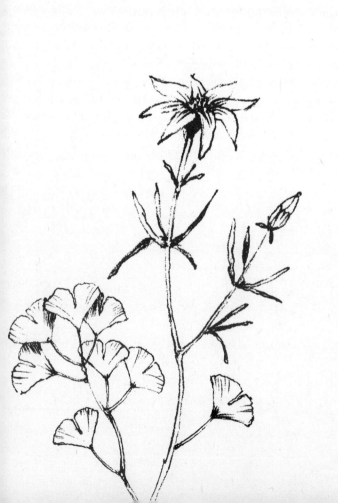

CHAPTER THREE

Brighton, East Sussex

ANNE, WEARING HER BLUE WALKING dress and her sturdiest shoes, stood before the dining room door of their Brighton townhouse. She took in a tight, though full, breath. The sea air still smelled of fish, just as it had yesterday afternoon when she and her mother had returned to this townhouse after their morning appointments, but she did not mind that one bit. Not if such air was the reason she had not needed to wipe her nose even once since retiring to bed last night. Back at Rosings, not an hour would pass without her having to pay such attentions to her health. Perhaps Dr. Crawford was right and the seaside was really, already, healing her. *I hope so.*

She inhaled again and entered the dining room. Brighton might be where her mother intended for Anne to regain her health and prepare herself to make an excellent match in London, but those facts, those entertainments, must not stop Anne from following her own pursuits.

"I am glad you are here, Anne," her mother said. "This is all so very vexing."

Avoiding her mother's gaze so as not to lose her courage, Anne leaned her least-plumed umbrella next to the door and set her reticule, bonnet, and leather-bound drawing pad on the tripod table beside it. She faced the other women. Mrs. Webb already sat in her assigned seat to the left of Anne's mother, who sat in the more intricately carved chair at the head of the table.

Anne clenched her skirt with both hands. "What is vexing?"

Mrs. Webb, Anne's new lady's companion, demurely bowed her head, and Anne took a tiny backward step. She should certainly be accustomed to seeing Mrs. Webb sitting there in pale-green calico rather than Mrs. Jenkinson in her austere black. It had been nearly a month since Mrs. Jenkinson had died of what Dr. Crawford had surmised were the results of old age or perhaps gastric fever. Yet every time Anne saw Mrs. Webb, she felt slightly taken aback. Why that was so she could not say with any sense of conviction. Perhaps it was because Mrs. Webb seemed to know Anne better than she did herself, quite often predicting her whims, interpreting her moods, calling for her lady's maid before Anne knew she wanted her. Mrs. Jenkinson had been more of a background fixture in Anne's life than was this youngish widow with smooth skin and strawberry-blonde hair. In truth, if Mrs. Webb did not so willingly always defer to Anne's whims, society would assume Anne was the lady's companion and Mrs. Webb the mistress.

"Of course I am speaking of the fire at Rosings." Lady Catherine motioned for Anne to sit in the chair at her right. "I have just had word from the man I hired to look into what caused it, and it is as I suspected. A woman in the village saw a thin, almost bald man running out of the wilderness shortly after it started."

Images of Mr. Soulden, of how he must have lain on the ground outside his cottage, filled Anne's mind, and her knees momentarily gave way. She took hold of her chair back for support.

"Miss de Bourgh?" Mrs. Webb jumped out of her chair and rushed to Anne's side. She wrapped her arm around her waist. "Are you well?"

"I will be in a moment," Anne said slowly. "I am afraid I am still upset about"—the deaths—"the fire."

"As well you should be." Mrs. Webb helped her into her chair. "You said Mr. Soulden was your friend."

"And an able gardener," Anne's mother said. "Soulden will be missed, but it is high time you put such things behind you, Anne. You can only mourn for so long. You must now collect yourself and move on with life. There is much ahead for you. Certainly you see that."

Anne nodded both to her mother and to Mrs. Webb, indicating she could now sit well enough on her own, then wiped her nose. Apparently Brighton's air had not healed her as much as she had hoped. "W-why would anyone intentionally set fire to Rosings Park?"

"I cannot say," her mother said. "But you can be sure if ever the man is found, he will pay for what he has done. Your father had a particular fondness for those woods, as do you, and he would never have let such nonsense go unrecompensed."

The woodlands . . . the daylilies Mr. Soulden grew just for me . . . "What is to be done?"

"The only thing that can be done. We wait for the culprit to be exposed. When he is, I will know what to do." Her mother hesitated as if seeing Anne for the first time. She scanned her attire. "I trust you slept well."

And just like that, the subject had changed. As if Mr. Soulden was nothing more than a check mark off her mother's daily task list.

Anne stared at her empty plate in front of her. She took her serviette from the table and placed it in her lap. "I did. Thank you."

Her mother nodded. "I understand from Mrs. Webb you slept longer than you had intended. I did wonder if I should have your lady's maid wake you earlier, but as our travels to Brighton were so wearying and our days since have been so filled with important visits with the local gentry, I saw no harm in letting you stay to your bed this morning. You will want all your strength for this afternoon. You may take a nap after breakfast, if you wish. Lady Barrington and her daughter are calling on us as a prelude to an invitation to their small soirée this weekend."

Anne, coughing slightly into her handkerchief, pushed her memories of Mr. Soulden's and Mrs. Jenkinson's funerals to the back of her mind. "I am well now, Mother."

Her mother, her eyes narrowed, scrutinized Anne. At last she nodded, and Anne inhaled with relief. She sat up taller, proving she was in better health. Talk of Mr. Soulden had made her momentarily forget her morning's purpose, but no more. *Courage, Anne.*

The butler brought in their breakfast: toast, hot chocolate, eggs, and sliced ham. Anne took a bite of her eggs. She swallowed it, took another bite, and glanced up at her mother. Lady Catherine stared at her. Anne stopped chewing.

Her mother buttered a piece of toast. "I see you and your companion are dressed to go out."

Anne swallowed her second bite. Despite all her practicing in front of her bedroom's full-length mirror, the words she had meant to say to her mother became a cottony lump in her mouth. "W-we are going out."

Her mother pursed her lips, and Mrs. Webb gave Anne such a pointed look Anne in no way could misunderstand her meaning. *Lady Catherine is not the queen of the world. She is only your mother—a woman like every other mother in every other sphere.*

Anne cleared her throat. "It has been at least two weeks since we left Rosings, and I last drove my phaeton." Mrs. Webb arched her eyebrow, and Anne spoke louder. "I find I miss the exercise." *And the freedom.*

"Even if we had brought your phaeton," her mother said, "I would not allow it. There are already far too many carriages on these roads. And pedestrians walking wherever they see fit."

"I did not mean I wished to drive my phaeton today. I-I only meant to say I wished to go out. To walk." Mrs. Webb gave her another nod of encouragement, and Anne added, "D-Dr. Crawford advised exercise, did he not? That it would, at the very least, heighten my complexion?"

Once again her mother narrowed her long-held gaze. "I am excessively concerned over such a prospect. And yet . . ." She stared blankly in front of her. "And yet, Darcy . . . no amount of telling him what to do helped him, did it?" She blinked and looked back to Anne. "Very well. As you must seize every opportunity to improve your health and heighten your complexion, you may have your way this morning."

Anne nodded but dared not smile. Too much hope might cast an evil eye on her efforts.

Her mother took another bite of her toast. Swallowed. Sipped her chocolate. "But you will not travel too far from this house. No matter how beneficial the sea air may be for you, Anne, doing too much too soon is never good for the system. Dr. Crawford agreed most heartily with me on that account, as I expect will Dr. Fletcher, the physician Dr. Crawford recommended we see while we are here in Brighton."

She turned to Mrs. Webb, scrutinizing her so acutely that if she had been Mrs. Jenkinson, she would have squirmed in her seat, but all Mrs. Webb did was smile prettily and lower her gaze.

Anne's mother continued in her severe tone. "Anne has been about Brighton with me enough these past days to become familiar with it, but if something happens, if she should even come down with another cold, I will hold you responsible."

"Yes, your ladyship."

"I will be careful, Mother," Anne said.

Lady Catherine bit into her toast once again. "Where will you go, Anne?"

"I had planned—"

"A walk along Marine Parade. Of course you have. While our townhouse here is not what it should be, at least this road is along Brighton's most respectable district."

"I—"

"Only you must be sure to take care, my dear. I see you have your parasol, but I insist you will not fail to wear your bonnet. It is overcast, to be sure, but any amount of sunlight reflecting off the ocean can sorely harm skin as delicate and snowy white as yours. You would not wish to look like a strawberry when Lady and Miss Barringer visit. And especially not at tomorrow night's ball."

"No, Mother."

"And when you have finished your walk, which I insist will be a short one, you will return home and rest. You will never gain your full strength unless you also take time to rest."

As her mother droned on about the Barringers' visit and the musical soirée they would attend that evening, Mrs. Webb motioned slightly toward the door, and Anne took a deep breath. She lifted her chin. *I must assert myself.* "I am afraid I will not be able to do all of those things today, Mother."

"Do not be ridiculous. Of course you will."

"Forgive me. I do not mean to be discourteous. I have simply made other plans." Another nod from Mrs. Webb. "P-plans I have been most anxious to begin since we first left Rosings."

Lady Catherine's eyes bulged wide—whether in surprise or irritation, Anne could not determine, but inside Anne's stomach roiled. *Do not back down. You have nearly succeeded.*

"What plans are these? I insist you tell me."

"An expedition of sorts. I-I hope to find some *Clematis fusca* and *Strobilanthes nutans.*"

"In English, if you please."

"One is a purple virgin's bower." Just as Anne feared, which is why she had used the Latin term in the first place, her mother's cheeks flamed at the title, while Mrs. Webb modestly lowered her eyelids. "The other—I do not know it's common name—has flowers that are—are such lovely pendulums of tassels I simply cannot w-wait to see them." Anne wiped her nose. "I have not found any in Kent, and I—they would make such fine additions to my drawing pad."

"I had hoped you had given up this fancy for plants, my dear. Sketching plants, unlike music, will never be considered a great talent among society, and especially among unmarried gentlemen of fortune. I suppose your drawing talent could be a slight diversion in some circles, but it will never be considered as fully accomplished if you insist on using pencils rather than paints and if you continue to bury your talent in simple plants. Surely there are more refined subjects you could put your ability to. I am well acquainted with many people of consequence who would happily sit for a portrait. Or perhaps a landscape. But you must use paint."

Anne, glancing at Mrs. Webb, set her fork next to her plate and lowered her gaze. If only her mother—or someone—would value Anne's enjoyment of plants as much as she did. "More refined subjects there may be," Anne mouthed. "But not more magnificent ones."

"Speak up, Anne. I must know what you said."

"I only meant—plants, having been created by God, are naturally perfect, and I-I find I enjoy sketching perfection."

"Hmm." Her mother studied Anne, pursing her lips.

Anne squirmed.

"Drawing does have a habit of brightening your eyes," her mother said at last, "which adds to your many charms. Very well. You may follow your planned diversion for a short while today."

I can? Really? "Thank you, Mother."

Her mother held up her hand. "However, in the future, you will consult with me on all your planned activities before you set your mind to them. Every night and even some of our days here in Brighton, there are medically prescriptive measures you must make and events you must attend to."

"Yes, Mother." Anne stood. Mrs. Webb did too.

"You and Mrs. Webb will return by one o'clock"—

That only gives me little more than two hours. How can I possibly locate and draw the plants in that short a time?

—"for you must be here to attend upon the Barringers."

So while her mother had given Anne permission to draw, the activity would not take away from her mother's plans. "Yes, Mother."

"And, as tomorrow night's ball is your first entrance into society, while we are limiting much of the pomp and circumstance due to your mature age, I have commissioned a topaz ring to be made for you to commemorate the day. The jeweler assured me he would have it ready for you tomorrow if we visit his shop and have your finger measured."

Anne groaned inwardly. Perhaps her mother believed they would attend the ball without pomp and circumstance, but Anne knew the moment her mother strode into the ballroom, with her head held high and Anne following behind her, every eye would turn to them as readily as if they were members of the prince regent's court. Why should they not? Her mother was the daughter of an earl, after all, as well as the wife of the late Sir Lewis de Bourgh, who had been the knighted and extremely wealthy gentleman owner of Rosings Park.

Mrs. Webb touched Anne's elbow. "Shall we leave, Miss de Bourgh?"

"Yes." Anne nodded to her mother, Mrs. Webb curtsied, and the two headed for the dining room door.

Before they reached it, her mother said, "As you will not walk along Marine Parade today, you will go to one of the nearby pleasure gardens. There are several near the Steyne Road. Some, I understand, are rather pretty and contain an ample number of plants. You will stop in at the Donaldson Library. Someone there will certainly be able to tell you where your specific plants might be found, if they are indeed here in Brighton."

"Yes, Mother."

And with that, Anne and Mrs. Webb quickly left the dining room. When they were partway down the hardwood staircase, Mrs. Webb said, "Upon my word, I hope you are proud of yourself, Miss de Bourgh. You were both assertive and bold without being unladylike or overbearing."

Was I? Anne bounced slightly on her toes. It was an indecorous action entirely unbefitting the heiress of Rosings Park, but thankfully, Mrs. Webb looked discreetly away. It was as if Anne's companion knew that no matter how stoically a girl controlled her thoughts and words, her actions simply had to defy them once in a while, or she would burst.

"I do wish my mother had allowed us more time. I doubt I can both locate the plants and sketch them within two hours."

"I daresay the time is unfortunate, but still, it is a step in the right direction, and we will do with it what we can." Mrs. Webb's smile, which was much more appropriate and certainly prettier than Anne's, disappeared the moment they rounded the final landing.

Mrs. Kelton, the housekeeper, and a young maid Anne had not seen before stood in front of the statue of a Roman goddess that filled the corner of the room closest to the grand entrance. Anne knew exactly how that goddess felt—or would have felt if she were alive, of course. It stood so quietly, just as Anne did, with her face veiled and with no one noticing the apple—the bounty—she would willingly share with them if ever they noticed her.

The housemaid glanced at Anne, curtsied to Mrs. Kelton, and hurried to the door that led to the back of the house. Mrs. Kelton, in turn, waited at the end of the railing until Anne and Mrs. Webb fully descended the staircase. Mrs. Kelton, wringing her hands in nervousness or worry—Anne could not determine which—glanced at Mrs. Webb and curtsied to Anne. "Good morning, Miss de Bourgh."

"Good morning."

After they passed her, the housekeeper headed to the same door the housemaid had just disappeared behind.

"I wonder if she knows where I might find the plants," Anne whispered to Mrs. Webb.

"Ask her," Mrs. Webb said. "Upon my word, if she knows, we can skip the library."

Anne bit the inside of her lower lip, nodded to her companion, and called out to the housekeeper, "Just a moment, if you please."

Mrs. Kelton turned back. "Yes, miss?"

Anne glanced at Mrs. Webb then took a deep breath. *Heaven and earth, why does my nose have to run now?* Anne quickly took her kerchief from her reticule, wiped her nose, and said, "As you are so much more familiar with Brighton than I am, Mrs. Kelton, I wonder if you could tell me where I might find two particular plants. I have heard they can be found here in Brighton. And I-I wondered if you might know in which garden I might best chance to locate them?"

"Plants, miss?"

"Flowers, actually." Anne described them.

Mrs. Kelton wrung her hands again, though slower this time. "I am not familiar with those particular flowers, but if anyone has them, I would expect they would be in one of Lady Talbot's gardens. I do not believe they are open to the public, but Lady Talbot's flowers always win Brighton's flower competitions. And my son is an undergardener there; he frequently tells me he has so many different watering and fertilizing schedules in his head to accommodate all of Lady Talbot's beauties, as she calls them, that he cannot put one more fact into his brain."

"Her gardens sound perfect," Anne said.

"Where are they?" Mrs. Webb added.

"It is not far. A little more than half a mile west of here is all—the estate at the end of Marine Parade. Seawind House, it's called. Belongs to Sir William Talbot."

Lady Catherine cleared her throat. Anne had not heard her mother arrive at the top of the staircase, but nonetheless, there she was, standing with her back so straight and her hand so decidedly poised on the bannister she seemed a queen gazing down upon her subjects. "You will go to Seawind House," she said to Anne. "Lady Talbot is a longtime friend of mine. Be sure to mention my name at her door, and I am sure her servants will accommodate you."

"That is most kind of you, Mother."

Mrs. Webb, smiling softly, curtsied to Lady Catherine, and she and Anne headed to the door. Mrs. Kelton came to open it for them.

"And if you chance to meet her son, Sir William Talbot," Lady Catherine called out, "be sure to mention we will be most pleased to see him at tomorrow night's ball."

"Yes, Mother."

CHAPTER FOUR

Brighton

Mr. Owen Talbot removed the shovel from the hook on the toolshed's wall. He hung his black tailcoat in its place and rolled up his sleeves. His mother had just finished her birthday breakfast, and judging by the three tick marks she had already penciled next to her list of ten riddles—er, *clues*—it would not be long before she would be nosing about the garden looking for her gift. He had better bury it directly.

He pressed his hand against his hip pocket, ascertained the small box had indeed not slipped out, and quietly limped out of the toolshed and along the cobbled footpath past the stable. It had only been two weeks since he had last inspected these gardens, but already the hedges of the maze his father had commissioned the year before his death had thickened. And the top and sides of the terrace that led into the flower garden bloomed with red and white roses. Owen smiled.

"Red, the color of blood, and white, the color of death," his mother would say the minute she stepped through it, which could be at any moment.

He hurried down the path toward the farthest corner and heard female voices. Surely his mother had not come out there already. "Hello?"

A slender young woman with thick dark hair that would not quite stay hidden beneath her bonnet and her not yet middle-aged, red-haired companion stepped out from behind the laburnum tree's cascade of thick golden leaves. The younger woman glanced at his corrective shoe and leg brace then lifted her gaze to his. Maybe he was imagining it, but it seemed her warm brown eyes softened not with pity—he was used to that—but with . . . was it understanding?

"There you are." She looked at her elder companion—the woman nodded—and moved toward him. "W-we called at the house a moment ago. A servant said we might find you here."

Owen frowned. He had not seen anyone about when he had crept out the door. Was he already found out? "Which servant told you I might be here?"

The young woman's gaze wavered. She pressed her hand against her upper chest and, rubbing her throat, looked back to the other woman. Had he upset her? He could not see how, but something was amiss. Was she nervous? "Are you unwell, miss?"

She shook her head. Her companion, however, stepped forward and said with an air of confidence he did not expect, "She is perfectly well, sir. She is only newly arrived in Brighton, and I am afraid she is not comfortable with—"

"The heat," the young lady cut in breathily.

He glanced back to the manor. Thankfully, there was still no sign of his mother. Perhaps his remaining riddles were more puzzling than he had believed. He hoped.

He turned back to the ladies. "Let us see what we can do to relieve your discomfort."

Owen did not believe the heat had anything to do with the young lady's pink cheeks, but it would not be appropriate for him to question her further. He again glanced at the manor then motioned for them to follow him toward the shade next to the section of the garden where he was headed. He limped rather quickly, he feared, but the ladies kept up with him.

A few steps before they reached their destination, the young woman, who walked directly behind him, said softly, "The servant was an elderly woman."

Owen looked over his shoulder. The young lady glanced up at him from beneath her thick eyelashes then dropped her gaze. It was most definitely understanding that filled her, not pity. He swallowed. At the same time, something inside him settled. "Thank you." Why had his voice squeaked? He cleared his throat. "The servant must have been the housekeeper, Mrs. Graham." At least Mrs. Graham could be trusted not to tell his mother where he had gone.

The three stepped into the shade.

"It seems you have recovered," Owen said to the young woman.

"I have. Thank you, sir."

"I am glad to hear it. Now, what can I do for you ladies?" He glanced toward his intended plant. It was only a few feet away. *Hurry.*

The older woman nudged the younger one, who then clenched the drawing pad in her hands and cleared her throat. "We heard of Lady Talbot's fine a-and varied gardens. We hoped she might have two specific specimens. Virgin's bower or *Strobilanthes nutans.* I want to—to sketch them."

"You are an artist?"

She glanced at her companion. The older woman squeezed the younger one's elbow and looked at Owen. "It is a passion of hers, sir. She is quite skilled."

"Not *quite* skilled," the young woman said. "But I do enjoy drawing."

Owen held the young woman's gaze. He ought not do so, for every time he did she quickly lowered her eyelids in obvious embarrassment. Yet he could not seem to help himself. On the chance moment when his gaze latched with hers, indescribable pleasure shot through his heart. Far be it from him to let such a moment pass. "You are in luck. We have the *Strobilanthes nutans.*"

The young lady nodded, and the older woman said, "If you would be so kind as to show us where it is, we would be most obliged."

"M-my mother, Lady Catherine de Bourgh, said to mention her name if there was a concern. She is a friend of Lady Talbot's."

Owen arched an eyebrow. After his mother had read in the *Morning Chronicle* of Lady Catherine de Bourgh's arrival in Brighton, she had told him that while the lady had been her closest friend in years past, most hereabouts knew her as a domineering *grand dame* who claimed control of all around her. His mother knew little of the daughter, however. Only that she had not been introduced into society when she was of age, and she had been recently snubbed in marriage to Mr. Fitzwilliam Darcy of Pemberley. Foolish man, to snub this delightful, quiet young woman. "You are Miss de Bourgh, then?"

"I am."

He peered back to the house.

"If you will only point us in the right direction," she prompted.

He turned back to Miss de Bourgh, but it was not she who had addressed him. He blinked, surprised he had made such a mistake, and focused back on Miss de Bourgh's companion.

"Pardon me," Miss de Bourgh said. "This is Mrs. Webb."

Mrs. Webb smiled slightly. Owen nodded and turned back to Miss de Bourgh. "The plant you seek is over there, in a square of earth we call 'Uncommon Ground.' I will warn you, however, it is likely you will smell my plant before you see yours. Mine is called the voodoo lily."

"You have a *Dracunculus vulgaris.*" Miss de Bourgh clamped her hand over her mouth. The smell of rotting meat must have already reached her just as it had him.

"Why would Lady Talbot want a plant with such a foul scent in her garden?" Mrs. Webb said.

He smiled, and capturing Miss de Bourgh's gaze—finally she did not pull it away from him—he folded his arms in front of him. "It is because it smells like a dead body. She and the late Sir William had a keen interest in solving murder mysteries together. After he died, she missed both him and the activity so much that when she heard of this plant, she immediately acquired it. It was not until she had it safely planted in this garden that her mourning lifted."

"How odd," Mrs. Webb said.

"I think it is sweet," Miss de Bourgh said. "Can we see the voodoo lily?"

"By all means." He continued a few steps farther into the garden and jabbed the point of his shovel into the moist ground at the foot of the voodoo lily. Its tall stock had thick foliage and a bloodred, leafless stem growing up through the middle of a large purple spathe.

"Does the *ton* know of this?" Mrs. Webb said. "What do they think of Lady Talbot's interest in the macabre?"

"I can only speak for those in Brighton, but they tend to think more along the lines of Miss de Bourgh here. In truth, my mother's propensity for crime-solving is the very reason I am out here. It is her birthday today, and as a gift, I have fashioned her a crime to solve. The resolution, as it were, will be planted beneath the voodoo lily just as soon as I can manage to bury it."

The companion stared at him. "Your mother? You are Lady Talbot's son?"

"I am. You did not know?"

Miss de Bourgh's face visibly paled. With disapproval, no doubt. Owen's reputation as Lady Talbot's "other" son, the crippled one, must have preceded him. But out of respect for his mother's position in society, people usually kept their opinions of him to themselves. Perhaps Miss de

Bourgh's character was not quite as far removed from the rest of society as he had thought.

"We have put you out, then! I am sincerely sorry, sir." Miss de Bourgh's voice dropped so low it was almost a whisper, and he searched her expression. He had been wrong. Disapproval of him sat nowhere near her. What troubled her, then?

She licked her lips. "I thought you were the gardener. If I had known you were Lady Talbot's son, I would not have addressed you so informally. I would not have been—"

"Charming?" His compliment had the complete opposite effect to the one he had hoped for. Rather than smiling, she paled even whiter. *Miss de Bourgh is shy. Remember that.* "What I mean is you said nothing untoward, Miss de Bourgh, and you have certainly not put me out. As you can see, my mother has not yet arrived, so I still have time to complete my burying."

"I . . ."

"Yes?"

Miss de Bourgh, her eyes wide, glanced between him and Mrs. Webb.

Mrs. Webb nodded to her and stepped slightly forward. "We are grateful for your hospitality, but we are certain, because of your generous instructions, we can find the way to the *Strobilanthes nutans* on our own." She lifted a parasol above Miss de Bourgh's head and took her arm.

"I wish you would not go," Owen said. "Not just yet."

Miss de Bourgh hesitated, looked at her companion, and faced him. "Is there something we can do for you?"

Owen could not be certain, but Miss de Bourgh's voice seemed a little louder than it had before. Was she growing more comfortable with his company? His thoughts bounced. He liked that idea. But at the same time, he did not. A woman of her station would never think of him as anything more than an acquaintance. Or perhaps a friend.

"As a matter of fact, there is something you can do for me." He took the small box from his waistcoat pocket. "This is my gift for my mother. They are pearl-drop earrings. Until this moment I have intended to bury them in this box at the foot of this plant. Now, looking at the dirt and knowing how valuable the earrings are, I am wondering if I should change my plan. What do you suggest?"

Miss de Bourgh looked askance at Mrs. Webb, but when she merely arched her eyebrow, Miss de Bourgh pressed her small hand and long slender fingers against her upper chest. "I know nothing of your mother's tastes, sir."

"Nevertheless, I would like to know what you think."

"I believe . . ." She pressed her lips into a tight line and swallowed. "I believe you might want to consider a different plan."

"Such as?"

"Surely something so—so valuable, and I expect . . . sentimental, would be better given in privacy."

She tilted her head so prettily that, for a moment, all Owen could do was study her eyes, her mouth, the outline of her neck. *Come back to your senses, man.* "I expect you are right, Miss de Bourgh, but I likewise believe my mother would find digging for her gift to be an exciting adventure. That is why I initially settled on this method."

Miss de Bourgh lowered her gaze. "As I said, you do know her tastes, whereas I do not."

"I suspect, however, she may have other tastes, too, more in line with yours, Miss de Bourgh."

She did not smile, but at last light warmed her eyes. "Perhaps, then, you should do both."

"What do you mean?"

Her cheeks reddened. She bit her lower lip and again glanced at Mrs. Webb, but just as he was about to apologize for his presumption in asking such questions of someone he had so recently met, she tore a clean sheet of paper from her drawing pad and handed it to him. "Perhaps you could bury a different kind of treasure—something like a note telling her of your love for her. Hearing how you speak of her makes me think she may be the kind of woman who would appreciate such sentiment."

He watched her.

She wrinkled her brows, shuffling her weight to her other foot. "You can, perhaps, if you wish, give her the earrings later. Or maybe—maybe you might find another, more appropriate hiding place. And write in the note where the earrings are."

Still all he could do was stare at her. And clear his throat. And rub the back of his neck.

Her expression drooped. "Forgive me. It was a foolish idea."

"Not foolish at all. I like it very much. What is more, I believe my mother will find your plan both heartfelt and exciting. I do hope, however, it is not asking too much for you to help me with it?"

Miss de Bourgh's lower lip trembled. She turned to Mrs. Webb.

Mrs. Webb frowned, but all she said was, "It is your decision, Miss de Bourgh. We promised your mother we would return soon, but if you are not able to finish your drawing in time, I expect this gentleman will allow you to return another day."

"Yes! Please do come back. As many times as you would like. Only now . . ." Owen glanced back at Seawind House. While so far luck was still on his side and his mother had not yet come out in search of her gift, that situation could change at any moment. He handed the blank sheet of paper back to Miss de Bourgh. "Will you be so kind as to write the note for me?"

She sniffed and touched her handkerchief to her nose. "Surely you would not want a near stranger to help you write such a personal note."

He glanced again at Seawind House. Miss de Bourgh's question was almost as bad as the task at hand, for both required him to speak of the feelings in his heart, and he had never been able to do so with any degree of ease. In truth, he was loath to do so. He felt quite comfortable with conversing about things, even intimate things that did not get too close to his deepest feelings. But those that were too close—he pressed his lips into a tight line—opening his heart had always led to deep wounds.

"My handwriting is not as tidy as it ought to be," he said. It was not the best of pretexts, but as it was all he could think of as a reason to keep her there with him, it would have to do. "And a note such as this . . . you are right. My mother is sentimental. This note will likely be something she keeps for the rest of her life, and I would prefer my messy handwriting was not preserved with it." Would his excuse suffice?

It must have, for in the next moment Miss de Bourgh offered him a sad, no, a consoling smile, set the paper on top of her drawing pad, and took a pencil from her reticule. "How shall I address it?"

Really? She will do it? "There is a bench around the bend up there. Would you be more comfortable sitting?"

"This will do nicely. I have become adept at standing while I draw. How shall I address it?"

"Oh—write, *Mother*."

"Dear Mother, You know I am a man of few words . . ." Her fingers trembled as she wrote, but her voice and gaze up at him held firm. "Is that a true statement?"

"It is." But how did she know? Was his character really that obvious to others? To her?

"What shall I write next?"

"I am a man of few words, but I do not want this day to pass without letting you know . . ."

She looked up at him and spoke so softly he almost did not hear her. "Letting you know I love you?"

"Yes. Exactly that."

She finished writing the sentence. "Anything else?"

He swallowed again. "Perhaps you should stop since, as you say, I am a man of few words."

Miss de Bourgh's face paled. "Is it too much? I have another sheet of paper. I can rewrite it and leave out some of the words."

Fool. You have embarrassed her. Owen touched her forearm. "Please do not trouble yourself further, Miss de Bourgh. The letter is excellent."

She smiled, but it was not until he told her to finish the note with, "You will find your prize for solving the riddle in my coat pocket," that a bit of color returned to her cheeks.

He signed the note, folded it, and took up his shovel.

"Do you have something to bury the note in?" Miss de Bourgh said. "To protect it from the dirt?"

"It will not be buried for long. My mother had only a few riddles left to decipher when I left her. In truth, I am surprised she is not out here already."

Mrs. Webb scrunched her nose in disgust. "I doubt any woman would appreciate touching, much less keeping, a note that had been covered in dirt for any length of time."

Miss de Bourgh, her head bowed, once more reached inside her reticule. She retrieved a soft leather case, removed three drawing pencils from it, and handed it to Owen. "You may bury your note in this."

"I would not wish to trouble you."

"It is no trouble."

Their gazes locked.

"Thank you," he said.

"I-I believe we should go now," Miss de Bourgh said. "I am afraid we have already intruded upon your privacy long enough. I will return another day to draw the *Strobilanthes nutans*, i-if I am still welcome to do so."

"I would be disappointed if you did not."

Seawind House's back door opened. "Son?" his mother called.

Both Miss de Bourgh and Mrs. Webb stiffened.

"Wait there," he called back to his mother. "I am not quite finished."

"What shall we do?" Miss de Bourgh whispered.

"Follow this path," Owen said. "It will take you through the trees, out of sight of my mother, and to a gate. From there, turn left and take the dirt road back to Marine Parade."

"Thank you," Miss de Bourgh said. They turned to leave, but before they had taken more than a few steps, Mrs. Webb clasped Miss de Bourgh's elbow and whispered into her ear. Owen did not hear what the woman said, but when her mistress turned back to him, her face had once again paled, and when she spoke her voice trembled. "I h-hope we will have the pleasure of seeing you and your mother at . . . at the ball at Castle Inn tomorrow evening."

If you, my dear Miss de Bourgh, are there, "I will be there."

She nodded, and the two women headed down the path. Owen, though he should be digging, watched Miss de Bourgh's retreating figure until he could no longer see her.

CHAPTER FIVE

ALMOST THE MOMENT ANNE AND Mrs. Webb stepped inside the townhouse, Mrs. Kelton gathered up their bonnets and, as she proclaimed it to be at Lady Catherine's insistence, led them into the drawing room. Her mother sat in the center of the cream-colored empire sofa, facing the door. She wore her best afternoon dress in obvious preparation for their visit from the Barringers, but otherwise, her air was one of stately ease. In the armchair at her left sat a gentleman not much older than Anne.

"Ah, come in, my dear," her mother said. "This is Dr. Sinclair. He has been waiting for your arrival."

The doctor stood and bowed. There was nothing singular in his movements, but he was so vastly different than the man Anne had spoken with a short time ago in the garden—the man she now realized was Lady Talbot's son . . . Sir William Talbot, her mother had said—she mentally, if not physically, shuffled backward. Not only was Dr. Sinclair shorter and a great deal slighter in shoulder span and muscular definition than Sir William Talbot but his blond hair was also thinner, almost to the point of baldness, whereas Sir William Talbot's dark hair was thick and, though not curly, had a sense of controlled disorderliness about it. It was not unlike Anne's own hair before her lady's maid took charge of it each morning.

"Dr. Sinclair works with Dr. Fletcher," her mother said.

"Dr. Fletcher, yes, the man Dr. Crawford referred us to." Anne spoke softly, but when her mother gave her a narrowed *Has-your-walk-been-too-much-for-you?* look, she said louder, "Is this a social call, Dr. Sinclair?"

"A professional one, I am afraid," he said. "I humbly beg your pardon, Miss de Bourgh. I normally would not dream of intruding upon you and your mother's privacy so soon after your arrival, but as it regards your health, I feel I must do so. I will, however, be brief."

"Please sit down," her mother said as much to Anne as she did to the doctor.

Anne and Mrs. Webb took their seats on the cushioned bench at Lady Catherine's right, and Dr. Sinclair again sat in the seat at her left.

"I am grateful for your concern, I am sure." Anne's voice was both louder and stronger this time, was it not? She glanced at Mrs. Webb, but her companion only gave her a thin-lipped smile. She must not have been loud enough.

Dr. Sinclair reached to the floor and opened the black leather medical bag sitting next to his feet. He lifted out two glass medicine bottles. One contained clear liquid and the other a burned-pink liquid. "Dr. Fletcher has had your health much on his mind, Miss de Bourgh. Almost as soon as he knew you had arrived in Brighton, he said he would call on you, but when I told him I would be in this part of town sooner than he could get away from his other duties, he asked me to bring these to you and bid you begin taking them immediately. They are a most delightful rhubarb wine and sea water. Alone, as I am sure you have heard, each has astonishing medicinal properties, but together they are pure perfection."

Anne had not, in fact, heard of the tonics, but still she said, "Yes, sir."

"Yes, yes," her mother said. "You told me these same things shortly before Anne arrived. What I require to know, however, is what causes these tonics to be perfection?"

The doctor smiled. "Simply stated, Lady Catherine, they have the power to cleanse human systems of sickly impurities and to put minds and bodies in perfect harmony with one another." He handed the two bottles to Anne. "Dr. Fletcher prescribes that you drink a tablespoon of sea water with a cup of wine every morning for optimal benefit. In order that your health may improve as quickly as possible, he also advises you take your first draught now, then every morning before you take your first bite of breakfast, and then again before you sea bathe."

Anne looked at the bottles in her hand. She glanced at her mother. *I have to drink sea water?*

"Dr. Fletcher prescribes this?" her mother said.

"Yes, my lady. The sea water is what is generally termed as 'the cure.' The wine is Dr. Fletcher's personal prescription. He has sent a bottle of the wine for you as well, your ladyship, as it is a favored beverage among all of society."

Her mother narrowed her gaze, studying him, it seemed to Anne, but after a moment she took his offered bottle and nodded to Anne.

Anne read her bottles' large printed labels. "I wish Dr. Crawford would have told me the cure was sea water. I could have prepared myself for it."

"I assure you drinking sea water is a common practice. I can provide you with endorsements from several of Dr. Fletcher's other patients, if you wish, but it will take me a day or two to contact them—two days in which you will not receive the tonics' benefits."

Anne tapped the corks. She scrutinized Dr. Sinclair's firm expression and his pinkish, healthy-looking skin. "Do you drink it?"

"I do indeed, especially when I am feeling poorly, and I am soon after in full health."

Anne nodded. She clenched her hands in her lap. *Speak louder . . . make your own decisions . . . exercise.* And now she had to drink sea water? Were improved strength and health worth such things? Of course they were. But oh, how she right then wished they were not.

"Thank you for visiting us so promptly, Dr. Sinclair," her mother said. "You may return to Dr. Fletcher and tell him Miss de Bourgh has taken her first dose and she will be pleased to take the remaining draughts as he has prescribed."

Anne bit the inside of her lip. She had to drink the concoction *now*?

"You may also tell him Miss de Bourgh has her first sea-bathing appointment set for the beginning of next week."

"I am pleased to hear it. To relieve any misgivings you may have about how much you should drink, Miss de Bourgh, I am happy to help you with your first dose."

"Oh. I am sure I can"—her mother gave her another hard look—"of course. That is most kind of you." Anne went to the occasional table next to the door and retrieved one of the clean cups. Her mother must have already had her tea.

She took the cup to Dr. Sinclair and held it out in front of her. He dribbled the sea water into it, and Anne pressed her lips together to keep from wincing. How could anyone make themselves drink cold, salty, dirty water that fish, animals, and even people had swum in? He poured in the rhubarb wine, filling the cup almost to the rim, and she gulped. If rhubarb wine was anything like raw rhubarb, it would be as sour as green apples. Or worse.

He handed the concoction to her, and she, staring at it, held her hand against her roiling stomach. It was unthinkable to drink such a mixture.

"Drink up, Miss de Bourgh." Dr. Sinclair's eyes were almost as bright, almost as comforting as his smile, and all at once, her mother arched her eyebrow. Her *left* eyebrow. She was skeptical. But of what?

"This tonic is the first step to making your dreams a reality," he added.

What did Dr. Sinclair know of Anne's dreams? She again turned to her mother. Lady Catherine no longer arched her brow, but she watched Anne with too-careful, too-narrowed eyes. Something had certainly caught her attention. If only it were the tonic. If it were, she would insist Anne not drink it.

Anne brought the cup to her lips and closed her eyes. She had not summoned the image, but there the man in the garden—Sir William—was anyway. His face filled her mind and spread warmth through her body like thousands of tiny, tingling prickles. Not only his face but also the brace on his leg, his limp. Years ago, Rosings Park's housekeeper had told Anne about her sister, who had been born crippled just as Anne assumed Sir William had been. The apothecaries and surgeons had tried to correct the girl's infirmity, and they did have some success, but every day, the housekeeper said, her sister felt pain. Did Sir William suffer pain every day too? Had he felt pain while she was with him in the garden, though showed no sign of it? If he could keep his misery to himself, could Anne not keep her discomfort with this tonic to herself? "Must I drink all of it?" she asked.

"Yes."

She stared at the cup, held her breath, and managed several swallows before the sea water's salty rotten-egg taste overpowered the sour rhubarb. She gagged and gave the unfinished cup back to Dr. Sinclair. "I cannot drink more."

"I am afraid you will not receive the medicine's full effects without drinking the entire draught, Miss de Bourgh."

"Do not worry, Doctor," her mother said. "It is only a mild hesitation. Miss de Bourgh knows it is both her privilege and her responsibility to herself and society to become as fit and comely as she possibly can. Come now, drink it up, my dear. I am certain you will not find it too difficult to finish after considering the benefits."

Dr. Sinclair handed the cup back to Anne. She took it. How could she not? His expression shined with hope, while her mother's narrowed gaze demanded she give up her ridiculous sensibilities and drink the mixture. Despite her sickly constitution, Lady Catherine de Bourgh's daughter must not be seen as weak-willed.

"I will drink mine at the same time," her mother said. "Will that help?"

"Perhaps." Anne waited while her mother went to the tea set, opened her bottle, and poured some of the wine into a cup. She held it in front of her, as if she were about to toast someone, and once again Anne closed her eyes. She held her breath. Then, picturing Sir William smiling down at her as she wrote his note for his mother, she downed the rest of the medicine. She cringed, but somehow she kept her grimace to herself.

Her mother set her own cup back on the table next to the wine bottle and pressed her lips into a tight line.

"Very good," Dr. Sinclair said. "I daresay the tonic is not good-tasting, but I expect your experience will be the same as Dr. Fletcher's other patients have had, in that by the time you have finished both bottles, you will no longer notice its flavor."

By then my taste buds will be dead. Anne nodded and handed the cup back to the doctor. When he turned away and set the cup back on the table, Mrs. Webb slipped Anne a handkerchief.

"For your mouth," she whispered. "If you so feel the need."

Anne sighed her gratitude and dabbed the cloth to her lips and tongue.

Dr. Sinclair turned back to them. Anne pulled the kerchief from her mouth.

"I will leave you now," he said. "But if I am not mistaken, I will see you both at tonight's ball at Castle Inn."

Lady Catherine's glance between him and Anne hardened, and Anne again touched the handkerchief to her lips. What was her mother about, to seem so suddenly suspicious of a man's intentions toward her after she had practically forced her to drink his appalling medicine? Her suspicion of them was laughable. Sad, too, if Anne let herself think on it for too long. For the truth of the matter was no one, not Dr. Sinclair or Sir William or any other respectable man, would ever look twice at her. Except, perhaps, as a marriageable woman of good fortune. And while that might be enough for her mother, it certainly was not enough for Anne. Her gut had twisted at the feelings she had seen in Mr. Darcy's face when he had looked upon Miss Elizabeth Bennet that day they had met at Rosings, but not because she wished he would look at her like that. No. It had been out of a longing to have the same kind of relationship in her life, to find a man she could love and who would love her in return with that same intensity.

"You will indeed see us at the Castle Inn this evening, sir." Her mother emphasized the word *see*.

He hesitated, as if waiting for her to say more, but when she did not, he said, "Very good. Sir William Talbot invited me, and I find I am quite looking forward to it." He bowed to each of them, including Mrs. Webb, and started for the door.

He knows Sir William Talbot? "Just a moment, Doctor," Anne said.

The others turned to her with various levels of surprise, and for a moment Anne felt as if she would be sick. Was that why drinking sea water was so beneficial? Because it made a person throw up any impurities that might exist inside them?

"Yes?" Dr. Sinclair said.

Anne clenched her hands in her lap. Perhaps she never would find a man who would love her as she wished to be loved, but that did not mean she should not make herself pleasing enough to catch such a man's fancy in case he did cross her path. "I wonder, Dr. Sinclair, if you might know of any other medicines or actions I might take to"—*make me beautiful*—"improve my health?"

"As it happens, my dear lady, I do indeed." He set his physician's bag on the table next to the tea set, removed a sheet of paper from it, and took out his quizzing glass, which he kept on a ribbon hung around his neck. He scanned over the paper. "I keep at least three copies of Dr. Fletcher's 'Regimens for Good Health' with me at all times in case they are needed for moments like these. I am certain if you take the medicines Dr. Fletcher has prescribed for you and religiously follow these instructions, you will find greater health than you have ever imagined."

If he truly believes so little in my imagination, he must think me very dull indeed.

He handed the paper to Anne. She read the first listed items.

1. *Rise at five o'clock in the morning.*
2. *Take a brisk walk for about one mile before breakfast.*
3. *Drink the cure.*
4. *Eat a simple breakfast no later than eight o'clock consisting of a plain biscuit, broiled beef steak, and a half pint of ale.*

"Thank you, Doctor," Lady Catherine said. "Please tell Dr. Fletcher my daughter and I will follow his instructions meticulously."

He bowed and, smiling slightly, left. The moment the door closed behind him, Anne's mother said, "How did you find my friend Lady Talbot?"

"We did not see her," Anne said. "But we did meet her son."

"Oh? That is most pleasing. Were you able to ascertain whether or not he would be at the ball?"

"Sir William said he would be there, but I am not certain he was pleased with the idea. I cannot imagine a man with his limp would find dancing enjoyable."

"A limp?" Lady Catherine's eyes pinched as tightly as the knots on the doily under the tea set. She shook her head. "Sir William Talbot does not have a limp."

"He said he was Lady Talbot's son."

Lady Catherine closed her eyes and opened them again. "You must be speaking of her eldest son, Mr. Talbot. Sir William Talbot is Lady Talbot's second son. Well, we will not concern ourselves with that now. If Mr. Talbot is attending the ball, I daresay Sir William will be there too. We can correct your acquaintanceship then. Now, Mrs. Webb, if you will please take Anne to her room. I will send Blanc up to help her dress. The Barringers will soon be here."

"Yes, your ladyship."

The two left the drawing room. Through every step Anne kept her expression blank, but inside her emotions drooped. The man she had met in the garden was *Mister* Talbot, *not* Sir William. Certainly the lesser title lowered his status, but why should that matter? He was a man of consequence, was he not? And her mother had vowed Anne would meet many such men over the course of the year, though most of them, she had claimed, would be in London.

Anne frowned. But Mr. Talbot's status did matter. Not to her but to her mother.

CHAPTER SIX

Aliston, East Sussex

KENNETH LEAPT OFF THE HORSE he'd borrowed from the farmer he used to work for, returned it to the stable behind his sister-in-law, Fanny's, cottage, and again checked his jacket pocket. He did not open the money pouch, as the strings were still tied shut, but feeling along the outside, he was quite certain he had not lost even one of the coins he'd had when he'd left the last village. Eight pounds. Remarkable what a few days' work could get out of trusting hands. Enough to pay off his gambling debts, give Fanny and her husband, Neil, a half sovereign for taking care of his seven-year-old daughter, Gracie, and even buy a bit of food to last until he finished that de Bourgh charade.

He left the stable and headed for the cottage. Five days ago, the last time he had been there, it had been at about this same time of day. Fanny's children, Kenneth's niece and two nephews, had been running about in front of the house, squalling over one thing or another, but today the yard was as silent as a churchyard. Were the children napping? It would be a nice thing for Fanny if they were. Even Gracie could be a handful if she got it into her mind to be so. Or maybe the lot of them were out with Neil grooming the farmers' hedgerows at the front of the lane. Not that Neil would need their help. He had been an earl's undergardener before the earl had died and his estate entailed to another who had hired his own servants. Work had been hard to find after that, but in the end, the farmer had noted Neil's skills and taken him on to help him with his yards and family garden. The job didn't use all Neil's skills, nor did it pay what he'd gotten from the earl, but it was work. He and Fanny were glad for that.

Kenneth knocked softly on the plank door in case anyone was sleeping. No one answered, and as there were no windows at the front of the house, he could not look inside, so he knocked again a little louder.

At last Fanny opened the door. A few strands of her dark hair drooped wet with sweat out of their bun and hung along the side of her face and neck. Her hair was the same dark brown—the same rich color his departed wife, Bridget's, hair had been. Kenneth supposed the state of Fanny's hair was to be expected, but something in the sorrow trailing her eyes yanked the breath from his gut and tore it into a thousand pieces.

"What has happened? Is it Gracie?"

Fanny inhaled. "The sickness caught her again. She's been abed for three days now."

Cold, deep and wretched, drained down Kenneth's spine. His muscles became ice.

"Hurry inside so she doesn't catch a draft," Fanny added.

Kenneth stepped into the meagerly furnished front-most room. He pulled the cap from his head. "What symptoms? A running nose?" He closed his eyes. *Please do not let it be a cough.*

"Fever. Chills too. And the poor girl's joints ache."

"How hot's the fever?"

"Hotter than I'd like. I sent for the apothecary yesterday. He prescribed bark tea to bring down her temperature, but I can't say it helped much. I even gave her more than he'd prescribed when she woke, but she's still hot."

Kenneth shoved his hand through the top of his brown hair. It was not the same dark brown Bridget's had been, or like Gracie's either. It was lighter, like wet sand. So much lighter that when Gracie was born and there was nothing of him in her features, only the spitting image of her mother, he had teased Bridget. "Who is that child's father?" he would say, even while he held the baby to his chest and rocked her in his arms. Both he and Bridget knew he hadn't meant it. For, while Gracie did not look like him, she sneezed twice, just as he often did. And when her clear blue eyes stared into his, it was like an invisible ribbon wrapped itself around their two hearts and said, *Welcome home.*

He glanced at the closed door that led into the smaller of the two bedrooms, where Fanny had been keeping watch over Gracie—the same room where Bridget had struggled against the same symptoms. And lost. "Putrid fever?"

Fanny nodded. "The apothecary said—"

"I can guess what he said!"

Fanny did not back away or tremble at his vehemence. Bridget had been strong like that too. *Bridget* . . . Kenneth stormed to the bedroom door, but as he put his hand on the knob, he paused and removed the half sovereign from his outer pocket. He turned back to Fanny. "I will secure a physician as soon as I can."

She stared at his hand before taking the money. "You found work? Where?"

"Odd jobs here and there." Before she could ask him more questions, he entered the bedroom and closed the door behind him. The setting sun's rays shone through the single window, brightening Gracie's flushed face enough that there was no need to light the rush candle. Instead he moved it off the wooden chair beside her bed, set it on the floor next to the large bowl of water Fanny must have been using to care for her, and sat in the chair himself.

"How are you feeling, my Gracie?"

She briefly opened her eyes. Sweat dripped along the side of her seven-year-old face. "Hot."

Kenneth took the rag from the bowl of water, wrung it almost dry, and dabbed it to his daughter's forehead and cheeks. "Better?"

"'Bout as cold as a tin kettle sittin' 'neath the summer sun."

He smiled. Bridget used to say that. It had been two years since she had passed, but praise be to God, their daughter had not forgotten her.

Gracie took a deep breath. "Where've you been?"

"Working"

"Makin' wheels?"

Or deals. "Something like that."

A tiny smile played on her lips. "You make good wheels."

Not good enough for the master to keep me on. "I am glad you think so."

"Ma said everyone thinks so." Her voice grew drowsy.

"It must be right, then."

She nodded. "I'm tired."

"You should be. With all those soldiers inside you trying to kill off that sickness, your body's got to be mighty worn out."

She didn't smile like she usually did. Had she fallen asleep? He leaned forward and touched her too-warm cheek. Panic shot through him. Was she still breathing? "Gracie, sweetheart?"

She opened and then closed her eyes.

He sighed in relief. "I'll go now so you can rest, but before I do, I need you to promise me you will do everything your aunt tells you to do so you can get well."

She wrinkled her nose. "Do I have to drink more of that tea?"

"Whatever she says to do, you must do it. Will you?"

"It tastes like wood."

"Will you?"

She took a deep breath. "All right."

"That's my girl."

"I don't like drinking wood."

"Neither do I." He kissed her forehead. "Tell you what. When you are all better, you will only have to eat and drink whatever you want for a whole week. Is it a deal?"

She did not move, but she breathed. He breathed too.

"Pa?"

"I'm here, sweetheart."

She opened her eyes, smiled, and while still smiling, closed them again. "Time for us to be happy."

An invisible blade twisted through the center of Kenneth's heart. More of his dear Bridget's words. Words that now cut when they used to heal.

All at once he imagined the fine clothes and carriages Evans would procure for him, the ones Kenneth would soon wear in Brighton. He thought on the sweet lies he would tell Miss de Bourgh. Of how he would convince her to marry him. And afterward, of how—where—the whole ruse would end. He would take no part in her murder—he hated murder. Hated lying in ways that broke hearts too—but her money would then be his. He would divide it with the others, and finally, deliverance would fill Leon's face. Evans's, too, for their vengeance on Lady Catherine, the woman who as good as killed Leon's and Evans's parents and left them to die as penniless paupers, would be complete. Such release, such vindication, was worth the cost. Especially if it helped Kenneth save his daughter.

CHAPTER SEVEN

Brighton

OWEN STEPPED OUT OF THE hat room and followed his mother, who followed his brother, into the Castle Inn's ballroom. The curved, classic white walls looked as if they had received a new coat of paint within the last few days. Even the domes on the upper walls and ceilings, adorned with elaborate *Dawn and Night* plasterwork, seemed pale in comparison. Or perhaps it was not the paint at all. Perhaps it was the candlelight reflecting off those white walls, gold fixtures, and the polished pinewood floor that caused the walls to look newly painted.

Owen scanned every nearby face. There were several young ladies, all wearing gowns of various shades of white and pastels, and almost as many gentlemen, including a few military men and some of the more prosperous local tradesmen among them, but no Miss de Bourgh.

He nodded to a group of young women who, standing in line ahead of him, had verified their seasons' public assembly subscriptions with the master of ceremonies before they had entered the hall. He glanced across the room to the musician's gallery. Its black backdrop stood out against the white statues of the Greek god and goddess guarding the entry as richly as black velvet behind diamonds, but not one of the ladies who stood near the gallery was Miss de—he caught his breath. There. A small, slim frame with a swirl of dark curls atop her head stood with two other young women next to the goddess statue. Her back was to him. He watched her, waited. At last she looked over her shoulder. He frowned. Her features were sharp, unforgiving even. She was most definitely not Miss de Bourgh.

"I truly do wish you would remain in Britain," his mother said from behind him.

"Must we continue this conversation here?" he asked, turning to her.

"As you felt inclined to bring it up in the carriage just now, I see no reason it should be left unresolved through the rest of the evening."

"What is there to resolve?"

She pressed her lips into a tight line and clasped her other son's forearm. "Tell him, Sir William. Tell him he must not go. I do not believe my heart can bear another loss to our family."

Sir William, Owen's younger brother by three years, stood to his fullest height, which was still two inches shorter than Owen's six feet, and cleared his throat. "Do change your mind, brother."

"You are not usually so quick to obey our mother's fancies," Owen said.

"In this case, they are my fancies too. At any rate, would it have changed your mind if I had spoken sooner?"

Owen dragged his gaze from the crowd and studied his brother's face. "No. But if you disagreed, I wish you would have told me."

"I saw no point in doing so. As you are the sensible one of the family, I trusted you would soon see the error in your decision and give up the scheme." Sir William nodded to a pretty blonde girl Owen had not seen before. She, like Miss de Bourgh, must have just arrived in Brighton.

"And I trusted you would agree with me, seeing as I am the sensible one." Owen lowered his voice. "And seeing as there is nothing for me here in England, which you well know."

"There is much for you here," his mother snapped. "Your father made certain your inheritance would leave you well prepared for the world."

"My stepfather, you mean." His mother's expression darkened, and he quickly added, "Forgive me, Mother. I was speaking only as others see me. I most assuredly consider him my father, and I am grateful for his care in providing for my future."

"See, there. You should stay," his mother said.

Owen exhaled, and Sir William shrugged once. At least his brother understood his need to get away.

"Lady Talbot." The woman's voice behind him rose so sharply above the hubbub it seemed all the guests in front of him not only silenced but also looked toward and beyond him. Owen allowed himself another quick glance across the ballroom then turned. A stately woman in a red velvet turban stood before him. Behind her—Owen's muscles, his stance, his breath relaxed—Miss de Bourgh had arrived.

"Lady Catherine de Bourgh." His mother briefly clasped the woman's hand. "I am glad to see you, my friend. It has been a long time."

Owen's gaze settled on Miss de Bourgh. She wore a white silk dress with a broad, square neckline and puffed short sleeves. Most certainly slips of lace, beads, and other furbelows adorned it, yet the only decoration that said to him this was, indeed, the essence of Miss de Bourgh was the Pomona green scarf she wore draped around her shoulders. That and the bits of artificial leaves and daisies woven within the curls pinned atop her head.

He planted his stance into the floor that he might not rush toward her. Miss de Bourgh, however, focused only on her mother or the floor. Owen furrowed his brows. Yesterday the young lady had seemed quiet, but her artistic skill, her quick knowledge of plants, her sense of ease when she noticed his crippled leg, and most especially her perceptions toward his mother's needs had made her seem far superior to any woman he had known. Yet, now she would not even meet his gaze.

"It has indeed been too long." Lady Catherine smiled at Owen's mother and looked past Owen to his brother. "And too long since I have seen you, too, Sir William. I believe the last time was when you were in your cradle."

Mr. Talbot stared at Anne. *Look at me.* But she did not. Her attention, like every other young lady of his acquaintance, had turned to his titled, wealthier, perfectly limbed brother. *Fool.* Owen should not have let himself hope for a different outcome.

"I am afraid I do not have the pleasure of remembering the moment of our meeting, Lady Catherine," Sir William said.

Lady Catherine smiled. "I believe you have also not had the pleasure of meeting my daughter." She motioned slightly behind her, and Miss de Bourgh stepped forward.

Sir William bowed. "Miss de Bourgh." She curtsied to him in response and smiled slightly.

Owen clenched and unclenched his hands. *Fool,* he told himself yet again.

Owen's mother moved between Owen and Sir William. "As I recall, Lady Catherine, you also met my firstborn that day. Lady Catherine, Miss de Bourgh"—she motioned to Owen—"my eldest son, Mr. Owen Talbot."

Lady Catherine nodded, and her eyelids lowered, but somehow her nose lifted. *This is why I am immigrating to America,* he thought. But when, at last, Miss de Bourgh's dark eyes met his, that lump in his chest bounced again. The kindness he had seen in her before was still there. She lowered her eyelids, and the lump thudded to the floor.

Lady Catherine addressed his brother. "It appears the musicians are about to begin the minuet. I hope, sir, you are anxious to dance. My daughter has long looked forward to this evening."

Miss de Bourgh's cheeks pinked. Owen could not tell if her response was due to embarrassment or pleasure, but it did not matter. Both emotions pinched that still-sitting-there pressure in his chest as tightly as his leg brace forced his foot and ankle into their proper positions. *Miss de Bourgh really will never think of me with anything but sympathy.*

The introductory music began, and the master of ceremonies announced the minuet. The lead couple moved to the front of the floor. Sir William bowed crisply to Miss de Bourgh. "Would you do me the honor of the first dance?"

Miss de Bourgh took Sir William's arm. "I would be honored, sir."

The pressure in Owen's chest pinched tighter.

Lady Catherine glanced at Owen then turned to Lady Talbot. "I would count it an honor if you would sit with me while we watch the young people. It has been years since we have sat together in such a manner."

"That would be delightful."

The two women started toward the cushioned chairs and benches set aside for spectators then hesitated. His mother turned back to him. "Will you join us?"

Owen glanced over his shoulder at Miss de Bourgh. "Thank you, but I think not."

Lady Catherine gave Owen a most disapproving scowl, but his mother, after also glancing at Sir William and Miss de Bourgh, said to Lady Catherine, "I believe there is a bench for the two of us near that window."

Owen turned away from them. Miss de Bourgh held his brother's gloved hand with her own. She moved gracefully beside him through the steps of the minuet. She smiled up at him. Unable to bear any more, Owen limped alongside the wall amid the other men and women without dance partners to an unoccupied spot of floor. While he could no longer see whether or not his mother or Lady Catherine were watching him, which had been his purpose in moving there in the first place, he might as well have been able to see them. Several men and women of all ages frequently stared at him before quickly looking away. Their expressions were just as the one his physician had held before he had forced Owen's foot and leg into his first brace.

"A crooked body is more a prison than a palace for your soul," he had said, "and it will not be accepted in polite society. It is therefore your moral duty to do all you can to restore its proper aesthetics to what God intended."

Owen had done as the physician prescribed and had suffered great anguish of mind and body in doing so. But what good had any of those years of pain done him? His body was still imperfect, and if it were not for his wealth and connections, society would not have accepted him at all. No society, for that matter. And Miss de Bourgh . . . His gaze clung to the smoothness of her cheeks, the softness in her eyes. And Miss de Bourgh, as the daughter of Lady Catherine de Bourgh—who, despite her friendship with his mother—would never be allowed to accept him into her society, either, even if she wanted to. Did she want to?

Sir William faced Miss de Bourgh. Moving with the dance, he clasped both her hands and smiled.

Owen growled under his breath. Sir William was a good brother and a friend to him in a way no one else had ever been. And Owen had never been jealous of him for anything he had. Not as a person, not as a perfectly formed man, nor even for his inheriting his father's title and all that went with it. But now, in the moment Sir William's hand clasped Miss de Bourgh's, all of that changed. If Owen had possessed all Sir William did, he would have a chance with Miss de Bourgh. He would not have to go to America, where all men were created equal, in order to be a man whose value was not so much determined by his parentage.

The minuet ended. Miss de Bourgh curtsied to Sir William, and the two returned to where she had originally stood with their mothers. Then Sir William walked away.

Owen scanned the men around Miss de Bourgh. None seemed to be heading her direction, perhaps intending to ask her to dance. Should he approach her? Speak with her? Would she welcome his company?

Erase her from your thoughts. You are soon leaving for America.

That was what his mind said and what he knew to be true, but something in the way Miss de Bourgh moved among the people drew him toward her as steadily as the moon's gravity tugged at the ocean's waves. He took a tentative step toward her.

Perhaps it was only the straightness of her posture or the soft, fluid elegance in her walk that attracted him. Or the intelligence in her eyes that frequented his memory. He took two more steps. Or maybe it was the friendliness in her demeanor when she nodded to the elderly woman next to a long table of what was very likely stale refreshments and watered-down lemonade. He stopped.

Lady Catherine and Owen's mother walked directly up to Miss de Bourgh with Mr. Stanton, a middle-aged gentleman of extreme wealth and a recent widower. Owen's mother, after briefly speaking with Mr. Stanton, stared at Owen. She said nothing, did nothing, but her gaze clung to his as if she were trying to impart some message into his heart. He had no idea what it was. Maybe one day he would ask Miss de Bourgh, and she, with the perceptive skills she had revealed so perfectly that afternoon, would know.

Lady Catherine, on the other hand, looked only at Mr. Stanton. She did not fold her arms like a queen might do, making certain a servant followed her commands to the letter, but her tightened jaw and pointed stare had the same effect. Owen furrowed his brow. Surely she had not coerced the man into asking Miss de Bourgh to dance. The only inducement any eligible man would need was to look upon her gentle features and to talk to her.

Mr. Stanton spoke. Miss de Bourgh said something, smiled slightly, and took his arm.

Owen glanced at his mother, who still watched him, then strode back to the empty floor space he had left a short time ago. Once again he crossed his arms and glared above the dancers at the opposite wall.

America, with its open spaces and rich farmland. That was where he belonged. A place of opportunity, where men such as he, men with wealth and determination, could buy and sell crops or land or whatever they wished. A country where, despite his infirmity, he could rule his own destiny, become his own man.

The dance ended. Mr. Talbot looked to where he had last seen Miss de Bourgh, but rather than finding her, he came face to face with his brother.

"Come now, brother, if you intended not to socialize tonight, why did you come at all?"

"It is my affair."

Sir William tilted his head. "I had initially thought it was because you were leaving for America and wanted to take one last look at the lot of us." He glanced over his shoulder toward their mother and Lady Catherine and then to Miss de Bourgh, who once again stood with them. "But now I believe your purpose has everything to do with a certain eligible young lady."

"Do not be ridiculous."

"Ridiculous to suggest an attachment to Miss de Bourgh might just keep you here?"

Owen cleared his throat. "Keep your thoughts to yourself, brother. The ladies are headed this way."

Sir William gave him a smirking glance and faced the approaching women. Miss de Bourgh's eyes momentarily lit up when Owen's gaze met hers but quickly moved to another approaching group of women. It was Mrs. Wycliff and two young ladies whom Owen could only assume were the woman's two daughters. He understood they had earlier that year returned from their French boarding school. The Wycliffs reached Owen and Sir William before his mother and the de Bourghs did.

"Sir William," Mrs. Wycliff said. "I am delighted to see you here tonight. My daughters have expressed a wish to know you, and I wondered if I might introduce them to you?"

The girls, standing a pace behind their mother, smiled at Sir William.

"I would be pleased to meet them, madam."

Mrs. Wycliff motioned her daughters forward. She first introduced the older, plumper girl, Miss Wycliff, and then her younger, slighter sister, Miss Henrietta Wycliff. Both had thick brown hair and dark eyes, but their expressions were too pink-faced for Owen's taste. Not that it mattered. Neither showed any interest in being introduced to him. In truth, when Owen sidestepped a few feet away from his brother, not one of the Wycliffs seemed to notice.

His mother did, though, and when her expression simultaneously flared and blanched, Owen turned away from her. He had no desire to deal with his mother's protective instincts or her sympathy. He was a grown man, and grown men did not need coddling.

But then—*then*—Miss de Bourgh's sudden gaze at him was clear and even a bit—dare he think it?—admiring. His heart tripped.

Lady Catherine moved beside and nearly in front of Mrs. Wycliff. She nodded to Sir William, obviously drawing his attention away from the Wycliff girls.

Mrs. Wycliff curtsied slightly to her. "Your Ladyship. It has been years since we last met. May I introduce you and your daughter to my daughters?"

Lady Catherine nodded, and Mrs. Wycliff did so.

"I believe your daughter was in her cradle when you first met Sir William," Mrs. Wycliff added.

"She was, yes." Lady Catherine glanced at Sir William. "But as you can see, she has grown into a lovely young woman with such vast interests I dare not keep her from them. That is the exact reason we have come to Brighton this Season. 'Mother,' she said, 'I believe I must take the waters.' And so she shall. Monday, in fact. We have hired a Mrs. Dramwell as her dipper. Perhaps you have heard of her? She comes well recommended."

Miss de Bourgh lowered her eyelids. She pressed her handkerchief to her nose. Owen had not had much use for the sea baths many newcomers used, but he had spent many hours swimming in the sea. Doing so was one of the few pleasures in England during which he felt fully whole. But Miss de Bourgh, despite her mother's pronouncement, did not seem as enthusiastic. *I hope she likes sea-bathing.*

"Perhaps Miss de Bourgh would like my daughters to go with her?" Mrs. Wycliff said. "They have no need of dippers, but they do so enjoy sea-bathing."

"Oh yes," Miss Henrietta said. "Sea-bathing is so refreshing."

"No matter how hard or dreary the day is," Miss Wycliff added, "we always feel much happier afterward."

Miss Henrietta giggled.

Owen frowned. He did not know what it was, but something in the two girls' expressions reminded him of the boys he had occasionally kept company with when he was a child. The ones who pretended to their parents they were Owen's friends but were more likely to laugh at him than enjoy his friendship.

"What time will you be there on Monday, Miss de Bourgh?" Miss Wycliff asked.

"In the morning." She glanced at Lady Catherine. "I do not remember the exact time."

Miss Henrietta nodded. "The cooler morning water is better."

"Then, we will meet you Monday morning," Miss Wycliff said. "If that is all right with you, Mother."

"Of course, my dear," Mrs. Wycliff said.

"We will watch for you on the beach," Miss Henrietta said. "And after you have met with your dipper, you can sea bathe longer with us."

Owen stared hard at Miss de Bourgh. *Do not agree. Something is not right.*

Miss de Bourgh did not look at him, however. Instead, she gave the girls a slight smile, a tiny nod, and clasped her mother's forearm. "I fear I am feeling a bit faint."

The two sisters glanced at each other, but at least they did not smile or giggle.

"There is a free window seat across the room behind that curtain," Lady Catherine said to Miss de Bourgh. "You will sit there for a few minutes and catch your breath." She turned to Owen's brother. "Perhaps Sir William will do us the honor of accompanying you."

"I would be most pleased to." Sir William glanced at Owen, bowed to the ladies, and held out his arm to Miss de Bourgh. They walked, unhurried, toward the window alcove. When they had at last settled on the seat in front of the pastel yellow curtains, the Wycliffs took their leave of Owen.

Lady Talbot sidled in beside him. She clasped his elbow. "Dr. Sinclair, the man standing next to the door there with his arms crossed, has not been long in Brighton. I spoke with him earlier this afternoon, and he expressed a specific interest in meeting your brother. He said he had an appointment with him this evening."

"I am at your disposal, Mother. What message would you like me to deliver to the doctor?"

"No message, son, but I did wonder if you would be willing to sit with Miss de Bourgh for a few minutes in Sir William's place."

Lady Catherine whirled. Until that moment, she had been watching Sir William and Miss de Bourgh as if afraid he might slip away at any moment. "Is that necessary?" Owen asked. "I am certain Miss de Bourgh will not need to rest for long."

"I believe it is necessary," she said. "Will you?"

Owen's pulse leapt to his throat. "I would be most happy to sit with Miss de Bourgh." Then, without waiting for Lady Catherine's rebuttal, he limped straight to the window seat. Miss de Bourgh looked up first, but Owen focused on his brother.

"Mother sent me to sit with Miss de Bourgh. She says Dr. Sinclair is waiting for you." He motioned toward the door.

"Oh?" Sir William glanced knowingly between Owen and Miss de Bourgh then stood. "Yes, of course. If you will excuse me, Miss de Bourgh." He bowed to her and headed toward the doctor.

At last Owen's gaze settled on Miss de Bourgh. Before this moment he had not had the right to look at her and keep looking at her, but he did so now without reservation. "May I sit with you?"

"You may." Her smile was not broad, but it lit up her dark eyes as if she had grinned.

He lowered himself onto the window seat next to her. They glanced at one another then directed their attentions toward the dance floor.

Miss de Bourgh dabbed her handkerchief to her nose. "D-did your mother like her gift?"

"I believe she did."

"And your note?"

His memory jumped back to the moment when, after digging out the leather case, his mother had brushed the dirt from it, opened it, retrieved the letter, and read the words Miss de Bourgh had written for him. Tears had filled her eyes. "It was perfect," he said.

Miss de Bourgh glanced toward Lady Catherine then looked down at her hands in her lap. Owen scanned the dance floor. Many couples moved back and forth across it, skipping, stepping, holding hands, but he observed none of their faces enough to recognize who they were. All he noticed was his pulse pounding in his throat and his fingers aching to reach out and touch the back of Miss de Bourgh's hand.

"It is rather quiet in this part of the room," he said.

"I am content with quiet."

So am I.

The dancers returned to the beginning of the set.

"Forgive me," he said. "I do not mean to be presumptuous, but I overheard you are going sea-bathing on Monday. With the Wycliff sisters."

"I am sea-bathing on Monday but not with the Wycliff sisters."

"I am glad to hear it. Not that I have anything against the activity. Swimming is one of my favorite pastimes. But I am glad you will not swim with them."

"Oh? I suppose they are much younger than I am."

"And rather silly."

She lowered her head and dabbed her handkerchief to her nose again, though this time it seemed the action was more out of nervousness than need. At last she peered up at him. She furrowed her brows as if she were assessing him—for what reason he did not know—and at last seemed to have come to a decision. She shifted taller, yet still she spoke softly. "And there was something . . . I am not certain what it was, for their speech was altogether correct . . . but there was something that made me feel . . ." She swallowed, studied him again, and finally said, "It made me believe sea-bathing for them was something different than it would be for me."

He tilted his head to the side. He had interpreted the sisters' actions differently, surmising they had more callous intentions rather than imprudent ones toward Miss de Bourgh. But now, thinking back on the girls' actions and words, he could see Miss de Bourgh may very well be correct.

The music grew louder. Anne gazed out at the dancers. Precious time Owen could use to get to know her slipped by.

"You now know I enjoy swimming," he said. "May I ask what your pursuits are? For instance, I know you draw."

She pressed her lips together and glanced down at her folded hands. "I do, but it is hardly worth speaking of."

"I do not believe it. Tell me. What do you draw? Anything besides plants?"

She whispered something in response, and he took the opportunity to lean closer to her. "I am sorry. I did not hear that."

"Only plants." She spoke louder and glanced about them as if she were afraid someone had overheard her. "I especially love flowers."

"All varieties?" He grinned. "I would love to see your sketches."

"Yes, all varieties, but I would not wish to spark your enthusiasm. There is nothing remarkable about my renditions." She laughed a little, as if she were discounting her very words, but her soft blush revealed its lie. Her drawings were important to her.

"I doubt that."

She tilted her head but said nothing.

"You surprise me," he said.

"I-I do?"

"In truth, your intelligence astounds me." Her eyes rounded, and her cheeks flushed red, but still he could not stop his thoughts from tumbling from his lips. "You are the most awe-inspiring woman I have ever met."

She lowered her gaze and pressed her hand against her chest. "Mr. Talbot, please."

"Have I embarrassed you, Miss de Bourgh? That was not my intention."

She shook her head.

He swallowed. "Have I done something to offend you?"

"No, it is only—" She looked beyond him and held her hand out in front of her. "You know my mother, of course."

Owen turned to the woman now standing before them. He stood and bowed. "Lady Catherine."

She nodded to him but stared at her daughter. Miss de Bourgh bowed her head. "Several men have asked me if you would be interested in dancing with them. I assured them you would. As you were smiling a few moments past, I expect you are feeling better now."

Owen's mother, watching them from across the ballroom, stood next to two other men, both in their late forties or early fifties. Were they the men Lady Catherine spoke of? *They are much too old. Much too—not right for Miss de Bourgh.* Owen clenched his hands at his sides.

"I am feeling better, Mother. Thank you," Miss de Bourgh said. Owen offered her his hand, helping her to her feet, and she added, "Thank you for your kindness, Mr. Talbot."

Was that a smile, albeit a small one? "I am happy to be of service."

She turned away from him and followed her mother to the waiting gentlemen. *Followed her mother.* Owen's thoughts paused. Anne was not weak-minded. Not at all. She was only silenced by her mother. But more than that, she was a young lady who would always follow her mother. That was another reason he should go to Amer—

Deuces! Anne glimpsed over her shoulder and gazed straight at him. *Him.*

The moment passed almost as quickly as it came, but it turned his world entirely upside down.

I will not go to America. Yet.

CHAPTER EIGHT

MISTER TALBOT. WHY WAS HE only *Mister* Talbot? His bearing was much more commanding than Sir William's stance. In truth, Anne could not seem to keep herself from looking at Mr. Talbot at every opportunity, even when she was in the company of Sir William. To be sure, Sir William was handsome, with his thick blond hair and Grecian profile, but Mr. Talbot had the more determined demeanor, the broader shoulders and stronger arms, and most especially a thoughtfulness for others that defined a true gentleman to her more than any other characteristic. Heat warmed Anne's cheeks. It was not the mortified kind of warm that dragged her confidence from her soul and buried it at her feet, but the elated kind that danced and squealed across the ballroom floor. Where was Mr. Talbot now?

Anne peeked over her shoulder to the window seat where she had sat next to him. Mr. Stanton caught her eye, nodded, and started toward her. He was—she swallowed—he seemed bent on asking her to stand up with him for the final dance. She turned in the full opposite direction.

What had happened to her? How could she behave so unjustly to someone she hardly knew? She glanced at her mother, who sat with Lady Talbot on the same bench they had claimed for most of the night, and slowed her step. The fact that Anne had found herself so entirely smitten by a man gave her no right to act so rudely to another. She stopped. If Mr. Stanton was still behind her, if he did indeed wish to dance with her, she would oblige him.

"Miss de Bourgh."

Warmth tickled the hair on the nape of her neck. She did not have to look behind her to know that voice did not belong to Mr. Stanton. It was Mr. Talbot's.

"Is your dance card free?"

She turned. Mr. Stanton stood only a few feet behind Mr. Talbot.

"I-I had not thought . . ." Anne glanced down at Mr. Talbot's crippled leg. "I am sure there is very little you cannot do, but as you have not danced with any of the other young ladies throughout the course of the evening"— *Oh dear! Now he knows I have been watching him*—"I had thought . . ." She shook her head. "My dance card is indeed free, sir."

"Then, would you do me the honor of walking with me around the room while we enjoy the last of the music?"

"I—" She swallowed. "Forgive me. I did not mean to disparage your leg."

"That is not the answer I had hoped for."

"I know. I—" She lowered her head. "It would be a pleasure." She sidled away from her mother's sudden hard stare and Mr. Stanton's frown and took Mr. Talbot's arm. He led her along the wall toward the musician's gallery at the back of the room. The musicians began the next song.

"Has the ball been to your liking?" Mr. Talbot asked.

"It has, thank you."

"I noted your partners have been among the best of Brighton's society."

All four of them, you mean? But Anne did not say that. She was quite happy she had not been required to dance frequently. While she felt the cure was healing her allergic rhinitis and the exercise regime was strengthening her stamina, she still felt more weakness than she cared to admit. Instead she determined she would not let that weakness show in her conversation with Mr. Talbot. "I also enjoyed our discussion in the window seat."

A slow smile spread across his face. "I meant every compliment."

Oh my. This time the heat in Anne's cheeks did come from mortification. How could he imagine she would refer to his compliments? She had only meant she had felt easy in his company, intrigued by his intelligence.

"Miss de Bourgh? Are you well?"

"Oh. Yes." She made herself look up at him. "I am perfectly well."

He tilted his head and, scrutinizing her face, placed his gloved hand over the top of hers where it rested on his arm. "Perhaps we should sit for a moment."

Perhaps I should not be such a ninny. "In truth, sir, I would prefer to take another turn about the room, this time close to the dancers, if it would not inconvenience you."

His stance stiffened. "Why would such a thing inconvenience me?"

Anne winced beneath his narrowed gaze, which scowled back and forth between her face and his leg. Heat warmed her cheeks. Did her embarrassment always have to show? "Forgive me, sir. Please do not believe I meant any manner of disrespect to you. I—" She swallowed. "Certainly everyone here knows how perfectly capable you are." *And strong. And kind. And everything wonderful.*

He glanced toward two young women standing close to them, staring at them, and turned back to Miss de Bourgh. He briefly pressed her hand where it still rested on his arm. "It is I who must beg your forgiveness. I am afraid that because of my infirmity"—he did not glimpse again over his shoulder at the girls, but Anne felt as if he had—"I have a tendency to take quick offense, even when none is intended."

Anne did not have his same self-control, for she did look at the girls. They, noticing her, did not even have the decency to turn away. "I hope you do not mind me saying further," Anne replied, "it does you great credit to have overcome such difficulties."

His slow smile returned. "Thank you." Mr. Talbot led her away from the staring girls and along the edge of the dance floor. "Perhaps some of the credit belongs to me, but my mother deserves most of it."

The dancers formed a circle in the middle of the room, and the musicians began the light, jaunty music of the cotillion. They continued around the room.

"I am glad you hold your mother in such esteem," Anne said.

"It is more than esteem. As a boy, when the doctor was forcing my foot into a brace, I begged my mother to let me die."

A sudden wave of compassion rushed over Anne and settled, hot and aching, in the back of her throat. "I am sorry you went through so much pain, but I am glad your mother did not let you give up. It would have been a great loss to us all"—*if you had died*—"if your leg had grown worse."

He peered hard at her. "I do not know that is true, Miss de Bourgh, but it is kind of you to say." They took a few more steps. "I do believe you and my mother must think a great deal alike or are at least equally empathetic. During one of my most difficult sessions with the doctor, she told me my life did not belong to me. It belonged to God. And it was up to me to do what good I could with the life God had given me."

Anne nodded, agreeing with his mother. Though she did not fully know what she believed about life and death, having never thought much on it, those words felt like truth.

"I was not certain I believed her," he continued. "But by then I knew my mother would never intentionally do or say something to harm me. There. As you can see, Miss de Bourgh, it was because I trusted my mother that I suffered through the brace."

"And became the man you are."

He smiled slightly.

"Does your leg still hurt? Even now?"

"I try not to think of it, but yes, it is frequently sore and stiff."

They reached the musician's gallery and started back in the direction they had come. They had only crossed half the distance when Sir William stepped out of the entrance, glanced about the room, and, seeing them, hurried toward Anne and Mr. Talbot. He lowered his voice. "I need you to come with me at once," he said to Mr. Talbot. "Dr. Sinclair is dead."

CHAPTER NINE

ANNE FROZE. DR. SINCLAIR, THE man who had visited her just the previous day, given her the cure, and prescribed exercises to strengthen her body, was dead? A man who, only a short time ago, Sir William had left to visit with?

"Where is he?" Mr. Talbot said. "Did he have some kind of accident?"

"I cannot say what has happened, but he is in the hat room."

"What has been done?" Mr. Talbot asked.

Sir William glanced at Anne. "I have sent for the magistrate."

The magistrate? Anne scanned back and forth across the room. People were laughing, smiling, and dancing while a dead man lay in this very establishment. Anne's knees gave way beneath her weight.

Mr. Talbot grabbed her elbow. "Miss de Bourgh, are you unwell?"

The warmth of his hand on her elbow and his arm against hers wiped the images from her mind and settled her nerves, but still her heart raced. She took a deep breath. "I think so. I am afraid my imagination was running wild."

He nodded, scrutinized her expression, and led her with him alongside Sir William toward the entry. She set her jaw. *Keep your head about you. Stay strong.*

"It will not be long before everyone here learns of the matter," Sir William muttered. "We need to learn what we can before then, before people come running—"

"And yelling about the sensation—" Mr. Talbot's voice was even softer than Sir William's.

"And destroy whatever evidence there might be."

"Mother will not like that," Mr. Talbot said.

"I will not like what?" Lady Talbot suddenly stood beside them. She took Anne's other arm and continued walking with them.

"The area surrounding the crime is destroyed," Sir William said.

"What are you talking of?"

"Dr. Sinclair is dead in the hat room, Mother," Mr. Talbot said.

"What? How can that be?" She stiffened upright, blinked several times, and looked about them. "Nothing seemed at all amiss when I spoke with him this afternoon."

"You spoke with him?" Sir William asked. "What about?"

"I had a question for him. But now he is dead?"

They reached the doorway that led into the entry hall. "Are you coming?" Sir William asked Lady Talbot.

"Go along. I will stay with Miss de Bourgh a bit longer."

Mr. Talbot gave Anne another quick, appraising once-over, released her into Lady Talbot's care, and limped after Sir William into the hallway.

"I do not understand," Anne said. "What are they doing? Should this not be left for the magistrate? Or at the very least the constables?"

"The magistrate might be of some use, but constables are little more than henchmen. They have no idea how to investigate a crime, much less how to secure evidence. And even if they did, while some men are honest, most would be more likely to fabricate so-called facts, if paid well enough, than to work to uncover the truth." Lady Talbot glanced over Anne's shoulder.

Anne followed her gaze. Her mother, though she stood among several other women, stared at them.

Lady Talbot gently tugged Anne in the opposite direction. "My sons, on the other hand, worked with my husband and me long enough to know something of what must be done."

"But it is such a sordid business." Anne pressed her handkerchief to her nose. She looked at Lady Talbot over the top of it and told her mind to focus not on where the men had gone but on where she was right then. "To pollute oneself with such an affair. How can you tolerate it?"

"Someone with a mind for such things despite their social class must tolerate it. Do you not agree? If such situations, such jobs, are always left to those in the lower classes, to men who have not the means nor in many cases the understanding to unravel them, injustices will only increase. We will be fixed in the world we currently live in. Progress will never come to pass."

Lady Talbot's words sounded like those Anne had read in the *Morning Chronicle* about the American and French Revolutions, but her thoughts paused on Lady Talbot's statement, "Someone with a mind for such things." Someone like Mr. Darcy, who had hunted down Wickham and Miss Lydia

Bennet even though no one else had been able to. "My cousin is such a man," Anne said.

The dance music grew louder.

Lady Talbot tilted her head and faced her. "Forgive me. I did not hear what you said."

"I was only thinking of my cousin Mr. Darcy. He is a gentleman, but like you and your sons, he went to extreme measures, investigating situations that would normally be beneath his class, in order to help another."

"I believe I would like to meet this cousin of yours."

"Perhaps you shall."

The two started back for the entrance.

"Will you go with your sons now?" Anne asked.

"Not until I know you are well."

"I am well enough. Please, do not let me keep you."

Lady Talbot narrowed her eyes, studied her. "Would you like to join me, Miss de Bourgh?"

"I could not." Anne glanced at the window seat where she and Mr. Talbot had sat not long ago. It was empty. Lonely. As lonely as she then felt. Anne took a deep breath. "My mother—the scandal of being associated with such a scene—she would never forgive me."

"Why do I not believe you?"

"About not going or about my mother?"

Lady Talbot smiled slightly but said nothing. Anne bit her lower lip. Otherwise no other exchange passed between them until they again headed back toward the refreshment table.

"Do not worry, Miss de Bourgh. I will not lure you to where you do not wish to go. But if it will set your mind at ease, and if you would like to go with me into the hat room, I will tell anyone who questions us that we simply came upon the scene unawares. We were there by accident. Completely unintentionally."

"And we left as soon as we realized what had transpired."

"Of course. We would do nothing else."

Anne moved to glance over her shoulder but stopped herself. One glimpse in her mother's direction, and Anne would lose her nerve. And right then she did not want to lose her nerve. She wanted to do something useful, to help someone other than herself. She wanted to be someone other than herself.

"I will go with you," Anne whispered.

Lady Talbot squeezed the top of Anne's hand, which was still looped around her arm, and headed them back toward the entrance. "Smile," she said. "Pretend we are merely walking together, enjoying one another's company. We are deep in conversation."

"If we do that, my mother will want to have her share in our conversation."

"What do you suggest we do, then?"

"You should leave me here." That was when Anne knew that was exactly what she did not want Lady Talbot to do. Anne was not simply curious, but she also wanted, truly wanted to go with Lady Talbot to see Mr. Talbot and to study the dead body's surroundings. And she wanted to do those things, in part, because she trusted Lady Talbot. Anne felt at ease with her, as if her opinions really mattered to the woman.

She felt that way with Mr. Talbot too.

"But I hope you will not leave me," Anne added.

"I will not."

They reached the entrance, only this time they walked through it and straight to the hat room.

"However, I am afraid I must hurry," Anne said. "My mother will be extremely put out if I do not return soon. Worse if she finds me here."

Lady Talbot opened the hat room door. "You may leave as soon as you wish. Will that satisfy?"

"It will. Thank—"

Lady Talbot stepped into the room. Inside, Mr. Talbot, his head bowed and his hands clasped behind him, limped slowly between shards of broken glass scattered across the floor. Sir William crouched in the center of the room next to Dr. Sinclair's body. It had been at least ten minutes since Sir William had first told them of the man's death, yet still he repeatedly checked Dr. Sinclair's pulse and held his hand in front of his vomit-covered mouth.

"The doctor is obviously not breathing," Lady Talbot said. "Give it up, son. There is nothing more anyone can do for him."

Both men looked up as if surprised to see Anne and their mother. Anne glanced at Mr. Talbot. His dark eyes wavered.

"One cannot be too careful," Sir William said. "Too many men who have been declared dead have outlived their burials."

Lady Talbot tiptoed between several shards of broken glass toward the body. She studied its surroundings.

Mr. Talbot stepped beside Anne. "Perhaps you would prefer to leave. Scenes such as this can sometimes be troubling."

"I want to stay." Anne glanced at Lady Talbot, who now bent over the doctor's body, and listened at the door. No sound. If her mother was out there, Anne would certainly hear her. "In fact, I am intrigued. What can I do?"

Mr. Talbot's lips quivered with what appeared to be slight amusement. "Look about you. Keep note of anything that seems out of the ordinary."

"What clues have you found?" Lady Talbot asked Sir William, who still knelt next to the body. "Do you have any idea what happened to the poor man?"

"I expect he had some form of an attack. Perhaps his heart gave out."

"The heart of such a young man? I do not believe it."

"There is no sign of a struggle."

"What about those red stains on his chest and shirt sleeve?"

"Wine," Sir William said. "I expect he spilled it when he collapsed."

Lady Talbot frowned.

"No scratch marks or cuts either," Sir William continued. "And his clothes are almost as neatly groomed as they were when I spoke with him earlier. It is as I said. He shows no signs of having tried to defend himself."

"A pity," she said.

Sir William gave up feeling for the man's pulse and stood. "A pity the man was not attacked before he was murdered? I believe, Mother, you must reorganize your priorities."

"I must do no such thing. You may be right, however. His death might have nothing to do with murder, but that does not mean we should not investigate the situation."

"I am afraid that is the medical man's job now," Sir William said.

She pressed her lips into a tight, thin line. "The best the coroner will do is determine what killed him. Not how or why." She turned to Anne. "Miss de Bourgh, what do you think of what you see before you?"

Anne blinked. With one ear craned toward the door, she had only taken in the conversations around her, not analyzed any of the scene before her.

Mr. Talbot clasped then released Anne's elbow. "You do not have to answer," he whispered. Then, louder, to his mother, he said, "It is hardly appropriate to put such a question to the young lady on such short notice. Not that her mind is not first rate—from our conversation earlier this evening

I saw proof positive it is sharper than any I have known—but she has had no experience with such things."

What had she said earlier that would prove such a thing to—? *The Wycliff sisters.*

"I appreciate your concern, Mr. Talbot, but I am happy to oblige your mother."

"You are? What I mean to say is, you do?"

"Let the girl speak for herself, Owen," Lady Talbot looked back to Anne. "Well then, what is your theory? What do you think happened to Dr. Sinclair?"

Speak quickly. While there was still no commotion outside the door, Anne's anxiousness wound so tightly through her she would not stay more than a moment longer. "I have no idea what happened to him, but I dis—I disagree with the suggestion there is no sign of a struggle. Dr. Sinclair had obviously been"—Anne swallowed—"drinking when it happened, but if it had been a natural attack of the heart or brain or some other physical system, would he not simply drop the glass?" She coughed. "And crumple on top of it? Instead, most of this glass shattered here by the door, as if he had thrown it."

"Or dropped it and then stumbled forward and fell," Sir William countered.

"True," Anne said. "But if he had been falling forward, would he not have fallen onto his face and not onto his back?"

Silence.

"I believe we have a puzzle to solve," Lady Talbot said at last.

Noise bustled outside the door. Anne stiffened and grabbed the doorknob. Was it her mother? "Forgive me. I am sorry, but I must leave."

Just then, five men rushed through the door and pushed past Anne. "Everyone out of the way," the front gray-haired man said.

He must be the magistrate, Anne thought. Another gray-haired man—perhaps the medical advisor?—and three younger men Anne assumed were constables followed him.

"Mr. Andrews," Sir William said. "I am glad you retained these men after last month's attack on the town hall. I believe Dr. Sinclair's death may be suspicious."

Anne left the room. Seeing no sign of her mother, she sighed in relief and headed for the dance hall, but she had barely crossed through the entry when a young man pushed into the room from behind her.

"Dr. Sinclair is dead," he yelled. "In the hat room."

A woman screamed. The master of ceremonies raced past Anne toward the entry. A man in a white mathematical-tied neckcloth followed him.

Anne pressed her free hand against her chest in somewhat pretended horror and stepped closer to the wall and out of the way of the suddenly rushing crowd. Surely her mother was there somewhere, but where?

Lady Talbot and Mr. Talbot slipped in beside Anne. Sir William, she noted, stood behind them, his arms outstretched while veering the throng away from them.

Mr. Talbot took Anne's arm. He wrapped it around his. "Stay close," he muttered.

Lady Talbot, Mr. Talbot, and Anne maneuvered through the crowd toward the empty window seat where she had earlier that evening sat with Mr. Talbot. The air was slightly cooler there. Even so, she wiped her nose with her handkerchief, wiped it again, and, breathing harder than any of the others about her, scanned the room. At last she caught sight of her mother. She stood on the opposite side of the hall, also near a window, only it was behind the refreshment table.

Anne lowered herself onto the window seat.

Lady Talbot sat beside her. She patted Anne's hand. "I am sorry this evening has turned into such an ordeal, but I do hope it has not discouraged your interest in our mystery."

"Mother," Mr. Talbot said. "Miss de Bourgh has hardly had a chance to catch her breath."

"It is all right, Mr. Talbot." Anne closed her eyes and inhaled. She sniffled slightly and wiped her nose once more. At length she said to Lady Talbot, "I am not discouraged."

"I am pleased to hear it." The lady regarded Anne and Mr. Talbot. "Miss de Bourgh, my sons and I would be most pleased if you would help us with our investigation into Dr. Sinclair's death."

Visit the Talbots? Mr. Talbot? Most assuredly. "I would be delighted to, your ladyship."

Lady Talbot glanced toward Lady Catherine, who was then moving toward them, and quickly added, "If you are not otherwise engaged, my dear, perhaps you can call on us early Monday afternoon to discuss the matter."

Anne glanced at Mr. Talbot. Something in his gaze at her reached out for Anne and drew her toward him as surely as if he had physically pulled her into his arms. She lowered her eyelids over the scandalous thought.

"I have no other engagements," Anne said. For, certainly, while Lady Catherine had invited Lady Allen and Mrs. Hancock, two of Brighton's leading members of society, to visit them on Monday afternoon, her mother would excuse Anne from the engagement when she learned doing so meant Anne would instead be in the company of Sir William Talbot.

"Shall we say two o'clock?" Lady Talbot said.

"That will be splendid."

Lady Catherine reached them. "Come, Anne. We must leave here at once."

Anne stood.

"I will see that your carriage is brought round," Mr. Talbot said.

"Thank you."

He nodded to Lady Catherine, glanced at Anne, and pushed back into the crowd.

"This evening has proven to be quite shocking," Lady Catherine said. "I should never have agreed to attend an event with so many mixed members of society."

"On the contrary," Anne said.

Lady Catherine stared at her, and Anne cringed. What had happened to her? How could she have spoken in such direct opposition to her mother? And yet she could not refrain from adding, "You have frequently told me it is our duty to concern ourselves with the lives of those around us, Mother. I believe helping others through this terrible event qualifies."

"Exactly my feelings," Lady Talbot said.

Her mother stood there, her arms hanging loosely and her posture as straight as ever, but something in her long-held gaze at Anne changed. "You are right."

"Other good has come from it too," Lady Talbot added.

Anne's mother arched an eyebrow. "What good?"

"I have taken quite a fancy to your daughter, and she has consented to call on me and my sons Monday afternoon. I hope that is agreeable with you?"

Anne's mother slowly turned to Anne. She stared at her and at last smiled. "I am certain an afternoon tea would be most agreeable."

"Monday, then," Lady Talbot said.

CHAPTER TEN

Near Lewes, East Sussex

KING'S PICTURES JINGLED IN KENNETH'S pocket. Usually he loved that sound as much he loved lifting the coins from one of the undeserving quality or winning them from some pigeon at the gambling table who was fairly flush in the pockets. But not tonight. Tonight the jingling was nothing more than a reminder his pockets would soon be empty. Again.

"Whatever it takes to save Gracie," he growled. When Bridget had the sickness, he had not had the means, nay, had not known there was only one physician in Sussex who had never lost a patient to putrid fever. If Kenneth had known, had convinced the man to attend upon Bridget, her life might have been spared. But now, now he did know about him, and no matter the cost he would get the man to attend to his daughter.

He climbed the manor's three front steps. He removed his cap and banged on the door.

A middle-aged woman holding a lit lantern opened it. She wore a simply made black dress overlain with a white apron, and her hair was askew beneath her cap. "I do not know whom you wish to see at this time of night," she said, "but the servants' entry is in the back of the house."

"I need to speak with Dr. Lambert, if you please."

She held the lantern farther in front of her and scanned the length of him. Her gaze hesitated on his muddy boots. "I am sorry, but he is taking his supper." She moved to close the door.

Kenneth reached up and stopped it. "I need to speak with the physician," he repeated. "My daughter is gravely ill. I have money."

Again she scanned him.

"I will not leave before I see him."

She frowned. "Wait here." She closed the door.

Kenneth shuffled his cap from one hand to the other. He slid his hand into his pocket, clenching and unclenching the coins. He paced from one side of the porch to the other.

The door opened. The housekeeper stepped to the side, and a middle-aged gentleman with a wig resting haphazardly atop his shoulder-length, gray-blond hair, which was tied at the back of his neck, filled the doorway. He wore a black waistcoat, white neckcloth, and similarly white breeches. "I understand you will not leave without seeing me."

"You are Dr. Lambert?"

"I am."

"I have come in behalf of my daughter, sir. She is ill—a bad case of putrid fever, we believe. Please, come with me and see her."

The gentleman stared at Kenneth. "Do I know you?"

"No, sir. I am from Aliston."

"That is nearly ten miles from here. Surely there is an apothecary much nearer your home."

"There is, and he has already seen her. My daughter needs more trained help than the apothecary can give." Kenneth clenched his fist as if he were once again clenching the quids.

Dr. Lambert nodded heavily. He held Kenneth's gaze. "Putrid fever is a grim business, but I am afraid I cannot help you. My fee is too dear."

"I will pay."

Dr. Lambert shook his head. He stepped backward and moved to close the door.

Again Kenneth stopped the door, holding it open with his splayed hand. "My daughter will die if you do not come."

"The fever is not always fatal."

"How much must I pay for you to see her?"

Dr. Lambert, a bit put out, it seemed to Kenneth, exhaled. "The travel alone will cost you five guineas one way. Beyond that I require five guineas per hour for my time and more for any prescriptions I may write."

The knot in Kenneth's chest collapsed. "Can I bring my daughter here?"

"If she is as ill as you say she is, the travel will do her more harm than good. I am sorry, but my best advice is leave her where she is, take the advice of your apothecary, and make her as comfortable as you can." Once again he moved to close the door.

Kenneth yanked the bag of coins from his pocket. "I have twenty pounds. It is not the coin you prefer, but I beg you to come with me."

"Where did a man like you get such money?"

Kenneth lifted his chin. The man didn't need to know where he got it, only that he had it. "I am good for the rest."

Dr. Lambert eyed the bag and pressed his lips into a fine line. "The fee could cost you up to twenty guineas more."

"Like I said, I will pay it."

"Within a month?"

Kenneth swallowed and nodded.

"Very well. I will come with you. But I will require the money in full by the end of the month, or it is debtor's prison for you."

Kenneth's mouth went dry. He clenched the money bag. Soon he'd be in Brighton. "I will get the money."

CHAPTER ELEVEN

Brighton

DR. SINCLAIR WAS DEAD. IT was such a terrible event to follow such a lovely evening. To think someone would kill—had killed—a man right under so many people's noses. Could it possibly have been an accident? Anne did not think so. Not with the oddness of the scene. But that meant there was another, more frightening, truth looming over them all. A murderer walked among them.

Anne's heart skipped a beat. A murder, a crime Lady Talbot had invited Anne to help her and her sons—*Mr. Talbot*—investigate.

Mr. Talbot . . . Anne stepped inside her bedroom and leaned back against the closed door. *Mr. Talbot.* Despite her memory of Dr. Sinclair's lifeless body lying amid shards of glass, Mr. Talbot's name wove through Anne like threads of sunlight. Not just his name but also his dark hair, so much darker than hers it was almost black. Each strand flitted in short, soft curls at the sides of his face and above his ears in such a haphazard way they reminded her of walking barefoot through a green field on a moonlit night. Not that she had ever done such a scandalous thing. But the thought of it seemed so delightful, so spontaneous, that for a moment she could almost feel the blades of grass between her toes, almost smell the scent of starflowers perfuming the air. And Mr. Talbot's chestnut-brown eyes! She could hardly breathe when she remembered how they'd flamed to life when she looked into them. Sometimes that fire was the single flicker of a candle and other times a raging inferno, but every time her breath fluttered. What her heart did, she did not know. She was too busy trying to keep her knees from weakening beneath her weight.

The doorknob turned, and the door bumped lightly against her back. "Miss de Bourgh?"

Oh! Anne stepped away from the door. "Come in, Blanc."

Ginger Blanc, the French lady's maid her mother had hired at the same time she had rented the townhouse, entered the room. Blanc was a younger girl than Anne's maid at Rosings, likely no more than twenty-one, but so far she had proven herself to be a very capable and efficient servant. It was a convenient arrangement, too, her mother had informed Anne, for the girl would be leaving service soon to marry a nearby farmer.

Blanc walked softly into the room. "Did you have a good time?" Her alluring French accent slid through her speech with such ease Anne barely noticed her softened inflections.

"It was wonderful and . . ." Anne's hands turned clammy. She removed her gloves. "What I mean is the ball was lovely, but afterward Dr. Sinclair, the physician who brought me the tonic yesterday, was found dead in the hat room."

Blanc caught her breath. "What a terrible ordeal for you, miss."

"Do not think of me. Think of him. From what I could see, Dr. Sinclair was alone. What if the poor man did not have a wife or children to mourn him? Or friends? I hope that is not the case."

"Very few people have no friends, miss." Blanc stared at Anne for another long moment before removing the scarf from around Anne's shoulders and draping it over the back of a chair. "What happened to him?"

"No one yet knows." But Monday Anne would see Mr. Talbot and his mother again, and together they would investigate the man's death. Anne had never before investigated anything more than the habitats and life cycles of plants. In truth, she did not know how she could be of any help whatsoever in this matter. But if Mr. Talbot—her toes tingled at the thought of him—and Lady Talbot, who seemed such an intelligent, strong woman, wanted her there, she would be there. And hopefully some good would come of their discussion.

Blanc removed Anne's white dressing gown from the wardrobe, draped it over the chair next to her scarf, and stepped lightly behind Anne. Then Anne straightened her arms at her sides, and Blanc slipped her out of her ball gown and into her white dressing gown.

A quick knock struck her door.

"Come in." Anne looked up as her mother's lady's maid stepped into the room.

"Lady Catherine bids you come to her bedchamber, Miss de Bourgh."

"Tell her I will be there in a moment."

The maid curtsied and left.

Blanc helped Anne into her white night cap. "Will there be anything else you need from me this evening?"

"I do not believe so. Have a good night."

"Thank you, miss."

Anne, watching the door close behind her maid, took a deep breath. She clenched and unclenched the sides of her dressing gown. What could her mother want to say to her now that she could not have said to her in the carriage on their way home? Had she somehow heard of her involvement with studying the scene and now feared scandal? Would she forbid Anne from seeing the Talbots again, even if it meant she would no longer associate with Sir William Talbot? She caught her breath. What would Anne do— say—if she did forbid their association? Could she bear never seeing them or associating with Mr. Talbot again?

Calm yourself. There was no point in chasing shadows she as yet knew nothing of. She again clenched her dressing gown then left her room and walked down the hall to her mother's bedchamber. Her mother, wearing her night cap and robe and looking a good deal paler than she had been a short time ago, stood up from her dressing table when Anne entered.

"Are you unwell?" Anne asked.

"What a ridiculous notion." Her mother frowned. "I expect you agree with me that this business with Dr. Sinclair is most alarming."

"It is."

"But after my conversation with Lady Talbot and seeing how attentive Sir William is with you, I believe all has turned out quite well." She walked to Anne and placed her hand on her shoulder. Her fingers trembled slightly. "I am sure you know I am excessively careful of you, that all I want is your welfare."

"Yes, Mother."

"You also know I will do whatever is in my power to help you achieve this match with Sir William."

"A match? I thought Brighton's amusements were only preparations. I thought—this is not London."

"Opportunities must be taken when they present themselves." Her mother flicked her hand. "But back to the point at hand. Sir William has proven himself to not only be a man of consequence but also of a self-willed mind—in the best sense. Therefore, you must make certain he knows of your interest in him."

Anne folded her arms across her middle. She turned away from her mother and, looking at the floor, paced to the window. She gazed out at the full moon that had no more than an hour before showered its light along Mr. Talbot's white neckcloth and across his broad shoulders, made broader by the cut of his tailcoat. "Sir William was polite and charming, but I saw nothing in him that indicated a particular interest in me."

"You must learn to be more observant. Did he not concern himself with your health when you felt faint? And sit with you in the window seat until he was called away? Did he not ask you for your first dance of the evening?"

Anne furrowed her brow. In some instances the first dance could be fraught with romantic meaning, especially if the partner was chosen out of personal interest rather than gentlemanly obligation, but the latter was certainly the case with Sir William's invitation, whereas Mr. Talbot, whom her mother had snubbed, had twice sought her company of his own accord.

"You are correct, Mother." Anne lowered her eyes. "Sir William did all those things just as you said he did."

"Anne?"

"Yes, Mother?"

"Turn around, child. Look at me."

Anne glanced once more at the moon then turned. Her mother studied her for so long it took all Anne's willpower not to shuffle her weight from one foot to the other.

"I see the problem," her mother said at last. "Despite all Sir William has to offer you, your interest has settled on Mr. Talbot. Do not try to deny it. I can see it in your eyes. Since this is the case, you must believe me when I say you must put Mr. Talbot from your mind. He is not a suitable match for a young woman of your station."

"Why not?"

"It is enough for you to know that he is not suitable."

"It is not enough—" Anne's eyes widened. "Forgive me. I spoke unguardedly."

Her mother narrowed her eyes. "Speak up, Anne. You will tell me what you mean by that outburst."

Anne glanced at the door, exhaled, and bit the inside of her lower lip. "It is only . . . if Mr. Talbot has feelings for me, and—and I for him . . ."

"Has he said anything to you of such things?"

"Of course not."

She nodded crisply. "Feelings have nothing to do with marriage. I warrant the lower classes believe such things, spewing the idea that love is most important. Such lies have even crept into the opinions of some in our own family"—

Mr. Darcy.

—"but I must insist you put them out of your mind. Marrying only for love is a vulgar, deceptive practice meant to undo the fabric of a society that has existed for centuries."

"But—"

"Marriage is about more than the union of people. It is about the joining of estates and inheritances. It is about keeping order in our world."

"What about love? Did you not love my father?"

"Enough of love comes after marriage." Her mother lifted her chin and slightly turned away from Anne, indicating the matter had been settled.

"I do not agree."

Slowly, so slowly Anne dared not breathe, her mother faced her again. Wariness laced the paleness in her expression, but there was surprise there too. A mix of disbelief and shock that Anne had only ever seen her mother show to the new Mrs. Darcy.

Anne forced herself not to smile. "I only mean I am an heiress, Mother. I have no need to marry for money or status. Why can I not do as I please?"

"The heiress of Rosings Park holds many responsibilities, Anne, including the preservation of our place in society."

Anne frowned and slightly shook her head.

"I see I must reveal the whole of it to you. I had wanted to save you from the unpleasant truth of Mr. Talbot's upbringing, for I am afraid you will find it extremely upsetting. But it now seems the most compassionate thing I can do for you."

Certainly there was nothing her mother could say of the gentleman that would lessen Anne's opinion of him. Even so, she took a slight backward step and asked, "What do you know?"

"Mind you, Lady Talbot is my dearest friend. It was she who brought your father and me together. She who, when you were"—she paused—"Leave me to say she is a woman to whom I owe a great deal and of whom I would never speak of such things if it were not necessary I do so."

"You owe her, care for her, yet you disapprove of her?"

"Not her, exactly. But her eldest son . . ." Anne's mother pursed her lips and stared up at the ceiling. At last she again looked at Anne. "When Lady Talbot—Miss Mary Reeves at the time—was a girl of seventeen, she had not yet come out into society, but what the vast majority of us did not know was she had already entered into an arrangement with a young man, a Sir William Talbot, whose father was a wealthy baronet with a vast estate. Of course, no one thought ill of the match; they were only displeased by its secrecy."

"There is hardly anything vexing in that," Anne said. "The couple might have been indiscreet in their actions, but surely, since they did marry, it is no longer of any consequence."

"Soon after news of their unofficial engagement spread, a wicked man by the name of Timothy Jones kidnapped Miss Mary Reeves and forced her to marry him."

Anne gasped.

Lady Catherine turned, pacing away from her. "Miss Mary's family and friends searched for her, Sir William Talbot most of all, but their efforts were in vain. Soon after her unfortunate marriage, Miss Mary—Mrs. Jones then—became pregnant."

Anne's stomach twisted as if someone had wrapped it in threads of ice. So that was the problem. Mr. Talbot was a ruffian's son. "What happened to her was terrible," Anne said, "but all must have turned out all right. She is Lady Talbot now."

"She is." Her mother returned to her side and once again placed her hand on Anne's shoulder. "When Mr. Jones learned of his wife's pregnancy, he informed Sir William Talbot of her condition and demanded a ransom for her return. Apparently money, along with some unwarranted sense of seeking justice against Sir William Talbot—for what, I do not know—had been his motives to Miss Mary's kidnapping and ruin. The only good part of the story is Mr. Jones's idiocy. When Sir William Talbot received the ransom note, he and Mary's father brought the authorities with them to the drop-off point, and Mr. Jones went to prison."

"Did he die there?"

"I know nothing more about him. What I do know is after Sir William had Miss Mary safely back with him, he and Miss Mary's father, Mr. Reeves, spent a great deal of time and money to have her marriage to Mr.

Jones annulled for incompetence. Mary had not been of legal age when the rites were performed, nor had the marriage been approved by her father."

"I am glad for that. For her sake and theirs."

Her mother frowned. Apparently *glad* was not the word her mother wanted her to use. "As I said, it took some time before the annulment could be completed. While they waited, Mr. Reeves took Miss Mary back into his household, and the child we now know as Mr. Talbot was born there. In time—two years later, as I recall—Sir William Talbot married Miss Mary Reeves, and soon after Sir William was born."

"Sir William Talbot's rightful heir."

"Yes. To be sure, Sir William was a good husband and father to Lady Talbot and her firstborn son, and he treated both boys as his own, but in the end, the legitimate son inherited the title and all that went with it. To Mr. Talbot's benefit, Sir William was also a shrewd man, much as your own father was, and through investments outside of the Seawind House estate, he was able to leave an ample amount for all his dependents. Or so Lady Talbot told me this evening."

Anne stared at the rug lying next to her mother's bed, at the red and blue and gold threads weaving in and around each other, forming patterns of suns and flowers. As it had done so many times that night, Mr. Talbot's face slipped in among those threads and held there, his gaze watching her. "So Mr. Talbot is rich and well-connected, but because of who his real father is, he must be ostracized."

"Not ostracized exactly. He is a member of society and, I expect, a good man, but you must allow the scandalous circumstances of his birth as well as his infirmity are highly against him. While I love Lady Talbot as my own sister, you must see Mr. Talbot will never be fully accepted into society. I did not raise you, my dear, to become less than who you are."

"I do not believe I am a lesser person simply because I know Mr. Talbot or because I am his friend."

Her mother's cheekbones flushed. "A friend? Your dishonesty is unbecoming and highly beneath you, Anne. All who saw the two of you together could not doubt there was more than friendship between you. You know full well I am not speaking of you associating with him. I am speaking of the two of you forming an attachment."

Anne rubbed her arm and glanced away. "An attachment? I have . . . All he has ever said is . . . We have only met twice."

"Nevertheless, now you understand why you must place all your attentions on Sir William. You must not give Mr. Talbot or his family the wrong impression as to where your true interests lie."

Anne took a deep breath. From the standpoint of the *ton*, she understood, but her own mind—her heart—did not. But how could she convince her mother of such things? "It is not—not Mr. Talbot's fault his father was a—a blackguard."

Her mother pursed her lips. "Monday when you visit Seawind House, you will make it clear to both men you are interested in Sir William and not in Mr. Talbot."

The sunlight Anne had been swimming in since she last saw Mr. Talbot shriveled into a puddle of blackness. She could not do that. She must not do that. And yet, what else could she do? "Yes, Mother."

CHAPTER TWELVE

Saturday and Sunday were such monotonous, rain-drenched days, diverted only by Anne's morning walks with Mrs. Webb and a dutiful visit from a local clergyman, that when Blanc woke her on Monday morning a few minutes before sunrise, Anne sat straight up.

Blanc grinned. "My mother smiles just like that when she wakes. She says morning is the best part of the day."

"And what do you think?"

Blanc lowered her voice. She glanced at the door as if she feared someone might overhear her. "I think if it ever happens I can choose the course of my day, I will stay to my bed as long as I want. Until midday if I choose."

Though Blanc did not look at Anne and her voice was as sedate as it ever was, her words pierced Anne's heart. True, the hope Anne had begun to feel for Mr. Talbot had slinked beneath her bed after her conversation with her mother, but all this young girl standing before her wanted was rest, something that was everyday life to Anne. Maybe Anne was unhappy with the life's course that had been placed before her, forcing her to choose propriety and genteel connections over the call of her heart, but that did not mean she had to be ungrateful for what she did possess. "Perhaps sometime I can give you a day in bed," she said.

"It is kind of you to imagine it could be so, miss."

Anne climbed out from under the light blanket and stood. Had she really only offered the girl a kind thought and not something she could actually give her? Was such a simple act, in truth, controlled by as many rules as, say, marriage was? All at once Anne's mother's face and stern expression filled Anne's mind. Anne, frowning, released a long, slow sigh. Blanc was right. No matter the circumstances or Anne's whims, there was little she could change. The working class must work; class distinctions must remain intact.

Blanc handed Anne the prescriptive list Dr. Sinclair had given her the afternoon before he had died and poured the tonics into a teacup. She had earlier arranged them on the small tripod table a few feet from Anne's bed. "Is there anything else I can do for you, miss?"

Anne glanced over the list, making certain she remembered the routine correctly. "I know it is now earlier than I usually dress for the day, but would you please help me into my walking dress? And wrap up my bathing gown?"

"It is a few hours too early for your sea-bathing appointment, is it not?"

"It is, but I wish to go for a walk first." *And maybe find a plant or two to draw.* It was too much for Anne to wish she could go to Seawind House before her tea appointment, but this was Brighton, and she still had not located the Virgin's bower.

Blanc removed Anne's red walking dress and beige flannel bathing gown from the wardrobe and draped them across the unmade bed.

Anne's mouth went so dry she almost wished to drink the tonic still sitting on the corner table. In a few short hours she would be wearing only this gown, which was little more than a long shift, in the middle of the ocean's cold, surging waves. "I believe I would also appreciate a shot of courage, Blanc, if you have it."

Blanc tilted her head. She studied Anne for a long moment and grinned. "I am afraid that is beyond my power, miss. But I can tell you, I have been swimming since I was an *enfante*. And we had no need of dippers. My papa taught us, the girls just as the boys. He said since we live by the sea, we must learn to swim in it, even if most of the people hereabouts didn't agree with him."

"And do you like it? Sea-bathing?"

"I do. And I believe you will too." Blanc folded the bathing gown, wrapped it in brown paper, and set it on the bed next to Anne's walking dress. "There now. You are ready for the day."

"I wish I had your confidence."

"You are only nervous because you have never been in the ocean before. I felt that way the first time, too, but I believe you will lose your fear as soon as you get over the first shock. That is how it was for me."

"I hope you are right."

Anne set the prescriptive list back on the table, and Blanc helped her into her walking dress. Red. Like blood. Dr. Sinclair's blood.

"Are you cold, miss? I can close the window, if you wish."

"Not at all. I was only thinking of Dr. Sinclair. Of what happened to him at the ball."

"I hear it was a terrible business. I cannot imagine what I would do if I had come upon such a scene."

Come upon such a scene. While Anne had mentioned the event to Blanc, she had certainly not told her how she had intentionally joined Lady Talbot and her sons in the hat room with the body.

Anne lowered and calmed her voice. "Have you heard something more of the good doctor's death?"

"Oh yes, miss. Everyone is talking of it. The servants, Mr. Robert Jonas, my betrothed. I can hardly walk down the street without hearing something of it." She tugged the dress into place around Anne's waist. "There now. Daylight is barely peeking into the sky, and you are already as pretty as an angel." She motioned Anne toward the mirror. "See for yourself."

Anne looked first at one side of her face and then the other. There was nothing out of the ordinary about her appearance, and nothing had yet been done to her hair, but she could not help but notice how striking her dark hair looked, falling over the shoulders of her red dress. She could not wear it that way, but when she was sea-bathing, would it slip from its bindings? Would Mrs. Webb, who would be the only servant with her on the beach, know how to repair it if it did?

Blanc must have inferred Anne's reservations, for she at once set about lifting and twisting Anne's hair into an extra-tight swirl at the back of her head. She then overlaid the entire ensemble with a simple red bonnet. "Now you are ready for your exercise regime."

"I am afraid my morning regime actually begins with drinking that tonic." Anne smoothed her dress at the waist, took a deep breath, and moved to the table. She picked up the filled teacup and lifted it to her lips. She glanced at Blanc.

Blanc smiled. "Go ahead, miss. I expect you will survive."

"I expect I will too." Anne had, after all, survived her last dosages. *If only it did not taste so dreadful.*

"Many in Brighton swear by the cure's healthful effects," Blanc added.

"I think it might already be working for me too." Anne closed her eyes and swallowed every—last—gulp. *Ugh.*

Blanc giggled into her hand and then, taking the cup, handed Anne a serviette. Anne wiped her mouth and turned away from Blanc so she would not see her also wipe the taste from her tongue. Anne's stomach churned, but at least the tonic stayed inside.

"I heard in town a relation of yours visited Brighton last year," Blanc said. "And went sea-bathing."

"A relative of mine? Oh. You must be speaking of Miss Lydia Bennet. I hardly think of her as my relative, but yes, she did visit Brighton last year." And foolishly ran off with Mr. Wickham. "Make certain you never speak of her in front of Lady Catherine."

"No, miss. I won't." Blanc watched Anne, looking as if she wanted her to say more on the subject, but as Anne had no desire to think anything of that botched marriage, and especially not on how the elopement had begun here in Brighton, she turned away from her maid and again glanced over her reflection in the mirror.

Someone knocked lightly on the door.

"That will be Mrs. Webb, come to collect me for my walk."

Blanc curtsied and opened the door.

Mrs. Webb, wearing a gray-blue walking dress and matching hat, filled the doorway. She glanced over Anne's shoulder at Blanc then back at Anne. "Good morning, Miss de Bourgh."

"Good morning."

Mrs. Webb nodded in a way that was almost a bow and backed to the side of the door. Anne handed her wrapped bathing gown and drawing pad to Mrs. Webb, gathered up her reticule, and crossed the threshold. Mrs. Webb followed Anne through the silent house until they stepped out the front door and closed it behind them.

"Lady Catherine has instructed me to have you back here as soon after your sea-bathing appointment as possible," she said. "She insists you must have ample time to prepare yourself for your visit to Seawind House."

Visiting the Talbots was the one part of Anne's day she looked forward to—not the part about having to give all her attentions to Sir William, but the part about seeing Mr. Talbot. Her heart simultaneously tripped, ran, and grieved. If only she were more courageous. If only her life could be ruled by her heart instead of the *ton*. Or her mother. "I will obey her wishes."

Anne and Mrs. Webb left the house and headed west along the boardwalk. Since it was so early in the morning, they at first passed only servants and livery men, but after they had traveled for at least twenty minutes, they turned back in the direction they had come and headed toward the women's sea-bathing side of the beach. By that time several gentlemen and a few ladies had also left their townhouses for what Anne could only assume were their morning constitutionals. Two of the young gentlemen tipped their hats to them. At first Anne did not recognize their faces, but when Mrs. Webb said, "Upon my word, did you overhear what they were speaking of?" Anne looked back over her shoulder at them.

"I did not, but I believe I saw them at the ball. Why? What did they say?"

Mrs. Webb hugged Anne's paper-wrapped bathing gown tighter against her middle. "It was the ball they were speaking of. Of Dr. Sinclair's death."

"Such a shocking business."

"To be sure."

They continued on, passing several men and women, and all, it seemed, were speaking of Dr. Sinclair. Some said he had magically appeared in Brighton like he was a ghost or a wizard. Others claimed he had very likely been the physician to the prince regent himself.

Anne shook her head. "So many fanciful ideas. I only spoke once with the man, but I can assure you he was none of those things." Anne's thoughts paused. That certainty over information she knew little about was exactly what her mother would have said. And Anne did not want to be her mother. True, Anne did admire her mother's physical and mental strength, her tenacity, but Anne did not want to become so caught up in her own viewpoints that she became the woman people, like Mr. Darcy, rolled their eyes at behind her back when she voiced her opinions as truths.

"I apologize," Anne said to Mrs. Webb. "The truth is, while Dr. Sinclair treated me with cordiality, I know nothing more than that of him."

Mrs. Webb stared at her.

"You are surprised," Anne said. "Why?"

She blinked. "I am actually more proud of you than I am surprised. I do believe, Miss de Bourgh, you are learning to trust your own thoughts."

It was a simple comment wrapped in even simpler praise, but it radiated through Anne as brightly as the sun reflecting off the Channel's waves. "Thank you."

Mrs. Webb nodded.

They continued down the boardwalk, crossed the road to the wide path along the beach, and headed toward the bathing machines. The machines were enclosed sheds on wheels lined along the shore and facing out to sea. The machine's drivers were there with their horses, along with several women Anne assumed were dippers, but she saw no sign of Mrs. Dramwell.

Anne wiped her nose for only the third time that morning. Her health was definitely improving. "Mrs. Dramwell has thick, sturdy arms and a large physique," her mother had said when she had first described the woman to her.

"I do not see her," Anne said. "Perhaps we are too early."

"Shall we walk up the Steyne while we wait? Perhaps we will find a garden that interests you. You did want to draw, and I believe there is still time before your appointment for you to do so, if you find the plant you are looking for."

"I like that idea."

The two started back, preparing to cross the road, when Anne heard a familiar giggle. She looked over her shoulder.

The Wycliff sisters, their arms hooked together, moved up the path toward them. Miss Wycliff held a parasol over their heads. Miss Henrietta carried two brown packages similar to the one Mrs. Webb carried for Anne.

Miss Henrietta grinned, and her voice bounced. "We came early, hoping we would see you before your dipping appointment. It looks to be a particularly hot day, and sea-bathing is always much more pleasant and better for the body in the cool of the morning."

"Do come with us," Miss Wycliff said.

The same warning feelings Anne had felt at the ball about joining the Wycliff sisters plowed through her, and yet only moments before, she had wished she had the courage to be more daring. Had her earlier impressions, in fact, been her own? Or were they merely due to her fear of the *ton*?

Anne clenched her reticule and looked back toward the bathing machines. "The beach is not open yet."

"The men's side is," Miss Henrietta said.

Anne's hand flew to her chest. Mrs. Webb gasped. "Miss de Bourgh, you must not—"

"No, no." Miss Henrietta released her sister and took hold of Anne's forearm. "We would never swim on the men's side, but the area between the women and the men is not so governed."

"And the beach grows out into the sea there," Miss Wycliff said. "It forms a natural kind of barrier. We will be quite safe."

"We do it all the time," Miss Henrietta added.

"There is even a rickety old bathing machine there. It is no longer sound enough to be pulled into the waves," Miss Wycliff said, "but it is safe enough to dress in."

Once again Miss Henrietta grinned. "Please come with us, Miss de Bourgh. You do not have to wade far out into the water if you do not wish to, but it will help you get used to the feel of the waves. You will see you have nothing to fear."

"And you can do so without being obliged to follow your dipper's rules or anyone else's, for that matter."

Anne's uncertainties still clutched at her empty stomach, but the young ladies' expressions were so open, so genial, and the idea Anne could first take the waters on her own terms sounded quite agreeable. And courageous. "Very well," she said.

Mrs. Webb stepped in beside her and clutched her elbow. "I am not certain this is the wisest course, Miss de Bourgh."

"It is. It is," Miss Henrietta squealed.

Anne looked hard at Mrs. Webb. Her usually open gaze was filled with so many misgivings, Anne could almost feel them traipsing over her feet, but there were so few parts of Anne's life she could control; surely it would be all right to try this one thing. Surely if either Mr. or Mrs. Darcy had wanted to try sea-bathing here, they would have done it. *Be courageous.* "All will be well," she said to Mrs. Webb.

So much sweat trickled from Mrs. Webb's hairline as she stared down the road toward their townhouse Anne at once feared she would rush back to Lady Catherine and tell her all Anne was about to do. *At least she cannot leave me without getting herself into trouble too.*

Anne and the other three ladies headed back to the west side of the beach, but the closer they got to the single bathing machine sitting on the shoreline, the tighter Anne's stomach clenched. *Courage. This is what I want.*

They stepped off the boardwalk and headed toward the rocky beach.

"Sea-bathing is as easy as slicing through melted butter," Miss Wycliff said. "We take turns going into the bathing machine, change into our bathing gowns, and step—"

"Or jump," Miss Henrietta said.

"Yes, jump, into the water."

The hair on the back of Anne's neck did indeed jump to attention. She looked about her. Was someone watching them? Her pace slowed.

Mrs. Webb clutched Anne's arm. "We should leave here."

"Do not listen to her," Miss Wycliff said. "Her nerves are all atwitter."

"Something is not right," Mrs. Webb pressed. "Trust me."

Miss Wycliff shook her head. "If something was wrong, my sister and I would not only know about it but would be the first to leave. Would we not, Henrietta?"

Miss Henrietta glanced up toward the top of the townhouses behind them and grinned. "I will go first." She slipped her brown paper package beneath her arm and ran through the splashing waves toward the front of the bathing machine. A few minutes later, she opened the door and jumped into the water. Her bathing gown floated above her knees. She again glanced toward the townhouses and waved to Anne and Miss Wycliff. "Come along. The water is perfect."

Anne bit the inside of her lower lip. Perfect how? Miss Henrietta was not smiling, and judging by the way she was shivering, the water seemed cold, not *perfect*.

Miss Wycliff looked at Anne. "Your turn?"

"I am not quite ready."

"I will go, then." Miss Wycliff hurried over the rocks and through the water to the bathing machine.

"Please, Miss de Bourgh. Let us leave." Mrs. Webb's words punched Anne in the gut and tugged her around to face her. Her companion motioned toward the top of one of the townhouses across the street. A flicker of steel flashed in the sunlight from an upper window.

"A spyglass," Mrs. Webb said. "It is difficult to see, but I am certain I saw a man up there in that window when Miss Henrietta stepped out of the bathing machine."

Anne's stomach dropped. Until that moment she had seen nothing of the debaucheries and overindulgences that had always accompanied descriptions of Brighton. She had even begun to believe her mother had been right on all accounts in bringing Anne there for the summer, that the rumors were merely exaggerations created by overly critical members of society. After all, Anne's health was improving, and Mr. Talbot, the best man she knew, lived in Brighton. His mother and brother did too. And Brighton belonged to this wondrous setting—the white ocean waves crashing with both beauty and power against the low-lying shore and distant crags. Such goodness should not be discounted. Good and bad. Why did they always live side by side?

Anne, edging closer to Mrs. Webb, looked back to the Wycliff sisters. "We should warn them."

"I am sorry to say this," Mrs. Webb said, "but I believe they already know the man is there."

As if on cue, Miss Henrietta faced the townhouses and, this time grinning, waved her arm high over her head. Mrs. Webb was right. Miss Henrietta did indeed know a man was watching them sea bathe. Not only that, she seemingly cared nothing for the scandal such actions could bring her. Scandal Anne would also partake of if she joined them. Was that why the girls had befriended her so quickly last night? Why they had led her there? She had thought they were merely silly, but had she in truth been a sort of prey to them? Worse, had she not assured Mr. Talbot she would not join them? *"They may wish for me to join them,"* Anne had said to Mr. Talbot, *"but I can assure you I will not."*

Praise be to the heavens Mr. Talbot was not there to see how she had almost gone against her assertion. That she had momentarily proven herself weaker and perhaps even less intelligent than he had proclaimed her to be. That she had disappointed him.

Anne took Mrs. Webb's arm with one hand and clenched her reticule with the other, and the two turned away from the bathing machine. They marched back up the rocky beach to the seaside path. "Thank you," she said softly.

"For what?"

Mrs. Webb knew perfectly well for what, but the insistence in her gaze told Anne she wanted to hear her say the words. She wanted Anne to once again speak up, to say what she wished to say.

"Thank you for your wisdom and your persistence. Thank you for keeping me from folly, and . . ."

"And?"

"And—thank you for—for letting me trust you."

"You are welcome."

CHAPTER THIRTEEN

ANNE'S DIVERSION WITH THE WYCLIFFS had consumed so much of her extra time that when she and Mrs. Webb finally made it back to the women's beach, they barely had time to locate Mrs. Dramwell, who was standing at the back of a sea-bathing machine. Mrs. Dramwell was a muscular, buxom woman with a businesslike expression, who wore a black bonnet and black dress. The dress was so black, in fact, Anne wondered if the woman was mourning. Had she, perhaps, known Dr. Sinclair? Or maybe—had someone died while she dipped them in the water?

Do not borrow trouble.

Anne and Mrs. Webb climbed past Mrs. Dramwell up the three steps into the bathing machine. A man, presumably the driver, waited at the front of the machine with his back gentlemanly toward them. He sat astride the horse Anne assumed would tug the machine into the water.

Before Mrs. Webb closed the door, Mrs. Dramwell said, "Would you like the driver there to wait a minute or more for you to put on your bathing gown, miss? Or do you want to dress while he drives into the waves?"

Anne, frowning slightly, glanced at Mrs. Webb. If riding to Brighton in a travelling coach on a dry road had pounded her nerves into a frazzle, how could she possibly endure changing her clothes amid the swells and dips of the ocean's waves?

"I would prefer if he waited for a few minutes," she said, "since this is my first time."

"And as I will not be swimming," Mrs. Webb added, "I wish to leave the machine before it leaves the beach."

Mrs. Dramwell looked at Anne, who nodded her consent. "Five minutes, then." She closed the door.

The two set Anne's belongings on the wooden bench attached to the bathing machine's wall and quickly, though not without several near-topples due to the unsteadiness of the wagon, changed Anne out of her walking dress and into her bathing gown. Soon after, Mrs. Webb secured Anne's street clothes in a raised compartment and opened the machine's back door. Mrs. Dramwell as well as another woman of similar size and dress stood at the bottom of the stairs.

"I will wait for you here on the beach," Mrs. Webb said to Anne. "I hope you have an enjoyable time."

Anne folded her arms in front of her barely clothed body and stepped back into the shadows. "Thank you."

Mrs. Webb, carrying Anne's reticule and drawing pad, returned to the beach, and Mrs. Dramwell closed the door. "Now," she called out.

"Yaw!" the driver yelled.

The machine jostled forward. Anne sat on the bench, pressed her back against the wall, and focused on the stream of sunlight filtering through the tiny window near the ceiling until the machine eventually stopped. In actuality, the ride could not have lasted more than a minute or two, but with the incessant joggling forward and hobbling back and forth over the rocks and amid the waves, it seemed longer than one of Mr. Collins's favored sermons.

Mrs. Dramwell opened the front door. She and the other woman— Cooper, Mrs. Dramwell called her—stood in the water to the side of the door, and the driver and his horse were no longer there.

Wet, salty wind blustered against Anne. She caught her breath.

Mrs. Dramwell held out her hand. "Take hold of our hands, miss."

Anne, breathing . . . breathing . . . against the chill and wind and her tremblings, clutched the women's hands and climbed down the stairs. Cold water swamped around her feet, her knees, her thighs. She climbed off the last step. But before she reached the ocean floor, Mrs. Dramwell and Cooper clasped each other's hands and arms, forming a makeshift chair, and scooped Anne into it. They carried her a few feet farther into the sea and dipped all but Anne's head beneath the waves. They did that three times. Then, still balancing Anne, they laid Anne back on top of the water. Anne closed her eyes. Sunlight blazed over her face and warmed her skin. The water muffled the sounds of the surging and crashing waves, the creakings of nearby bathing machines, and the laughter of other women likewise enjoying the sea. Though the dippers still held her, Anne felt as if she were floating above the water. She breathed in and out, quickly at first then slower.

"Time's up," Mrs. Dramwell said.

"Can I stay? Just a bit longer?" *I have never felt so free before.*

"A minute or two, but no longer. More customers are waiting for their dippings."

"Thank you." Anne, her eyes still closed, arched her neck farther back and spread her arms. Was this what it felt like to be a fish swimming wherever it wanted through the sea? Or a swan floating on the water as if it had no cares in the world? Freedom . . . freedom. Was this why Blanc enjoyed swimming so much? And also why Mr. Talbot did?

Mr. Talbot. Swimming did not require walking. It only required strong, strong arms like Mr. Talbot's. Anne swallowed.

"Do you know how to swim?" Anne asked.

"We could not be dippers if we did not," Mrs. Dramwell said. "Some clients get a bit too certain of themselves and venture too far out into the sea. If we could not swim, we could not save them."

"Oh."

"Would you like to, on your own, stand in the water?" Cooper said. "It is not too deep."

"I would."

They lowered Anne to her feet. As the woman said, the water was not too deep—it covered Anne's chest—but they did not release her hands until she bid them do so. *Complete freedom. Amazing!*

Anne walked a few feet in several directions, mostly forming a circle, swishing her arms through the water as she went.

"We must go back now, miss," Mrs. Dramwell said.

"Very well."

Mrs. Dramwell and Cooper took Anne's hands and led her back to the bathing machine. They set her feet onto the stairs. Water slogged off Anne, but the freedom, the courage she so recently felt still whispered through her.

"Until tomorrow," Mrs. Dramwell said.

"Yes, tomorrow," Anne said. "But I do have a request."

"What is it?"

"During our sessions, would you teach me how to swim?"

Mrs. Dramwell told Cooper to return to the beach and see to the needs of their next clients and looked back to Anne. "I must say no one has ever asked me a question such as that. Common folk learn from friends or family, and most gentry do not care to swim."

"Some of my friends do and quite enjoy the pastime."

Mrs. Dramwell gazed out toward another bathing machine still on the beach. Her dipping companion, now there, waved at her. "We'd best be leaving, miss." She turned back to Anne. "Perhaps you should ask one of your gentry friends to teach you."

A boulder thudded at the base of Anne's stomach. She could never ask Mr. Talbot, a man, to teach her how to swim. Merely thinking of it was scandalous. And the Wycliff sisters—the image of the spyglass flashing in the sunlight made her cringe. Anne would rather remain on dry land for the rest of her life than swim with them. "Sadly, that is not possible."

Mrs. Dramwell studied Anne's face. "I will teach you what I can during the time we have, but it will not be enough. Swimming requires practice time, which I do not have to give you."

"If I purchased more sessions with you, could you do it?"

"Perhaps I could find other dippers to take over my duties. If you paid enough."

"Thank you." Anne rushed up the stairs to the bathing machine. "You will hear from me after I speak with my mother."

CHAPTER FOURTEEN

Aliston, East Sussex

KENNETH HANDED DR. LAMBERT A dish to catch the blood from Grace's too-thin arm and replaced his rag. When Kenneth had last stood in this spot, Grace's face had been red with fever and sweat had not only pooled on her forehead but had also dripped down her face and wetted the back of her neck. Kenneth gritted his teeth. Now, in the few short minutes he had been in the other room, changing out the doctor's supplies, Grace's skin had paled whiter than the tin cup of daisies sitting on the window's ledge. Neil, knowing Grace loved daisies, must have picked them for her. Fanny had indeed married a thoughtful man.

Grace's breathing shallowed.

"How much blood will you take from her?"

"Only as much as is needed to get the sickness out." Dr. Lambert looked up at Kenneth. "You may wait in the other room if my ministrations are too much for you."

"No." Kenneth focused on his daughter's face. Was her paleness turning blue? "She is so small, so frail. It seems there is more sickness in her than blood."

Dr. Lambert got up from where he sat next to Grace on the bed and fully faced Kenneth. "If you wish your daughter to live, you must let me care for her as I see fit."

Kenneth swallowed. "Yes, sir." He took the bloodied supplies from the doctor and turned back to the door.

"If you would prefer it, I can leave," Dr. Lambert said from behind him. "As my fee has already surpassed your payment, you may now believe it is best to consult an apothecary."

Kenneth faced the doctor once again. "We went through this before. I will get the money. All you have to do is keep as close a watch on my daughter as you do your pocketbook."

"I cannot work long on credit for someone who already sits next to the poorhouse." So much arrogance laced the physician's frown it took all Kenneth's self-will not to grab the man by his waistcoat and shove him out the front door. Instead Kenneth yanked open the bedroom door and stormed out.

CHAPTER FIFTEEN

Brighton

IF ANNE HAD NOT JUST spoken with her mother and if her mother had not just refused to allow Anne extended dipping time, she would have been excited to at last stand before Seawind House's front door. As it was, her mother's words scratched the back of her thoughts like a not-quite-healed wound.

"Dr. Fletcher will certainly agree with me that the dipping time you have is the exact amount you need to improve your health," her mother had said. "As for your sudden desire to swim, while I am glad you enjoy the amusement, an heiress such as yourself must concentrate on more important pursuits. You will put the matter out of your mind and set your thoughts to your upcoming visit with Sir William."

Anne groaned and stared at Seawind House's still-closed door. *Blanc knows how to swim. I will ask her to teach me.*

"Are you all right?" Mrs. Webb said.

"Merely lost in my thoughts."

Mrs. Webb nodded, but Anne had the distinct impression her nod was double-edged. Yes, she agreed with Anne's feelings on the sea-bathing matter, but at the same time, as she had said when Anne had first told her of her mother's reply, *This is what comes when you do not speak your mind.*

It was also what came when Anne had to obey her mother. In all things. And relationships.

At last Mrs. Graham, the Talbot's housekeeper, opened the door and led Anne and Mrs. Webb into Seawind House's sitting room. Lady Talbot, wearing a white afternoon dress overlain with such a dark-forest-green robe that in some lighting it seemed an evening gown, sat in the center of a pale-gold couch on the far side of the rather vast room. Sir William and Mr. Talbot, with their hands clasped behind their backs, stood behind their mother and in such close proximity to one of the four large western-facing windows that the sunlight gleaming into the room haloed both men—Mr. Talbot, especially, even though his features were darker than Sir William's.

Mr. Talbot's gaze caught Anne's. Her palms turned wet inside her gloves. *"You will make it clear to both men you are interested in Sir William and not Mr. Talbot,"* her mother had said. But if Mr. Talbot kept looking at Anne like that, how could she do so?

Sheer will. Until then she had considered will as something good, an actual power she must develop in order to find whom she was and acquire what she wanted in life. Now she realized such will had a downside too; sometimes a person had to exert it toward an undesirable outcome.

Anne ignored the fresh slice that thought made in her heart, dragged her gaze away from Mr. Talbot, and nodded her greeting to Lady Talbot.

"Thank you for coming, Miss de Bourgh." Lady Talbot motioned for Anne to sit in the chair closest to her. Mrs. Webb sat in the chair on the other side of Anne. "Is your mother in good health?"

"She is quite well, thank you."

"I am glad to hear it. I had worried the events at the ball might have overpowered her. I understand many in attendance were quite scandalized."

Anne took a deep breath and glanced about the room until she had calmed herself. Scandal. Had hers and Lady Talbot's pretense that they had merely come upon the body quite by accident been believed? Anne had heard nothing more of it, but the *ton* could be as blatant or as secretive as it chose to be.

"Thank you, ma'am," Anne said. "I assure you she is quite well," she repeated. The others watched Anne for so long, embarrassment prickled up her spine and across her face. *They expect me to say something more. But what?* She shifted in her seat, clenching her drawing pad tighter against her waist.

Mr. Talbot watched the movement and looked back into her eyes.

"May I hold your drawing pad for you?" Mrs. Webb whispered.

"Oh yes, thank you." Anne handed the leather book to her companion and looked back to Lady Talbot, Sir William, the pianoforte situated behind Lady Talbot, and the two brass candelabra with four sconces each sitting in the middle of the dark hardwood table. She scanned across the window draperies and— "What a lovely painting."

"Thank you," Lady Talbot said. "We have a few family portraits, but this one is my favorite."

Quiet returned.

Exert yourself. Anne stood. She crossed the carpet that filled the middle of the sitting area to the large painting hanging on the wall between the window where the Talbot men stood and its neighboring window. "I suppose the man standing next to you is your late husband, Sir William."

"It is," Lady Talbot said.

Anne turned back to them. "When was it made?"

Lady Talbot, her sons, and Mrs. Webb joined Anne at the foot of the portrait. Mrs. Webb frowned. What had displeased her?

"Several years ago," Lady Talbot said. "My husband had it commissioned soon after we moved from London to Brighton."

Anne focused back on the painting. With no one looking directly at her, she let her gaze linger over the image of Mr. Talbot, of the upward tilt of his lips and the curls of dark hair where they brushed the tops of his eyebrows.

"I do not think I have seen this girl before." Anne bit the inside of her lip. Since this was a family portrait, the girl must be a Talbot, but had Anne made a mistake in asking after her? She hoped not.

Thankfully, Lady Talbot simply touched Anne's forearm and smiled softly. "That is Susanna, my daughter. She is away at finishing school."

"She bears a strong likeness to your husband."

"She does." Lady Talbot rested the back of her forefinger against the side of the man's face. His features, though older than the two young men in the portrait, provided the same contrast Mr. Talbot had with Sir William; for while Mr. Talbot had inherited his mother's dark features, Sir William's straight blond hair and blue eyes were nearly identical to both his sister's and his father's. *His* father's. Not Mr. Talbot's. *Remember that,* Anne could almost hear her mother's voice say inside her mind.

"The artist's skill was quite remarkable," Anne said.

Mr. Talbot opened his mouth, hesitated, and closed it again. Lady Talbot looked at him and turned back to Anne. "What makes you think so, my dear?"

Anne's breath froze. Everyone was staring at her, waiting for her to respond, but all she could think to say was *because Mr. Talbot's expression has the same seriousness, the same studiousness as he wears now,* which she absolutely did not want to say aloud. Such a statement would certainly hint at her interest in him, and she could not allow any of them to know of it.

"Perhaps," Mr. Talbot said, "it is because Miss de Bourgh, being an artist in her own right, recognizes the brush strokes of a master."

"You draw, do you, Miss de Bourgh?" Lady Talbot asked.

Anne nodded. She glanced at Mr. Talbot—*whether you realize it or not, you just saved me from embarrassment*—then looked back to his mother. "The reason I know the man who painted your family portrait is an accomplished artist is because when I look at it, I feel as if I am looking not at a picture but at a moment in time. The artist depicted each person exactly as they are."

"What moment?" Sir William teased. "I bet you cannot guess it."

"Come now, brother," Mr. Talbot said. "That is not a fair question. You may disregard everything he says, Miss de Bourgh."

Anne pressed her finger against her lips and once again scrutinized the portrait. Sir William's painted smile was every bit as playful as it was at that moment. "All I will say is I can almost see Sir William running away from the artist and going off to play a game of battledore with the neighborhood lads."

Sir William laughed. "Gads, you are good, Miss de Bourgh. Though battledore was a bit too sedate for me."

Anne closed her mouth. Her thoughts reeled. She, soft-spoken, sickly, frightened-of-her-own-shadow Miss Anne de Bourgh, had spoken outright, unguardedly even, of a painting—a subject she knew something of—without first worrying about herself. And yet no one had seemed to mind. In truth, Mrs. Webb's earlier displeased expression was replaced with greater pride than Anne had ever before seen in her. Was that the key to the inner strength Anne had been missing all these years? She simply had to forget herself?

Can I do it again?

"My brother would more likely be out racing than playing battledore," Mr. Talbot said, "or playing hide-and-seek."

Anne let herself look at Mr. Talbot. She lingered over every movement of his expression while he spoke before reluctantly turning her attention back to Lady Talbot. "And that is why I admire the artist."

Lady Talbot continued to study the painting. "I believe you are right, Miss de Bourgh. I have often wondered why this portrait, separate from the others I have of my husband, would provide me with such comfort. I had thought it was because of his quizzing glass. See how it hangs from his neck there? He used to wear it whenever we were investigating a crime. It was a sort of ritual of his."

"Pardon me. You are likely more right than I am."

"No, dear." She turned away from them and walked toward the center of the room. "Mrs. Graham," she said to the housekeeper, who stood near the door, "please ask Morin to bring my investigation journal to me."

"Yes, my lady." Mrs. Graham curtsied and left.

Lady Talbot returned to where Anne and the others still stood in front of the painting. "As I was saying, I see now, Miss de Bourgh, your summation of my situation is correct. My feelings are connected with the perfection of my husband's expression in this likeness." Her voice slipped through the air like softened mellow sunlight. "As a girl I believed chivalry and compliments were the true marks of love, the only ingredients for a happy marriage, but marriage to Sir William taught me differently."

She turned to Anne. At first her eyes were like glazed glass, but in the next moment, her gaze cleared. "Forgive me, my dear. You will think me a foolish old woman for such talk."

"Not at all." From what Anne's mother had told her of Lady Talbot's early life, Anne could guess the shades of the woman's memories, of how she would see sacrifice and commitment as greater measures of true love than politeness. That made sense for Lady Talbot. And, from what Anne had seen, even for Mr. and Mrs. Darcy. But such romantic notions were not the stories of all love affairs. Anne's parents had known almost nothing of each other when they had taken their vows, but from what Anne could remember of them, it seemed their minds and wishes had grown together as certainly as their lives had. And Mr. and Mrs. Collins—they were happy, were they not, though they had known very little of one another when they had wed?

Anne exhaled. If there was one thing she, a single woman in want of a husband, could definitively say about the marriage state, it was that while there were as many ways to fall in love as there were people in the world, love, though pleasing to think on, was not always possible before marriage. Nor was it required. Or in many cases, wanted. In truth, every so-called romance Anne's governess had read to her when she was a youth had either ended in tragic death or unrequited love that led to agony of heart.

"You have grown quiet," Lady Talbot said to Anne. "And, I daresay, thoughtful. Have you seen more in the painting? Pray, please enlighten us. I would dearly love to hear your thoughts."

Anne's muscles, breaths, heartbeats stumbled.

Sir William studied her. She crossed her arms over her chest.

"I wager you were thinking of something much more pleasing than the painting," he said.

Anne lowered her gaze to hide her embarrassment. If he, a man so unlike herself and of such short acquaintance, could read her so well, how could she hope to show definitive interest and pleasure in his attentions when she did not truly feel them? He would certainly see through her façade. But then, perhaps that would work to her advantage. Perhaps if he recognized the façade, he would definitively turn his attentions away from her, and Anne's mother would believe it was his actions and not hers that had kept them from forming an attachment.

"That is enough, Sir William," Lady Talbot said. "Do not tease the girl."

Sir William chuckled softly. "Forgive me, Miss de Bourgh."

"I believe Miss de Bourgh's thoughts on the subject of art can be more fully defined through her own work," Mr. Talbot said. "Perhaps, Miss de Bourgh, as you have brought your drawing pad with you, would you do us the honor of sharing your drawings with us?"

Finally, the heat burning her cheeks cooled enough she dared look up. Sir William, Anne was mildly gratified to see, actually did seem apologetic, and Lady Talbot's gaze was openly curious, but Mr. Talbot's expression, while likewise curious, held Anne's gaze with such a mixed expression of fierceness and gentleness she could not misinterpret their significance. He, noticing her discomfort, had acted solely in her behalf and had changed the subject. Once again heat blazed her cheeks, only this time it was from feelings of gratitude and something else she did not quite know how to label.

Mrs. Webb held Anne's drawing pad out to her, but Mr. Talbot took it first. "May I?" he asked.

Cheeks, I command you to cool. They did not listen. *So much for sheer will.* "You may," she said aloud. "But as you might remember, there is still a plant in Lady Talbot's garden, which I am particularly keen to draw."

"I remember." He opened the cover and scanned the first page.

Lady Talbot peered from Mr. Talbot to Anne and back again. "Which plant?"

"The *Strobilanthes nutans.*" Mr. Talbot turned to the second, the third, the fourth page. "This one is . . ." He looked up at Anne. "Might I have this one? If you have no other use for it?"

As he did not turn the book toward her, she stepped around it and next to him. For the briefest of moments, the fresh, citrusy scent of his cologne whiffed her back to a moment in early spring when her favorite flowers first bloomed in the garden Mr. Soulden had planted in her honor.

Anne peeked over Mr. Talbot's broad forearm at her drawing. "You want my picture of a daylily?"

He nodded. "It interests me."

His words distilled through Anne with the warmth of a heated blanket on an icy winter night. Perhaps no one would ever consider her artistic ability to be a true accomplishment, but someone—Mr. Talbot—was interested in her drawings. In her plants. "Why?" she said aloud.

He turned to her. "Must I have a *why*?"

"I-I suppose not."

Lady Talbot stepped to his other side and glanced down at the drawing. "Of course Miss de Bourgh needs a why. This is her work, which she is likely keeping for some purpose of her own."

"Very well. I have a need for it. Will that suffice, Miss de Bourgh?"

"I admit it is my favorite flower," Anne said, "but lilies are not difficult to come by. I can draw another."

He nodded, folded the parchment, and slipped it inside the chest pocket of his tailcoat. "I believe, Mother, your lady's maid is here with your investigative journal."

A tall, slight-framed woman crossed the drawing room toward them. She, like Mrs. Webb, had red hair, though it was much darker and not nearly as flatteringly fashioned, neither was her stance quite as elegant, but otherwise they seemed so close in age and appearance that Anne briefly wondered if they might be relations.

"Thank you." Lady Talbot took the book from her lady's maid and once more positioned herself on the gold couch. Sir William sat in the chair to her left.

"Sit next to me, Miss de Bourgh," Lady Talbot continued. "I believe you will be quite interested in my book. And while you are looking through it, the four of us can determine our first step in determining who killed Dr. Sinclair."

Mrs. Webb, who had clearly been discounted from Lady Talbot's "the four of us," sat in the chair to Anne's catercorner right. Mr. Talbot sat in the chair directly across from Anne, where he kept watching her. Was he worried she would faint or something? Anne sat up straighter. *I will not be a weakling.*

"Really, Mother." Sir William said. "We do not even know for certain Dr. Sinclair was murdered."

"He most certainly was murdered. Miss de Bourgh's observations with regards to the broken glass were entirely correct."

"I appreciate your trust in me," Anne said, "but I am not at all certain I was right. I have had no experience with"—*murder*—"instances such as these."

"Well, I have, and I immediately recognized the truth of your words." Lady Talbot smiled at Anne. "Instinct, you see—or dare I say talent?—can sometimes be more valuable than experience, no matter the endeavor. Which brings me to the case at hand. The two foremost answers my husband and I needed before we could effectively solve any murder were, first, how did the victim die, and second, who would want him dead? As I have an easy correspondence with the coroner and he was always wont to help my husband with our investigations, I will take on the first question. The other, I believe, can be carried out by my two sons. And you, Miss de Bourgh."

"I already made a few inquiries," Mr. Talbot said. "I learned the good doctor had been at the tavern on St. James's Street prior to the ball. Perhaps Miss de Bourgh would like to help me question the proprietor?"

Mrs. Webb caught her breath.

Anne shifted in her seat. After having so recently escaped the debaucheries of the beach, she certainly had no intention of walking into a tavern, even if she were in the company of Mr. Talbot.

"St. James's Street Tavern is no place for a respectable woman," Lady Talbot said.

"Forgive me. I did not mean any impropriety. We would of course not visit the tavern." Mr. Talbot's gaze settled on Anne. "I meant only Miss de Bourgh and I could visit the proprietor, Mr. Reddington, at his home."

"What would be the point in going there and not to the tavern?" Lady Talbot said. "You can learn much more where the deceased was than you ever would at the proprietor's home. No, you, Owen, must investigate Dr. Sinclair's actions at the tavern alone."

Mr. Talbot frowned slightly and looked at Anne. Anne quickly looked over to Sir William, who checked his pocket watch. "Well, Mother," he said, "I have enjoyed today's bit of sleuthing, but I am afraid I must take your leave. I have business in town I need to take care of before I set off for London."

"Surely whatever it is can wait a few minutes more while we make our plans."

Her voice held no inflection, but something in her words affected Sir William, because he narrowed his eyes, glanced across the group, and folded his arms. He sat back against the chair. "I suppose a few more minutes will not hurt. I will, however, remind you a man cannot spend all his time playing at diverting games."

Anne furrowed her brows and tilted her head. *Diverting games?* Sir William could not possibly be referring to Dr. Sinclair's murder. That night at the ball, he had been the one who had suggested his mother take the event more seriously.

Lady Talbot smiled. "May I remind you that your father, a *man*, felt as strongly as I do about uncovering the truth of such matters? Just because a person enjoys an endeavor does not mean he or she does not take it very seriously. I am also certain a victim's family would welcome anyone who made their loved one's murderer face justice."

"Justice, yes, but I am not certain justice is your greatest motivation. You agree with me, don't you, Owen? Most of Mother's investigations are games, like the one you created for her birthday."

"Leave me out of this," Mr. Talbot said.

"You can hardly call Dr. Sinclair's murder a game," Lady Talbot said.

"I did not say his murder was a game," Sir William said.

Lady Talbot pursed her lips, and a glint sparked her eyes. "You must not listen to him, Miss de Bourgh. My son is determined to make me seem a calloused trickster intent on my own entertainment."

"Nonsense, Mother!"

Anne stared between the two of them. Their conversation certainly rang of unkindness, if not impropriety, but there was nothing of those traits in their expressions. If anything, the lighthearted twinkles in their eyes and the gentleness in their voices revealed deep caring for one another.

"Very well," Lady Talbot said at last. "I will concede my investigations are diversions if you will concede they are *important* diversions. Murderers must be caught, and as the constables will not look far to find them, I will do so."

Sir William lifted his hand to her as if he were toasting her words.

"You will indulge me, won't you?" Lady Talbot added. "You will help us find who murdered Dr. Sinclair?"

Sir William sighed. "For a while."

"Thank you." Lady Talbot sat taller, and though she held Mr. Talbot's gaze, she spoke to Sir William. "Now that matter is settled, put your mind to calling on Dr. Fletcher. Since he worked with Dr. Sinclair, he may be able to shed some light on the man's death. Perhaps tomorrow or the next day—whenever it fits in your schedule. And take Miss de Bourgh with you, if she is interested." She looked askance at Anne.

Anne's mouth turned dry. She had not thought of it until then, but what if, after she spoke with Dr. Fletcher, he was to tell her mother of her visit? And of her and Sir William's questions? Would she forbid her from investigating? Or would she set her scruples aside since Anne was, in fact, working with Sir William?

Mr. Talbot frowned.

Sir William slid to the edge of his seat. "Tomorrow, then, Miss de Bourgh?"

But then, was it not just as possible Dr. Fletcher might say nothing to her mother of the matter? After all, why would he? Once Anne saw him and received his real cure, he would have no other reason to call on them.

"Yes," Anne said. "I-I would be happy to join you, Sir William. At two o'clock?"

"As you wish. And since Mrs. Webb will of course join us, I will bring the barouche."

Mrs. Webb nodded and smiled so brightly an onlooker might assume Sir William had offered her a roomful of gold rather than a seat in a carriage that anyone in her position as Anne's companion would have. But then, maybe she had a right to be so affected. Generally no one paid her any mind. Anne had sometimes envied Mrs. Jenkinson's and now Mrs. Webb's invisibility. It was, after all, much better to go unnoticed than to be seen and ultimately thought little of as Anne often was. At least, Anne used to think that was the case. Now she was not so sure.

"And when we have all made our inquiries," Lady Talbot said, "we will meet here again to discuss them and determine our next courses of action."

Sir William stood and helped Anne and Mrs. Webb to their feet. "In other words, we will determine our next move on the game board."

Mr. Talbot helped his mother.

"Think of it as you will," Lady Talbot said.

Sir William arched an eyebrow. "When would you like us to reconvene?"

"Three days from hence, for afternoon tea." Lady Talbot, smiling again, clasped her hands in front of her and scanned the group. Had she focused a little longer on Mr. Talbot? On Anne? "Yes. That should do quite nicely."

Anne nodded her goodbye to Sir William and Lady Talbot, but when she faced Mr. Talbot—er, when her momentary glance latched with his glare . . . his clenched jaw . . . all sense of warmth spiraled to the floor and slid under the door. What had happened? Why was he angry?

CHAPTER SIXTEEN

Aliston, East Sussex

Kenneth stopped outside his sister-in-law's front door. There was no way he could snuff out the cigar smoke or wipe the brandy stains from his clothes, since he had practically lived in them throughout the whole of the night, but he could hide the false playing cards he had used to bilk that naïve young gull out of his sovereign.

Kenneth slid the cards out from among his newly acquired coins, tucked them in an inside pants pocket, and knocked on the door. Fanny immediately opened it. She tugged him inside and closed the door.

"What's wrong?" He scanned the small living area. There were a few dirty dishes on the plank counter, and Fanny still held a flour-covered rolling pin, but otherwise all seemed in order. "Gracie?"

Fanny stopped him before he reached the sickroom. "She still lives, but I implore you calm yourself before you see her. Dr. Lambert said the more agitated she is, the more the sickness will spread through her blood."

"I expect he also offered up another prescription."

"Aye. For a poultice. I sent Neil to the apothecary for the ingredients."

Kenneth, scowling, pulled the coins he had won at the gambling table from his pocket and handed them to Fanny.

"Where did you get these?" she said.

"An odd job. Like last time." He glanced at the sickroom door. "And there will be more soon. I will be leaving in a few hours for a job I found in Brighton."

Fanny's gaze both narrowed and wavered. When they were children, playing together as their two families had done, Fanny would have yelled her skepticism at him. She would have demanded proof of his claims. But now that she had grown, her silence bit his conscience harder than any amount of shouting ever had. Not that it mattered whether or not Fanny believed him. All he cared about was she asked no questions.

"Where is the doctor?" Kenneth said. "In there with Gracie?"

"He left a bit ago. Said he had to clear his head."

"To clear his head? What about Gracie's? She's been delirious for hours."

"That has passed. The fever broke too. Around sunrise."

The tension that had been clenching Kenneth's shoulders drained into the puncheon floor. "My Gracie," he breathed. "She made it through."

Fanny squeezed his arm. "The poultice is for . . . The rash has set in."

New dread dropped over his head even as tension shot back into his shoulders. Bridget had died soon after the rash had struck her.

"I know it is hard to do, but please try to stay calm."

Kenneth looked at the ceiling, took another deep breath, and after again glancing at Fanny, stepped into the sickroom. Gracie opened her eyes. The skin on her arms was still clear, but red rough-edged spots dotted her neck. *Praise be to God.* The rash did not cover her entire body.

"Papa?"

"Yes, my girl." Kenneth stepped to her side. "How are you feelin' this mornin'?"

She closed her eyes again. "I hate my stomach."

"I expect it itches?"

"On the outside. Inside it hurts."

He set his hand over the top of the quilt that covered his daughter's stomach. "You only have to bear through this a while more, sweetheart. When it is over, I promise you will feel stronger than ever."

Again she opened her eyes, only this time she watched him for a long moment. "It is all right, Papa."

He smiled. Everything was always all right in Gracie's world. Every day he prayed it would remain so. "It is. And you will be even better tomorrow."

"No."

He shuffled back a step. "What do you mean?"

She set her hand on top of his, where it still rested above her abdomen. "I mean it will be all right even if God takes me to live with him. Mama will be there."

Kenneth's breath leapt from his chest and raced for the door. "Do not say such things. You are going to get well."

She smiled, and when she did, her eyes got all misty, but just like her mother would have done, she did not let even one tear fall. "I'm not worried, Papa."

Kenneth squeezed her hand between both of his.

"Mama wasn't worried either, was she? Before she died?"

"Wipe that idea out of your mind right now. That not-worrying feeling is not death coming. It's strength, strength alive and well inside you, that says you are getting better."

"Strength?" Gracie furrowed her brows. "The kind Aunt Fanny told Cousin Eli he'd lose if he kept lying about hiding rocks in her pickle barrel?"

"I don't think I heard about that."

"She said he had the makings of a great, strong man inside him, but if he didn't start living up to that greatness, he would wind up losing everything."

Everything good about life. Gracie didn't add those last words, but he heard Fanny saying them anyway. Gracie, like his wife, always had a way of connecting goodness with strength.

"Is that the kind of strength you mean, Papa?"

He leaned toward her and brushed a matted strand of her blonde hair from her eyes. "Can't say I know much about that. I only meant your body is getting its health back—getting so strong that quicker than you can say *pickle barrel* you will find yourself climbing out of that bed, walking through that door, and telling Aunt Fanny it is about time you ate a big ole slab of bread doused in butter."

She giggled then slumped back against her pillow. "I don't believe you, Papa."

"It is true. You are already feeling a bit better now, aren't you?" He stared into her eyes, willed her to find strength and life inside her not-worrying.

"Maybe."

Kenneth had heard of children sometimes speaking words beyond their years. Gracie had even done it once or twice. But he had never seen anything even close to wisdom settle into a child's expression until that moment.

"I think it is like what Mama whispered to me before she died. When the worryin' was gone."

Pressure that felt like wet fire pulsed against the back of Kenneth's eyelids. He remembered his wife holding their daughter that last time, remembered how she had whispered into her ear before he had taken Gracie from her arms, but he had never known, never felt he could bear to ask Gracie what she had said.

"Mama said there are some things we can't run away from, like death. But all that matters is we must be good. If we are good, and even if our bodies do not work like they should, we can stand all healthy and strong on the inside. That is the kind of strength you mean, isn't it, Papa?"

He could not answer, could not speak, could only slip his arms around his daughter and pull her against his chest.

"That is right, isn't it, Papa?" she asked again.

"Yes," he whispered. But inside, his heart screamed.

CHAPTER SEVENTEEN

Brighton

WHILE ANNE'S MOTHER WOULD NOT consent to Anne learning to swim, and while Anne had not yet figured out how she might slip away long enough for Blanc to teach her, which she had agreed to do, it did not mean Anne could not acquire some skill during her dipping sessions. She would take advantage of every moment she had with Mrs. Dramwell, which meant, first and foremost, Anne would never again let the dipper do for her what she could do for herself.

Anne pushed open the bathing-machine door. She braced herself for the onslaught of cold, took a deep breath, and jumped into the ocean. Unlike Mrs. Dramwell, who stood alone, hip-high in the gently lapping waves, Anne splashed and sank to her knees. The water covered her to the top of her neck. She gasped.

"No, no," Mrs. Dramwell said. "Do not stand yet. Get used to the sea."

Anne, breathing hard, swished her arms through the water. She enjoyed the feel of its flow between her fingers just as she had during her last session. Soon her skin melded with the ocean's temperature, and her breathing calmed.

"Now let's go out farther," Mrs. Dramwell said. "Not so far you cannot touch the bottom but far enough you are not sitting on the ground."

Anne, crouching, walked alongside the dipper for several more feet until, fully standing, the water came up to her chest.

"Good," Mrs. Dramwell said. "Now, let's teach you 'ow to float on your back."

"Do you mean lying on top of the water, like I did last time?"

"Yes. Only, today you will do it alone."

Shivers spread across Anne's shoulders and down her back. She could not possibly lie on the water alone. She would sink. *Have courage.*

"W-what do I do first?"

"Trust me. Can you do that?"

"Y-yes. I will."

Mrs. Dramwell, standing next to her, slid her right arm into the water a short distance behind Anne. "Take a deep breath . . . good . . . now spread your arms a bit and lie on your back. Softly."

Anne stiffened.

"Relax, miss. I will catch you. Take another deep breath. That is right. Close your eyes so the sunlight don't blind you. Now—"

Anne closed her eyes and fell backward as if she were dropping into bed.

Mrs. Dramwell's hand slid beneath her shoulders. "Perfect, miss. Arch your back, your neck . . . Keep breathing . . . there. You are doing it."

"I am floating?"

"All by yourself. Floating as prettily as a leaf on a lake."

Anne grinned. "Now what?"

"Why, you try to get used to it, but do it fast. Two minutes more is all we have."

"Finished already?"

"Afraid so. Dippins always go by too quickly."

Anne floated for several more seconds.

"You are tense again."

"I am just not ready to end this."

"I suppose your mother would be surprised to see you now."

Surprised, yes, but happy? Proud? Not likely. Not unless swimming caused Sir William to make her an offer, which was also not likely. Sir William had already intimated he would be leaving for London soon. Though Anne need not tell her mother that. She need only obey her mother by going about each day, following her health regime, visiting those her mother deemed necessary she visit, and taking every opportunity she had in associating with the Talbots, Sir William especially. Which opportunities, when compared to how many times she thought about the Talbots—Mr. Talbot—seemed all too few.

But she would put that out of her mind for now. She would think only on how many of her clothes she could put on without help before the bathing machine returned to the beach and Mrs. Webb stepped inside.

* * *

Anne knew something was wrong the moment they stepped through the front door. Not because her mother did not meet her in the drawing room, insisting Anne quickly ready herself for the Evanses' late-morning visit, nor because Anne smelled nothing of breakfast cooking from the kitchen, but because tension vised the air.

Anne peered toward the door at the back of the hall. She started up the staircase.

"Surely they cannot all still be abed," Mrs. Webb said.

"I will be surprised if they are." Even so, Anne lightened her step the rest of the way to the top of the staircase. She paused. Everyone was definitely not asleep. It was late morning, but candlelight spread outward from every door. All were open. Her mother, still in her dressing gown and bed cap, walked out from her bedchamber. Dark purple rimmed the skin beneath her eyes. Had she not been sleeping?

"There you are," her mother said. "Come, Anne. I am most seriously put out."

"What has happened?" Anne hurried toward her, but her mother, rather than waiting for Anne, returned to her bedroom. Anne and Mrs. Webb followed. Several female servants, including her mother's lady's maid and Blanc, bustled about the room, looking inside drawers and behind furniture.

"My broach is missing," her mother said. "The one Sir Lewis gave to me the night we formally announced our engagement."

"I cannot imagine it could have gone far," Anne said. "I have not even seen you wear it since we have been in Brighton."

"I had intended to wear it when the Evanses called on us." She furrowed her brow, clenched her hands in front of her waist, and scanned first one side of the room and then the other. "They have been most anxious to make our acquaintance—since the first day of our arrival, in fact—and now this. How is it to be borne?"

Anne clenched her reticule and glanced at Mrs. Webb. Lady Catherine was a strong woman whose opinions were never to be taken lightly, yet at that moment, she seemed younger, or maybe it was more vulnerable than Anne ever remembered seeing her. Never in Anne's life had she been unable to count on her mother's strength. It was not a pleasant feeling.

Her mother raised her voice. "No place must be left unchecked."

The maids quickened their paces.

"Search the other bedchambers again if you must," her mother continued. "And all the rest of the house. The broach must be here. And when it is found, the culprit—for surely someone in this house must have taken it—will face the ultimate punishment."

Anne blinked away the image of a hangman's noose that filled her mind at her mother's mention of "the ultimate punishment." Not long ago she and the Talbots had been talking about the death of a murdered man, and now there she was, investigating another crime. Burglary was miniscule compared to murder, but having it happen in one's own home, becoming the victim rather than an onlooker, made it seem many times worse. "Is anything else missing?" Anne asked Blanc.

Blanc turned from where she had been searching behind the open window curtains. "No, miss. Not that anyone has noticed."

"The thief had better pray to God there is not," Lady Catherine said.

Blanc and the other maids quick-glanced at one another and, though it had not a moment ago seemed physically possible, hurried their search.

Her mother, yawning, paced to the open jewelry box sitting on top of the dressing table. She glared from the full-length mirror to the wardrobe to the open window to the bed.

"Mother!" Anne moved to Lady Catherine's side. "When did you begin sleeping with the window open?"

"What do you mean? I never sleep with the window open. I always—" Her mother looked again to the open window, and her eyes widened as broadly as her second yawn.

"Perhaps no one in the house did take it," Mrs. Webb said at length.

"The opening is certainly large enough for a man to climb through," Anne added.

"Surely no man would be so undignified, so callous, as to creep into my home during the night and steal such a valuable piece. It is unfathomable. No one could have so little respect for women of our stations."

Anne tried to push away the thought of a shadowy figure creeping into their home while they slept, but the image would not leave. It sat right in front of her eyes, taunting her. *No one is safe in Brighton.*

CHAPTER EIGHTEEN

Anne had been pleasantly surprised to find Mr. and Mrs. Evans to be such personable guests, especially considering Mrs. Evans was the niece of Lord Backwell, a member of the prince regent's court. In truth, Mrs. Evans, with her round cheeks and merry expression, had been so taken with Anne that almost immediately upon entrance into the de Bourgh's sitting room, she invited them to attend the next ball at the Pavilion as their special guests.

And Mr. Evans! Anne could definitely see why his fair-complexioned good looks, solicitous manners, and easy charm were the talk of society. A young woman would have to be dead not to be affected by them. And yet, through every moment of their visit, Mr. Evans's devotions had been most certainly settled on his wife. Mrs. Evans, it seemed, though she had married slightly beneath her status, was likewise one of the few lucky women to have found a devoted and trustworthy husband, proving once again that Mr. Darcy had been right. Rank did not equal happiness.

Anne sighed. How very different Mrs. Evans's, Lady Catherine's, even Anne's own life were from that of Lady Talbot's life. For while all their worlds were wrapped around managing their households and maintaining their positions in society, Lady Talbot's days were also spiced with hours of unraveling riddles and uncovering intriguing details. No wonder the lady insisted on keeping her diversions.

Thank you, Lady Talbot, for letting me take part in those diversions too. Anne smiled.

"Here we are." Sir William's coachman stopped the horses in front of Dr. Fletcher's home, a white-brick gabled structure south of the Steyne. Sir William climbed out of the barouche and helped Anne down the steps. Once she was safely on the cobbled walk, he likewise helped Mrs. Webb, and the three walked to Dr. Fletcher's front door, where Sir William knocked. A middle-aged housekeeper answered.

"My name is Sir William Talbot, and this is Miss de Bourgh. May we please speak with Dr. Fletcher? I informed him yesterday of our visit, and I expect he is waiting for us."

"Yes, sir. Come in." The housekeeper opened the door wider and backed into the house.

Sir William courteously waited for Anne and Mrs. Webb to enter ahead of him, and once again Anne wished she were entering with Mr. Talbot rather than with Sir William. Indeed, though all her associations with Sir William had proven him to be both courteous and thoughtful to everyone, no matter their social or monetary status—a trait Anne highly admired—she found she still preferred Mr. Talbot to any other man of her acquaintance.

And yet Lady Catherine, who was always excessively attentive to Anne's welfare, believed Sir William to be the better choice. After her mother's first insistence, Anne had thought that choice was based solely on Sir William's greater rank and wealth, but after further consideration, Anne wondered if there might be more to it. Her mother frequently told Anne her welfare was her highest priority, and her mother did know Anne's character and tastes. Perhaps Sir William was the better choice for Anne in other ways too.

Anne's feelings rebelled at that thought. Even so, she tucked them behind her heart because her mother would wish her to do so and waited as the housekeeper closed the door behind them. *I will give my mother's choice for me a chance.*

"I will let the doctor know you are here," the housekeeper said.

Anne glanced about the home's entrance hall. Neither it nor the staircase was as elegant as the de Bourgh's current residence, but its paneled walls and green simple-patterned carpet indicated such a serene yet masculine elegance Anne could almost see Mr. Talbot—she blinked—*no,* Sir William in a formal tailcoat descending the staircase toward them. She sighed and glanced back at him. He was such a handsome man.

Sir William quirked an eyebrow at her. Mrs. Webb pursed her lips and glanced back and forth between them. Anne, realizing she had been staring at him, suddenly felt as if she had stood too long next to the fire.

She quickly faced the man walking through the door behind them. He was only a few inches taller than Anne, and while the creases round his eyes and mouth showed him to be of late middle age, his short-cropped hair had only a few trails of gray mixed in with the brown.

"Sir William. Ladies." His voice was almost as quiet as the click of the door when he closed it.

Sir William shook the man's offered hand. "I believe you have not yet had the pleasure of meeting Miss de Bourgh or her companion, Mrs. Webb."

"I have not."

Anne nodded, and Mrs. Webb curtsied.

"But I have long looked forward to meeting you, Miss de Bourgh," Dr. Fletcher continued. "Your physician in Kent, Doctor Crawford, spoke highly of you and your mother and asked I take especial watch over your health. It is your intent, I understand, to strengthen your body, putting your allergic rhinitis—a frailty that has long affected you—to an early grave, you might say." His eyes twinkled.

Sir William gave Anne such a disbelieving expression that while he said nothing, Anne could almost hear his voice in her head saying, "I did not know you were sickly."

That aspect alone made each of his other qualities grow a hundred times taller in her mind. And her heart, or maybe it was her breath, for both paused. Mrs. Webb glanced at Anne out of the corner of her eye.

"You are correct," Anne said to the doctor. This introduction was just as it should be. Come to think of it, why had Dr. Sinclair not referenced anything about her medical history when he had first spoken with her?

"I hope it will not be long before you make an appointment with me about your health," Dr. Fletcher continued. "I am sure you are anxious to begin 'the cure.'"

"I have already begun the cure. Dr. Sinclair delivered it to me when we first arrived in Brighton."

Dr. Fletcher furrowed his brows. "Dr. Sinclair? Is that not the name of the man who died at the ball?"

Anne stiffened. What could the doctor mean? Had he misunderstood Sir William, for he most certainly must know Dr. Sinclair. "Yes, that is him. Dr. Sinclair delivered the tonic along with a health regimen to our home on Marine Parade. He said you bade him bring it to me. And as he worked with you, my mother and I saw no harm in my taking his advice."

"I am sorry to tell you this, Miss de Bourgh, but there has been some mistake. Perhaps you misunderstood the man. Except for the reports of his death, I have never heard of Dr. Sinclair. I also do not work with any other physicians. My techniques and skills are my own. I would be happy to set an appointment with you, if you would like, but in the meantime, I advise you not to take whatever 'cure' this man prescribed until I can ascertain its safety."

Mrs. Webb gasped. Anne covered her mouth with her hand. She stared at Mrs. Webb. Certainly there must be some kind of mistake. Perhaps Dr. Fletcher had misunderstood them.

Sir William clasped Anne's elbow. "You know nothing of Dr. Sinclair?" he said to Dr. Fletcher. "He did not work with you?"

"He did not."

Sir William looked at Anne, and she, her fingers trembling slightly, opened her reticule. "Dr. Sinclair clearly said he worked with you. He gave me this list, which he said was from you. It is a regimen explaining exactly how and w-what I must do in order to improve my health." She removed the list from her bag, which, thankfully, she had that morning tucked inside the notebook. She handed it to Dr. Fletcher. "There. At the top. That is your name, is it not?"

Dr. Fletcher scanned the document, turned it to the back side—it was blank—and frowned. He handed it back to her. "This list is indeed from my office, but I have given out dozens of them this year. This Dr. Sinclair must have collected it from one of my patients."

"It is yours, then?" The physician had already said it was, but Anne needed to hear the words again. How could she have been so foolish as to have taken the advice of a man whose credentials she had not checked? *My mother believed him too.* She is not infallible. Anne felt very little comfort in that knowledge.

"It is my list," Dr. Fletcher repeated. "And despite where you attained it, if this is the regimen you are following, I am certain your health will improve. I do, however, again advise you to stop taking the tonic he prescribed and bring it to me immediately."

"Of course."

"In the meantime, if you will wait here, I will bring you a sample of the real cure and a prescription for more. You can have it filled at the apothecary's shop on Grand Parade." Dr. Fletcher headed back toward the door he had originally entered through.

Sir William, still holding Anne's elbow, stopped the physician. "I hate to harp on a moot point, Doctor, but will you please tolerate me asking it one last time that I may be certain I have understood you correctly? You state without reservation you have never worked with Dr. Sinclair?"

"I have not."

Sir William frowned. Anne tilted her head and pursed her lips. While she had passed over the shock of the good doctor's announcement, her thoughts now reeled with questions. Who was Dr. Sinclair, and why had he called on her and her mother? Especially so soon after they had arrived in Brighton? He could have gained nothing by their meeting. They had not even given him any money in exchange for his services.

"If you will excuse me," Dr. Fletcher said, "I will get the cure and write your prescription for you, Miss de Bourgh, so you and your companions can be on your way."

"Thank you."

Dr. Fletcher left, and Sir William looked back at Anne, who was still staring at him. "It appears you are thinking the same thing I am," he said.

If he meant his blue eyes and blond hair—more than that, his goodness—were stuttering round each other through the base of her chest, then yes, she was thinking the same thing he was. "I am not sure."

Mrs. Webb furrowed her brows at Anne. *Be decisive.*

Sir William smiled. "You were thinking St. James's Tavern was where my mother assigned my brother to go."

The stuttering stopped, dropped, and slipped inside her memory of Mr. Talbot's warm brown eyes. Anne's mother was right. Sir William was a good man. A respectable man. A man any woman would be blessed to marry. The man her mother would insist she marry if given the chance. But he was not the man Anne's heart cried out for. "Indeed," she said.

Sir William offered her his elbow. "My brother headed out on that errand at the same time I left to call for the two of you. Let us see if he is still there. He may already have the answers we seek."

Anne winced. While she would dearly love to see Mr. Talbot, she could not go to the tavern.

He briefly pressed his hand over hers where it rested on his arm. "You need not worry, Miss de Bourgh. The driver will wait with you and Mrs. Webb in the barouche."

"Thank you."

* * *

Owen pressed his palm against Miss de Bourgh's drawing of the daylily, where it lay tucked inside his waistcoat pocket. It was the only physical thing he had of hers, an object she had not only possessed but that had also come from within that beautiful, sensitive, intelligent mind of hers. He was loathe to let it out of his hands, but he would do so for this purpose. For her.

He glanced up the three-story gray rock building in front of him. He took a deep breath and stepped through the heavy wooden door. Miller, Owen's friend from university, and a few other members of London's Royal Society had a few years ago formed a small Brighton group of scientists, engineers, and physicians. Now they regularly met in this building to drink, dine, and in all ways support subjects related to science. Normally Owen would not intrude upon Miller in this setting, but as his several attempts to contact him at home had failed and as his butler had assured Owen his employer was at this establishment, Owen determined this was his best option.

Again he touched his pocket, but before he lowered his hand, a young man stepped up to him.

"May I help you, sir?"

Owen glanced behind the man to the gentlemen sitting at the few tables spread about the large hall. Miller was among them. "You can. Would you please inform Mr. Joshua Miller that Mr. Talbot is here to speak with him on a matter of science?"

The man bowed and headed farther into the large room. Within moments Miller stood before Owen and shook his hand. Then, in his usual fashion, he went straight to the point. "Mr. Young said you wanted to talk to me on a matter of science."

"It is good to see you too."

Miller smiled. Though Miller was a small man in the physical sense, and weak-eyed, as he had so often described himself back at university, Owen had always considered him one of the greatest men of his acquaintance. The man was more intelligent than any of his other associates at the school, including some of his professors, but he never wore that intelligence like a royal crest. To Miller, a person's mind, attitudes, and actions toward others determined one's rank in his life, not one's monetary or social status, nor even one's gender. In truth, looking back on those days, Owen believed those attributes were the reasons they had become such good friends. Those and, Owen supposed, the fact that their worlds sat on the outskirts of society— Owen's because he was a cripple of scandalous birth and Miller's because his mousy features and blunt manners tended to repel rather than attract.

"My information is in relation to the book you have been commissioned to write and illustrate." Owen reached inside his waistcoat pocket, removed Miss de Bourgh's drawing, and handed it to his friend.

Miller pulled out his quizzing glass. He studied the sketch. "Where did you get this?"

"A young woman of my recent acquaintance drew it. She has a strong interest in plants and a skill, as you can well see, which I believe you may find useful."

"I admit I have been considering the possibility of procuring someone to help me." Miller looked up from the picture. "Did the young woman ask you to show this to me?"

"She did not."

"So you decided of your own accord to do so." This time Miller studied Owen through his quizzing glass. "Who is this woman? And what is she to you?"

"Her name is Miss Anne de Bourgh." Tingles spread up the back of Mr. Talbot's neck. "Our mothers are friends."

"I see."

"Drop the quizzing glass, will you?"

Miller grinned and lowered the glass. "Is this better? Even if it does not change the fact that I can see you have feelings for this woman? Perhaps my congratulations are in order."

Owen glanced over his shoulder. He tugged at the hem of his left coat sleeve. "There is nothing of the sort between us."

"Why not?"

Owen tried not to look down at his leg, but he must have done so anyway—that, or his friend correctly interpreted his silence—because Miller said, "You are a man of wealth and consequence, Talbot. Any woman worth your notice will overlook your infirmity."

"It is possible she might, but her mother will not."

"But—"

Owen lifted his hand. "And even if by some miracle her mother did overlook my infirmity, her pride would never permit her daughter to marry someone with my background."

"I thought you said your mothers were friends."

"They are."

"In name only, I take it."

"So it would seem."

Miller furrowed his brow. "Your lady's name—"

"She is not *my* lady."

"The young woman's name is Miss de Bourgh, you say? Why does that name sound—" His eyes widened. "The daughter of Lady Catherine de Bourgh?"

"Yes."

He folded his arms. "I have heard the lady is most attentive of everything and everyone around her. No one's business, I understand, is beneath her scrutiny."

"It does not seem I am counted among them."

Miller studied Owen for a long moment. Then, obviously trying and failing to suppress a smile, he said, "Perhaps congratulations are in order that Lady Catherine de Bourgh will not be your mother-in-law."

Sir William's image jumped into Owen's thoughts and stomped on his heart. Lady Catherine de Bourgh may never be his mother-in-law, but she most certainly intended his brother to marry Anne. If that happened, Owen would still be connected to the woman, and Anne would be—he swallowed—his sister. "Returning back to my purpose in seeking you out, what do you think of Miss de Bourgh's work?"

Miller again scrutinized the sketch. "It is most impressive. Most impressive. Tell her I may have a use for her talent. If she is interested, bid her come to my home Monday afternoon, and we will discuss the terms." He put Miss de Bourgh's drawing into his own pocket. "And have her bring more of her work."

CHAPTER NINETEEN

THREE MEN HAD GONE INTO the red-brick tavern, and only one had left during the fifteen overlong minutes Anne and Mrs. Webb had been waiting in Sir William's barouche. Before Anne and her mother had come to Brighton, fifteen minutes would have seemed little more than a moment in an otherwise long, unvarying day. But now, with Anne's regular walks and daily sea baths, her body felt as if it must move, must exercise, must grow stronger and stronger—which was already happening, Anne had realized when she had climbed into the carriage with little support from Sir William's offered hand. She exhaled a long, relieved sigh. At least the regimen Dr. Sinclair had given her was authentic.

Mrs. Webb touched Anne's arm. "Try to calm yourself, Miss de Bourgh. Upon my word, Sir William is too much a gentleman to leave us out here on the side of the road for much longer with only the driver for protection."

Anne sighed again, in gratitude this time, that God had seen fit to bless her with such a companion, such a friend as Mrs. Webb, a woman who seemed to sense Anne's thoughts even before Anne herself was aware of them. "I believe you are right."

"But . . . ?"

Anne shifted in her seat. "It is only I feel so useless sitting here doing nothing but watching seagulls peck at the ground while Sir William is inside finding answers to our questions. I feel like . . . it is hard to explain."

Mrs. Webb squeezed the back of Anne's hand. "Try."

Anne furrowed her brows, shifted in her seat. "I do not know what it is, but something—I feel like we need to hurry. Like—like something is about to happen."

Mrs. Webb frowned, one of the few frowns Anne remembered her ever offering. "What could . . . ?" Her voice sounded odd, tight even, but the peculiarity disappeared after she cleared her throat. "What do you think we need to hurry and do? Find out from Sir William what is taking him so long?"

"No. I mean, I do not know. You must think me ridiculous."

"I have never thought any such thing." Mrs. Webb glanced beyond Anne. She narrowed her eyes. "Upon my word. Is that Mr. Talbot?"

Anne's cheeks warmed even as she followed her companion's gaze. Just as Mrs. Webb had indicated, Mr. Talbot moved up the cobbled walk toward them. He reached the carriage and scanned past both of them.

"Miss de Bourgh, Mrs. Webb. How fortunate to have met you here. Where is my brother?"

"Inside." Anne nodded toward the tavern door, from where a rotund man had just exited. "It turns out Dr. Fletcher had not heard of Dr. Sinclair."

Mr. Talbot stared beyond her toward the other side of the carriage.

"But like you," Anne continued, "Sir William thought we might find answers here. He is in there now. He had thought you might be there as well."

Mr. Talbot glanced over his shoulder to the tavern. When he turned back, his gaze latched with Anne's for a glorious moment then slid to Mrs. Webb. "I can well imagine that is the case, but as it turns out, I have not yet been inside the tavern today." He opened his mouth as if he were about to say more, but then, apparently deciding against the idea, he closed it again. He stepped back from the carriage and stared decidedly away from them and up at the driver. Why did he seem so uneasy?

Mrs. Webb bumped Anne's knee with her own. Anne was not sure if her bumping was intentional or not, but in either case, it reminded Anne she must speak up. "Perhaps, Mr. Talbot, as your brother is inside, would you be so kind as to offer us your protection while we wait?"

Mr. Talbot shifted his stance. He leaned on his cane, again glimpsed over his shoulder toward the tavern, and finally looked back at them, but only at Mrs. Webb. Mrs. Webb lowered her eyes.

"As you wish," he said.

A lump formed at the base of Anne's throat. Why was Mr. Talbot ignoring her?

The tavern door creaked open. This time an elderly gentleman staggered through it.

"How long has my brother been inside?" Mr. Talbot said.

"Long enough that several people in the next shop have peeked out their window at us."

Mr. Talbot peered to where Anne referenced and turned back to her—no, to Mrs. Webb. The lump in Anne's throat constricted tighter. She most certainly must have done something to upset him, but what?

"Miss de Bourgh?" At last he faced her, but an invisible wall clouded his gaze.

"Yes?"

He reached inside his tailcoat pocket and removed a card. "My brother was correct in supposing I would be here before he was, for I did not tell him I would make another stop first. This card is from Mr. Joshua Miller. He is a friend of mine and a natural scientist who has been commissioned by the director of botany at the University of Vienna to write and illustrate a book on England's unique and rare plants. I gave him the drawing you so kindly offered me yesterday, and he wants to meet with you."

Anne took the card from him. She should not have noticed, or at least not have put stock in the noticing, that Mr. Talbot's gloved fingertips brushed hers, so pretending her heart rate was still as sedate as it had been before he arrived, she slowly scanned the name and address on the simply printed card. "You showed Mr. Miller my drawing? Why?"

"I confess, I thought of his book the moment I saw your work." Mr. Talbot again looked back to the tavern. "Your artistic skill impressed him, Miss de Bourgh. He asked me to tell you, if you are interested in helping him illustrate his book, to please join him Monday afternoon to discuss the details of your working arrangement."

"Work!" Mrs. Webb said. "You could not do such a thing, Miss de Bourgh."

Anne's thoughts and emotions swirled. She stared at Mr. Talbot. Never in all her life had anyone had such regard for her art or for her feelings about it. And yet, why would Mr. Talbot not look at her?

"I realize if you were to agree to such an arrangement," Mr. Talbot continued, "every detail would need to be kept in the strictest of confidence. But I do believe the decision should be yours and not society's. Nor your mother's."

"That is very kind."

"Not kindness, my—Miss de Bourgh. All I did was show him your drawing. The rest of it—his interest in your work—you earned on your own merit." He shifted his stance. "If you will both please excuse me, I believe I will see what is taking my brother so long." He made to move toward the tavern.

"Wait." Anne leaned against the side of the carriage. Mr. Talbot whirled back to her, and Mrs. Webb grabbed her arm, but Anne shook her off. "I do not know how to properly thank you for your generosity on my behalf, but please let me do so before you leave us."

"No thanks are necessary. It was simply an opportunity I knew someone with your talents could make use of."

And that was the wonder of Mr. Talbot's kindly heart. He did not even recognize he had such a one. For just as certainly as he had helped his mother indulge in her mystery-solving interests, he had recognized Anne's talents and found a way to strengthen them. Anne pressed her palm against her chest. *He understands me.* "Thank you, Mr. Talbot."

Finally, his expression softened, and a tiny smile lifted the corners of his lips. "You are welcome."

"Brother!"

The softness in his gaze hardened.

"I am surprised we made it here before you did."

The three of them looked at Sir William, who had just stepped out of the tavern. Within moments he stood before them.

Mr. Talbot frowned. "Yes, well, what did you find out?"

"Not much. The owner said Dr. Sinclair gambled, but he always paid his debts in full. He did believe the doctor must have had higher connections than anyone realized, however, because sometimes the debts he owed were much higher than a person of his station should be able to pay in a short time, yet he always did so."

"That is all you learned?" Mr. Talbot said. "Did he have any enemies?"

"Not that anyone could recollect."

"Mother will not be pleased to hear that. It gives us very little to go on."

"Maybe someone at the inn where he was staying will know something," Sir William said.

"You found out where he lived?" Anne asked.

Again Mrs. Webb clasped her arm, and Anne caught her breath. She pressed her hand over her mouth. It was one thing to be bold when the moment called for it, but twice in a matter of minutes she had acted outside of restrained etiquette. What was wrong with her?

Sir William, on the other hand, chuckled softly, and Mr. Talbot, as before, stared beyond them at what seemed to be nothing and stepped backward.

"My dear Miss de Bourgh," Sir William said. "If my mother were here, your outburst would thrill her."

Anne bowed her head. "I am glad to hear it, but my mother would have felt exactly the opposite."

"Mothers. What would we do without them?" he said.

"I am sure I do not know."

Sir William smiled. "In answer to your question, yes, I did learn Dr. Sinclair had been living at the inn on North Street. I say we go there now and find out what we can." He opened the carriage door and motioned for Mr. Talbot to climb in ahead of him.

"Excuse me," Mr. Talbot said. "I wish I could go along with you, but I am afraid I have business I must take care of."

"Now? Surely it can wait."

Mr. Talbot glanced at Anne. His expression appeared calm, but his muscles seemed stretched to their breaking points. What could she possibly have done to upset him so deeply?

"Forgive me." He bowed, nodded to his brother, and limped away, slapping the ground with his cane.

Sir William climbed into the barouche. He sat on the bench across from Anne and Mrs. Webb and told the driver they were ready to leave, but Anne noticed no other part of the ride. All she could do was think over each of the last few moments she had spent in the company of Mr. Talbot. Up until she had last left Seawind House, he had been completely amiable. And even a little, though she hardly dared think it, interested in her. But now . . . what could have possibly happened between then and now? She straightened her spine and glanced at her companion. If Anne were to consult Mrs. Webb on the matter, she would certainly tell her to be the woman she was born to be and do what she wanted to do. So far, the few times Anne had taken Mrs. Webb's advice, all had worked out well. Anne's mother had given her a bit more freedom, had she not? Anne was learning to swim, albeit a little, and . . . come to think of it . . . Anne had not stuttered her words in she did not know how long. Mrs. Webb's wisdom had blessed Anne's life. *The next time I see Mr. Talbot, I will ask him what I did to upset him.* Anne bit the inside of her lower lip as if her body did not quite believe her mind, but even so she clenched her fists. *I will.*

CHAPTER TWENTY

It took the driver only about ten minutes to reach the inn and about five minutes after that for them to gain permission from the innkeeper to search Dr. Sinclair's apartment. The room would, after all, be cleared out within the next day or two in order to allow for new guests.

"All I can tell you is the doctor was only here 'bouts a week," the innkeeper's wife said to them when she unlocked the apartment door. "He also had so many questions 'bouts where the stores and taverns and such were, I felt sure he must be new to Brighton."

"Did he ask about any businesses more than any others?" Anne asked.

Mrs. Webb offered Anne a quick smile. Anne could not say why. Maybe her question had shown some amount of self-fortitude. Whatever the reason, Mrs. Webb's smile gave Anne hope she would indeed, and soon, see Mr. Talbot again, find out what she had done to displease him, and apologize. After all, the service he had done her in seeking out Mr. Miller had to mean he was not entirely indifferent to her, did it not?

"I do not recall any extra mentions regarding any businesses around here," the woman said.

"Thank you." Sir William handed her a few coins.

She curtsied and left.

Anne removed her notebook and pencil from her reticule. She almost sketched the one-room apartment, but noticing Sir William and Mrs. Webb watching her, she instead briefly described it beneath the other information they had learned about Dr. Fletcher, which she had written during their ride there. She wrote,

1. *A mahogany four-poster bed*
2. *A rectangular green carpet next to the bed. The rest of the hardwood floor is bare.*

3. *An unlit coal fireplace*
4. *A single chair and small table*
5. *A wardrobe*
6. *A vanity*

Mrs. Webb, still standing next to the door, wrung her hands. "What should we be looking for?"

"Anything that might tell us something more about Dr. Sinclair," Sir William said. "Who he was, where he was from, or what he was doing here in Brighton."

"Perhaps a calendar or a schedule," Anne suggested. "Something that might tell us where he last went or whom he last saw."

"An excellent idea." Sir William crossed the room to the table. He picked up a used ale cup, studied it, and set it down again. "This place is quite sparsely furnished. How could a man of such limited means have afforded a physician's education?"

"Perhaps he had a benefactor," Anne said.

"Or perhaps he was a gentleman's youngest son," Mrs. Webb said, "and he used the whole of his small inheritance on his education."

Anne glanced between her two companions. Within the last hour Mrs. Webb had spoken out more often than a woman in her station usually did when in others' company. Had her familiarity with Anne given her a sense of equality? Or could she, having been widowed at such a young age, possibly have an interest in Sir William?

Anne studied her companion's downcast eyes, her ever-present, pretty smile. She was quite well-looking, to be sure, and—having at one time lived a comfortable, independent life—quite refined. But it would be utter folly if she did have an interest in Sir William. Not because their stations were so vastly separated but because, while Sir William showed them every gentlemanly consideration, Anne saw no depth of feeling in his expression toward either of them. In truth, the only sensation Anne noted at all was the small connection she herself felt with Mr. Talbot because she was with his brother.

"Both suggestions as to how Dr. Sinclair gained his education are possible," Sir William said.

"Another idea might be he was intentionally living below his income," Anne said.

"To what end?" Sir William said.

"Some people do save their money," Anne said, "rather than spending it on expensive furnishings and such."

Sir William shuffled through a stack of papers. "A man of consequence would have no need to retrench."

"He might if he was trying not to bring attention to himself." Heavens knew Anne had had a great deal of practice in staying away from attention.

"Hiding in open sight, you mean?" He looked up from the papers. "From whom, do you suppose, would he wish to hide?"

"Perhaps an enemy, as we have already considered. Or a relative. A long-lost love even."

Mrs. Webb cleared her throat again, and Sir William, glancing at her, smiled. However, Mrs. Webb's expression revealed no sign of attraction. If anything, she seemed indifferent, thereby proving she did not have an interest in Sir William.

"I see, Miss de Bourgh," Sir William said. "I must keep tabs on your mind. It is likely to run off without me if I am not careful."

"It certainly is," she teased.

Sir William laughed.

Anne bit her lip, and Mrs. Webb offered her a half smile. Anne must be feeling quite at ease with her companions to have once again become so bold, but was that easiness due to Sir William's presence, her own growing personal strength, or her thoughts of Mr. Talbot?

"It is no wonder my brother likes you," Sir William said under his breath.

Anne's cheeks heated. Did Mr. Talbot like her? But as her companions were then staring at her, she clasped her hands in front of her and steered the conversation back to more comfortable ground. "For my part"—she cleared her throat—"I believe Dr. Sinclair must have been a man of some means. For while he does live in this somewhat rundown place, the tavern owner did say he quickly paid his debts, some of which were quite high."

"I believe you must be right." Sir William again shuffled through the papers, slower this time. "Ho-ho! An appointment book."

Anne crossed to his side. Mrs. Webb did, too, only she pressed her arms tightly against her sides. Was she afraid of brushing against Sir William?

"Is there anything of interest in the book?" Anne said.

Sir William flicked through the pages. All but the first one were empty. He turned back to it, and the three studied the untidy scrawl listed under the date Dr. Sinclair had died:

1:00 MAB

Sir William frowned. "Only one entry in the entire book? I must say that is quite odd. And MAB? I wonder what that could mean."

Mrs. Webb, furrowing her brow, cupped her chin and concentrated on the writing.

"MAB," Anne said. "A person or a thing, do you think?"

"A person, I wager," Sir William said. "It *is* an appointment book."

"To be sure. M. Mister A-Algernon . . . Anthony . . .

"I know an Andrew, but his surname does not begin with a *B*."

Anne frowned. "Let us start with the *B*, then. Bennet . . . Barrington . . . Bingly . . ."

Sir William, studying the notebook, paced away from her. "Burnett, perhaps? Or—I know a Mister Burk."

Burk was Anne's housemaid's name back at Rosings. Anne's thoughts paused. She tilted her head and stared at Sir William. "I know what it is."

He whirled to her. "Well?"

"*MAB*. Miss Anne de Bourgh. They are my initials. One o'clock is when he visited my mother and me at the townhouse—when he gave me the tonic, which was not, as it turned out, from Dr. Fletcher."

"Hmph." Sir William, pursing his lips, looked back to the appointment book. He flipped through the pages, hesitated, and turned a few pages back. "Ah. Here is another entry: *4:00 LT*. No date though. Any ideas on that one?"

Anne thought for a moment. "I am afraid not."

He took a deep breath, closed the book, and slid it into his inside pocket. "I will give this to Headborough Powell. You will, I trust, write the information in your notebook?"

Anne nodded.

Sir William walked to the bed, and Anne, after she had recorded the information, went to the narrow wardrobe cupboard that stood against the wall close to the bed. She scanned the length of it with a tight, critical eye. Mrs. Webb, following suit, stepped beside her.

Sir William lifted an edge of the blanket in his gloved hands. He looked under the bed. "Nothing here. You would think the man, being a doctor, would have a medical bag or other such supplies around. Like tonics. Or at least empty bottles in which to put the tonics."

Anne opened the wardrobe cupboard. A waistcoat, two pairs of pants, and a few white shirts hung on a rod. "Nothing but clothes in here." She moved to close the cupboard, but before she did so she glanced down. "Hold on." She opened the door wider and removed a small, open crate sitting on the floor in the far corner of the cupboard. She set it on the table. "Pears's White Imperial Powder? A cosmetic brush?"

"Perhaps Dr. Sinclair had a sister visit him here," Mrs. Webb said. "Or a mother."

Anne, frowning, picked up a thin strip of what might have been mouse fur and dangled it in front of her. "What do you think this is?"

Sir William furrowed his brows. "It looks like some sort of costume."

"A *costume*? Like an eyebrow?"

"Or side-whiskers." Sir William's half smile held the same humorous glint Anne had seen in his family's portrait back at Seawind House. He removed the last object from the crate: a closed burlap bag. "Any guesses what might be in here?"

Anne shook her head, and Sir William, watching her, opened the bag and peeked inside.

"Interesting," he said.

Anne leaned over the bag too. "A wood box? Not so curious, but I do wonder why Dr. Sinclair would keep it in a bag."

"There is something else here too." Sir William took out the box, set it on the table, and pulled out the other object. It was a lidded rectangular box about the same size as the one Anne kept her art supplies in. "Would you like to do the honors?"

"Do be careful," Mrs. Webb said.

Anne wanted to roll her eyes at their theatrics. It was, after all, just a box. But she instead frowned, took the box from Sir William with a small huff—he chuckled—and opened the lid. Inside were pencils of varying tip sizes, two quill pens, a small bottle of ink, and at least a dozen cards—no. She rifled through the documents. There were a few calling cards with Dr. Sinclair's name on them, but the other cards had other names. There were miscellaneous notes, too, written in varied hands, and several certificates. One proclaimed Dr. Sinclair had in fact graduated as a physician from Cambridge.

"I am glad for this one, at least," Mrs. Webb said, referring to the certificate.

Anne inhaled and set the box on the table. "Your turn," she said to Sir William. "What is in the box?"

He, glancing at Anne, removed the box's contents: dozens of ten-pound bank notes. "At least they show the doctor was not a pauper. I was beginning to wonder if he was a gentleman at all, that perhaps he was an apothecary pretending to be a physician in order that he might gain a greater income."

Anne shook her head.

"You disagree, Miss de Bourgh?"

"Entirely. However, I think your idea that he was not a physician at all is exactly what these items do indicate."

"I was only in jest."

Mrs. Webb gaped between the two of them.

"I realize that, sir." Anne fanned the name cards and certificates between her hands. "But look here. These varied names, the ink and pencils, the cosmetics, the money . . . and no doctor's bag? I believe all of them indicate Dr. Sinclair was not a physician at all. That he was a charlatan. Perhaps even a confidence trickster."

"Those are some pretty large assumptions to make with such little evidence," Mrs. Webb said.

"Perhaps they are," Anne said, "but that does not mean they are incorrect."

Anne searched Mrs. Webb's gaze. Maybe the woman did not agree with Anne's assessment, but surely she was pleased with her behavior. Anne had not kept to herself as if she were a mouse afraid of being trampled upon. She had spoken out, and she had done so even when the odds of her companions believing her were miniscule. If only she had had bravery enough to confront Mr. Talbot about his anger earlier. If she had, perhaps they would already be friends again, and he would be there with them that very moment.

Sir William squeezed Anne's hand between both of his. "My mother is going to be most pleased with your assessment of *Dr.* Sinclair, Miss de Bourgh."

"I am glad to hear it." Anne curtsied, continuing on with his theatrics. As she had noted earlier, Sir William was an eligible match, but now she realized she also enjoyed his company. Was this what it felt like to have a brother? *My mother deems I should be your wife, not your sister.*

"I believe we should return home now, Miss de Bourgh," Mrs. Webb said.

"Quite right. We have likely learned all we can here." Sir William released Anne's hand and led the two ladies from the inn.

As the Steyne was quite busy with both carriage and pedestrian traffic, it took them all of half an hour to make it back to the de Bourgh's townhouse where, in a very uncharacteristic fashion, Anne's mother, leaning slightly against the doorframe, greeted them at the door. Mrs. Webb, quickly excusing herself, went inside.

"I hope, Sir William, you will stay a little longer and join my daughter and me for tea?" Anne's mother said. "I am sure after such a long and I hope pleasant afternoon you are quite hungry."

"Yes." Anne, again feeling the familial amity for him she had felt a short time ago, briefly touched his forearm. "Do stay."

Anne's mother beamed at her.

"There is nothing I would enjoy more, Lady Catherine, Miss de Bourgh, but I am afraid I have business I must attend to."

"Some other time, then?" Anne's mother pressed.

"I would be pleased to." He bowed to both of them and left.

When her mother closed the door behind them, she took Anne's arm, and they headed toward the door at the back of the entry hall.

"Are you all right?" Anne asked her.

"I seem a bit dizzy this morning, but it will clear up in a few minutes. I expect it is due to my worry over our morning's misfortune."

Dizzy? When was her mother ever in anything but perfect health?

"Did you find your broach?" Anne asked

"I did not. Neither was that Headborough Powell of much help. He said there have been frequent thefts among the gentry these days, but he would do what he could."

"Which is very little, I understand." *I wonder what he will do with Dr. Sinclair's appointment book.*

"Very little indeed," her mother said. "I should never have brought the broach with me. I only did so because it was a way to keep your father and a bit of Rosings with us on our journey. But now . . . if I'd had any idea such a thing could happen, I never would have done so."

"I am truly sorry, Mother. I know how important the broach is to you."

They reached the drawing room and crossed the entire length of the floor to Lady Catherine's favored couch before she spoke again. "What is done is done, and I cannot do anything about it now."

If Anne were an outsider looking in upon this scene, her mother would have seemed a stoic, regal woman who felt nothing more than a slight irritation over her broach's disappearance, but as Anne was not an outsider, she noticed the almost imperceptible waver in her mother's voice, which could be due to her dizziness, and the slight hunching in her shoulders. Her mother had been emotionally wounded.

Lady Catherine rang a bell for a maid to bring their tea. "Your complexion is looking rather rosy, my dear," she said to Anne. "I believe your outing with Sir William has done you a great deal of good."

"I believe you are right."

"And I must say his fondness for you has increased."

Anne helped her mother into a cushioned, straight-backed chair. "Perhaps it has."

"There is no *perhaps* in it, my dear. He is fond of you. Perhaps we will not go to London after all."

Anne coughed. She could not possibly tell her mother she believed such a thought had not even entered Sir William's mind. But if she could say something, could tell her that while she had obediently given Sir William a chance, nothing had come of it, what then? Anne could not answer that question, but just imaging herself standing up to her mother with such ease overwhelmed her with so much wonder she lowered her head.

"Has your outing taken so much out of you?" Lady Catherine said. "This evening you will take your tonic, but you will do away with your evening walk. You must preserve your energy."

Anne pressed her palm against her chest. She would prefer to go on her walk, for it always invigorated her, and she would not take the tonic, nor would her mother wish her to do so if she knew the truth about Dr. Sinclair, but—Anne's breath hitched. *Mother takes the tonic.* Anne had to tell her something.

"I-I saw Dr. Fletcher today," Anne said. "He asked me about the tonic Dr. Sinclair had given us. Are you still taking yours?"

"Not anymore."

Anne exhaled in relief.

"I finished it this morning," her mother continued. "And as you have taken your medicine as prescribed, I am certain you will soon finish yours.

I must say I am glad of it. For all the cure's reputation, I feel no healthier today than I did before I took it."

"I believe you are right." As Anne felt no inclination to explain any of the rest of it to her mother, and as neither of them were any longer taking the tonic, nor did they seem any worse for the wear in having done so, Anne said nothing more about it. Instead she followed through the quiet motions of the afternoon tea before returning to her room.

There, she sat on her bed and collapsed onto her back. She stared up at the ceiling. So many things had happened today. Dr. Sinclair . . . who was he really? Sir William . . . his good humor and gentlemanly kindness toward her. Mr. Talbot . . . how he had shown her art to the scientist . . . Anne sat up and rushed to her desk, where she kept her drawing pad. The scientist, Mr. Miller, wanted to talk to Anne about her art. He wanted to perhaps utilize her talents.

Thank you, Mr. Talbot, for this opportunity.

And yet, at the same time, Mr. Talbot had seemed so angry with her. Why?

CHAPTER TWENTY-ONE

North of Ditchling, East Sussex

Moonlight shadowed the slope when Kenneth shoved through the prickly hedge at the top of the hill that overlooked the Old Bamber Cottage. Last year, he and the rest of the gang had reunited there and devised their plan against the de Bourghs. This place, they had said, would be their refuge.

Evans, the fun-loving youngest son of a moderately prosperous landowner, had acquired it upon his father's death shortly before Evans had married his rich heiress. At that time, Evans had stood as tall and proud as if the cottage had always been his, as if he had owned it even back when their band had broken up because people were starting to wonder too much about the four young people with little to recommend them. When their gang had moved into town, they had no occupations as far as anyone could see, but when they left a few months later, people had talked about how they were seemingly better off. That was when the group had determined they must acquire their fortunes alone, before their frauds were revealed and they were sent to the gallows.

After that, Evans used his charm and good looks to win his heiress, and Evans's cousin Leon had likewise married well. Seymour still lived by his wits, moving from one scheme to another as the gang had once done. Kenneth had settled down with and lost Bridget; he still had Grace, but the way Kenneth had left Leon . . . He clenched his hands at the memory. Perhaps the gang's coming back at Leon's request and Kenneth's taking part in Leon's scheme would now make up for that offense.

Kenneth started down the grassy slope toward the shadowed shrubbery and full-leaved trees encircling the cottage. Candlelight through the window nearest the door flickered twice. The signal.

Kenneth ran. Evans, stouter than Kenneth remembered but still as tall as any wild oak, stepped out of the darkness. His blond hair, almost the same color as his buckskin trousers, glinted in the remaining moonlight. "You are later than I had expected." He brushed a leaf from the sleeve of his perfectly cut brown riding coat.

"At least I am here," Kenneth said.

Evans, the gang's designated costume procurer, grinned and waved Kenneth to follow him around to the back of the cottage. "That may be, but I advise you to be prompt from here on out. Lady Catherine de Bourgh has little patience for anything less than perfection."

"That fastidious, is she?"

"More than that."

"I expect I'll enjoy the challenge."

"I expect you will." Evans's voice seemed to smile. "But the first thing you'd better do is fix that accent. The scheme is over now if you do not."

Kenneth straightened his spine. *Crash the slang, improve the accent.* He arched his voice. "How is this?"

"I believe it has been a while since you spoke like quality. Never mind. I am certain it will come back to you. It always did. Simply think a little taller in the back of your throat. More refined."

Kenneth rounded his voice even more. "What about now?"

"Better."

Behind the cottage Kenneth drew back his shoulders and thought through the words he'd memorized after the gang had first come up with his new identity. *My mother was born to English gentry, and my father was suave and rich. Very rich.* "Good enough, to pass for a wealthy American come to visit his mother's cousin?" he called out. "The esteemed Mr. Evans, the husband of the niece of Lord Backwell, who is a member of the prince regent's court?"

"It is close. Keep working at it. Above all, do not slip back into your own voice until we finish this. If you do, I do not believe even my impeccable connections could save us from being found out and strictly punished. Society does not welcome infiltrators."

"Or confidence men."

"Unless you marry one of society's elite." Evans chuckled over his own joke, for he himself had duped and ultimately married one of them. How long he intended to stay married, to not use Leon's services and abscond with his wife's money as Kenneth was to do to Miss de Bourgh, Kenneth did not know.

Evans pulled a bulging cloth sack off the back of one of the two horses tied to a tree and handed it to Kenneth. "Hurry and get dressed. We have a three hours' ride down to Brighton."

Kenneth examined the pack's contents: a white shirt, a gray riding coat, tan buckskins, and black boots. "Miss de Bourgh. Is she like her mother?"

"I cannot say what Miss de Bourgh's tastes are. She spoke very little when Mrs. Evans and I visited them, but I do not believe she will give us much trouble. Her disposition was docile, though she did not seem as sickly to me as society claimed her to be. Lady Catherine said she has allergic rhinitis, which Dr. Fletcher in Brighton is working to help her cure."

Kenneth removed his clothes. "Does Mrs. Evans suspect us?"

"Not at all. She did not even blink when I told her I had offered you the phaeton and two horses to use during your visit. I believe she secretly hopes you will marry one of Brighton's fine young ladies."

"A lucky guess for someone who knows nothing about our plans."

"She only hopes for another female relation she can visit with."

"My Bridget said something like that to me when I told her I'd found work in another village. I believe she was lonely."

"Mrs. Evans is most definitely not lonely. She has all of Brighton's society at her beck and call. And possibly all of London's too."

Kenneth's stomach soured. "It must be nice." *To have so much.*

"Wealth has its benefits."

Kenneth pulled on the buckskins. "How is the scheme going so far?"

"On schedule, but. . ."

Kenneth shrugged into the white shirt. "But what?"

"Seymour is dead."

Kenneth froze. "What happened?" As if he could not already guess the answer.

"All I know is Leon was not happy with Seymour's performance as Dr. Sinclair."

"Poisoned him?"

"What else?"

Kenneth clenched his teeth. He stuffed the hem of his shirt into the buckskins. "Leon had no call to do that. Seymour was only playing the part Leon had assigned him. He had nothing to do with Lady Catherine and her late husband cheating your aunt and uncle out of that tract of land or of the destruction of their livelihoods."

Evans faced Kenneth. He tightened his glare and crossed his arms. "I am sorry Seymour paid such a heavy price for his mistakes, but I am with Leon on this. Nothing must get in the way of Lady Catherine at last facing justice. She must see what it is like to suffer at the hands of another whom she thinks she can trust. It is like her husband, Sir Lewis de Bourgh, told them: 'Business and wealth are not subservient to emotion. They are kings, and as such, they can only be handled by those who know this.'"

Kenneth turned away from the bitterness slicing the air between him and Evans and slid on the boots. They fit as if they had been made for him, which they may have been. While ten years had passed since their last sham, Evans had not forgotten Kenneth's clothing and boot sizes, which fortunately had not changed since then.

"You have not gone soft on us, have you? Leon said bringing you back was like playing a wildcard."

"I am as in as I ever was." Kenneth tied his neckcloth. "You had no reason to doubt me then, and you have no reason to doubt me now." He shoved his arms into his riding coat and once again faced Evans. "I need the money."

"Badly enough we can trust you no matter what?"

"No matter what." Kenneth shoved his own clothes into the bag.

"One more thing from Leon." Evans handed him a folded piece of paper. "You are to complete that assignment before I introduce you to the de Bourghs."

Kenneth read the note.

> *Rescue Miss de Bourgh from an "accident," and ingratiate yourself into both her and her mother's affections. Miss de Bourgh will be at the address listed below at eleven o'clock.*

He scanned the address then looked up at Evans. "No other instructions?"

"Leon left it to your imagination."

Kenneth growled. Miss de Bourgh would die in the end, of course, but something about knowing that and hurting her now niggled at his conscience. "I am not a hangman."

"Not yet."

Kenneth stared at Evans.

"Think of it as part of the ruse," Evans said. The two men climbed onto their horses. "What are you calling yourself?"

Kenneth pictured Grace's pale face, the doctor standing over her. "Mr. Lambert."

"One of England's old family names. Good choice." Evans flicked the reigns, and the two men's horses took off toward the main road that led back to Brighton.

CHAPTER TWENTY-TWO

Brighton

RUN. IF ANNE HAD TO choose one word to describe Friday it would be *run*. She had rushed between her morning walk and breakfast even though she had wanted to continue speaking with Blanc about their upcoming swimming lesson. Blanc had worked it out with her father and her intended, Robert, that she would teach Anne on her last day in Anne's mother's employ. Likewise, Anne had hurried to and from her sea-bathing—swimming—exercise, thinking all the while about how she could sneak away with Blanc to that swimming lesson without her mother knowing. And finally, though Anne had not fully been able to keep up with Mrs. Webb, she had hastened along the boardwalk the entire way to Seawind House. Even so, Mrs. Webb reached the Talbots' front staircase a moment before Anne did.

Anne, breathing hard, came up behind Mrs. Webb on the first stair. "One day soon I hope I am healthy enough to move as easily as you do."

Mrs. Webb stepped down beside her. "Forgive me, Miss de Bourgh. I do not know what I was thinking to run ahead like that."

"Perhaps you are as anxious as I am to learn what Lady Talbot knows about Dr. Sinclair."

"Perhaps." Mrs. Webb straightened her spine. "Though I doubt the activity is as diverting for me as it is for you."

Mrs. Webb mentioned nothing of Mr. Talbot, yet still heat brushed Anne's cheeks. What a way to begin her meeting with Mr. Tal—the Talbots.

Anne turned away from Mrs. Webb. "What is your opinion about Dr. Sinclair's death? I have been going over everything I know about the incident, and I am weary to the bone of replaying the same thoughts."

"I cannot come to any conclusions either. But as you have such a good eye for details and an understanding of people, I do not doubt you will uncover the whole of it soon enough."

If Anne was so good at understanding people, why could she not figure out what she had done to upset Mr. Talbot?

They continued up the steps to the front door. Anne reached for the knocker, but as she clasped the sun-warmed metal, new nervousness shivered through her. Soon she would see Mr. Talbot, and soon she must find a way to apologize to him for whatever she had previously done to upset him.

Mrs. Graham answered the door and showed Anne and Mrs. Webb into the sitting room. Just as they had done when Anne had last entered this room, Lady Talbot sat on the pale-gold couch on the far side of the room, and Sir William and Mr. Talbot stood behind her. Mr. Talbot nodded to Anne. Not with sharp movements or a tightened expression, the way he had done when she had last seen him, but with downturned lips and slumped shoulders. Was he no longer angry? Was he instead sad? She could not say, but her heart leapt. *He is here. With me.*

"How lovely to see you, Miss de Bourgh," Lady Talbot said. "Come. Sit here next to me."

Anne looked only at Lady Talbot as she crossed the carpet to her hostess, but when Sir William suddenly stepped around the couch and took her hand, helping her into the seat next to his mother, out of the corner of her eye Anne noticed spots of pink touch Mr. Talbot's cheeks.

"Tell me," Lady Talbot said to Anne. "How is your mother?"

Anne handed her reticule and drawing pad to Mrs. Webb, who sat next to Anne. "She is well, thank you."

Sir William sat on the settee next to Mr. Talbot and across from his mother.

"I am sure you have ascertained my sons have already told me what the three of you learned during your investigations," Lady Talbot said. "I will also add, in case you have not heard, that this morning's *Brighton Herald* reported Dr. Sinclair had likely been poisoned."

Though Mr. Talbot now stared at a square of white marble tile in front of him, there was something in his forward-leaning posture that made Anne feel as if he would, if he could, rush from the room—from her—at his soonest opportunity. And yet, like she had previously noted, that feeling did not seem to originate from his previous anger at her. Nor from sadness. *What is this about?*

"My sons likewise told me they did not find anyone who knew much about Dr. Sinclair," Lady Talbot continued. "But they believe he may, in fact, not be a doctor at all."

"That is what we have begun to believe," Anne said.

"They also told me you kept notes on your findings. How very prudent of you. I knew you would be an important asset to our investigation. Will you share with me what you have written?"

"Of course." Mrs. Webb handed back her reticule, and Anne removed her notebook from it. She quickly read aloud the information she had written there, starting with what they had learned from Dr. Fletcher and ending with what they had found in Dr. Sinclair's apartment.

Sir William placed his hand on Lady Talbot's shoulder. "I am glad Miss de Bourgh took such careful notes. While I told you we found that appointment book and I gave it to Headborough Powell, I had not remembered exactly what it said. *MAB*, it seems, stands for his meeting with Miss de Bourgh."

"It does?" Lady Talbot said.

"It has to," Anne said. "One o'clock was when he showed up at our townhouse. And *M-A-B* must be Miss Anne de Bourgh."

Mr. Talbot stared so hard at Anne she could not mistake the anger, sadness, and some other emotion—was it betrayal?—tightening his expression. What had she done? *Find out. Apologize.*

"We do not know what Sinclair's other appointment meant though," Sir William continued. "It was at four o'clock, but *LT*—"

Lady Talbot flicked her hand. "*LT* must be me. That is the time I met with him that day."

"That's right." Mr. Talbot said. "I had forgotten you had met with him. What about?"

Mr. Talbot, looked straight at Anne, held her gaze—her breath stopped—and looked back to his mother.

"Well?" he said. "Why did you meet with Dr. Sinclair?"

Lady Talbot glanced between the two of them and ultimately focused on Mr. Talbot. "It was nothing worth all this fuss. Remember the riddle you made up for me for my birthday?"

He nodded.

"I solved it quite quickly, as you know, but while doing so, I came across this real mystery in the newspaper. You have heard of it, I am sure. It is about a man and woman who suddenly died in their homes some weeks past."

"Arsenic poisoning, as I recall," Mr. Talbot said.

"Yes, that is it." She repeated what she had learned about the crime scene, how there had been all forms of food about, from stale chocolate truffles and raspberry fudge conserves to dried-up salads and moldy soup. They were the most likely culprits, but, "So far, no one knows exactly how they were poisoned, and as I had heard we had a new doctor in town, one I hoped would not mind me asking him a few out-of-the-ordinary questions, I made an appointment with him."

"You talked with Dr. Sinclair about arsenic poisoning on the same day he died, likely from poisoning?" Sir William said. "Did you tell the constable about your meeting with him?"

"I did. I thought the event was such a great coincidence the matter might interest him, but he did not seem in any way concerned. He dismissed himself quite quickly, as I recall."

"Headborough Powell did that?"

She shook her head. "One of his associates. Now, let us put that incident behind us and set our minds to what I found out."

Anne stared at the woman. How could she be so cavalier about her situation? And yet, if the constables also thought nothing of her conversation with Dr. Sinclair, why should any of them? Perhaps no one considered his murder as anything but a distraction.

Lady Talbot took a letter from the end table beside her and held it out to Anne. "This is the report from the coroner. Would you be so kind as to read it aloud for us, Miss de Bourgh?"

Mrs. Webb winced, and Anne looked askance at her.

"Forgive me," she whispered. "Go ahead, but do speak up."

"I will." Anne turned back to Lady Talbot. "I would be happy to read the letter." She unfolded it and cleared her throat, for Mrs. Webb had been quite right in reminding her to speak up. Often when they read together, Anne did have a tendency to let her voice trail too softly. Anne read:

> "Dear Lady Talbot,
>   My results from the autopsy of Dr. Charles Sinclair remain
> somewhat inconclusive at this date. While I am certain he

died of arsenic poisoning, I have not yet determined how the
substance entered his system. His body shows no signs of having
been gradually poisoned, nor does it exhibit signs of struggle.
Though, oddly, the skin on his face, lips, and hands were tinted
by a vegetable-based powder commonly worn by women. I am
sorry I cannot at this time give you more conclusive help.
   Sincerely—"

"Dr. Sinclair wore the cosmetics?" Sir William said.

"Perhaps he used it to cover something up," Anne said. "A scar or—or a wound from an illness. Or maybe . . ." All at once, everyone focused on Anne. She lowered her gaze, folded the letter tighter than necessary, and pretended that insufferable heat had not again crept up from her neck and across her cheeks.

"Please tell us what you were about to say," Mr. Talbot said. Softly. The creases at the corners of his eyes drooped, but otherwise the same emotion, the same energy that had connected the two of them the night of the ball blazed from his gaze. But that other unfathomable emotion was there, too, standing between them like an impenetrable barrier.

Anne slipped the letter back inside the box. She pressed her feet harder against the floor and straightened her spine. She stared straight back at Mr. Talbot, silently pleading to know what had happened, and said aloud, "Since it appears Dr. Sinclair, or perhaps we should say *Mr.* Sinclair, was not in actuality a physician—was possibly nothing more than a confidence trickster—perhaps the cosmetics were part of a disguise."

"I believe you are exactly right, my dear," Lady Talbot said.

Mr. Talbot swallowed, and Anne at last dragged her gaze from his.

"Which also means we know nothing more than we did before." Sir William shoved his hands across the top of his legs and stood. "Forgive me, Mother, I know how much this investigation means to you, and under normal conditions I would be happy to continue helping you with it, but I believe I must now bow out if I am going to make it to London in time to take a late evening meal with Susanna."

"Surely you need not leave immediately. Your sister has been homesick for the past three months. Surely she can bear another day." Lady Talbot turned to Anne. "Miss de Bourgh, please, convince him to stay."

Anne offered Sir William a slight smile. "Do heed your mother, Sir William."

While Lady Talbot and Sir William stared at one another, Mr. Talbot's gaze at Anne hardened, and that barrier between them grew wider.

"You do not mean that, Mother," Sir William said. "After all, you are the one who, after receiving her letter earlier today, insisted I visit her."

Lady Talbot sighed. "You are right. I do not mean it. It is only a man is dead, and I cannot help feeling those who care for him—his mother, perhaps—yearn for someone to unravel the truth as quickly as possible."

"I am certain the three of you will get along well enough without me." Sir William regarded Mr. Talbot. "I bid you, if you would be so kind, to make my apologies to Lady Catherine in my behalf? I am afraid I will not be able to keep my dinner engagement with her and Miss de Bourgh."

"Consider it done."

Lady Talbot frowned, but as she spoke, her expression turned into a gentle smile. "Please, son, give sweet Susanna my love."

"I will be happy to do so." Sir William bowed over his mother's hand and left the room.

When he was gone, Mr. Talbot stared between the closed door and Anne, especially at Anne. "You do not seem to mind that my brother has left."

"He will be missed, of course," Anne said, "but I believe the rest of us will manage without him."

His eyes widened, and just as quickly as Lady Talbot cleared her throat, that impenetrable barrier between him and Anne disappeared. He inched toward her, and the look in his eyes clasped her heart and did not let go.

"I am happy you think so, Miss de Bourgh," Lady Talbot said. "For I have determined our next steps."

"You have?" Anne's mind had been dancing so quickly over the fact that something had finally healed the breach between her and Mr. Talbot that she could hardly think of anything else.

"I have. While we wait for further information from the coroner, the three of us must ask more questions around town. There must be someone who knows something else about the poor man."

"I am happy to help you in any way I can." While Anne was curious about what had happened to Mr. Sinclair, she greatly wished to please Lady Talbot. And acquire more opportunities to associate with Mr. Talbot.

"Shall we go into town now?" Mr. Talbot asked his mother.

"I believe I will wait until tomorrow morning." Lady Talbot, glancing much too innocently between Anne and Mr. Talbot, pressed her fingertips to her forehead. "I find I have a sudden headache."

"I am sorry," Mr. Talbot said. "May I get you anything?"

"No, I will be well. I need only a bit of tea and rest. But please do not let me stop the two of you from going."

Mr. Talbot caught his breath, bowed over his mother's hand, and whirled to Anne. "I would be happy if you would allow me to escort you into town. We can take the barouche."

"I wish I could, but I am afraid I have an appointment with Mr. Miller at eleven o'clock."

"Then, how about I escort you to the Millers'?"

"Oh." Anne shifted her stance. "Thank you, yes."

Mr. Talbot stood. He sent a servant to call for the barouche and held out his hand to Anne. She took it and stood. "Thank you."

He offered her his arm. Then Anne, Mrs. Webb, and Mr. Talbot bade farewell to Lady Talbot and left the sitting room. Outside, Anne said, "Mr. Talbot?"

He turned to her.

"I have wanted to apologize. I know I have recently angered you somehow, and I am sorry for whatever it was I did. Please believe me when I say I never meant to do or say anything that would upset you."

"Do not trouble yourself. You did nothing wrong. My actions were entirely of my own making and were based on what I now see was nothing. I hope you will forgive my boorish behavior."

"You are forgiven."

He smiled slightly, pressed his hand over the top of hers where it rested on his arm, and motioned for her to follow him down the stairs toward the barouche that waited for them at the end of the walk.

"Please, will you not tell me what I did?" Anne pressed. "I do not want to repeat it."

"There is nothing for you to change, Miss de Bourgh. As I said, you did nothing wrong. It was me. All me."

Anne bit her lip. She held her breath, but still her heart raced. If ever there was a time when a woman could let a man know of her feelings for him, this moment, when nothing but good feelings existed between them, was it. And yet, how could she do so? Should she do so?

She peered over her shoulder at Mrs. Webb. Her companion did nothing, said nothing, but her manner was such that Anne thought she heard her say, "Be assertive. Follow your heart. Be the woman you want to be."

The footman opened the carriage door. Mr. Talbot helped Mrs. Webb inside and held out his hand to Anne. She took it, hesitated. "Nothing was just you. It was the two of us. You and I. The way we feel. Together."

His mouth fell open, and she jumped into the carriage.

CHAPTER TWENTY-THREE

THOUGH THE FASHIONABLE, NIGHTTIME PROMENADE hour of nine o'clock was still a few hours away, so many of Brighton's elite had already gathered along the Steyne that Mr. Talbot's driver slowed the horses' pace even more than he had while they had driven along Marine Parade. He also frequently veered between the park and the boardwalk to avoid colliding with an impeccably dressed pedestrian or two. Not that many of them seemed to mind. When Anne, studying the architecture of the shops, gentlemen's clubs, and spacious libraries, saw a few ladies and even one gentleman unnecessarily fall against a member of the opposite sex, they merely laughed and occasionally stayed against the other longer than what Anne considered necessary. *The bad and good living side by side,* she thought.

Their surroundings changed from busy and boisterous to quiet and sedate almost as soon as they turned off the main thoroughfare onto Church Street. They stopped before a modest, white brick home.

"Mr. Miller's residence." Mr. Talbot's crippled leg brushed passed Anne's knees as he moved past her and Mrs. Webb. He climbed out of the carriage and held his hand out to Anne. She took it, and finally, after all his quick glances on the ride there between the floor and Anne, directly faced her.

"I hope you enjoyed the ride," he said.

"I did, thank you."

He released her hand—*Had he squeezed it first?*—and turned to help Mrs. Webb from the carriage. Anne took a few steps up the cobbled walk that led through the small yard to Mr. Miller's front door.

"It is not a grand house," Mrs. Webb said behind her.

Anne looked over her shoulder. Both her companions stared at her, but it was Mr. Talbot's fixed gaze that simultaneously bounced through her senses and quavered through her stomach. Had her earlier hint worked? Did he suspect he meant something to her? *Please let me mean something to him.*

Anne nodded at Mrs. Webb, who tilted her head, obviously not understanding Anne's communication, but it did not matter. All Anne meant was to show her gratitude to the good and wonderful woman who had encouraged her to not only stand up for herself but to also act on the wishes of her heart. Because of her, Anne's hopes had the possibility of coming true.

Mr. Talbot stepped next to Anne and led them to Mr. Miller's front door. "I feel I ought to clarify something before we go inside. Mr. Miller is a good man and my friend. I never hear better sense than I do from him, but some people find him a bit difficult to understand."

"Does he not speak coherently?" Anne said.

"It is not that. It is only he is sometimes considered peculiar because he does so much of his work alone. But I do hope you and Mr. Miller will get along. I believe he is in great need of your artistic abilities, though he may not admit it."

"I can understand how it is. Sometimes I too have found it is easier to deal with the disappointment of friendlessness than the condescension or indifference of society."

"Quite right." Mr. Talbot's gaze settled on Anne's. Her breath leapt from her chest and somersaulted into the sky.

"Perhaps someone should let Mr. Miller know we are here," Mrs. Webb said.

"You are right." Mr. Talbot laughed a little and knocked.

Almost immediately a short thin-haired man with squinting eyes opened the door. "Talbot."

"Miller."

They shook hands. Mr. Talbot motioned toward Anne. "This is Miss de Bourgh, and this is her companion, Mrs. Webb."

Mr. Miller quick-nodded to both women and glanced between Anne and Mr. Talbot. "Miss *Anne* de Bourgh? The woman you told me of? The girl—"

Mr. Talbot stiffened.

"The gifted artist?"

Though Mr. Talbot's posture relaxed, he angled decidedly away from Anne. "Yes. This is the gifted artist." Mr. Talbot, still not looking at Anne, rubbed the back of his neck. He cleared his throat. Was he uncomfortable?

All at once Anne remembered that moment when Mr. Talbot had stood in the garden next to the voodoo lily and asked her to write his letter to his mother for him. He had said he was a man of few words. She had not seen that characteristic in him, exactly, but new understanding sat squarely on her chest. *Mr. Talbot has difficulty expressing some of his feelings.* Was that why he would not explain his earlier anger?

Mr. Miller grinned at Mr. Talbot and motioned them to follow him inside. The entry was half the size of Anne's townhouse and much more austere. In truth, the small, shadowed paintings; intricately carved wooden animal skulls; and thick green ivy that ran like tapestries down the dark-paneled walls made the room seem more a backwoods hunting lodge than the home of an esteemed scientist. But then, it was not as if Anne had met any other scientists. Perhaps they all lived amid such unique surroundings.

Mr. Miller held out his hand. "May I see your drawing pad, Miss de Bourgh?"

Anne handed it to him, and he gave her a sheet of paper from the table next to him.

He flipped to the last page of her book and pursed his lips. "Do you know what that paper is?"

She scanned it. "A list of plants. Their Latin names."

He pointed to the sixth one down. "What is that?"

"*Parnassia palustris*? It is the grass-of-Parnassus."

Mr. Miller handed her drawing pad back to her. "Talbot was right. You are indeed capable of this work. When can you start?"

"I am—what I mean to say is my mother will certainly not allow me to actually work for you. She would consider it a great scandal."

"Why did you come here, then?" He glared at Mr. Talbot.

"I believe Miss de Bourgh is very interested in—"

Anne, glancing at Mrs. Webb, touched the back of Mr. Talbot's elbow. "Thank you, but I would like to take care of this myself."

Mr. Talbot nodded and stepped slightly back.

Anne turned again to Mr. Miller. "I came to visit you because I am very interested in helping you with your book. I love plants, and I have yearned for many years to find a good use for my interest."

"You have more than interest, Miss de Bourgh. You have great talent."

"Thank you. I am, however, the daughter of Lady Catherine de Bourgh, and I would not wish to displease her. I have been thinking on this situation for some time now, and I believe I have come up with a solution."

Mr. Talbot, Mr. Miller, and even Mrs. Webb stared at her with such incredulous expressions that Anne almost lost her nerve. She clenched the side of her dress skirts and said, "First, my contributions to this project must be kept solely between the four of us, which indicates my name will not be associated with any of my drawings."

"But Miss de Bourgh," Mr. Talbot said, "everyone should have the privilege of knowing the artist."

She shook her head. "I am certain this is the only way. But I do not mind. Truly. It is enough for me to know others appreciate my work."

Mr. Talbot crossed his arms in front of his chest and pressed his lips into a tight line.

"Very well. I agree," Mr. Miller said. "What are your other conditions?"

"I have only one more," Anne said. "I will draw for you, but you will not pay me for my illustrations. You will instead donate any moneys coming to me back into the needs of the University of Vienna."

"As you wish. That is everything?"

"It is."

"When can you start?" Mr. Miller asked again.

"I suppose I can begin as soon as you need my help."

"I need it immediately." Mr. Miller opened the top drawer of the table and pulled out another piece of paper. He exchanged it for the one he had originally given to Anne. "This is a real list of the pictures I need. Deliver your drawings to me as soon as you complete them."

Anne read over his list. "I hope you know where I can locate the subjects. Some of the plants I can find without difficulty, but others—"

He waved off her comment and went to the door. "If you have any trouble in that regard, you can consult the library."

You. That meant the burden of location would be on her, but Anne did not mind. Researching the locations of plants would give her another reason to leave the house for purposes other than mundane tasks and maintaining her connections with society.

"Now I need to get back to my work." Mr. Miller opened the door. "Oh. One more thing. Please use ink on your drawings. It will preserve them better."

"I will be pleased to, sir."

Mr. Miller smiled and waited with Mr. Talbot next to the door while Anne and Mrs. Webb stepped outside. Mr. Talbot followed them.

"I look forward to seeing your work, Miss de Bourgh," Mr. Miller called. "And Talbot, feel free to join Miss de Bourgh any time. I would enjoy your company too."

Mr. Talbot glanced at Anne out of the corner of his eye while Mr. Miller, grinning, closed the door.

Anne glimpsed between the list in her hand and the closed door. "You were right, Mr. Talbot. Your friend is very singular."

"He is that. Do you mind?"

"Not at all."

Mr. Talbot smiled so broadly Anne could not help but smile back at him.

"Shall we?" He motioned for them to return to the carriage.

Mrs. Webb touched Anne's arm, and when Anne turned to her, she lowered her voice. "Forgive me, Miss de Bourgh. I do not wish to interfere with your endeavors, but I do believe it is time for your mid-morning constitutional."

Anne frowned toward the barouche. It was true she felt too wound up to sit in a carriage just then. "You are right, of course. I wonder, Mr. Talbot. Would it be too much to ask that we walk for a bit before your driver takes Mrs. Webb and me home? I need more art supplies, and I expect one of the nearby shops might be able to accommodate me."

"It is no trouble at all." He held out his arm to her, informed the driver to meet them at the shop, and the two, followed by Mrs. Webb, headed down the walkway.

"I hope this endeavor will not keep you from helping my mother with her investigation," he said after they passed a house and a vacant strip of land.

"I would not dream of letting it stop me. Helping your mother investigate a murder only adds to my enthusiasm for Brighton."

"Brighton suits you, then?"

"I believe it does."

"I admit I am surprised. Many, I believe, find Brighton lives too much up to its wild reputation."

"It does that, but I find there is also much that is good here."

"I have found that to be the case with everywhere I have been."

"Have you traveled much, sir?"

"If you consider all of England as being much, then yes." He opened his mouth, as if he was about to say more, but when he did not, and when the silence dragged between them, Anne said, "Thank you, Mr. Talbot."

"For what?"

"For your kindness in showing my art to Mr. Miller."

"You have already thanked me for that. There is no need to do so again."

They stepped off the boardwalk, preparing to cross the road. "Perhaps, but I am truly grateful for the opportunity to draw plants for Mr. Miller's book. I can think of no better gift you or anyone could have given me."

Mr. Talbot's cheeks flushed lightly.

Anne stared at him. Why did he seem so suddenly embarrassed? He must surely receive many such thanks for his frequent kindnesses. However, it was not her place to judge, only to ease his discomfort if she could. She turned quickly away from him and, heading across the road, stepped out beyond a parked carriage.

"Miss de Bourgh!"

Anne did not know who yelled her name, Mrs. Webb or Mr. Talbot or both, but when she whirled to the sound, two galloping black horses, an even blacker carriage, and a driver looking off to the side rather than where he was going, filled her view. She screamed.

"Miss de Bourgh!" A hand clamped her arm, yanked her backward, and flung her into the side of the parked carriage before the galloping carriage hit her. Smashed nose . . . jarred neck . . . aching forehead. She slumped to the ground. Darkness.

"Miss de Bourgh."

All was black, but hands as warm as sunlight pressed her forehead and brushed her hair from her cheeks. Mr. Talbot's suddenly gentle voice said, "Miss de Bourgh, open your eyes."

Anne squirmed, groaned. Somehow she obeyed his command. Mr. Talbot's tightly furrowed brows and now-pale face filled her view. "What happened?" she asked.

"Anne." He said her name. Her actual name, without a title. Anne should be offended by such intimacy, yet instead, his whisper—half reproachful, half tender—danced through her heart.

"Oh, Miss de Bourgh!" Mrs. Webb edged Mr. Talbot to the side. "You are bleeding."

All at once a man ran up to them and crouched next to Anne. "Are you all right, miss? I do not know what happened. The horses suddenly spooked."

Anne glanced at the sandy-haired man then focused on Mr. Talbot. "My head hurts. And my nose."

"Right. Your nose." The man whose carriage had hit her pulled a handkerchief from inside his tailcoat pocket, balled it up, and held it out to her.

Mr. Talbot took it from him and pressed it to the warm liquid dribbling from Anne's nose and onto her lips. Salt and rust. She gagged.

"Stay still." Mrs. Webb grabbed Anne's arm. She felt along it and her other limbs. "Nothing feels broken."

"I am well," Anne said. "Just a little bruised. Someone help me up, please."

"I cannot tell you how sorry I am," the stranger said. "Please, let me be of some service."

"There is no need," Anne said. "My friends will take care of me."

"Can you hold the handkerchief?" Mr. Talbot asked Anne.

"I think so." Anne lifted her hand to her nose. Mr. Talbot rested his hand over the top of hers and pressed it ever so slightly. "Got it?"

She nodded.

He slid his thick, muscled arms under her, pulled her against him, and, following Mrs. Webb, carried her the short distance down the road to where their driver, hat in hand, waited for them next to the barouche's open door.

Mrs. Webb climbed inside. Mr. Talbot positioned Anne on the seat next to her. The stranger peered at her over Mr. Talbot's shoulder.

"Please, miss," the man said. "There must be some help I can give."

"Rest assured we have the situation in hand." Mr. Talbot sat in the seat across from Anne and Mrs. Webb and pulled the carriage door closed. "Drive slowly," he said to the driver.

The stranger, frowning, stepped back from the carriage as it pulled into the road.

Mrs. Webb held Anne's reticule on her lap. Seeing it, Anne groaned. The fabric was torn, and several pages of her drawing pad had ripped.

"I am sorry for that," Mr. Talbot said. "I am afraid it fell when I yanked you out of the way of the horses. I hope you can replace them."

"The reticule is not particularly important."

"I meant your drawings."

"I know." Her voice broke.

He reached out as if he were about to touch her, hesitated, and lowered his hand to his lap.

"I will replace them with something new," she said. "Perhaps with the *Strobilanthes nutans*. I've not yet been able to sketch it."

"You know you are welcome to Seawind House anytime."

She pressed her hand against her ribcage. It hurt slightly, but not as much as her backside. "Will tomorrow be convenient for me to visit your mother's garden?"

The driver turned onto Marine Parade.

"Should you not take at least a day to rest, my—Miss de Bourgh?"

"It is kind of you to worry, but I think resting for the remainder of the day should be sufficient."

"Very well. If that be the case, my mother and I will expect to see you at Seawind House tomorrow."

While the horses' slow pace did protect Anne from being jounced in her seat and allowed Mrs. Webb to gently minister to her wounds, the drive took longer than Anne had expected. In truth, it was perhaps as long as an hour before they reached their townhouse.

At last the carriage stopped, and Mr. Talbot climbed out. He helped Mrs. Webb out first and reached for Anne. She carefully maneuvered herself from her seat, held his hand with one of hers and the handkerchief to her nose with the other, and stepped down to the cobbled walk.

"I am pleased to see you are managing so well," he said.

"Thank you. So am I."

"I also hope, if you are feeling up to it, and if you do indeed visit Seawind House's gardens tomorrow—"

"I will be there."

He smiled. "Perhaps you might also accompany me into town to visit with the coroner Mr. Hunt about his findings in relation to Dr. Sinclair's body."

If senses could waltz, Anne's did. She took Mr. Talbot's offered arm. "I would be pleased to accompany you tomorrow, Mr. Talbot."

Another horse-drawn carriage—the one that had hit her—reigned in behind theirs, and the sandy-haired man alighted from the driver's seat.

He had followed them?

CHAPTER TWENTY-FOUR

"Truly, sir," Anne said to the man as he approached her, "it is kind of you to be so concerned, but you need not trouble yourself."

"On the contrary," he said. "It is my fault you are in this condition, and I must find a way to make amends. Is this your home?" Without waiting for her reply, he hurried ahead of them and knocked on the front door.

Mrs. Kelton opened it. She peered at him and then beyond him to Anne. Her eyes widened. "Miss de Bourgh! What has happened?" She bustled past the man, but Anne, Mr. Talbot, and Mrs. Webb had already reached the steps.

"I was in an accident," Anne said.

"Oh, miss. Come inside." She glanced at the man, pushing past him once again, and hurried into the entry hall. "Blanc, Mary!"

Anne, with Mr. Talbot, Mrs. Webb, and the stranger, followed after her, and the stranger closed the door. Mary, the young housemaid, stepped out from the hallway. "Yes, Mrs. Kelton?"

"Find Blanc. Tell her Miss de Bourgh needs her immediately."

"Thank you for your trouble," Anne said, "but there is no need. I assure you I look much worse than I am."

Mrs. Kelton started for a chair in the far corner of the entry hall.

"Let me get that for you," the stranger said.

Mrs. Kelton, wringing her hands, gave Mary a hard look. Mary curtsied and rushed up the stairs. Anne excused Mrs. Webb, who nodded and followed Mary.

"You must not trouble yourself," Anne said again to Mrs. Kelton. "I need only to rest in my room for a bit. I would like to see my mother first though. Where is she?"

The stranger set the chair next to Anne, and Mr. Talbot once again took Anne's arm. He urged her into the chair. "Perhaps it would be best if I leave you now," he said.

"Please stay at least until after I have told my mother how you rescued me."

The stranger looked up sharply. Anne supposed he also glanced between the two of them, but Anne saw only Mr. Talbot's grin at her. She smiled into his eyes.

"Oh my," Mrs. Kelton said. "With your injuries, with all the blood and commotion, it completely left my mind. Lady Catherine asked to see you as soon as you—"

The door to the drawing room flew open, and Anne's mother stepped into the entry hall. "What is all the—Anne!" She glanced at the stranger and Mr. Talbot. "What have you done to her?" She clasped Anne's hands. "Are you all right, my dear?"

"I am afraid Miss de Bourgh had an accident on the road a short time ago," Mr. Talbot said. "She assures me she is well, but I do hope you will see that she rests the remainder of the day."

The stranger straightened and stepped forward. "Forgive me, my lady, but I must confess the accident was my fault. My horses lost control, and when I saw what had happened to this lovely young lady, I could not rest until I had seen her home safe and well."

Lady Catherine's expression softened slightly when the man referred to Anne as lovely, but she quickly turned her full attention back to Anne. "Are you certain you are all right?"

So much concern bled from her mother's expression that Anne's strength wilted. She moved closer to her. "I am a bit shaken, but like Mr. Talbot said, I would like to rest."

"Of course, my dear." She squeezed Anne's hands and glared up the staircase. "Where is Blanc?"

"I have already sent for her," Mrs. Kelton said.

Lady Catherine turned back to Anne. "Are you certain you are all right?" she repeated.

"Yes."

She sighed in obvious relief, glanced at Mr. Talbot with a pinched expression, and faced the stranger. "I do not believe we have met, sir."

"Mr. Lambert, at your service." He bowed.

"Lambert. Hmm. An old family name."

"It is. And from what I have seen of you, you must be Lady Catherine de Bourgh."

"Oh?"

"You are highly thought of in this district, madam. While I have been in Brighton only a short time, my cousin has spoken highly of you. And often."

Anne's mother scanned the length of the man, and for the first time, Anne did too. He was thickly built in the shoulders and chest, much like Mr. Talbot was, but he was not nearly as tall nor as handsome as Mr. Talbot. How old Mr. Lambert was, Anne could not tell. To be sure, his facial features were full and youthful looking, much as hers had been when she was not much older than twenty, but there was a seriousness in the set of his eyes that could not possibly belong to a very young man. Most likely, he was about Anne's age, for just as it was with her now, not one bit of gray or white touched his light-brown hair. It was not as thick as Mr. Talbot's hair, but she had to admit the color was quite pleasing. It reminded her of wet sand.

"And who is your cousin?" her mother said.

"Mr. Evans. Of Grandfield Hall. To be sure, I will have him properly introduce me."

Anne blinked. "The Evanses did mention a cousin was visiting."

Her mother arched an obviously pleased eyebrow toward Anne. She would not say it, but Anne knew her words all the same. *The Evanses are connected to Lord Backwell.*

"And where do the Lamberts hail from, sir?" her mother asked.

"My family lives in Derby, my lady, but I now reside on my estate in America."

"I have a relation from Derby. She resides in Kent now, and though I have not seen her for some years, she will not mind me inquiring from her after your family." She glanced between him and Anne then focused back on him. Anne squirmed. Most certainly her mother was assessing his fine clothes, his straight posture, his flawlessly trimmed hair. *Would he be a good match for Anne?* she was certainly wondering.

"Anne." Her mother clasped the chair back. Her arms wobbled slightly. "If you are indeed all right, I expect you will be rested enough by dinner."

Anne shifted in her seat. Her muscles were stiffening, screaming at her to curl up in her bed and sleep until morning. "Yes, Mother."

Lady Catherine looked back to Mr. Lambert. "And you, sir, will stay for dinner. I insist on it."

Mr. Lambert took a deep breath and bowed. When he lifted his face, he looked directly at Anne. "Miss de Bourgh, Mr. and Mrs. Evans have spoken highly of you, too, and now that I have made your acquaintance, I see they were not wrong. I would be very pleased to dine with you and your mother this evening."

Anne nodded. He had a slight accent she did not recall hearing before, but in all other respects he seemed gentlemanly and amiable. Anne glanced at her mother. Lady Catherine in turn gave Anne such a hard, insistent stare, Anne at once understood her meaning. Mr. Lambert was yet a new, marriageable opportunity she must lend her interests toward. As such, Anne saw no other course before her than to demurely lower her eyelids and say, "I am pleased to meet you, sir, but if you will excuse me, I feel a bit faint."

Instantly, Mr. Talbot helped her from the chair and wrapped his arm around Anne's waist, steadying her. Anne leaned slightly into his strength. If only she could stay there.

Mr. Talbot looked over to her mother. "I regret to tell you, my lady, but my brother bade me offer his apologies. He has been called to London, and I do not know when he will return."

Mr. Talbot's voice was sedate and polite, but her mother's behavior toward him bristled through Anne's senses like the pine needles that scraped the bottom of her shoes when she walked through the gardens at Rosings. True, her mother had silently commanded Anne to shift her attentions to Sir William, and Anne had obediently, albeit momentarily, done so, but the endeavor had been useless. Anne preferred Mr. Talbot. What was more, she believed Mr. Talbot preferred her. Those were reasons enough for her mother to act with civility toward him. Yet there her mother stood, entirely disregarding his feelings. And hers. Never before, not even when her mother had chastised Miss Elizabeth Bennet for her interest in Mr. Darcy, had Anne felt such embarrassment for her mother's actions.

"I am sorry to hear it," her mother said. "Anne and I were looking forward to his visit."

"Actually, mother," Anne said, "one might consider it providential that Mr. Talbot and not Sir William was with me this afternoon. Mr. Talbot pulled me from the path of Mr. Lambert's charging horses. He saved my life." She motioned to Mr. Talbot. "May he not also join us for dinner?"

Her mother pursed her lips. Anne halfway expected that reaction, but what she did not expect was for Mr. Talbot and Mr. Lambert to suddenly stare at one another, both tight-shouldered, clench-jawed, and stiff-postured.

"Yes, Mr. Talbot," Anne's mother said tightly. "You are welcome to dine with us."

Mr. Talbot released Anne. "Thank you for the invitation, Lady Catherine, but I am afraid I am not at liberty this evening."

"Perhaps another time," Anne said softly.

"Perhaps." But there was nothing of softness in his voice. In truth, anger once again replaced the affection that had so recently filled his gaze, only this time Anne knew she had done nothing to cause it. She frowned. How could a woman bear with, much less trust, a man whose feelings for her seemed as changeable as the sea? She lifted her chin. Perhaps it was better he would not join them for dinner.

Mr. Talbot edged closer to Anne, and this time, though he did speak softly, his every word lashed at her conscience. "But I expect another invitation will only come if your mother gives you permission to invite me." He turned away from the others and headed for the door.

Anne hurried after him. "What do you mean?"

Mr. Talbot looked down at his hand on the doorknob. "You are an intelligent, capable, grown woman, Miss de Bourgh. You do not need your mother to approve every step of your life."

"Of course not, but she is my mother, and this is—"

He grabbed her hand. "Until you learn that truth there is no point in us." He squeezed her hand, bowed over it, and left.

The door closed behind him. Anne stared at it as Mr. Talbot's footsteps clicked away from the door . . . scuffed down the path to the carriage . . . and mixed in with the whir of the carriage wheels, the outside's clattering, and the sound of her heartbeat pulsing against her breath. Mr. Talbot was not the changeable one. She was. For no matter how she felt about him, or anything for that matter, she always submitted to her mother's will. That had to stop. Just as Mrs. Webb had taught her during so many other instances, Anne did have to stand up for herself. Stand up to her mother. Now. Before she lost Mr. Talbot.

She turned back to her mother and Mr. Lambert.

"I hope now we are finally rid of the man," her mother said. "I admit Mr. Talbot has been a help to you, my dear, and for that I am grateful, but

I am sure you will agree with me in saying, now that you are safely at home with me, his help is no longer needed."

Anne's vision swirled. She began to fall.

"Miss de Bourgh!" Mr. Lambert rushed to her side and wrapped his arm around her waist. She had to admit his strength was as sturdy as Mr. Talbot's, but it possessed nothing of his comfort.

"Perhaps you would like to sit," Mr. Lambert said.

Anne closed her eyes. She took a deep breath. "Thank you. I did feel faint for a moment, but I believe it has passed. Now, I wish only to retire to my room."

"Blanc," her mother called.

At last Blanc hurried down the stairs and to Anne's side. Mr. Lambert handed Anne into her care.

"See that she has all she needs," Anne's mother told her.

"Yes, your ladyship."

CHAPTER TWENTY-FIVE

Anne slowly pushed herself up from her bed, pulled off the sheet, and stared down to her bare toes. The white dressing gown Blanc had helped her into after she had bathed Anne's wounds still lay as evenly and unruffled over her body as it had when Anne had first climbed into bed. Had she not moved at all?

She glanced at the clock on the mantel. Seven fifteen. *Oh dear!* Her mother had said they would postpone dinner until half past six o'clock to give her time to rest. Why had Blanc not wakened her earlier? Had she actually missed dinner? Or, which was most likely the case, were they bearing through their hunger while they awaited her arrival?

Anne growled in frustration. She had no appetite. More than that, Mr. Talbot would not be there. If only she could stay in bed for the rest of the night, partly to rest her wounds but mostly to think on Mr. Talbot's parting words and determine what she should do about them. However, staying in bed and thereby forcing her mother and their guest to wait on their dinner would be impolite. And she did not want to be impolite.

Anne pulled the bell pull next to her bed, stood, and stretched. Her backside ached slightly, as did the scrapes on her knees and palms, but otherwise . . . *Hmm.* She stared down at her hands, front to back. She touched the bridge of her nose, rolled her shoulders. Much of her ached, but none of it—she widened her eyes—none of that aching was enough to worry over. She really, truly, did feel quite well. Back home at Rosings she would never have recovered her strength this quickly from someone pulling her out of the way of racing horses, much less after tumbling to the ground.

"A miracle," she whispered.

Whether that miracle was the tonic, her new exercise routine, Brighton's sea air, or—she swallowed—or her new friendship with Mr. Talbot, she could not say. Maybe it was due to all of them combined. Whatever the case, she did indeed feel better and even, dare she think it, stronger?

Mr. Talbot had lifted her into his strong arms . . . carried her to the wagon. *Mr. Talbot rescued me.* Then left.

Blanc entered the room. "I am glad you are awake, miss."

"Have I missed dinner?"

"No. Lady Catherine, she held dinner for you." Blanc stood taller, forced her already slightly pursed lips into a deeper pucker, and arched her voice. "'Eight o'clock,'" she said, mimicking Anne's mother. "'Only then, if Miss de Bourgh is not yet able to come down, will we go ahead without her.'"

"We'd better hurry, then. They must be famished."

Blanc seemingly floated, as she was wont to do, to the wardrobe and opened the cupboard. She pulled out Anne's red dinner gown.

"I will wear the dark-green one," Anne said.

"Your mother said you would wear the red one."

Anne ran her hand down the side of one arm. Since her mother often said Anne looked her best in red, she likely wanted Anne to look well for Mr. Lambert. And to be sure, Mr. Lambert, as a relative to the Evanses, was well-connected. He was also handsome, and he might perhaps turn out to be as kind and charming as Sir William, but none of that mattered. Mr. Talbot wanted Anne to make her own decisions, and Anne's heart—her will—had chosen Mr. Talbot.

She turned away from Blanc. "You need not worry. If my mother questions you, I will tell her the green dress was my choice."

"Yes, miss." Blanc, hiding a frown, removed the green dress from the cupboard, draped it across the bed, and after helping Anne out of her night clothes, slipped the gown over her head. "If I were Lady Catherine, I would not mind you wearing the green. It brings out the dark brown of your eyes."

"Thank you." If Mr. Talbot were there, would he agree with Blanc? Would his eyes light up with appreciation? Or would anger still rule them?

Anne furrowed her brows, and as Blanc continued helping her into her dress, she thought on the events of the day, especially on her last moments with Mr. Talbot. Once Sir William had left and she had regained Mr. Talbot's favor, all had moved along splendidly. Even after the accident she had seen only concern in his expression. His earlier anger had not returned until her mother had so discourteously invited him to dine with them. After that, Mr. Talbot and Mr. Lambert had glared at one another the way Anne imagined two opponents might do in a boxing ring.

Anne caught her breath. *Two opponents.* For what? For *her*? She did not care one whit why Mr. Lambert had behaved as he did. She hardly knew the man. But Mr. Talbot . . . was he, in truth, jealous? Was that the reason for his anger?

You do not need your mother to approve every step of your life. Until you learn that truth there is no point in us.

No. Jealousy may have contributed to Mr. Talbot's anger, but he had also meant what he had said. Anne needed to get beyond her need for her mother's approval.

Anne smoothed and resmoothed her skirt.

"Are you nervous, miss? I would be if I were about to have dinner with such a handsome man."

Anne smiled slightly. "I am not nervous. I am only worried about something that happened earlier today."

"Your accident?"

"No. I hardly think of it."

Blanc, frowning outright this time, fastened the topmost clasp of Anne's dress behind her neck. "Perhaps talking of the future will help you not worry over the past. Is all in order for tomorrow?"

"It is."

Blanc took a hairbrush from the vanity and motioned for Anne to sit in front of the mirror. "I admit I have been looking forward to this since we planned it, but I do worry. You do know you will need more than one lesson from me for to learn to swim?"

"I do. Do not concern yourself about the rest of it," Anne said. "I am grateful for all you have done."

Blanc, grinning, gathered Anne's hair to the top of her head and caught Anne's gaze in the mirror. "I can hardly believe it—a morning off to swim. My last morning before I marry Robert."

Mrs. Webb entered Anne's bedchamber. "It is nearly eight o'clock."

Blanc pinned the remaining strands of Anne's hair into place.

"It looks as if Blanc was right when she said you would be both awake and ready for dinner by this time," Mrs. Webb added.

"Indeed she was," Anne said. "Thank you, Blanc. You may go."

Blanc pressed her earlier smile into a tight-lipped line, curtsied to Anne, and walked past Mrs. Webb and out of the room.

"The butler will be announcing dinner in a few minutes," Mrs. Webb said. "I have come to take you down."

"Thank you." Anne took another quick look in the mirror. She patted the lower edges of her hair, making certain none of the strands had slipped from her hairpins, and walked with Mrs. Webb from her room.

"I must say you are looking a great deal better," Mrs. Webb said shortly before they reached the top of the staircase.

"I feel better, thank you. The rest did me a world of good. And you? I hope you have not suffered because of my mishap."

"On the contrary. At first I thought I might find myself with nothing to fill my evening hours, but your mother kindly invited me to sit with her and Mr. Lambert in the drawing room until it was time to dress for dinner. He is a very agreeable man, Miss de Bourgh. So charming, and I daresay more handsome than either of the Talbot gentlemen. Upon my word, I predict you will soon be as smitten with Mr. Lambert as I expect every young woman of his acquaintance is."

He is like Mr. Evans, then. "Pray, please do not speak so loudly of such things."

Mrs. Webb laughed lightly and lowered her voice. "Why not? Finding you a suitable marriage partner is the reason your mother brought you to Brighton, is it not?"

"It is not." They started down the stairs. "I thought you knew. Brighton is only a stepping stone for London. Mother plans for me to take part in London's little Season this fall."

"I did know. But your mother has been so insistent on you meeting some of the area's young men, I thought surely she must have changed her mind."

"No," Anne said, stronger this time. "Mother brought me to Brighton to cure me of my ailments. What is more, I do believe the cure is working. That and your good sense and encouragement."

Mrs. Webb smiled prettily. "Your countenance is most certainly more radiant than I have ever seen it. I would not be surprised if the young man waiting downstairs for you notices that about you right off."

Heat flushed Anne's cheeks. "I do believe you are getting a bit carried away with your own fancies, Mrs. Webb. Mr. Lambert and I are as yet casual acquaintances, and I would not be surprised if we continue to be so."

Mrs. Webb smiled—a bit smugly, Anne thought. "We shall see."

Anne arched an eyebrow. "If I did not know better, I would think you were the one who had an interest in the gentleman."

"Upon my word, Miss de Bourgh! Marriage is well beyond me now. I am much too old."

"You are not. You are only a few years older than I am. So if marriage is not well beyond me, it is certainly not well beyond you."

"That is kind of you to say."

"It is not kindness; it is truth. You are beautiful and refined and quite free. I believe many men would consider themselves lucky to gain your favor."

Mrs. Webb pressed her fingertips against her mouth and turned her face away from Anne. "Such sentiments, for me at least, are unrealistic dreams, Miss de Bourgh."

"No. Truly, it is possible. I have seen many marriages take place after one or the other's spouse has died."

They reached the bottom of the staircase. At last Mrs. Webb looked back at Anne. "You are right. I have seen marriages like that, too, but in this case, I am quite sure you are the one who has caught Mr. Lambert's fancy. Not me."

They headed to the drawing room.

"What about you?" Anne asked. "Has Mr. Lambert caught your fancy?"

"Not at all. It is true I have assessed his qualities, but I have only done so in your behalf."

Anne wanted to frown, but she did not want to offend Mrs. Webb, since it was very kind of her to be so solicitous of her well-being. So she instead stepped in front of her and entered the drawing room.

Her mother immediately noticed Anne's gown, but though she lifted her chin and flattened her lips into a tight, almost-frown, she said nothing.

Mr. Lambert, on the other hand, stood in respect of their entrance. "Miss de Bourgh. I hope you are feeling better."

"I am. Thank you."

Mr. Green, the butler, stepped into the room from the dining hall. "Dinner is served."

"Mr. Lambert," Anne's mother said, "you will please lead Anne into the dining hall."

He smiled and obediently offered Anne his arm, but Anne stared at her mother. As she was the highest-ranking person there, Mr. Lambert should be walking in with her.

Her mother arched an eyebrow, and in that small movement Anne saw a truth she had not known before: her mother may appear to be fully attached to society's conventions, but the reality was she was willing to flout them when it convenienced her.

Anne took Mr. Lambert's arm, and the two entered the room behind Anne's mother. Mrs. Webb brought up the rear. They took their places at the table, and the servants brought in the artichoke soup.

After each of them had taken their first sip, Anne's mother said, "My dear Anne, I made an appointment with Dr. Fletcher for you to meet with him tomorrow after your morning sea-bathing exercises. He will assess your current health and make certain, after Dr. Sinclair's most unfortunate passing, that you are indeed following the best health regimen."

"Thank you, Mother, but—" Mrs. Webb gave Anne a pointed look, and Anne sat up taller. *Be strong. Take courage. Speak up for yourself.* "Mother, I—"

"Mr. Green," her mother said. "We are ready for the fish. What will it be this evening? Mackerel, I expect."

"Yes, your ladyship. With fennel and mint. Cook insists it is most delicious."

"Very good. Have the servants bring it in."

He bowed and left.

Mr. Lambert, watching Anne, nodded to her but spoke to her mother. "Pardon me, Lady Catherine, but I believe Miss de Bourgh has something she wishes to speak with you about."

Anne smiled at him. "Thank you, Mr. Lambert."

Her mother frowned and stiffened, but when she glimpsed the two of them smiling at one another, her features softened. "What is it, my dear?"

"I wish I had known your plans for me to visit with Dr. Fletcher tomorrow, for I agree it is important I see him soon"—she swallowed—"but I am afraid I cannot make that appointment. I have another engagement."

"What engagement?"

Meeting with Mr. Talbot. "Lady Talbot invited me to luncheon with her and to afterwards help her with a project we are working on together."

Oh dear. She should not have said the word *project*. Now she would have to explain how their project did not include *work*. But Anne need not have worried. Her mother went straight to "I thought you said Sir William was in London."

"He is."

"Well, then, I am certain Lady Talbot can do without you for one afternoon. I will send word that you will not be able to attend her. And I have no doubt she will most readily agree with me. Your health, after all, is more important than almost anything else."

"But I do think—"

Her mother arched an eyebrow, cutting off Anne's complaint, and turned to Mr. Lambert. "If it is not too much to ask, sir, I do hope you will accompany my daughter to her physician's appointment."

Anne stared hard at him. *Say no.*

Mr. Lambert looked at Anne. He most certainly saw her expression, but he either did not understand her silent command, or he ignored it, because he said, "I would be most happy to accompany your charming daughter wherever she needs to go."

"I will see that my barouche is brought out."

"There is no need. I am happy to offer my carriage, as it may be easier to maneuver through town."

Her mother sighed. And smiled. "Anne and her companion will be ready at one o'clock."

He frowned. "Actually . . ."

"Is something wrong, sir?"

"Forgive me. Perhaps we should take your barouche. As I said, I am most happy to offer my carriage, but it is a gig and I had not considered Mrs. Webb's attendance."

"I commend you for your sensitivity to our needs, and yet, now that I think about it, a gig is better suited to maneuvering through town. And as you are such a close connection to Lord Backwell through the Evanses, there can be no harm. Mrs. Webb will remain here, and you will accompany my daughter."

Mrs. Webb glanced out the corner of her eye at Anne in such a way that Anne heard her companion's voice inside her mind saying, *See? I was right. You are the one who has caught Mr. Lambert's fancy.*

Anne, however, pulled at her skirts. She shifted in her seat. She would not get to draw the *Strobilanthes nutans* tomorrow. She would not get to discuss Dr. Sinclair's murder with Lady Talbot. And worst of all, she would not be able to see Mr. Talbot. Instead she would again obey her mother and spend time with a man she barely knew. How could her mother submit her to such a situation? Regardless of Mr. Lambert's noble connections, her mother should not force, much less condone, such a situation. Yet, what could Anne do about it?

You do not need your mother to approve every step of your life.

Anne shivered.

"Are you cold, Miss de Bourgh?" Mr. Lambert said.

"She is not cold," her mother said. "It is not cold outside, and no breezes blow through the room."

He nodded to Anne's mother but scrutinized Anne. Anne, in turn, looked at the door where Mr. Green and another servant entered with the next dinner course.

If only Mr. Talbot could see she was not letting her mother control every step. Yes, her mother had spoiled most of her plans for the morrow, but one plan still remained. Tomorrow morning she would go swimming with Blanc instead of sea-bathing with Mrs. Webb.

* * *

Late that night Kenneth, disguised as Mr. Lambert, returned to Stonewith Manor to find that while Evans and his wife had not yet returned from the prince regent's party at the Pavilion, Evans had left two notes in his room next to a bottle of port. The first was from Evans:

> *Detained courier with note from LC to Derby to check your credentials. Will soon send her a "correct" response.*

The second was written in Leon's hurried scrawl:

> *Must move faster. MAB—Willow Pond early tomorrow morning.*

CHAPTER TWENTY-SIX

IT SEEMED ANNE HAD BARELY closed her eyelids when gray, early-morning sunlight slipped between the cracks of the window shutters. She groaned and flopped her arm over her forehead. But that would not do. It was a little after six o'clock, and Blanc might already be waiting for her.

She jumped out of bed and, alone, quickly put on Blanc's simple pale-blue dress, white apron, and white cap. She took Dr. Fletcher's tonic from off the top of her vanity and carried it to the window. She opened the shutters, stared out at the waves crashing into the shore with the incoming tide—beautiful, turbulent, and perfect. Just like this cure.

She rolled her eyes at her own jest and plucked off the lid. "To greater health." She took a deep breath, closed her eyes, and gulped down two large swallows of the detestable tonic. She grimaced and glared at the bottle. *This liquid had better be worth the misery.*

She returned the tonic to her vanity and took up her packed and ready carpet bag from the floor next to the door. Soon after her first sea-bathing appointment, she had realized the bag was much better suited than paper packaging for carrying her wet bathing gown, and she had used it ever since.

Anne peeked into the dark hallway. Mrs. Webb, as they had agreed last evening, stood at the top of the staircase. She pressed her forefinger to her pursed lips and beckoned Anne forward.

"Have you seen Blanc?" Anne whispered when she reached her.

"I saw her from my bedroom window before I came down. She is waiting for you outside on the boardwalk in front of the neighbor's house."

Anne nodded and peered down the staircase. She pressed her hand against her chest. "You are certain you are happy to stay in your room all morning?"

"I am quite content to do so," Mrs. Webb said. "And I sent your message to Mrs. Dramwell, letting her know you will not be there today."

"Thank you." Anne hesitated.

"Is there something else?"

Anne inhaled and bit her bottom lip. "Do you—am I doing the right thing?"

Mrs. Webb clasped Anne's upper arms. "I would be remiss in my duties if I did not say you, Miss de Bourgh, are doing an entirely wrong thing."

Anne frowned.

Mrs. Webb raised a finger. "As far as your mother and society are concerned. But that is what you want to do, is it not?"

Anne nodded. Was that—this disobedience—really what she wanted?

"However, there is no need for you to worry," Mrs. Webb continued. "You have arranged every detail beautifully."

I have? Warmth bathed Anne's worries. "My mother—"

"Has been sleeping long for the last few days. If her current pattern holds true, she will not wake before ten o'clock. Be back by then, and she will never know you have been anywhere other than where she intended for you to be."

"I do hope you are right." Anne squeezed Mrs. Webb's hand in return then scanned the entry hall. After ascertaining there was, indeed, no one else about, she hurried down the staircase and rushed out the door. The moment she stepped onto the small porch, though, her senses prickled to attention. She scanned every direction, even up to her mother's bedroom window, but saw no one watching her.

"Do not be paranoid," she muttered. *I am a grown woman. I can and will make my own choices, despite my mother's disapproval.*

Anne took a deep breath. She lowered her head and, dressed as a servant, scurried straight down the boardwalk in the direction Mrs. Webb had pointed her. But after a few steps, she stopped. She stared out to where Blanc certainly waited for her and back up at the townhouse. Did Anne really want to leave with Blanc without her mother's approval? If Lady Catherine discovered Anne had crept out of their home like a criminal and swum in a pond like—with—her servant, she would be horrified. But the *ton* . . . Anne's breath stopped, and her stomach knotted. What was she thinking? If Anne did this, she—not only her but also her mother—would be forever scandalized. They would be cast out of society, uninvited from every social event. Anne's future would be destroyed. Was sneaking away to learn to swim worth all of that?

No.

She hugged her carpetbag against her chest and turned back to the townhouse. She had been so caught up in trying to become her own person, someone who did what she felt was right rather than what others told her to do, that she had not included her position in society in those thoughts. Her status was part of her identity. True, Anne wanted to learn to swim, but she did not want the scandal that could follow it. And yet . . . Again she stopped. And yet if scandal, if society's approval, were her biggest concerns, she would, as her mother had demanded she do, have to stay away from Mr. Talbot.

No, no, no.

Once more Anne turned and headed down the boardwalk.

All would likely be well in the end anyway, would it not? While the *ton* simultaneously disdained and delightfully gossiped over the indiscretions of others, they frequently forgave or at least tolerated those same indiscretions, especially if the transgressor's circumstances and birth were of a high station—just as they had done with Lady Talbot. What was more, had her mother not only proven that she, too, only followed society's rules when they suited her needs?

Within moments Anne met up with Blanc, who immediately reached for Anne's carpetbag.

"Thank you, but I believe I should carry it today." Anne glanced east down Marine Parade. A few men and women had ventured outside at that early hour, but not one of them seemed to be looking her direction. Why did she feel like she was being watched?

Blanc grinned. "That is right, miss."

But if she were being watched, was it too much to ask that it would be by Mr. Talbot? Anne again scanned her surroundings. There were people, yes, but not one of them had Mr. Talbot's height or breadth of shoulders.

She frowned. She was being ridiculous. Why ever would Mr. Talbot be out there at that time of day? As far as Anne knew, he had no particular business to bring him this direction. And after yesterday, after her mother's discourteous behavior—what if he never came this way again?

He must come back. If he does not . . . Anne furrowed her brows, clenched her carpetbag tighter, and closed her eyes on the image of her mother's disapproving glare. *If he does not come back, I will go and find him.* If she had the courage.

Yet, I am doing this. This takes courage, does it not?

"Robert will meet us at the corner of Margaret Street with the wagon."

Anne glanced over her shoulder to the west and then up the length of their townhouse to her mother's curtained bedroom window. Still seeing no one, she once again gazed down Marine Parade. Going east of Brighton meant they would pass Seawind House.

"Is something wrong, miss?"

"I did not know we would be going so far."

"It is not very far, miss. Only a short drive. There's Robert now. Come along."

The two hurried east down the boardwalk and soon reached the corner of Margaret Street. Robert, a short, wiry man with a tanned complexion and black hair stood next to his wagon. Out of habit, Anne headed to the front seat.

Blanc went to the back of the wagon. "Robert will drive. We will ride back here."

Anne stiffened. She had never before ridden in a farmer's wagon, much less the back of one. Her mother would be livid. Anne bit the inside of her lower lip. Perhaps that was reason enough to do it. She glanced about her, gazing toward Seawind House, but then, noticing through the corner of her eye Blanc watching her, Anne turned in the opposite direction and jumped onto the backside of the wagon next to Blanc. Robert pulled the wagon onto the main thoroughfare.

"It is very kind of your betrothed to drive us to Willow Pond," Anne said.

"He did not mind," Blanc said, after which Robert looked back at them and added, "I told Ginger I wanted to get a look at the young lady who wants to swim in spite of Lady Catherine's wishes."

Blanc grinned. "Robert called you an adventuress."

"What a notion. Me? An adventuress? I have spent more days indoors with my nose running and my head aching than I can count. Why, Brighton is only the third place I have seen outside of my home. And the farthest away, I might add."

Blanc smiled. "But now you are changing that." The wagon bumped over a rocky patch of the road, and Blanc, having bounced forward in the jostling, scooted to her original position. "Robert is right. A woman who is willing to go out into the world, take it by its britches, and shake it until it changes her life for the better is an adventuress."

Anne smiled. Anne the Adventuress. The phrase had a nice ring to it. And truth be told, the longer she thought on those words, the more they seemed like they could one day be true. If only Mr. Talbot had heard them.

She scanned both sides of the road.

Blanc gave her a curious look. "Willow Pond is not much farther."

Anne hugged the carpetbag on her lap and watched the townhouses disappear into the countryside. Soon after, the people disappeared and farms and trees dotted the north side of the road. The slope at their right led down to the seashore's high, craggy cliffs.

At length, Robert turned north off the main road and onto what seemed more of a wide, two-wheel-grooved path than a road. "It will not be long now, miss. We will reach my house before you can count to twenty."

"I thought you said we were going to Willow Pond," Anne said to Blanc.

A teasing glint lighted her eyes. "I didn't think even an adventuress like yourself would wish to change into your swimming gown out in the open."

Warmth crept up Anne's cheeks. "Oh yes, of course." She had been so caught up in thinking about Mr. Talbot that it had not crossed her mind there would not be a sea-bathing machine at the pond.

Robert pulled up to a white farm house with a thatched roof. It was about the same size as the home her mother had provided for Mr. Soulden at Rosings. Though Anne had never had reason to venture inside the gardener's home, she had imagined it looked much as this house did, with a single room that made up the kitchen and what one might call a sitting area, and two small bedrooms, one on the side of the front room and one in the back. Anne and Blanc changed their clothes in the side room.

"Leave your things on the bed," Blanc said. "Robert's sister will not mind. We will use blankets to cover us when we are not in the water."

Anne smiled, nodded, and, holding one arm in front of her, took the offered blanket. She hugged it around herself. To be sure, heat already touched the air, but the cool breezes that had frequently blown over her from the sea on their journey there had made her feel more vulnerable than usual. What was more, once she stepped into the water, her gown would cling so closely to her body the blanket would be a welcome shield indeed.

She returned with Blanc, who was wrapped in her own blanket, to the wagon, where Robert waited for them. He drove them back down the dirt road for a short distance before veering off through a small village. Finally, they stopped next to a large pond. Tall green grasses dotted with purple and yellow wildflowers surrounded it, and a small island grew up in the middle of it. It looked like it was once only a large boulder but was now covered with the same grass and flowers.

"I will return after I feed the animals," he said. "Should take near an hour."

"We'll be here," Blanc said.

He nodded in response to Blanc's wave, and after he had gone, Anne and Blanc folded their blankets, left them next to their shoes, and made their way through the foliage, down to the pond. The water, unlike the ocean, was so clear and blue Anne could see the brown sand beneath the shallows next to the shore. Farther out, that clearness revealed mossy some-smooth-some-jagged rocks and earthy brown bleeding into rich liquid green. At her soonest chance, she would draw that image.

"This water is quieter than the Channel, no?"

"It is." Anne dipped her right foot into the water and immediately pulled it back. "And colder."

Blanc grinned and jumped into the pool. She stayed so long beneath the surface Anne had already started back up the shoreline in search of help when she heard Blanc laughing behind her. Anne whirled.

"You look as if you've seen a ghost." Blanc, grinning, stood waist deep in the pond. Her wet hair plastered to the sides of her head, and water dripped down every inch of her skin.

"I thought you were drowning," Anne said.

"Not here." Laughing again, Blanc reached out to Anne. "Come along."

"Very well." Anne clenched her teeth and ran into the pond. When the water was waist high, she plunged beneath the surface. Mrs. Dramwell had told her the faster her body grew accustomed to the temperature, the better.

Anne shoved her head above the pond's surface and, crouching, swished her arms in front of her. She crawl-walked toward her lady's maid.

"This is good," Blanc said. "Now, if you will please show me what you already know about swimming."

"I can float."

"Show me."

Anne closed her eyes. Then, just as Mrs. Dramwell had taught her to do, she flopped gently onto her back. She floated for several seconds.

"Can you float facedown too?" Blanc asked.

"No." Anne glanced back at the empty shoreline and rubbed the base of her neck. Mrs. Dramwell had wanted her to do so, but each time Anne had tried, she'd felt as if the water were smothering her.

"Ah. Then, floating on your stomach is where we will begin." Blanc stepped in front of Anne and took hold of both her hands. "There's no need to worry. I will be here the entire time."

Anne tried not to breathe too quickly, but with the water suddenly feeling colder than it had when she had first jumped in, she did anyway. At length, Blanc's ever-kindly words and careful teaching calmed Anne enough that she, alone, eventually floated and kicked on both her back and her stomach as calmly, as freely, as perfectly as a swan gliding through a glassy pond. Or so Blanc had said.

"Hello there!"

Anne whirled. Mr. Lambert stood before them. He wore only tan trousers and a white shirt, which opened halfway down his torso. What was he doing there?

Suddenly aware of her thin, wet gown clinging to her body, Anne dropped beneath the surface until only her head showed above the waterline. Had Mr. Lambert been watching them since they had arrived? An image of a man with a spyglass ogling Miss Wycliff while she swam on the beach flashed through Anne's mind, and she cringed. Hopefully Mr. Lambert was not so ill-mannered.

Blanc, staying beneath the water just as Anne did, moved protectively beside and slightly in front of her.

"Hello." Anne's voice barely broke above the sound of the rippling water, so she swallowed and called out louder. "I am afraid you have caught us at a disadvantage, sir. We had not expected anyone to be out here at this time of morning."

"Nor did I." He covered his eyes and turned his back to them. "I thought you were going sea-bathing with Mrs. Dramwell."

Blanc giggled. Anne said nothing.

Mr. Lambert motioned to his gig a short distance away. "A man at Raggett's Club recommended this place as his favorite, relatively private, swimming hole."

"I believe it is Blanc's favorite swimming hole too. Excuse me, this is Miss Blanc, my lady's maid."

He did not turn around, but he gallantly bowed toward the road. "I am pleased to make your acquaintance, Miss Blanc. And you, Miss de Bourgh? Do you enjoy the water?"

"I did until—"

"Until I came along. I am truly sorry for that. I hope you will forgive me."

Anne swallowed. What else could she say, but, "Of course."

"I also hope you will not fault me when I say I am also not entirely sorry."

Anne caught her breath. She pressed her hand against her chest and edged backward.

"What I mean to say," he continued, "is while I am sorry I have undoubtedly caused you some embarrassment, I am pleased to have come upon you, as it were. I know I have not been blessed with your acquaintance for long, but I have found myself unable to keep you, Miss de Bourgh, from my thoughts. I hope this occasion will not keep you from increasing our association in the future."

Anne gaped at the back of him. He wanted to associate more with her after knowing her for such a short time? It was incredible. Unless, of course, it was not her he sought but her fortune or her connections, which he could unite with his own.

Blanc nudged her with her elbow. "Say something."

Anne glanced at her. What could she say? As Mr. Lambert himself had indicated, they hardly knew one another, and his marked interest in her made her feel different than she felt when she was with Mr. Talbot. Fluttery inside, she imagined. Honored too. She kind of liked that, actually. Knowing exactly where she stood—in the eyes of a man who found her . . . attractive? Interesting? Rich?—was quite refreshing. And relieving. For, while she was quite certain she felt nothing beyond a slight friendship for Mr. Lambert, his company might keep other would-be fortune hunters away from her while she tried to figure out how to win Mr. Talbot's affections. Not that she would intentionally use Mr. Lambert to her advantage, but if the opportunity presented itself . . . why not?

"In any case, my dear Miss de Bourgh," Mr. Lambert continued, "I believe I will go over to the other side of the pond to swim if you have no objection?"

Anne, still standing neck-high beneath the water, hugged her arms in front of her chest. "I believe that would be best." But she definitely had an objection. As gentlemanly and appealing as Mr. Lambert was proving himself to be, how could she and Blanc modestly leave the water without him seeing them?

Mr. Lambert cupped his hands on either side of his eyes, blocking his view of them, and marched through the grass toward the far side of the pond. This time both girls laughed outright, and at length, the island obstructed their view of him.

"Will this do?" he called.

"I believe so," Anne called back. "Thank you."

Blanc tilted her head and studied Anne's face. "Everything was so lovely before. I hope you are not too disappointed."

Anne glanced around both sides of the island. "I am disappointed, in a way, but it seems it cannot be helped."

She smiled. "*In a way*, miss?"

Anne lowered her gaze.

"He is handsome, isn't he?"

"I did not notice."

"I don't believe you."

As Anne did not yet know how she felt about their current situation, or especially about the man swimming a few feet away from them, she simply said, "We are trapped here, though, are we not?"

"It seems we are. Though I expect Robert will be here before long."

A shiver like the one Anne had felt earlier when she had thought someone might be watching her shot through her skin. She glanced about her, saw no one, and rubbed her hands up and down her arms. Blanc paced from one edge of the island to the other.

"Miss de Bourgh?" Mr. Lambert called from the other side of the island.

"Yes, Mr. Lambert?"

"Are there mosquitos over there?"

"We have not met with any. I assume that means you have?"

"Hundreds of them." Anne heard slapping. "I believe I'd better leave."

"No," Blanc burst out.

"What are you about?" Anne said. "If he does not leave, he will want to come over here."

"Robert. I see his wagon. He will be here any minute."

Anne stared at Blanc and called out, "Mr. Lambert?"

Slapping. "Yes?"

"If you can bear with the mosquitos a few minutes more, our ride is almost here. We will be leaving, and then you may come over to this side of the pond."

Smack. "You are not only lovely, Miss de Bourgh, but you are also my savior. Thank you."

"That is a bit dramatic for what I am, sir."

"You would not agree if you were on this side of the pond. Miserable creatures. They caught me quite by surprise."

Robert pulled the wagon up to the road. He glanced between them and what Anne assumed was Mr. Lambert and looked discreetly away.

"Our ride is here," Anne called. "We must ask you for privacy."

Water sloshed. "You are safe," he called back.

"Thank you."

Anne and Blanc climbed out of the pond, quickly grabbed their blankets and shoes, and hopped into the back of the wagon.

Mr. Lambert was already walking to what had a short time ago been their side of the pond as they drove away. He waved his hand to them. "The Evanses and I will be visiting with several gentlemen and ladies at Donaldson's Library this afternoon," he called out. "If you find yourself free, I would be honored if you would join us."

"Thank you."

"He is so far away," Blanc said. "I do not believe he can hear you."

Anne took a deep breath, preparing to yell louder but, at the last moment, gave up the notion. He was indeed too far away.

CHAPTER TWENTY-SEVEN

Owen gazed out his library window. In a few short hours Miss de Bourgh would enter his home. Her footsteps would grace their floors. Her voice would delight the air. Her very presence would warm the dark-paneled walls. But would she forgive him when he apologized for his rudeness last night? He should not have said what he had said to her. He should not have left her as angrily as he had left her. To be sure, her continual compliance to her mother's wishes frustrated him, but if bearing with Lady Catherine de Bourgh was what it would take to win Miss de Bourgh's affections, he would do it.

The Channel's waves dashed against the rocky coastline. Sometimes they plunged against the legs of the men and women wading into the incoming tide, and sometimes they splashed white foam onto empty boulders, but always the sunlight sparkling off its blue-gray-green waters reminded him of the delightful, mysterious, intriguing Anne. Especially because right then, Anne was somewhere in that ocean, feeling the sticky salt on her skin, holding on to her dipper's strong arms, and drifting—sometimes plunging up and down—through the water. He pictured her smile. Did she enjoy sea-bathing as much as he enjoyed swimming? He did not know the answer, but something deep inside him proclaimed she liked it well enough, and when they married—*when* they married?

He whirled away from the window and strode to the opposite side of the room. Normally this secluded corner was a place of refuge, but today the bookshelf-lined walls and the two empty yet intimately placed wingchairs whispered loneliness, not safety.

He whirled again, tramping back to the window.

Very well. He would admit to himself, and himself alone, that he wished to marry Miss de Bourgh. It was a wish that tortured his senses more deeply than his leg brace ever pained his body. But what did it matter how much he yearned to win her? While he sometimes fancied he saw interest, even caring for him, in her glances, Lady Catherine had made it perfectly clear she would never allow Anne to join herself to a scandal-ridden cripple. No, Miss de Bourgh would marry a respectable, whole-bodied man. Someone like—Owen scowled, clenched his fist, and stormed back to that awful, lonely corner—someone like Mr. Lambert.

Fight for her.

He shoved his hand through his hair. To what end? Anne was a lovely, intelligent, desirable woman, not an infirmity to be overcome or a business venture to be conquered. She had to have her own life, had to have the ability to choose her own course.

Her mother is choosing that course, not her.

He grabbed his business ledger from the top of the desk, snarled over the figures he had placed there last evening while calculating the times and necessities of his upcoming voyage to America, and shoved it into the top drawer.

Perhaps Lady Catherine was choosing Anne's course, but who else but her own mother had a right to do so? Not him. He was entirely unconnected to Anne.

Your heart is connected to hers. If only that were true for her as well.

A quick knock tapped the door.

"Come in," he growled.

Mrs. Graham opened the door. She quick-scanned the room and stepped toward him. "Excuse me, sir. These messages came this morning. Your mother asked me to bring this one down for you with the other."

He took them from her. The first was addressed to him, the other to his mother. "Thank you."

When Mrs. Graham left, he opened the first note. It was a dinner invitation from the Wycliffs. Mrs. Wycliff must have heard his brother had left and had decided to try her daughters' marriage fortunes with him. He frowned. That or the other eligible bachelors in town had at last recognized the imprudence Anne had noted in them after a few minutes' association. He tossed the invitation onto the table. He would write his refusal later.

He opened the other, already-opened, note.

My Dear Lady Talbot,

I regret to inform you Miss de Bourgh has an appointment with her doctor this afternoon and will not be able to meet with you. I expect you have heard of her accident in town yesterday, but please let me put your mind at ease in saying her appointment has nothing to do with that alarming event. She is simply overdue meeting with him, and I have insisted she not break this appointment. I am sure she would be pleased to meet with you another day.

Sincerely,

Lady Catherine de Bourgh

Owen wadded the note and flung it at the wall. Even if Anne did care for him enough that he could court her, this note was proof Lady Catherine would never allow such a possibility. He had no choice; he must put Anne out of his mind.

He closed his eyes. Her image smiled back at him. He opened his eyes and glared at the ceiling. *I have no choice but to let her go.*

Once again Mrs. Graham knocked and entered the library. "The magistrate and constable are here to speak with you and Lady Talbot, sir."

Owen furrowed his brows. Yesterday, when he had told Headborough Powell about the meaning of the notes in Dr. Sinclair's appointment book, the man had thanked Owen but had not offered any indication he would want to speak with him or his mother again. "Very well. Show them in."

"I am sorry to bother you so early, Mr. Talbot," Mr. Andrews, the magistrate, said.

"Not at all. It is best to get to the root of such matters as quickly as possible."

"Exactly." Mr. Andrews glanced at Powell. "I am sure you realize we have some questions for your mother about her meeting with Dr. Sinclair, but we would also like to speak with your staff."

Mr. Talbot started. "Our staff? Whatever for?"

"Some routine questions." Mr. Andrews looked at Mrs. Graham, and she, frowning, looked at Mr. Talbot.

"It is all right," Mr. Talbot said to her. "Show the constable into the dining room and gather the staff."

"Yes, sir." Mrs. Graham led the constable from the library.

When the two were gone, Mr. Talbot looked at Mr. Andrews and motioned to one of the two chairs. "Will you sit?"

"Thank you." Mr. Andrews moved to the chair, but before he sat, Lady Talbot entered the room. She glanced at Owen. "Mr. Andrews, what is this about?"

"I have a few questions for you, my lady, about this nasty business with Dr. Sinclair."

She took the seat opposite the one Mr. Andrews stood by, and he too sat. Owen took a stool from near the window, set it next to his mother, and joined them.

"How can I help you?" Lady Talbot said.

Mr. Andrews rehearsed for her the information Owen had given him yesterday about the address book. "You asked the doctor questions about arsenic."

"I did. Like my dear late husband, I am very fond of investigating crimes, and at the time I had been looking into, on a very unobtrusive and unofficial basis, mind you, the deaths of that poor couple who were found dead in their library. I understood they died of arsenic poisoning, and I wondered if Dr. Sinclair could apprise me of the properties of arsenic. But I expect you know all this, as I did already give this information to your associate."

He nodded slightly. "What do you mean by properties?"

"Oh, things like how arsenic can be administered and how long after it is internalized the poison takes effect."

"And did Dr. Sinclair answer your questions?"

"No. In fact, I found him to be very vague on the matter. It was as if he knew nothing of arsenic whatsoever."

"You have your answers now, though, I expect?"

"I do."

"May I ask where you attained your information?"

"From another man."

"May I ask who? Was it from Mr. Hunt?"

She glanced at Owen.

"Come, my lady. You need not be alarmed. Mr. Hunt has told me you have been in correspondence with him on both matters, and he, in respect for your late husband, has given you the information you requested."

She sighed. "I am glad to hear it. There is nothing to be concerned about, but I would not want to send him trouble."

Mr. Andrews cleared his throat. "It is, however, a rather large coincidence that you contacted Dr. Sinclair about arsenic poisoning on the very day he died of it."

Owen's mother sat taller. More often than not, while she had a great curiosity, she was a genteel, kindly person who would more likely take hardship or ill-treatment upon herself rather than inflict it on others. But right then, with her hands clenched at her sides and her posture stiff, she seemed to Owen more a military man preparing for battle. "As I told the constable, my meeting with Dr. Sinclair and the questions I asked him were indeed coincidences, as you say, but nothing more."

Mr. Andrews watched her. "Will you tell me what you learned from Mr. Hunt? What are the properties of arsenic?"

Lady Talbot frequently paused through her descriptions, but she at last proclaimed she had rehearsed all she had learned, which was quite a bit more than she had even told Owen.

Powell entered the library.

"Well?" Mr. Andrews asked him.

Powell focused on the magistrate. "There is arsenic on the premises, sir."

Owen stood. "See here."

"It is all right, son." His mother stood and, though it seemed Powell was about to say more, Owen's mother added, "We do keep arsenic here. In the stables, mostly, as most everyone else in Brighton does, as a rodent poison."

"Powell?"

He nodded. "Rodent poison. That is what its use seemed to me to be, sir."

Mr. Andrews frowned, glanced at each of them, and once more focused on Lady Talbot. "I hope I have not put you out too much this morning, my lady. I expected this would be the result of our visit, but we had to be certain. I hope you understand."

"I do understand, and you have not put us out. Now that this unfortunate business is behind us, would you like to stay for tea?"

"That is kind of you, but we must be going." He started for the door, but after only a few steps, he stopped and turned back to her. "I would appreciate, Lady Talbot, if you learn of anything else applicable to this case, if you would share it with me. I know it is rather untoward of me to ask, but I have twice now found the information you have gathered to be not only interesting but also, in two cases, helpful."

"It has? How delightful. Tell me how, please."

"I will only say that your questions to Mr. Hunt have made us look as these situations differently than we had before."

Owen's mother's eyes rounded. "You said I helped you twice?"

"That is right, I did." He smiled slightly. "It was a few moments ago when you were describing the properties of arsenic. Until then I had not realized arsenic could be immediately deadly in some instances while prolonging death in others. I expect Mr. Hunt overlooked telling me that detail, but nevertheless, it gives us helpful information. Thank you."

Her smile gradually grew so broad that by the time she had seen the men out, her face beamed. "Think of that!" She clapped her hands together in front of her and turned to Owen. "I have helped the police with a real crime. Your father would be proud."

"And jealous, I expect."

She laughed softly. "I expect your father is not the only one with jealousy in his blood, or whatever liquid, if any, is inside his ghost."

"Ghostly blood is a rather macabre image, Mother."

"Not at all. But do not change the subject. Murder is not the only thing that holds my notice."

He arched an eyebrow.

"Play innocent if you wish, son, but I know very well you are in love with Miss de Bourgh, and I want to know what you intend to do about it."

He pursed his lips, took a deep breath, and, after glancing at the floor, rubbed the back of his neck. "There is nothing I can do."

"Do not be ridiculous. I have no doubt she likes you, too, and with a little encouragement—"

"Does she like me?"

"She does. Now, as I said, do not change the subject."

"Even if Miss de Bourgh does care for me, her mother will never allow a union between us."

"And?"

"There is no *and*."

She stepped in front of him and looked him straight in the eyes. "You have never been a person to let obstacles stop you from getting what you want."

"This is different. She is different."

"Which is why you love her."

He folded his arms across his chest. "She deserves better than me. She should have what she wants."

Owen's mother took hold of both his hands and edged closer. "Miss de Bourgh should have the person she loves. The person who loves her. She should have you."

Mr. Talbot glanced toward the sunlight shining through the window then back at her. "I am going to America, Mother."

The tips of her mouth quivered, but still she squeezed his hands tighter. "Take her with you, then."

"She will not want to leave England."

"Tell her, Owen. Tell her you love her and want to marry her. Only then, when she knows the truth, when she knows all her options, can she decide her own best course."

"I am not sure I could bear it if I asked her and she said no."

"Can you bear it if you do not ask her?"

He looked away from her.

"You have overcome many difficult things in this life, son," she continued. "And you can overcome more. Remember that."

* * *

Two hours. One hour before Miss de Bourgh's appointment with Mrs. Dramwell and one hour after. That was how long Owen had stood next to the fish market, scanning the faces beneath each parasol and decorative hat that passed him, counting the moments until he would finally see Miss de Bourgh's lovely face. He knew just how it would be. She and Mrs. Webb would come up the boardwalk. They would be gazing out at the sea or perhaps conversing with one another, but whatever the case, Miss de Bourgh would be smiling. And when she saw Owen walking toward her, that smile would broaden, brightening all around her as if she were the very sun.

Much too slowly he would reach her. Mrs. Webb would then discreetly step back from them, and he would take both Miss de Bourgh's hands in his, and then—heat splashed through Owen's skin—and then he would apologize for his idiocy of yesterday and tell her the things of his heart. She would forgive him and tell him the things of her heart too. Which were—what? He clenched his cane and tapped the butt of it on the edge of the boardwalk. Did she care for him? Did he really have any chance of winning her?

Passersby numbers one hundred twenty-seven and twenty-eight passed him. Surely Miss de Bourgh should have finished her sea-bathing by now, unless her run-in with the carriage yesterday had hurt her more than he had thought. Was she hurt? Ill? Her mother had said she was well, but even so, his mouth turned dry, and he again scanned down the boardwalk and out at the growing crowd on the beach. Still no sign of her. Perhaps her mother had told them a falsehood. Perhaps Miss de Bourgh was still at her townhouse.

He headed that way, even-paced at first, but the farther he walked, the quicker he moved until a farmer's wagon followed by a black gig pulled to the side of the road in front of the de Bourgh's townhouse. Miss de Bourgh, with wet hair, water splotches on her dress, and a muddied hemline, climbed out of the back of the wagon and walked toward the townhouse. Another young woman, one much shorter and slighter than Mrs. Webb but as equally wet as Anne, followed her. Immediately after that a gentleman as wet as the ladies jumped out of the gig. Owen swore under his breath. *Mr. Lambert.* Where had the three of them been?

"Hold up a minute, if you please," Mr. Lambert called after the ladies.

Miss de Bourgh and the other girl turned and waited for him to catch up to them. Miss de Bourgh smiled at Mr. Lambert, Mr. Lambert smiled at her, and then he offered her his arm. She reached for it, but as she did so, her gaze turned to Owen. She whirled to him. Her stance stiffened. Her eyes widened.

She was surprised; there was no mistaking that. But there was something else in her expression he could not define, something that gathered his fears over whether or not she cared for him into a tiny ball and shot them into the air. Owen gave her a half smile, a shrug. *How are you?*

Miss de Bourgh narrowed her gaze and cocked her head to one side as if she were trying to understand the words he had not said, but as she was both too far away from him and too surrounded by others for him to dare walk up to her and say what was in his heart, he simply tipped his hat to her, as if she was nothing more to him than a casual acquaintance. *Fool.*

Mr. Lambert glanced toward Owen and back to her. He said something. She nodded but looked only at Owen.

Do something. Say something. Anything. Owen stared at her.

Mr. Lambert spoke again. Miss de Bourgh lifted her hand to Owen—Goodbye?—and, turning away from him, took Mr. Lambert's offered arm.

Mr. Lambert sidled in next to her, blocking Owen's view of her face, and the three walked into the townhouse. The other young woman glanced at Owen before closing the door behind them.

Owen stared at that closed door. He stared until the words he had not said clenched his throat. At last he stormed off and whipped his cane through the air. Why had he just stood there? Mute? *Fool.*

CHAPTER TWENTY-EIGHT

Perhaps their housekeeper, Mrs. Kelton, had been right when, after Anne had returned from her appointment with Dr. Fletcher, she had suggested Anne and Mrs. Webb wait until early evening to walk to the Pavilion. The *Gentiana verna* the librarian had yesterday told Anne she would find there would be just as admirable in the evening hours as it was in the morning. Besides, the current crowds along the beachfront and boardwalks were, as Mrs. Kelton had warned, an ever-shifting maze of people they would have to continually work their way around.

But Mrs. Kelton being right about the discomfort they would find did not change the fact Anne simply could not abide one more minute of sitting quietly in her room, waiting for a slip of cool air to chance through the window while she watched those very crowds moving forward in their lives, enjoying the day, and especially *not* wasting their time.

After all, Anne had plants to find, sketches to complete, and the memory of Mr. Talbot's pinched expression to ease from her nerves. If only he had approached her when she had last seen him that morning. If only he had said something to give her reason to speak with him. If he had, she could have explained to him the reason she was in that unseemly situation at that time of day. She could have told him she was in fact doing as he had suggested and following her own desires rather than her mother's. She might even have urged that smile she craved back into his eyes. She sighed. *I will do so the next time I see him.*

She clenched her reticule in her left hand, her drawing pad in her right, and in turning off Marine Parade and onto the Steyne, stepped around a picnic basket, which the father of a rather large family carried. Finally, the boardwalk opened up enough she and Mrs. Webb no longer had to walk single file.

Several minutes later, when they, side by side again, reached the Pavilion, Mrs. Webb said, "You have been even quieter than usual."

"Forgive me. I suppose I am lost in my thoughts." When Mrs. Webb smiled, Anne quickly added, "I have been thinking of Lady Talbot's investigation into Dr. Sinclair's death. I wish there was something more I could do to help her with it."

"Surely you do not have reason to worry on that account. Lady Talbot has already been quite pleased with the information you have given her, and I doubt she expects you to do more."

"Perhaps you are right."

"I believe I am. In any case, let us think of more pleasant things."

"I cannot imagine what you mean."

Mrs. Webb grinned. "Can you not? Very well. If you are too reticent to speak your feelings, let me do it for you. I suggest you are thinking of a certain eligible bachelor. There. You are blushing, which means I am right. You are thinking of the handsome young man you spent most of the morning with."

The heat that had indeed spread to Anne's cheeks cooled. "You are speaking of Mr. Lambert."

"How could I not be? His interest in you is quite marked. But even more importantly, Lady Catherine's inquiries into his family and connections have returned with most satisfactory commendations. You would be a fool *not* to be thinking of Mr. Lambert."

Following the directions the woman at Donaldson's Library had outlined for her—Mr. Lambert and the Evanses had left an hour earlier, the woman had said—Anne led Mrs. Webb through the gardens and stopped before the tiny mounds of blue flowers. *Gentiana verna.* "Your praise of Mr. Lambert is exaggerated, surely."

"Not at all."

"Then, I can only assume it is your fancy he has caught, and not mine, for while I admit he is handsome, I am not at all sure of his character or his temperament." Or his heart. "What if he is vicious?"

Mrs. Webb's gaze wavered. She looked back and forth, first one direction then another, and pressed her hand against the top of her chest. "You are right, of course."

Anne took her pencil from her reticule. She would trace over her picture in ink when she returned home.

"What I mean to say," Mrs. Webb continued, "is my only wish is to see you happily matched."

"*Happily* matched? Or *well*-matched?"

"Is something troubling you, Miss de Bourgh?"

Anne opened her sketch book to the next blank page. While Mrs. Webb and Blanc, she supposed, were the two women she could talk to about mundane things, she had never in all her life had anyone she could trust with the inner workings of her heart. Yet at that very moment she felt if she did not tell someone, she would burst, and as Mrs. Webb had previously been wed, and as she had been such a kind and helpful companion, it seemed the lot would fall to her. "I know Mr. Lambert may very well be a good marriage partner. He is by all accounts a man of good breeding and consequence, and I do not dislike him, but I find my heart is attached to another."

Mrs. Webb clasped then released Anne's forearm. "Please do not tell me you are speaking of Mr. Talbot."

"To be sure."

Once again Mrs. Webb's gaze wavered, but this time it seemed to be with indecision rather than embarrassment. "May I speak frankly?"

"Please do." Anne handed her reticule to Mrs. Webb to hold for her and drew a quick outline of the *Gentiana verna*'s inch-high stem. "While you are my companion, not long ago you were also a gentleman's wife and are not so far beneath me we cannot speak openly."

"Thank you." Mrs. Webb licked her lips. "Please forgive me if my speech is unkind. I do not mean it to be so. It is only that I can think of no better words to express my thoughts."

Anne made herself unclench her pencil and sketched the first of the three elliptical leaves.

"I believe a match with Mr. Talbot would be, for a woman such as yourself, a form of trading your birthright for a mess of pottage," Mrs. Webb continued. "No, I am not speaking of his infirmity or even of his scandalous parentage. Many fine men and women have lifted themselves from the ashes of such situations."

Anne exhaled. "What, then?"

"I am speaking from experience. You have been acquainted with Mr. Talbot for only a matter of weeks, but in that short time he has already proven himself to be one who runs away when troubles or hardships come."

Anne kept her expression blank, but her thoughts whirled. More than once she had wondered over that exact thing.

"Marriage is the best institution for a happy and prosperous life," Mrs. Webb continued. "But what elders do not often tell young people before they enter into the marriage state is it is also a very difficult undertaking. It requires not only kindness and more than a little understanding but also steadfastness. You doubt me?"

Anne shook her head. "I only wonder what any of that has to do with the situation at present."

"You are contemplating marriage, are you not?"

Anne stared at her. While it was true she frequently thought of the possibility, not once had she or Mr. Talbot brought up the subject.

Mrs. Webb pressed her lips into a tight line. "A few years before I met and married Mr. Webb, I was engaged to another—a young man who was handsome and charming but was as poor as a field mouse. At the time I did not mind he was poor. He was so headstrong and resourceful I felt sure he would find a way out of his poverty. But that stubbornness . . . I am afraid I was stubborn too . . ." She turned away from Anne and stared, glassy-eyed, down the Steyne and out toward the empty, open sea.

"What happened?" Anne outlined the five-lobed flower.

"We quarreled, and when I would not forgive him, he stormed off. Upon my word, I had planned to forgive him later, after he had agonized a bit, but he never came back."

"Oh, Mrs. Webb. How tragic."

She glanced at Anne as if surprised to see her then looked back to the sea. "I admit I was sorry at first. I wished I had forgiven him when he had asked me to, but in the end I realized his leaving was for the best. He eventually died at sea, still a pauper, but more than that, I had come to see, through my meeting of Mr. Webb—he was a widower with a grown family—and our subsequent marriage, that a man who did not love me enough or was at least committed to our partnership fully enough to stick through hard times could never be trusted."

Anne clenched her pencil so tightly she could not have drawn a competent line if she had tried. Mr. Talbot did emotionally run from her, but it was certainly out of jealousy. And he had always come back, even though part of his jealousy was wrapped around her allegiance to her mother. Coming back disproved Mrs. Webb's assessment of him, did it not? "So you married Mr. Webb."

"Mr. Webb shared all he had with me, provided me with a comfortable home, and stayed committed to our marriage until his death and his properties were entailed to his oldest son."

"That is when you visited my mother."

"I told her of my predicament, and she said she would think of how she might help me."

And then Mrs. Jenkinson died. "I suppose you had no idea that visit would lead you to becoming my companion."

"No, but I am glad it did."

That was the most Anne had heard of the late Mr. Webb, but Mrs. Webb's words spoke to Anne what she suspected the woman did not want her to hear. While many women did forsake love for worldly comforts, Anne was the sole heir of Rosings Park. As such, she would one day be as wealthy and independent as her mother was. Anne could do whatever she wanted. And right now what she wanted was to somehow claim Mr. Talbot's affections before she forever lost the opportunity to do so.

Just as it had been during her wagon ride that morning, Anne suddenly felt overwhelmed with a sense of Mr. Talbot's presence. The feeling was likely due to the fact that she was thinking of him, but even so, Anne scanned the gardens, the crowds, even the windows of the neighboring buildings for some glimpse of his face, his profile, or even his top hat. *Nothing.*

"Do you understand what I am trying to say?" Mrs. Webb said.

Anne inhaled. "You are saying constancy in marriage is more important than all else."

Mrs. Webb, smiling slightly, nodded, and Anne turned her attention back to the *Gentiana verna*.

"The hottest part of the day is quickly approaching. I had better get on with my drawing."

"Of course."

Anne stooped over the Gentiana verna. She lightly touched its stem and leaves. She had drawn enough of it now that only the textural details remained, but the sun's heat burned so hotly through the top of her bonnet, she opted to finalize only the most unique details then and finish the others when she returned to her room at the townhouse.

* * *

All afternoon Owen occupied his mind with managing the business concerns of Seawind House in behalf of his brother and continuing his preparations for his voyage to America that he might relegate Miss de Bourgh to the back of his mind. Not his feelings for her. They filled him no matter where he was or what he did. But his memories of that very morning, of how he had stood only a few yards away from her, stared into her questioning expression and did absolutely nothing, tormented him. Such memories should never again see the light of day.

He shoved his list of needed voyage supplies across the desktop and slouched back in his chair. *Foolish.* Just as his mother had said, he had never accomplished anything by standing around and doing nothing. He had set goals, kept them firmly at the front of his mind, and chased after them, fought for them, accomplished them no matter what. The same principles applied to winning a wife. He knew that, yet still he held back when it came to his feelings for Miss de Bourgh. No one would want to attach themselves to a cripple. Yet, what if Miss de Bourgh did? She had not acted embarrassed by his attentions, and in many instances, he could have sworn she welcomed them.

Familiar hope prickled his senses. Maybe she did care for him. Maybe she would discount her mother's decrees and accept him. Maybe. One thing was certain. If he did not declare himself to Miss de Bourgh, and soon, he would lose whatever chance he had in attaining her, and Mr. Lambert would certainly do so instead.

A quick tap struck the door. Mrs. Graham entered. "Lady Catherine de Bourgh wishes to see you, sir."

He stood. "By all means, show her to the study."

"She insists she will wait for you in the entry hall."

He exhaled. Must the woman always dictate terms, even in his own home? "Very well." He followed Mrs. Graham from the study to the entry hall. Lady Catherine was studying the portrait that filled the wall at the base of the staircase. It was of his father, Sir William Talbot. "Lady Catherine," he said.

She turned away from the portrait and walked toward him with such a determined stride that, for a moment, he thought to do away with the niceties and move right to asking her the purpose of her visit, but when she then nodded, he opted, as decorum warranted, for the niceties.

"What a pleasure it is to see you. I hope your family is in good health."

"By my family, you mean my daughter."

Ahh. No niceties today.

"And you know very well she is in perfect health, due to my insistence she come to Brighton and take the cure."

You may have provided the opportunity, but Anne has done the work. "Of course. What can I do for you today?"

She stared at him. Then, just as he thought she was about to speak, she closed her eyes and pressed her fingertips to her left temple. A red rash rimmed her wrist at the base of her sleeve.

"Lady Catherine, are you unwell?"

She inhaled and opened her eyes. "I am perfectly well. A brief moment of dizziness is all."

"Perhaps you would be more comfortable in the parlor."

"Thank you, but I will not keep you long. This is not a social call."

"Oh?"

She pursed her lips, stood taller, and drew back her shoulders. "Believe me, sir, when I say I find no enjoyment in the pain I fear I am about to cause you, but as your mother's friend, I cannot in good conscience keep my news from you."

"What news?"

"It is about my daughter. About her situation."

"Miss de Bourgh? You said she was well."

"She is well. You need not concern yourself on that score. But that hopeful expression you gave me just now, the one when you said her name—that is the reason I am here."

"I do not understand."

Somehow she looked down her long nose at him even though she lifted her gaze. "As I said, I have come only because I am your mother's friend, and I feel I must warn you that the union I am certain you aspire to contract between yourself and my daughter cannot come to pass. From her birth she has been nurtured and trained for the best possible future—for greatness, in fact—and I will not allow you to stop her from achieving that greatness."

"A greatness by your standards, you mean."

"There can be no other standard."

Owen took a backward step, but when Lady Catherine glanced down at his infirm leg, his courage riled and he planted his stance and crossed his arms in front of him. "Lady Catherine, as you have spoken so openly, I will do you the honor of replying with the same candor. I must confess I am at a loss as to why you have come all this way to tell me what I already know. You have always made it quite clear to me, and no doubt to Miss de Bourgh, you do not approve of her association with me."

"How dare you accuse me, and in such a manner? I have always shown you the utmost civility."

"Very little civility, ma'am."

She glared at him for so long he imagined her pooling her thoughts, one drop after another, into a cask of venom. "I have come because I believe it is only fair for you to know my daughter is engaged to Mr. Lambert."

"Is she? I grant I am surprised. I saw Miss de Bourgh and Mr. Lambert this morning, and neither of them intimated such happy news to me."

"I admit their engagement has not yet officially taken place, but I assure you it will soon come to pass."

"What you mean to say is the man in question has spoken to you, and you have given him your consent, but he has not yet spoken to Miss de Bourgh. Well, then, I am glad you are happy. For now."

"How dare you!"

"How dare I what?"

She scowled. "You are in love with my daughter. Do not deny it."

"I will not confirm or deny your allegations. Yet."

Lady Catherine did not stomp her foot, but something about her suddenly tightened posture made Owen feel as if she had. "What do you mean, yet? Are you intent on destroying her chance at happiness?"

Owen opened the door for her. "Good day, Lady Catherine."

She walked toward it and paused next to him. "Perhaps your cares are only for yourself, but my daughter's happiness is my only concern. To that end, she will soon marry Mr. Lambert." She lifted her chin and left.

Owen closed the door and scowled up at the ceiling. *Only then,* his mother's voice said inside his mind, *when she knows the truth, when she knows all her options, can she decide her own best course.*

He stormed away from the door and up the staircase to his bedroom to change into his best tailcoat. He had declarations to make and a question to ask. Now. Before it was too late.

CHAPTER TWENTY-NINE

THE LATE-AFTERNOON SUN WARMED THE side of Anne's face when she at last finished drawing the *Gentiana verna*. She closed her drawing pad and slid the pencil back into her reticule. "Shall we return?"

Mrs. Webb, who had stood beside Anne through all that time, turned away from the sea. "Yes. If you are ready."

"I am."

They left the Pavilion's gardens and continued south along the Steyne. Mrs. Webb spoke to her from time to time, but Anne's thoughts were so focused on Mr. Talbot that when her companion said, "Shall we stop in?" Anne jolted.

"Forgive me. Would you mind repeating your last question?"

Mrs. Webb gave Anne a sidelong glance and, sighing, motioned toward *Finch's Chocolates and Ices* across the street. "I merely suggested you might like to stop in for one of your favorite chocolate rolls. I believe you told me a few weeks ago the last one you tasted was at Christmas."

"It has been since Christmas, but I hardly feel like eating candy in this heat."

"Perhaps an ice, then? Or to purchase a sweet for your mother?"

"I can think of nothing my mother would want from there." Anne hesitated. "It is not normally like you to want to stop in at a shop."

Mrs. Webb smiled—a bit sheepishly, Anne thought. "I believe I saw a gentleman not unlike Mr. Lambert go into Finch's a few moments ago. And as we had been speaking of him, I thought you might not want to pass up this opportunity to see him."

Mr. Lambert was not the man Anne was looking for. However, the word candy had been sitting on her mind since Mrs. Webb first said it.

Lady Talbot's description of the crime scene where the couple had been found dead had included candy. Certainly the magistrate would have checked into the food sources. And yet, if they were indeed as incompetent as the Talbots said they were, maybe, for Lady Talbot's sake, she should ask questions about the candy. Might they have come from this shop?

"On second thought," Anne said, "I would like to go inside. Perhaps a scoop of ice cream would provide an antidote to this heat."

Mrs. Webb grinned and gave her a knowing look that implied Anne did, or at least should, fancy Mr. Lambert, and Anne, trying not to frown, headed for the shop.

A bell rang as a couple, both carrying small dishes of chocolate ice cream, opened the glass door. Anne and Mrs. Webb waited for them to pass before stepping inside. The whitewashed wood floor reflected the light shining through the window and spread it throughout the room. Two small square tables, each accompanied by four chairs, filled in the narrow space that divided the counter from the door. Signs with listed prices and illustrations of icy confections and chocolate drinks covered the wall behind the counter. But it was the man standing before that counter that most caught Anne's eye. His back was to them, and he was talking to a middle-aged gentleman on the other side of the counter. He wore a gray tailcoat that looked a bit too small for him across the shoulders, but there was no mistaking his accent. Mr. Lambert.

Mrs. Webb touched Anne's elbow. "It is him."

Perhaps it was happenstance, or perhaps he heard Mrs. Webb's whisper, but whatever the cause, he at that moment turned to them, took a deep breath—in surprise?—and bowed. "Miss de Bourgh, Mrs. Webb, it seems Providence shines upon me again."

Anne nodded to him. "Finding another way to keep cool today, I see, Mr. Lambert."

"Quite. As, I see, are you and Mrs. Webb."

"We are indeed."

He stepped to the side and motioned for them to move ahead of him. "Please, sir," he said to the man behind the counter. "I would feel it an honor if you would serve these ladies first and allow me to pay for whatever it is they choose."

"As you wish," the man said.

"That is very good of you," Anne said, "but there is no need."

"Perhaps not, but I insist."

She smiled slightly and lowered her gaze. "Very well. Thank you." She and Mrs. Webb stepped up to the counter. "While it was kind of Mr. Lambert to let us order before him, Mr. . . . ?"

Behind the counter, the man's yellow-toothed grin disappeared behind his gray beard. "Finch, miss."

"Finch. This is your shop, then?"

"It is indeed."

Anne clenched her skirt. *Be assertive. Gain his trust.* "I must say I am pleased I have come inside." She swallowed and glanced from one side of the room to the other. "This room is just what an ice café should be."

"I am gratified you think so, miss."

"H-how could I not think so? There is even a cool breeze to erase the outside heat. However do you manage it?"

"The cool breeze? Open windows near the ceiling."

"Oh yes, of course."

He waited. She fidgeted, smiled a little.

"May I take your order?"

"Yes." She lifted her chin and glanced over the list of ice-cream flavors. "They each sound so wonderful it is difficult to decide. Mrs. Webb, do you know what you would like?"

"I will take chocolate," she said.

"Very good, madam," Mr. Finch said.

"Chocolate does sound good." Again Anne clenched her skirt. "But I believe I will go with punch today. It sounds both delicious and refreshing."

Mr. Finch wrote their orders on his pad of paper and looked at Mr. Lambert, who ordered parmesan ice cream then motioned them toward the nearest table. "Or would you prefer we eat outside?"

"This will do." Anne exhaled. She had made it through the first part; now to ask the man about his candy.

Mr. Lambert held out a chair for her, Mrs. Webb sat next to Anne, and he at last sat across from them. "May I say again how pleased I am to see you, Miss de Bourgh, especially since I missed you at the library."

"Thank you." Fortunately, Anne was not required to say anything more, for Mr. Finch arrived with their ice cream.

"Before you go," Anne said to the proprietor as he started back to his counter, "I wonder if you could tell me about your candy."

He turned back to her. Mrs. Webb gave Anne a slight nod.

"I have been thinking of—of a gift for my mother. I had heard you make the best chocolate truffles and raspberry fudge conserves."

"I am most grateful for the recommendation, miss," Mr. Finch said. "But I am afraid you must be speaking of *Baldwin's Tearoom*. It is a few shops north of here."

"Baldwin's Tearoom?" Anne repeated.

"That is right. I hate to send anyone there, as they are my competition, but they are the only business in Brighton who sells truffles and conserves. If, however, you find yourself wanting chocolate rounds sprinkled in sugar, come to me."

"I will."

He nodded and headed back toward his counter.

"Come to think of it," Anne said, "perhaps I will decide on the rounds."

The man hesitated. "Aye, miss?"

Mrs. Webb sat upright, and Mr. Lambert stared at Anne, but neither said anything.

Anne took a deep breath. Information for Lady Talbot meant an opportunity for her to see Mr. Talbot. *I can do this.* "After all, I did hear that dreadful story about the couple who were found dead in their home. They had been poisoned, I understand, and some of the food they had eaten previous to their deaths were truffles and conserves, which I now assume came from Baldwin's Tearoom."

"I read the same thing in the paper a few weeks ago, miss."

"You did?" She pressed her serviette to her lips and lowered her voice. "Maybe the murderer was one of the Baldwins."

"I do believe the magistrate considered them as well, but I understand they have been cleared of it," Mr. Finch said.

"Really?"

He nodded. "I suppose they initially thought, as you implied just now, Mr. Baldwin had both the motive and the means to do the deed, seeing as he was not happy with the Rowes for calling in their debt on him like they did. But from what I hear—wait a moment, miss. I still have the newspaper in the back room."

Anne shifted in her seat. Mrs. Webb and Mr. Lambert stared at her with marked incredulity.

"I am curious," she said.

Her announcement did not change their expressions, but as Mr. Finch returned a moment later, Anne thought nothing more of it.

"The report is right here." He set the paper on the table in front of her and pointed to the article in the middlemost column.

Anne scanned the article. The Baldwins and the Rowes had worked out their differences. The Rowes had ordered candies from them, including those Anne had mentioned, but the authorities had found no trace of poison in them.

Anne pursed her lips. *Keep talking. You are doing well.* "I suppose it does not make sense the Baldwins would want to kill the people they're indebted to. What would they gain from a different loaner? They already run their business under terms they are used to, and someone else could possibly make things worse."

"As I understand it, that is exactly what has happened. The Rowes's children are not as merciful as their parents were."

Anne frowned. "Well, I am glad it was not the Baldwins, at least."

"I agree. To think of someone selling poison, selling it to someone who trusts them—well, it is quite unsettling."

Someone who trusts them. Anne's breath paused. Facts connected in her mind. From what she had heard of this matter, the Rowes had shown no sign of a struggle, which made the authorities believe they had known their murderer. Similarly, Dr. Sinclair had not put up a fight—not much of one, that is—either. Had he known his murderer? She shivered. "I do not suppose they have figured out who did it, have they?"

"No, miss." His expression softened. "It worries me too."

"I hope they figure it out soon."

"Aye." He held her gaze for a moment longer. "Would you like to order the chocolate rounds, miss?"

"I believe I will. Six, please."

Mr. Finch's eyes lit up. He rubbed his hands together. "Very good. Very good. As it happens, I made rounds this very morning. I will go now and box up the best for you."

When he had gone, Mrs. Webb reached across the table and touched Anne's forearm. "I did not know you wished to give Lady Catherine a gift."

It had been nothing more than an excuse to help Anne procure information from Mr. Finch. That might even have been what had given her the courage to speak up as she had done. But as neither Mrs. Webb nor Mr. Lambert would wish to know any of that, especially considering she had done it in hopes of seeing Mr. Talbot again, she simply said, "My mother will not be expecting it, but as she has been looking rather peaked lately, I thought a bit of sweets might lift her spirits. Was I too bold, do you think?"

"Not at all," Mr. Lambert said. "I thought you were quite charming."

Anne gave him a small smile and set about eating her ice cream. She savored each bite of the cool delicacy, swallowing it slowly that she might enjoy it as long as possible, but even so, it was little more than twenty minutes later when they left the shop.

"I would be most grateful if you would allow me to carry your box of chocolates for you, Miss de Bourgh," Mr. Lambert said.

"Thank you. I admit it is a little awkward." Anne handed it to him.

"I suppose if we do not get them back to your cook's icebox in time, you will have squares rather than rounds."

"Or puddles." She smiled.

He slowed his stride as they reached the corner of Marine Parade and lowered his voice. "Or ponds."

Anne's breath stumbled. Mr. Lambert was teasing her over their morning's escapade. Surely he was. But that look was so flirtatious, so suggestive, she turned away from him and picked up her pace. He would not tell her mother about the incident, would he? But then, he could not do so without revealing his own actions.

"Is all well, Miss de Bourgh?" Mrs. Webb asked from behind her.

Anne glanced at the nearest passerby. "Yes. It is only Mr. Lambert is right. We do not want the chocolates to—" Her heartbeat jumped to her throat. *Mr. Talbot!* He was moving up the walk toward them.

Mr. Talbot noticed her at nearly the same time she noticed him. He quickened toward them.

"Mr. Talbot," Anne said. "What a pleasure to see you again."

"You as well." He glanced at Mr. Lambert, who tipped his hat to him, and Mrs. Webb, who pressed her lips into a thin line. Though he kept his own expression relatively sedate, Anne had seen that hard look in his eyes enough times to know he was not sedate. His emotions were churning. Jealousy again?

Reassure him. "We are on our way home," Anne said.

"I was just there. I was disappointed to find you were out."

Anne made herself not grin over that announcement. "Is there something in particular you wish to speak with me about?"

"There is." He glanced at Mr. Lambert then back to her but said nothing more.

"Walk with us home," Anne said. "Perhaps that will ease your disappointment."

Mrs. Webb scowled, but Anne took no care for it.

"I would be pleased to accompany you, Miss de Bourgh." He quickly moved to her left, since Mr. Lambert remained on her right, and Mrs. Webb stayed behind them.

"Mr. Talbot," Anne said.

He turned quickly toward her. "Yes?"

If only they were alone. If only she could speak to him of her feelings rather than being forced by decorum to wait—and pray—for him to speak his first. She stopped. "I have been thinking of my last visit with Lady Talbot, and I have some information that might please her." She tore a blank page from her drawing pad, quickly wrote out the key points she had learned from Mr. Finch, especially the part about her thinking Mr. Sinclair might have known his murderer, and after folding it, handed it to Mr. Talbot. "Will you be so kind as to pass this information on to her?"

"I would be happy to."

Soon after, the four reached Anne's townhouse. They paused at the front door. Mrs. Webb looked as if she wanted nothing more than for them to go inside and leave Mr. Talbot outside, but Anne lingered.

Mr. Talbot motioned to her drawing pad. "Did you locate one of Mr. Miller's plants?"

"I did."

"May I see it?"

"It is not finished."

"I do not mind."

Anne's mother opened the door. She eyed each of them, scowled at Mr. Talbot, and focused on Anne. "Ah, my dear. I expect you had a pleasant afternoon. And Mr. Lambert, how good to see you."

Mr. Talbot cleared his throat. "Perhaps another time, Miss de Bourgh." He tipped his hat.

"Yes," Anne said as he walked away. "Another time." Most definitely. When she could no longer pick out his form from among the others on the street, she turned back to her mother. Anne scowled at her, but in the next moment she wished she had not, for her mother's skin was a pasty yellow color. Anne clasped her hands. "Mother, are you unwell?"

"I seem to be a bit out of sorts today. Perhaps I ate something that has not agreed with me. But it is nothing for you to worry about."

"But I do worry, Mother. I will call for Dr. Fletcher."

"Nonsense. All I need is a good night's rest. I will be better tomorrow." She bid them follow her inside, and after closing the door, she said, "I insist you get a good night's rest, too, Anne. Lady Talbot has invited us—you as well, Mr. Lambert—to a card party tomorrow evening, and I wish you to look your particular best."

Anne's heart leapt. They were going to Seawind House. She would again, soon, see Mr. Talbot.

"Pardon me, your ladyship," Mr. Lambert said, "but Miss de Bourgh always looks her particular best."

Her mother beamed. Anne squirmed. Did everyone have to stare at her?

"Why should tomorrow night be of any more importance than any other evening?" Anne asked.

"Only that I believe it will be the beginning of good news." Her eyes twinkled as she gave Mr. Lambert a knowing look, but Anne's insides churned. Surely he could not be ready to make her an offer after such short an acquaintance? And in Mr. Talbot's home? It was unthinkable.

"Go along to your chambers now, Anne. I am certain Blanc, as it is her last night in our service, is waiting for you. And, Mr. Lambert?"

He bowed to Lady Catherine and took Anne's hand. He squeezed it. "Until tomorrow evening, Miss de Bourgh."

CHAPTER THIRTY

OWEN STRAIGHTENED HIS BEST TAILCOAT and walked from one end of the drawing room to the other. Just as his mother had directed, the servants had exchanged the regular furniture with card tables, chairs, and new packs of playing cards; lit candles sat on every table and filled every wall sconce; and a bouquet of daylilies adorned the center of the sideboard, which was surrounded by a punch bowl, dishes of fruit, and platters of cold cheeses, meats, and breads. Would Miss de Bourgh notice he had remembered her favorite flower? Would she realize he had procured them in her honor?

He took a deep breath, straightened his tailcoat yet again, and imagined Anne in various places throughout the room, sometimes at a nearby table, winning a game of cards, sometimes gazing out at the stars through the window while drinking a glass of punch, but most often smiling into his eyes in that quiet way of hers that simultaneously turned his stomach and settled his nerves. *Tonight is the night,* he told himself for the hundredth time. Tonight, no matter how often Lady Catherine discounted him or how many times Mr. Lambert slithered between them, Owen would, once and for all, declare his feelings to Miss de Bourgh.

The butler entered the room behind him. Voices filled the downstairs entry hall. "The first of your guests have arrived, sir. Shall I show them into the drawing room?"

"Yes."

Owen ran his hand along the side of his hair. He leaned his other hand against a chair back. He stood upright again, straightened his spine, and crossed his arms. Finally, he lowered them back to his side. The first guests stepped into the room. "Miller! I am glad you have come." Owen shook his friend's hand and, while bowing to Miller's wife, glanced behind them at the others entering the room. No sign yet of the de Bourghs—only two single gentlemen and three young ladies with their mothers, all who were permanent residents in Brighton. But as this was an intimate party, Owen felt certain Miss de Bourgh must not be far behind them.

"Welcome," Owen said to all within hearing range. "My mother will be here shortly. In the meantime, she has asked me to make certain you avail yourselves of the refreshments or take a seat at one of the tables. You may even begin a game of Whist or Loo or whatever strikes your fancy. The most important thing is you must, I beg you, enjoy yourselves."

Miss Wycliff, newly arriving with her mother and sister, curtsied to him and, after thanking him for the kind invitation and smiling rather flirtatiously at him, walked with her younger sister to the nearest table, where, Owen assumed, they could best assess the merits of each of the other young men as they arrived.

"I do hope Miss de Bourgh will be here," Miller said. "She sent a sketch to me this afternoon while I was out, and I am most anxious to tell her how pleased I am with it."

"She will be here."

And then, all of a sudden, she was at the door, standing in front of him and gazing at him with those warm, dark-brown eyes. His breath tripped.

"Miss de Bourgh." He walked to her and bowed over her hand. "I am glad you could make it."

She released Mr. Lambert, who stood beside her, and curtsied. "I am the glad one. I was most pleased when I learned your mother had invited us to this party this evening."

Lady Catherine stepped around and in front of her daughter. The woman's skin seemed a bit yellower than it had when last Owen saw her, and her stance seemed a bit off-kilter, but the set of her jaw was as strong as ever. "Where is Lady Talbot? I would also like to thank her for the invitation."

"She will be here shortly, my lady. She had some trouble with the servants she needed to attend to."

Three more people filled the doorway behind Lady Catherine. Two more guests after that, and their party would be full.

Owen motioned Lady Catherine into the room. "You are welcome to dine or play cards or even visit if you prefer," he repeated. "The only thing I ask is you enjoy yourselves."

"Thank you; we will." Lady Catherine took Mr. Lambert's arm. "Come along, Anne. With the heat of the day settling through the walls, that table nearest the open window will be the most comfortable."

Miss de Bourgh moved to follow after her mother and Mr. Lambert.

"Miss de Bourgh?" Owen said lowly.

She looked up at him.

"I want to—" The remaining guests entered the room. *I must welcome them. I am the host.* "You look lovely."

She blushed prettily, which was the only way she could blush.

Lady Catherine turned to them. "Anne?"

"Yes, Mother." Miss de Bourgh nodded to Owen and, still blushing, followed her and Mr. Lambert to the table next to the window. Lady Catherine sat—rather shakily, it seemed to Owen—into the chair closest to the window, and Miss de Bourgh and Mr. Lambert sat on either side of her. That left one chair across from Lady Catherine. Providence willing, Mr. Talbot would take that chair before someone else—Miller was moving toward it.

Owen lifted his hand. Miller caught the movement, paused, and tilted his head quizzically. After a couple of meaningful looks and head nods, Miller approached the de Bourgh's table and spoke with Miss de Bourgh long enough for Owen to finish greeting the guests. Fortunately, with Miller there, no one else took the open seat. Both Lambert and Lady Catherine's expressions seemed as if they wanted nothing more than for Miller to leave, but Miss de Bourgh appeared so pleased with Miller's conversation Owen found himself wishing it was his words and not Miller's that had caused her delight.

Lady Talbot entered the room. The gentlemen stood.

"Please do not trouble yourselves," she said. "Think only of enjoying the evening." They sat again, and within moments, all had settled into their card games.

Owen's mother stepped next to him. "I see an empty seat next to a lovely young lady."

"I do too." He kissed his mother on the cheek and limped to Miss de Bourgh's table. Perhaps he should have asked if they minded if he joined their game, but as Lady Catherine and maybe even Mr. Lambert would likely refuse him, he merely sat and, appraising the setting of the cards, said, "Whist, I daresay? It appears I have chosen the right table."

"You have indeed," Miss de Bourgh said.

Lady Catherine pursed her lips as if holding back a scowl. "I hope your enjoyment of the game means you play well, Mr. Talbot, as you will be my partner."

"I hope so too."

Mr. Lambert shuffled the cards. "Not too well, I hope."

Miss de Bourgh cut the cards.

Lady Catherine dealt them out and revealed her last card to the others. "I believe we will soon find out the truth of the matter."

From there the game began in earnest. Miss de Bourgh and Mr. Lambert won. At first Owen thought their winning had displeased Lady Catherine, but when she then handed the deck of cards to Anne, indicating she would be the next dealer, he noted an extra-pleased glint in her eyes that, while he had often seen it in his own mother's eyes when she had looked at him, he had never noticed it in Lady Catherine's eyes before. *A mother's pride.*

Miss de Bourgh handed the deck to Owen. His fingertips *accidentally* brushed hers as he took them from her. Then he cut them and handed them to Lady Catherine to shuffle.

"I believe Mr. Lambert is much more adept at shuffling than I am," Lady Catherine said.

"Thank you, your ladyship." Mr. Lambert, frowning in a way that seemed almost a smirk, took the cards from her and shuffled them.

Miss de Bourgh dealt them out. Partway through the dealing, one of the cards fell to the floor beside Owen. She leaned down to get it—so did Owen—and as his hand once again brushed hers, he whispered, "I must tell you how I feel."

That blush. But she said nothing. When they sat up again, Lady Catherine's and Mr. Lambert's gazes narrowed. They glanced back and forth between the two of them. Owen and Miss de Bourgh, however, paid heed only to the cards on the table.

The next game went about the same as the previous one, and once again, Miss de Bourgh and Mr. Lambert, especially Mr. Lambert, won.

"I am not unhappy the two of you have won," Lady Catherine said, "but I believe I need a new partner."

She is getting rid of me. But when Miss de Bourgh shook her head and said, "Why do we not play a different game?" every candle in the room glowed brighter.

Mr. Lambert pressed his hand over the top of Anne's—*did she cringe?*—and stood. "I would be most pleased to choose another game, but right now I am feeling a bit hungry. Would you join me at the sideboard, Miss de Bourgh?"

Miss de Bourgh glanced at Owen.

"Yes," Lady Catherine said. "I could do with a bit of food as well. Anne, you will bring me a plate."

"Yes, Mother."

"Nothing too heavy, mind you, or too sweet. I already ate more of those chocolates than is good for me."

Anne nodded. Owen stood.

"Mr. Talbot, you will sit with me until they return."

Mr. Talbot held back his grimace and sat again. If only he was not that night's host. If only he was not responsible for the comfort and enjoyment of his guests. He tried not to watch Miss de Bourgh walk away, but he most certainly did, because Lady Catherine cleared her throat and said, "I was polite earlier today, but you have left me no alternative but to outright say I will never allow you to marry my daughter."

"As I said before, I am fully aware of your opinion, your ladyship. But I believe in this instance, Miss de Bourgh should decide for herself what and whom is best for her."

"I am her mother."

"But not her jail warden."

"How dare—"

He held up his hand to stop her. "I do not wish to argue with you, Lady Catherine, for I know Miss de Bourgh has no wish to displease you, but I also know she yearns for a life of her own. My only wish is to help her find that life. I will not deceive you by saying I do not wish to marry her. You already know I do, and I can only hope the life she wants will include me."

"A girl such as she is—"

"A woman."

She scowled. "The man Anne chooses to marry will affect the rest of her life, and a *girl* like her is too naïve and gentle-hearted to be burdened with such a decision."

"I wholeheartedly disagree. The person who must live with the choice is the one who should be allowed to make it."

They glared at one another.

Soon after, Miss de Bourgh and Mr. Lambert returned to the table. Mr. Lambert sat. He took a piece of cold ham from his plate. Miss de Bourgh, glancing between Owen and Lady Catherine, set a plate of fruit and bread in front of her mother. "You two look quite serious. What are you talking of?"

"Futures," Owen said.

She raised her eyebrows, but when neither he nor Lady Catherine said anything more, she said, "I believe I will get something to eat for myself. I will return shortly."

"I will join you." Mr. Talbot stood and, ignoring Lady Catherine's "If you please—," followed Miss de Bourgh. He stood next to her in front of the flowers. "Do you like the daylilies?"

"They are beautiful." She set a strawberry on her plate.

"Daylilies are your favorite flowers, as I recall."

She quickly lowered her gaze. "They are." Then, just as quickly, she lifted it again. She glanced over his shoulder and said, "Thank you."

He followed her gaze. Mr. Lambert strode toward them. *Time is short. Be bold.* "You are the most wonderful woman I have ever known."

She smiled. "Next to your mother, you mean."

Mr. Lambert reached them and clasped Anne's elbow. "May I get you a glass of punch, my dear Miss de Bourgh?"

"Yes, thank you."

Mr. Lambert released Miss de Bourgh's elbow, but before he had even edged away from them, Owen, looking only at Miss de Bourgh, said, "Equal with, if not above, my mother."

Mr. Lambert furrowed his brows. "I am afraid I do not understand you, sir."

Miss de Bourgh's gaze, focused on Mr. Talbot's, sparkled brighter than the candlelight reflecting off the window. "You need not worry, Mr. Lambert. His message was meant for me."

Yes!

"Mr. Lambert," Lady Talbot said from behind them.

Each faced her. Owen, catching his mother's quick glance, stood taller and nonchalantly brushed his left sleeve.

"Lady Talbot." Mr. Lambert bowed. "How may I be of service?"

"I understand you are Mr. Evans's cousin."

"I am indeed, my lady."

She stepped next to him and took his arm. "Mr. Evans, I hear, is a connoisseur of apricot cakes. My cook assures me hers is every bit as good as the Evans's cook's, but to me it seems something in her recipe is not quite right. I wonder, would you be willing to taste hers for me? It is just over here, and I assure you, it will not take much of your time, but I would be indebted to you."

He glanced at Owen, at Miss de Bourgh, and frowned. "I am happy to be of service, your ladyship."

"Thank you." Lady Talbot took his arm and led him to the opposite end of the sideboard.

"Well, Mr. Talbot?" Miss de Bourgh said. "I suspect that display from your mother was in your behalf."

"It was." He swallowed. "She knows I want to tell you, however I can, that I—" Miss de Bourgh's gaze was so open, so warm, so, so . . . his mouth went dry.

"Yes?" She glanced over her shoulder at his mother and Mr. Lambert, who had just taken a bite of the apricot cake.

Hurry. "Quite right." Mr. Talbot stood taller. "Miss de Bourgh, I must tell you I-I'm never so happy as when I am with you." *They are returning.* "You mean everything . . . what I want to say is . . . I will be"—*They are only a few steps away*—"I will be leaving for America soon, and I hope you will—"

Mr. Lambert and Lady Talbot were once again at their sides. Miss de Bourgh's gaze, though still warm, drooped. Lady Talbot quirked an eyebrow at Owen, and he shook his head. Once. He should have spoken faster. Why had he not simply said, "I love you. Will you marry me?"

"Come, Miss de Bourgh." Mr. Lambert offered her his arm. "I have been most anxious to speak with you all evening, and I see now I must make my own opportunity."

She glanced at Owen as she took Mr. Lambert's arm and walked with the man away from him—all the way across the room to the quiet and devilishly empty window seat. And there they sat, their heads somewhat close together. Why had Owen not taken her aside like that? Why did he not do so now?

I will. Mr. Talbot started toward them, but after two steps he stopped and growled softly. Mr. Lambert leaned toward Miss de Bourgh in such a way that one knee almost touched the ground. He spoke. He held out a—a ring? No, it was merely a flower with its stem formed in the shape of a ring, but Owen knew its meaning. Mr. Lambert had proposed to Miss de Bourgh in *Owen's* home, in front of all these people. How dare he? And Miss de Bourgh . . . She looked at Lady Catherine, who beamed at her from the table where they had last left her, and took the flower from Mr. Lambert.

"Oh dear," Mr. Talbot's mother said from beside him. "Lady Catherine requested a few moments to make an announcement this evening, but I had no idea it would be that."

Owen clenched his fists.

His mother wrapped her hands around his arm. "Stay calm, son. All may be different than it appears. Perhaps Mr. Lambert has only given her a flower. We know nothing of what was said or of her response."

"I intend to find out." He shook off his mother's grasp and limped past the guests still occupied with their card games and straight toward Miss de Bourgh. Mr. Lambert sat next to her, but Miss de Bourgh stared at Mr. Talbot. "May I speak with you, Miss de Bourgh?"

"I—" She glanced at her mother, who was now also walking toward them; at the other guests, whose attentions were now focused on them; at Mr. Lambert; and finally, at the flower ring in her hand.

"Ladies and gentlemen," Lady Catherine said above the low din. "Lady Talbot has given me permission to announce a most pleasing event. Please lift your glasses in congratulations. My daughter, Miss Anne de Bourgh, and Mr. David Lambert, Mr. Evans's cousin, are soon to be married."

Owen's muscles pulsed beneath his skin. His blood screamed through his heart. "My congratulations," he said in conjunction with those around them. He then bowed and headed for the door.

CHAPTER THIRTY-ONE

THE BITTERNESS IN MR. TALBOT's voice thundered so deeply through Anne's core she jumped to her feet. *Stop! It is all a mistake.*

Mr. Lambert sidled in closer to her. He clasped her lower arm and, glancing at Mr. Talbot's retreating figure, lowered his gaze to hers. "My dear Miss de Bourgh, is all well?"

She pressed her hand to her chest. *Everything is wrong.* "I am well."

Mr. Talbot walked out the door. He left quietly, but Anne's emotions gathered into a misshapen rock, flew across the room, and shattered through the window.

Several guests smiled at Anne from behind their lifted glasses. She could not be certain—perhaps it was only a fancy formed from her own anxieties—but it seemed many of their expressions were cold, flat even, as they gazed between Anne, Mr. Lambert, Lady Catherine, and Lady Talbot. Why had her mother of all people arranged such an announcement in another person's home? Did she really want her to marry Mr. Lambert so much that she would defy common decorum? Anne curtsied to Lady Talbot, who smiled sadly at Anne and moved away from her.

Mr. Lambert stepped closer to Anne's side. "Are you certain you are well, my dear? Indeed, you look quite pale."

"Truly, I—" *I must go after Mr. Talbot.* But so many people were still staring at her that Anne pressed her stance harder into the floor. If only she could now refute her mother's proclamation without embarrassing her. If only she could run after Mr. Talbot, chase him through his house if need be, and explain the whole of it without bringing society's judgements against any of them. If only . . . *I will tell him the truth first thing tomorrow.*

Though that thought shot hope through her heart, her knees gave way beneath her weight, and she grabbed Mr. Lambert's hand on her arm to steady herself. "Perhaps I am out of sorts. Maybe I ate something that disagreed with me."

"Why do we not we sit for a moment?" Mr. Lambert urged her back onto the window seat and sat next to her. "Is this better?"

How could it be better with Mr. Talbot so upset? *Where did he go?* "It is better. Thank you."

Her mother, clasping the back of one chair after another, moved toward her. She briefly clasped Mr. Lambert's hands in congratulations and turned to Anne. "My dear, I am so pleased with this news." But when she leaned over to clasp Anne's hands, her gaze narrowed. "Anne? What is it?"

"She is feeling unwell, my lady," Mr. Lambert said.

"As I have not been feeling particularly well, either," Lady Catherine said, "the two of us must have caught some sickness."

"I think we should take her home immediately," Mr. Lambert said.

"Is your betrothed right, my dear?" Lady Catherine asked Anne. "Do you wish to go home?"

No. I want to stay here, where Mr. Talbot is. I want to find him and tell him the truth of what happened. And yet her mother had called Mr. Lambert her betrothed. Anne needed to clear up that misunderstanding immediately. "Perhaps going home would be best."

"I will let the driver know to bring around the carriage," Mr. Lambert said.

"I would rather you stay with me a bit longer," Anne said. "Mother can order the carriage."

Her mother's eyes gleamed. "Of course, my dear. You will remain here in your betrothed's capable hands."

"I am most happy to accept the charge," Mr. Lambert said.

They nodded to one another, and Anne's mother headed toward Lady Talbot, who stood near the doorway, where Mr. Talbot had just left. Anne's head throbbed.

"Mr. Lambert?"

He pressed his hand over hers where it rested on the window seat between them. "Yes, my dearest?"

"I-I thank you for the compliment of your proposal. You are a charming man, and I do like you, but I am afraid I cannot marry you."

His smile drooped. The color evaporated from his face.

"I know this is not the news you wish to hear, and I am sorry for the misunderstanding that has already gone on longer than I would wish, especially because of the embarrassment it will likely cause, but I hope you will believe me when I say I had not meant for any of this to happen."

"You had not meant for me to propose? But your mother assured me of your wholehearted approval. You cannot be blind to my affection for you, and with my name, my connection with Mrs. Evans and therefore Lord Backwell, you must surely see the benefit of a match between us."

"Again, I am sorry. I wish my mother had spoken with me first. I could have saved you all this trouble."

Such a hard glint filled his eyes that when he sat up taller, Anne feared anger was about to overpower his manners. Would he shout at her? Cause a scene? Instead he only rubbed the back of his neck. "You do not wish to marry me? You are most certain of that?"

"I am. Forgive me."

His gaze darkened. He released her hand, slid slightly away from her, and scanned the room. She likewise turned her attention away from him. They sat like that, as if both were encased in ice, until her mother returned.

Mr. Lambert stood. He opened his mouth and backstepped, but before he could make his excuses and leave, which Anne fully believed he wished to do, her mother claimed his arm.

"Our barouche is waiting for us."

"Very good, madam." He stiffly offered Anne his other arm.

Anne took it, and the three followed a manservant from the house. When the outside door closed behind them, Mr. Lambert added, "Forgive me, Lady Catherine, but I am afraid I will not be able to accompany the two of you home this evening."

Anne glanced up the front of Seawind House. Candlelight brightened a few of the rooms, but most were dark. Which rooms were Mr. Talbot's? Was he up there somewhere now, staring down at them from within the shadows? Angry at her for leading him to believe she cared for him? For certainly he had seemed to be about to make his own offer. If only she could scream up to him, "I love you," and he would hear her.

"You cannot accompany us?" her mother said to Mr. Lambert as he walked with them to the awaiting carriage. "Has something happened?"

"Something has happened. Yes, that is it." He glanced at Anne. "I have pressing business I must attend to."

"Business? At this late hour?"

"I am afraid so." He opened the carriage door and helped the two of them inside.

Anne faced the other side of the carriage. She closed her eyes and bit the inside of her lower lip. Would this evening never end?

"Business always calls at the most inconvenient times," her mother said. "Very well. I suppose there is nothing to be done about it. We shall see you tomorrow, I hope?"

He half smiled and closed the door.

Her mother nodded to him. "Until tomorrow." Then, as the driver pulled their barouche into the road, she faced Anne. "Congratulations, my dear. I must say your self-will has grown as much as I ever hoped it would, and I could not be more pleased. You must agree his proposal was the perfect icing to tonight's event."

"Thank you, Mother." Anne again looked away from her.

"However, while I do not wish to give you cause for alarm, especially tonight, I feel there is something I must tell you. As you know, I have not been well lately."

Anne faced her again. She furrowed her brow. Not one prior hint had prepared her for that statement.

"No, do not worry yourself, my dear. I expect whatever this illness is will pass soon enough. But it has made me realize how short life is. You must see, Anne, my age being what it is, that something could happen to me at any time. And if, no, when, the unthinkable happens, I will rest easier knowing you are well cared for."

Anne gazed down at her mother's hand where it then clasped hers. Her mother's illness. Her quick acceptance of Mr. Lambert. Her worry for Anne's future. None of it excused her behavior toward Mr. Talbot, but at least Anne now understood why her mother had become so hurriedly insistent that Anne marry Mr. Lambert.

"You are very quiet, my dear," her mother continued. "Have tonight's events put you so out of sorts? Of course they have. That is why we are leaving at this early hour. Well, I will not press you. Rest yourself now, and we will speak of these happy things in the morning."

Anne exhaled. *Yes, tomorrow.* Tomorrow, when Anne's head cleared and her strength returned, she would find a way to tell her mother the truth, to somehow convince her that a life with Mr. Talbot would be—would be wonderful. But even if she could not convince her . . . Anne closed her eyes and took a deep breath even as worry for her mother's health trickled through her. She loved her mother, but whatever happened, whatever the results of her confession might be, she would tell her mother the truth. And then she would find and speak with Mr. Talbot.

* * *

The next morning Anne took the cure but skipped her early walk so she might be on hand to speak with her mother the moment Lady Catherine came down to breakfast. As it turned out, her mother stayed to her bed longer than usual, and Anne was also obliged to miss her sea-bathing appointment and instead spent the whole of her morning waiting in the dining room. It was not at all what Anne would have wished, but at least it gave her time to rehearse the words she would say to her mother as well as devise how she might properly contact Mr. Talbot. After all, a young woman simply could not write to, much less call on, a young man without a prior understanding between them.

It was nearly noon when her mother entered the dining room. She looked more ill, weaker than Anne had ever seen her. Should she not wait to confide her news? Perhaps she should comfort her mother's physical distresses. Perhaps she should not tell her of Mr. Talbot. *Mr. Talbot.* Anne straightened her spine. Too much time had already passed without him knowing the truth.

"Good morning, Mother," Anne said. "I am sorry to trouble you when you have just wakened and are so obviously not feeling well, but I simply cannot wait. I must speak with you."

A maid, carrying a cup of hot tea, followed her mother into the room and set it at her mother's place at the head of the table.

"It is no trouble, my dear," her mother said. "Soon-to-be brides have many worries to contend with, and I am most happy to help you through them. I do ask you to sit with me though." She lowered herself into her chair. "I realize you must have taken your breakfast hours ago, but I will have only a little tea this morning. I hope it will settle my stomach."

"As you wish." Anne forced away her frown and sat. She wrung her hands in her lap, focused much too fully on the teacup, and twice caught herself jouncing a knee.

"Be still, my dear. My stomach cannot handle all that movement."

I must insist Dr. Fletcher call on her. "Forgive me. I will be still." Anne looked toward the clock ticking in a most indifferent manner from its place on the fireplace mantel: 12:14 . . . 12:15 . . . 12:16 . . .

Finally, at 12:22, her mother set her half-empty teacup away from her and lowered her hands to her lap. "Very well, my dear, what is it? I suppose you are worried we will not be able to have your gown made in time for the wedding. Or perhaps that is not it at all. When will the wedding be, my dear? The fall, of course, when the leaves are blazing their reds and yellows. It must be the fall—neither too hot, nor too cold."

"Please, Mother, I need to tell you—"

Her mother pursed her lips. "If you are worrying over who might perform the ceremony, I insist you put your mind at ease. It must be Mr. Collins. I will see to it as soon as I feel more myself, and you—"

"No, Mother."

"It will certainly be Mr. Collins. He, as well as our neighbors, will consider it an affront if we do not have the man who has personally attended so long and well upon us perform such a service. I admit there might be some difficulty, if you and Mr. Lambert have set your minds on having your wedding here in Brighton, but I strongly urge you—"

"I do not mean we should slight Mr. Collins. I only—"

"I am glad to hear it. Well, then, when you and your betrothed tell me the date, I can get to work on the—"

"*Mother*. There is not going to be a wedding between me and Mr. Lambert."

Lady Catherine opened her mouth, but this time no words came.

"Mr. Lambert did propose to me last night, but I refused."

"Tell me you are not that foolish."

"If refusing him means I am foolish, then I am afraid I am."

"Have you lost your senses, girl?" Her mother straightened her spine, but her expression drooped as if the yellow of her complexion weighed too heavily for her muscles. "We must find Mr. Lambert and apologize for your mistake. I will write to him, as it is not appropriate for you to do so, and give him some excuse. With any luck, he will take you back."

"It is not a mistake. Mr. Lambert seems a very amiable man in many respects, but I do not love him. And I do not believe he loves me."

"Love has nothing to do with these matters."

"It should. A marriage without love can only bring disappointment."

"Nonsense. You have obviously read too many of those silly gothic novels."

"On the contrary, I have not read any. But I have observed many marriages, and I see no reason why I, a woman of means, must accept a second-best situation. Perhaps such circumstances were good enough for you, but I would rather live alone than succumb to a life without love."

While her mother's frown tightened, the creases round her eyes softened with what seemed to be sadness. "Loneliness has very few merits, Anne. I would not wish it to be your bedfellow longer than it has been mine."

"I only meant—"

"Furthermore, you know nothing of my marriage. Your father died long before you could have any recollection of it."

Her father's smiling face, his hands balancing Anne as she sat on his lap. Those were Anne's only memories of her father. "You are right. I spoke unkindly and rashly."

"Traits I have never known you to have."

Anne turned in her seat until she fully faced her mother. "I do not wish to offend you, Mother."

Her mother lifted her chin. "I insist you change your decision. Marrying Mr. Lambert is your only hope, I fear, for a happy and fulfilled life."

There it was. In her heart her mother believed as all polite society surely did, that Anne was too old, too sickly, and in some opinions, too cross to ever make an equitable match. Perhaps they were right. If so, and if Anne had indeed lost what she considered to be her only chance for an equitable, nay, a *happy* match with Mr. Talbot, what did it matter? She could live alone. In relative terms, she had done so all her life. "I will not change my mind, Mother. I will not marry Mr. Lambert."

"Foolish, headstrong, ungrateful girl!"

Anne folded her arms in front of her. "I will not accept Mr. Lambert's proposal of marriage."

Her mother's fingers trembled, but still she glared at Anne. "If the man you think of is Mr. Talbot, you can forget about him. I went to Seawind House yesterday and told him you were soon to be engaged and he must forget about you. He, as I expected from such a man, had the presumption to refuse my request."

"He said that?"

"He did, which further proves my point that he is not the man for you."

"I think his words prove the opposite."

"Do not contradict me, girl. His words did nothing of the sort. I was there, and you were not."

But Mr. Talbot was. "I wish I had been there. I wish—" Anne pushed up from her chair and rushed to the door.

"We are not finished with this conversation."

"You may not be finished, but I am." Anne opened the door.

"Where do you think you are going?"

"To see Mr. Talbot. It is high time the truth was out between us." She rushed from the room.

"Anne!"

Anne did not even look back as she raced through the hall, up the staircase, and to her room. On the way, she told Mrs. Kelton to summon Dr. Fletcher to see her mother, knocked on Mrs. Webb's door, and opened it. Mrs. Webb sat at her writing desk.

She looked up at Anne. "Miss de Bourgh, whatever has happened?"

"We are going to Seawind House. Change into your walking dress, and come to my room."

Mrs. Webb stared down at her pad of paper. After a moment she set her quill in the ink bottle and stood. "I will be there in five minutes."

* * *

True to her word, Mrs. Webb entered Anne's room five minutes later just as Danton, Anne's new lady's maid, finished fastening the back of Anne's green walking dress.

Anne grabbed her reticule and handed Mrs. Webb her drawing pad.

"Why the rush?" Mrs. Webb asked. "I expect the *Strobilanthes nutans* will be there in an hour as well as in a few minutes."

"Today drawing the plant is only an excuse." Anne bustled from the room, and with Mrs. Webb behind her, hurried down the stairs. Her mother met her at the door.

"I forbid you to go to Seawind House."

"I am of age, Mother. I do not need your permission."

Her mother's glare tightened.

"Please stand aside," Anne said.

Her mother stepped more fully in front of the door. Anne growled and brushed past her. "Come along," she said to Mrs. Webb, who still stood at the base of the staircase. Mrs. Webb stared between Anne and her mother as if they had lost their senses. Maybe they had.

"Keep here, then," Anne said to her. "I will go alone."

Her mother shook her head, looked up at the ceiling, and at last stepped to the side. She leaned against the door frame. "Perhaps you would like Mr. Lambert to accompany you instead of Mrs. Webb."

"I doubt Mr. Lambert would have the stomach for watching me confess my love to another man."

This time Mrs. Webb blanched. Why? Was a woman confessing her love to a man so much more unseemly than a woman sneaking off to go swimming with her maid? Perhaps it was, but Anne did not care. Right then all that mattered was, come what may, she would confess her feelings to Mr. Talbot before she lost all opportunities to do so.

Anne headed to the boardwalk. Mrs. Webb hurried after her. As they walked, so many memories of Mr. Talbot and of Anne's questionings over whether or not she was taking the right course tumbled through her mind that it seemed to take an hour, though it could only have been a few minutes, by the time she and Mrs. Webb reached Seawind House. Mrs. Graham showed them into the entry hall, and a few moments later Lady Talbot stepped into the hall.

"Miss de Bourgh." Lady Talbot moved quickly to her side and clasped Anne's hands. "How good of you to come to this lonely place so soon after last evening's party. But then, I see you have your drawing pad. You have no doubt come to draw the *Strobilanthes nutans*. Go ahead, my dear. I will have Mrs. Graham show you out to the garden."

Anne stared at Lady Talbot. The woman's eyes were red and puffy. Her lips trembled into a frown. She had called Seawind House a lonely place. "Thank you, but what has happened?"

"Forgive me. I am afraid you have caught me out of sorts this morning." She sniffed, glanced at Mrs. Webb, and forced a smile. "I did not have the chance last night, but let me wish you joy on your engagement."

"No! I am not engaged to Mr. Lambert. It was a mistake. I came—"

Sudden tears filled Lady Talbot's eyes.

"What is it?" Anne said.

Lady Talbot pressed the back of her hand to the tears on her upper cheek. "I had hoped he had given up his idea of going to America, but last evening when Owen learned of your engagement, he decided he could wait no longer. He left for London early this morning to purchase supplies, and from thence he will be going on to Falmouth."

Anne stared at her. Her voice knotted in her throat. "He is gone?"

"Oh, Miss de Bourgh, I fear I will never see him again."

Anne's knees weakened, but somehow she kept upright. "Do you know where I can locate him?"

"I do!" Lady Talbot stared at her. "If anyone can stop him, you can." She grabbed Anne's hands. "The Crowne Inn in London. I expect he will be there for at least three days."

Anne swallowed, lifted her chin, and did not look at Mrs. Webb, who kept nudging her arm. She would be right in indicating her mother would never allow her to make such a journey, especially in pursuit of Mr. Talbot, but Anne replied, "I will do my best."

* * *

Kenneth, waiting, watching, wondering what he should do next and when that next move should be, stared out his bedchamber window.

A knock sounded at his door. He turned.

Evans entered. "Tonight." He handed Kenneth a folded note. "Here are the details."

Kenneth glanced over the note and growled. As Miss de Bourgh would not marry him, he must now abduct her? He scowled, looking up at Evans. "We are not prepared for a kidnapping."

"Nevertheless, that is what we will do."

CHAPTER THIRTY-TWO

Outside of Brighton, Rural East Sussex

LATE AT NIGHT WOULD HAVE been a much better time to abduct Miss de Bourgh. A time when shadows were ever-present and only a slit of moonlight brightened the road. But now, since, as Leon had told him, Anne had determined she would leave before sunrise and would not be swayed otherwise, this time would have to do. At least the black rainclouds would shield the approaching sunrise.

A horse neighed over the air. Kenneth peered into the darkness across the ups and downs of the road that led back to Brighton. He couldn't see it yet, but most certainly the *crack crack crack* lumbering toward him must be a carriage.

Kenneth pulled his hat farther over his face, blocking the pounding rain, and lifted the black cloth he'd tied over the beard he'd glued to his face. He backed his horse off the muddy road and beneath the trees. He scowled. All of this could have been avoided if Miss de Bourgh had consented to marry him as she was supposed to do, as they'd planned for her to do. She would have simply, willingly, after her money had been placed into his hands, gone off with him to France, where Leon would ultimately kill her, and the three of them would disappear with no one knowing who they really were and with Lady Catherine devoid of all she held dear—if she still lived by then.

If only Miss Anne de Bourgh had not met Mr. Talbot.

All at once the memory of the first time he'd seen his own true love, his Bridget, with her hair blowing every which way in the wind as she had gathered firewood for her family's hearth, trembled into his heart. *It is not the same thing.* He growled. *Bridget and I were meant to be one. We were*

meant to bring our Gracie into the world. Miss de Bourgh and Mr. Talbot—we don't need more high folk about us. He sneered past the image of his daughter smiling . . . coughing . . . telling him to stand on the inside.

Dr. Lambert, the real Lambert, had better be worth his pay.

Horses' hooves splashed. The carriage could not be more than thirty feet away from him. Soon it would be more than shadows approaching him. Soon he would see the driver's face. Soon he would . . . Kenneth clenched his pistol in one hand, his horse's reins in the other, and charged out of the trees. He stopped in front of the closed carriage. The carriage's horses neighed, straining against the driver's pull on their reins.

"What the devil?" the driver yelled.

"Stand and deliver!" Kenneth yelled.

"Nothin' doin'." The driver cracked his whip.

Again the horses lurched forward, but when Kenneth shot his gun into the air, they veered north off the road. Kenneth chased after them. The carriage joggled through the uneven ground and tall wet weeds. It barely missed crashing into three trees, but at last it plowed into a bog of thick mud and stopped.

Kenneth took on his roughest voice. "Get down. Now," he told the driver. "Walk away if you want to live."

A bullet whizzed past Kenneth's shoulder.

Kenneth ducked low in his saddle. He hadn't been told the driver would have a gun. "Foolish move. Now you're out of ammunition, and I have a double-barrel flintlock."

"You think I don't have another gun ready and waiting?"

"If you did, you would have used it already. Now, get out of here."

"I will not leave without the passengers."

Kenneth jumped down from his horse, rushed at the man, and yanked him to the ground. "I said, *get out of here.*"

The carriage door inched open. A lady's reticule filled the space. "Please, sir. I have money." It was Miss de Bourgh's voice. Gads, she'd developed more mettle than he'd realized. Not that it would do her any good.

"Take it," she continued. "All of it, if you will, but please let us go."

Kenneth grabbed the reticule from her hands and slammed the door closed. The women huddled together on the opposite side of the carriage. They stared back at him through the slightly fogged window.

"Do not move." He pulled the ransom note from his pocket with his free hand and threw it at the driver. "Take this to Lady Catherine."

The driver's eyes bulged. He looked at Kenneth, the gun in Kenneth's hand, the letter lying in the mud and weeds, and then, still staring back at him, scooped up the letter and ran back toward the road. When Kenneth could no longer discern between him and the surrounding shadows, he opened the carriage door. "Get out."

The women obeyed, Miss de Bourgh dismounting first. Cold rain pelted their skin and hair. He resisted the urge to offer them his hat and coat and instead motioned his gun between them and the distant rolling hills. "Walk."

"Through this mud? We can hardly see where we are going as it is." Miss de Bourgh's companion, Mrs. Webb, did have a tendency to speak out more than she should.

"And where do you suppose you are going? To a ball?"

"You have the lady's money; let us go."

Miss de Bourgh grabbed Mrs. Webb's hand. "I believe silence would be more prudent."

"If you had any decency," Mrs. Webb continued, "you would let us be on our way."

Kenneth grabbed her arm, yanking her from Miss de Bourgh's grip, and shoved her around in front of him. "Move."

He forced them far from the main road and deep into the woodland, moving more uphill than not through the mud and tall grass, to where no travelers could see them if they chanced by. They had barely traveled a mile when the wind stole the ladies' hairpins, but that in addition to the rain soaking their clothes through the remaining five rougher miles brought Miss de Bourgh and even, occasionally, Mrs. Webb to tears. *Foolish women.* It wasn't his fault they'd planned that morning to run away. He'd rather not have kidnapped them in this rain either. But, as this was their lot, he pressured them forward until hours later, when the clouded sky grayed with late-morning light.

They crossed another muddy bog and stopped before a tall, tangled hedgerow.

"Through there," Kenneth said.

"You have nearly drowned us," Mrs. Webb said.

He frowned at Miss de Bourgh. *Drowned.* How appropriate. "I said, *through there.*"

"Where are you taking us?" Miss de Bourgh said.

Kenneth shoved them into the mess of shrubbery and trees. Branches clawed their sleeves and hair, and more than one thorn scratched his face, but moments later they pushed their way through to the other side and clambered down the slope to the cottage. He pushed open the wooden door. It creaked.

"Inside." He shoved them through several strands of spiderwebs into the darkness. "Remove your shoes and stockings and throw them out here."

"Why?" Mrs. Webb asked.

So it will be harder for you to run away. "Do it."

The women stared at one another, and though Miss de Bourgh lifted her chin slightly, her lips trembled.

* * *

Owen stepped into the small pub next to the Crowne Inn. Shadows as black and empty as his mood filled all but the tables closest to the two front windows, but even they were dulled by the afternoon's grayness.

"The sun detests this day as much as I do," he muttered.

"What was that, sir?"

He turned to the woman—a dark-eyed barmaid in a worn, pale-green frock. She smiled up at him.

When he didn't answer, she said, "What can I get ye?"

"Something to make me forget."

She curtsied and headed to the bar.

Owen made his way through the crowd to the darkest corner of the room. He plunked his top hat onto the middle of the only empty table. He sat and scowled at the window. He should have looked about him before he had chosen this wretched table, where straight in front of him there was nothing more to look at than the dismal gray shops across the road—shops that needed something alive to drive customers into them. A tree, a plant, even a colorful picture would do. A picture painted by Miss Anne de Bourgh.

He clenched his fists across the top of the table and faced the wall. He focused on his travel preparations. So far, though he had not been long in London, he had already purchased the bedding he would need for his cabin on the packet ship. He still needed a few personal articles, a solid pair of shoes, and a coat thick enough to withstand the New York winters. He was not certain he could find a ready-made coat like that at this time of year, but he would look. If he did not find one by tomorrow night, he would make do with what he had until he could buy one in America. *America.*

All the way across the ocean from England, from his family, from Miss de Bourgh.

"Mr. Talbot?"

Owen turned. A man in a gray split tail coat stared down at him. Owen sat up taller. "Deuces, Fry. What are you doing here?"

"Lady Catherine bade me bring this message to you, sir."

"Delivering messages is a coachman's duty now?"

"There was no time for a regular courier, sir. The message is urgent."

Owen, frowning, took the sealed note from Fry. He tapped its edge against the tabletop. The gall of that woman. How dare she contact him for any reason?

"What does she want?"

"I can't say exactly, sir, but I believe it has something to do with Miss de Bourgh. She was stolen this morning."

"What?" Owen tore open the letter.

> *Dear Mr. Talbot,*
>
> *Last night a highwayman stole my daughter and her companion and sent me a ransom demand. The note says the ransom must be delivered to them tonight at eight o'clock or Miss de Bourgh will be killed.*
>
> *I have sent for the help of the constables, but as time is short and you are closer to the exchange point than we are here in Brighton, and as I cannot find Mr. Lambert or Mr. Evans, I beg you, if you truly do care for my daughter as you say you do, to immediately go to that place and keep watch for her. I will collect the necessary money and send someone to deliver it at the assigned hour, but I am sure I do not need to say I have no trust in this villain. I fear even after he receives the money he will not return my daughter. Someone must find her before the worst happens.*

Beneath her signature, Lady Catherine wrote the exchange point's directions. It was near Brighton Road, a few miles southwest of Crawley.

Owen grabbed his hat, jumped to his feet. "Tell her ladyship I will leave directly." He headed for the door and called out to the barmaid, "I am sorry, but I will not need that drink after all."

CHAPTER THIRTY-THREE

ANNE HUGGED HER KNEES TO her chest. She tucked her bare feet beneath the hem of her dress and leaned against the plank wall behind her. The cold from the wood chilled her backbone as deeply as the storm had soaked her clothes.

Mrs. Webb sat next to Anne. Her hair and dress were as askew and crumpled as Anne's were, but her legs were stretched in front of her, revealing she also had bare feet. Was she not as cold as Anne was? Perhaps her superior fortitude provided its own heat source.

"What are you going to do with us?" Mrs. Webb asked.

Their kidnapper walked a few feet away from the dirt-smudged window and peered through the shadows at Mrs. Webb. The wind had long ago blown away the kerchief he'd worn over the lower half of his face, and he'd cursed when Mrs. Webb had called him by name, but the truth was, Anne had seen through his disguise soon after he'd forced them from their carriage. His stance, his height, his walk, even elements of his voice. Mr. Lambert. What Anne could not understand, though, was why he would do this. Was he not a gentleman? Had he not only last night proposed marriage to her? Certainly his finer, kinder instincts would soon take over and he would release them.

"What am I going to do with ya?" Mr. Lambert spoke to Mrs. Webb, but he instead stared at Anne. "Just like quality not to see what is in front of their faces."

Anne's hope disintegrated. Mr. Lambert's glare spoke of hate, not kindness, and certainly not love.

Mrs. Webb rubbed the back of her neck.

He whirled. "Did I tell ya to move?"

"No, sir." Mrs. Webb slowly lowered her arm.

"Exactly. I'm in charge. And you will do as I say until I've traded Miss High 'n Mighty for a bag o' gold."

Anne cringed.

"And me?" Mrs. Webb said.

"I haven't decided what to do with you yet."

Anne pressed her mouth and nose into her propped-up knees. Her breath against her skirt warmed her nose, but her lips trembled. She quickly pressed them together. Trembling indicated weakness, and she must not be weak. She must be strong enough to bear whatever the near future held, strong enough to get away. For, while her mother would certainly pay whatever ransom Mr. Lambert demanded, he had revealed too much of himself to her and Mrs. Webb. He would not allow them to live long enough to turn him in. Escape was her only hope.

She scanned the room. Beneath the boarded-over window lay a toppled stool with legs so decayed it looked like it would collapse beneath a child's weight, and next to it was a splintered piece of wood that might have once been the lower half of a table. A pile of broken rocks sat at the base of the otherwise empty fireplace. And nestled in the corner next to her was a rusted link from a chain tangled within a narrow strip of net. A fisherman's net perhaps? Not that it mattered. Such a thing could hardly help Anne and Mrs. Webb. Or could it?

"What are you thinking?" Mrs. Webb whispered.

Anne looked up. Sometime in her reverie, Mr. Lambert had stepped outside.

"Where did he go?"

"He only said he would be watching the place so to not get any ideas. Miss de Bourgh, I am so afraid. He seems a—a monster."

"That is why we have to get away."

Mrs. Webb caught her breath and shook her head.

"Listen. We do not have much time." Anne, glancing between Mrs. Webb and the door, rehearsed her half-formulated plan.

"Are you certain it will work?" Mrs. Webb asked as the two stood.

"No, but we have to try something."

"Try what?" Mr. Lambert had returned.

Mrs. Webb inched toward the window, and Anne, staring at Mr. Lambert, who stood just inside the doorway, moved in the opposite direction. As she had hoped, his attention followed her rather than Mrs. Webb. "We can *try* to convince you to let us leave."

He stared at her. She stared back at him. Mrs. Webb picked up the piece of wood and crept toward him.

"You will not get away with this, Mr. Lambert," Anne said.

Mrs. Webb lifted the wood over her head.

"Ah, my dear, like every other of your kind, you are entirely mistaken." He sneered.

"Grab her!" Mrs. Webb yelled.

Mr. Lambert stepped sideways, grabbed Anne's arm, and yanked her forward. Mrs. Webb slammed the piece of wood down on Anne's head.

Pain. Anne reeled and collapsed.

* * *

Anne had no idea how long her mind whirled with blackness, but when her senses roused, her head throbbed, she lay on her side with the bottom of someone's shoe beneath her cheek, and she felt her hands being bound behind her back with what felt like that netting she had seen earlier. She groaned.

"She's coming to." Mrs. Webb's voice was hard, raspy in a way Anne had never heard before. Close too. Was she free? Anne kept her eyes shut. Perhaps if she pretended unconsciousness long enough, she would learn something that would help her escape.

"She'd better wake soon." Mr. Lambert's voice came from several feet away. "I'm not carrying her to the exchange."

The shoe Anne now realized belonged to Mrs. Webb pulled out from under her. Mrs. Webb had put her shoes back on. Would Mr. Lambert let Anne do so too? Mrs. Webb's foot nudged Anne's chin. "I would not worry."

"You never were one to worry, were you?"

"What is the point in worrying?" Mrs. Webb said. "It gets a body nowhere."

"Hanging's a big worry in my book."

"Only if a body gets caught."

Steps scuffed the ground near Anne and moved away. Light-footed steps. Mrs. Webb's steps. Was Anne dreaming? That was it. This was a nightmare. In the real world, Mrs. Webb was her companion, her friend, her strength. She would not be involved in this, would not be her enemy. *I trusted you.*

"Speaking for myself," Mr. Lambert said, "this body is not going to get caught."

"You always were a runner," Mrs. Webb said. "Ran from our engagement all those years ago. Still running, it seems."

Anne clenched her teeth. *A runner? Engagement?* Mr. Lambert was the man who had run from Mrs. Webb's engagement years ago? *So many lies.* And now Anne's own runner, the man she loved, was every moment moving farther away from her because of a lie.

"It never would have worked between us, Leon."

Who is Leon? Mrs. Webb?

"How do you know?" Mrs. Webb said.

"We wanted different things. My life is different now. I have different responsibilities. So do you."

"You could run away from your daughter if you wanted to."

"I could not. Guilt—caring for someone beyond myself—that's part of what's different between us."

"Tell yourself that if it pleases you."

Silence. Pacing about the room.

"Look, Leon. Money to help my daughter is the only reason I'm doing any of this."

"Money is what I want too."

"Of course it is. It's what Miss Eleanor Leon always wanted, always thought she deserved—to have the means to buy all her heart desired by taking everything away from the de Bourghs."

"Why shouldn't I?" Her voice snarled with so much bitterness that Anne cringed. Mrs. Webb continued. "It is high time Lady Catherine found out what it is like to have everything that is important to her taken away from her just as she and her husband took everything from my and Evans's parents after promising they could keep it—their home, their land, their livelihoods—and all in the name of business. Only this time, it is my business."

Anne swallowed. Her parents—her mother—had taken everything from Mrs. Webb's parents? Surely the woman must be lying. Never had Anne heard anything close to such a tale. And with Hunsford as small as it was, such a happening, if it were true, would have been noised long and loudly about the village. It simply could not have been hidden . . . forgotten . . .

discounted because . . . Anne's thoughts paused, twisted. Through all the days Anne could remember, her mother had been excessively involved in the concerns and affairs of the people around her, always making certain everything from clothes to closets to gardens were just right for them. Anne had often wondered why she would worry over such things when she had an entire estate to watch over, but now . . . was Mrs. Webb's story the *why* of it? Had her mother been trying to make amends for those earlier actions?

"I only wish Sir Lewis had not already died and gone to the devil," Mrs. Webb added. "I would have loved to have seen him suffer when he learned I stole his family's broach."

Anne's stomach hardened as her newfound sympathy for her mother crashed into the memory of her scouring the townhouse for the heirloom. Her mother would never get over that loss.

"You did get good coin out of it," Mr. Lambert said.

"And oh, how Lady Catherine is suffering—will suffer!"

"What's fair is fair," Mr. Lambert said.

"Exactly. She will learn of Miss de Bourgh's pains and know there is nothing she can do to relieve them. She should be glad she will not have to go on living with that knowledge—that want—the way we did."

Anne gritted her teeth and tugged at the netting binding her wrists. All this time she had been nothing more than a wooden puppet waiting for Mrs. Webb to hold up in front of her mother and burn.

More pacing.

"You know what?" Mr. Lambert said at last. "I don't care about any of that. All I want is the means to pay off Dr. Lambert and get back to my daughter. You can have the rest of it."

"I like the name."

"It seemed appropriate."

Once again footsteps scuffed the ground. It sounded as if they were on the other side of the room, so Anne chanced a glimpse at them through her eyelashes. Fortunately, her captors faced the window.

"I want nothing to do with another one of your deaths, Leon. I'll help you get her there, but then I'm gone."

Deaths? Anne inhaled.

Mr. Lambert and Mrs. Webb whirled toward her.

Anne closed her eyes. She held her breath until she had control enough to slowly release it. Who had Mrs. Webb killed?

"You are already involved."

Mrs. Webb's voice sounded a bit softer than it had before, like she was once again facing away from her, so Anne again risked peeking then fully opening her eyes. As she had hoped, the two had their backs to her and were again looking out the window.

"You would have done the same thing if you were in my shoes." Mrs. Webb drew away from Mr. Lambert. "Seymour was too much of a risk. He was a good tracker, I will give you that, and he got away—barely—with burning Sir Lewis's favored woodland, but one more visit as Dr. Sinclair to the de Bourgh's and Lady Catherine, maybe even Miss de Bourgh, would have realized he was not a physician, and the ruse would have been up."

"So you killed him."

Anne's breath froze in her gut. Her heartbeat pounded in her throat. *Mrs. Webb* had killed Dr. Sinclair? If only she, Lady Talbot, Mr. Talbot, the constables, anyone, all of them, had taken more serious care over investigating Dr. Sinclair's death, maybe they would have discovered the truth in time. Maybe none of this would have happened.

"He was my friend," Mr. Lambert growled. "And yours, as I recall."

"Friends? Is that what we were? We used each other. Made a lot of money until our luck ran out."

Mr. Lambert grabbed her upper shoulders. "Is that what you and I were too? People who merely used one another?"

She yanked away from him. "I had not thought so. At first. But your leaving proved it was."

He stared at her. "I'm sorry. I hope now, after this, you can forgive me."

"We will see."

He released her and slowly lowered his splayed hands. "You should have just sent Seymour away. You did not have to kill him."

"You say that now, but you would have changed your tune if he had given us away."

Mr. Lambert scowled.

"I grant you, he did get Lady Catherine to drink her first draught of poison, but beyond that . . . you must see I was the only one strong enough, the only one able to take care of the situation. Who else did you suppose could slip into the ball, talk with him, and lace his drink with arsenic without anyone noticing? No one pays any heed to a lady's companion. Look at how easy it was to get rid of Mrs. Jenkinson. Only it was even simpler with her. All I had to do was visit the de Bourghs one time and offer to pour their tea." Her voice seemed to smile with satisfaction. "No one thought twice about an old woman dying."

Anne's stomach rolled over for what seemed the hundredth time. If Dr. Sinclair had given her mother her first poisoned draught, who had continued with the rest of them? *Mrs. Webb,* of course. Mrs. Webb was the one who had killed Dr. Sinclair and Mrs. Jenkinson. Before Mrs. Webb's visit, Mrs. Jenkinson had shown no symptoms of ill health, but . . . Mrs. Webb was right. None of them had questioned her death. That poor woman. She had served and lived among Anne's family for as long as Anne could remember. She had not deserved such treatment.

"Congratulations, Leon," Mr. Lambert said. "Your scheme, despite its few setbacks, is moving along just as you planned it would."

"Yes. Even Lady Catherine, who is proving to be more resistant to arsenic than I expected, will at length succumb to it. But this way she will suffer over her daughter's fate even longer than I had planned she would."

Anne, peering again at them through her eyelashes, carefully clawed at the netted binding around her wrists. She had to get away from them. From Mrs. Webb especially. Not only did Mrs. Webb have no sympathy for her, but she, like Mr. Lambert, also knew Anne knew too much about them. Anne was nothing more than a loose end to them. *My life, this life I'm finally learning to really live, is forfeit.*

Mr. Lambert glanced toward Anne. Anne closed her eyes and stilled her fingers. How could she have been so blind? For as long as she could remember, she had prided herself on her ability to notice the details of her environment, to discern the true intents behind the actions of those around her. Their selfishness, their pettiness, and in Mr. Talbot's case, his superiority of character. They had all been open books to her. Now, to find Mr. Lambert and Mrs. Webb—the two people who had been among those closest to her in recent days—had not only blinded her to their truths but had also held her future, her life, in their cruel hands . . . It was too much to be borne.

"Pick her up," Mrs. Webb said. "It is getting late."

"I already told ya, I'm not carrying her. It'll be easier if she walks." Mr. Lambert grasped Anne's shoulders and pulled her upright. He shook her.

"Wake up," Mrs. Webb said.

Anne flopped, pretending to slumber.

"I said, wake up," Mrs. Webb repeated.

Slap!

"Aaaah!" Anne opened her eyes as her head jolted backward. "Mrs. Webb? What is going on?" She struggled against the net wrapped around her wrists, but still it held her fast. "Why am I tied up?"

"Enough with the questions," Mrs. Webb said. "It is bad enough we need you here at all."

Anne exaggeratedly gaped at Mrs. Webb as if she were learning of her deceit for the first time. Then she scowled and looked away from her. "What do you need from me?"

"That needing is only temporary, Miss de Bourgh. As soon as we get our money, our use for you is finished."

I will die, Anne thought.

Mrs. Webb shoved Anne through the door. Anne stumbled. Jagged stones pricked her bare feet. She peered up at the black clouds hovering over the afternoon horizon. If her only choice was death, what did it matter if she fought now, died now, rather than gave them what they wanted and died later? *I do not want to die.*

She trudged forward. *Be strong.*

* * *

Early evening had not yet drowned into night when Owen left his horse tied in a grove of trees and set off through the grass and underbrush. The lake, the kidnapper's exchange point, was on the other side of the hill about a half mile away, if he had calculated the distance correctly. In any case, he would definitely reach it before eight o'clock and hopefully long before the kidnapper showed up with Miss de Bourgh and Mrs. Webb. But was it long enough for him to brace his emotions? Ever since last night when Miss de Bourgh had become engaged to Mr. Lambert, Owen had told himself he would never see her again, that he would symbolically throw his feelings for her off the ship and into the sea on his way to America. But now Owen would do everything in his power to see her again. And then let her go. Again. He closed his eyes as if the movement might assuage the pain, but it only tore wider the ache in his heart.

He scowled at the landscape before him. He would not let her suffer the same fate his mother had suffered. Not even the betrayal he had felt when Miss de Bourgh had succumbed to her mother's interference and accepted Mr. Lambert mattered now. His scowl tightened. How could he ever have hoped, sought, yearned to be the son-in-law of Lady Catherine de Bourgh? "Miss de Bourgh."

He didn't know whether he had spoken her name aloud or only felt the breath of it cross his lips, but her name, Miss de Bourgh, seemed to shoot into the sky, wrap itself around her wherever she was, and connect once again with his heart. "Miss de Bourgh." Despite her mother, despite her setting him aside for another, and despite the hole in his heart that would never be filled, he would rescue her, make sure she was well, and figuratively hand her back to Mr. Lambert.

Owen hunched his shoulders and hurried from one thicket to another until he reached the top of the hill. He shadowed his eyes from the sunset's direct glare. He peered down at the lake and across the countryside beyond it. There were very few places in which he could hide—only clumps of tangled hedgerows and small copses or the thick woodland that filled the southernmost section of the lake. Or, he supposed, the pile of fallen logs that lay between the woodland and the flatter land to the south. Actually, the log pile might provide his best covering. At least it would when darkness hit. What about before then?

The woodland.

He growled as if the kidnapper already stood before him, loosened his collar, and charged down the hillside to the woodland as fast as his limp allowed. He chose a tree far enough away from the meeting place that he would not be readily seen yet close enough he might hear their voices—a tree with branches spaced no farther from each other than his arm span. He grabbed the closest branch, heaved himself upward, and, hand over hand, climbed the rest of the way until he had fully situated himself within its leafy branches. He pulled his spyglass from his waistcoat pocket. The woodland shadowed most of the day's remaining light, but he could still see all of the lake. "Perfect," he muttered. "They will not get past me undetected."

CHAPTER THIRTY-FOUR

ANNE HAD ALWAYS ENVIED THE less fortunate—not the starving, emaciated ones who had no hope beyond their bleakness but the hardy, good-souled among them. Those who toiled for their livings, faced with optimism the hardships life threw at them, and shared their means and hope with others. Such people were the healthiest she knew. They would never tremble through a few-miles hike the way she did, no matter the terrain. And they would have ignored their grumbling stomachs, thought them more as motivations than obstacles. Even better, their strong, calloused feet would have withstood the land's every sticker prick, fallen tree branch, or rock jab; such feet would not have offered their blood to the soil the way that mouse that crossed their path had after Webb stomped on it.

Soon after they had left the cottage, Anne had wiped the *Mrs.* in relation to Webb from her thoughts. Murderers did not deserve titles. Neither did kidnappers.

I may not be as robust as the less fortunate are, but I will get through this. I will escape.

Anne tripped on a bramble and plowed onto the ground. Lambert yanked her back to her feet and pushed her forward. "Keep moving. We have an engagement to meet."

Anne ignored the sting on her knees. *Be forceful.* "There is no need for this. Let me go, and I will make certain you are paid whatever you ask."

"Payment before prison?" Lambert said. "There's no point in that."

"I won't tell anyone. I give you my word."

"You cannot be trusted," Webb said.

I cannot? How ironic.

They trudged onward, still heading north. Toward London? As Anne had no way of knowing where they were or where her captors planned to take her, she had instead focused her thoughts over various escape plans, but it was not until they had crossed a narrow stream a while back that her ideas fully took shape. What she needed now was for them to come upon a forested place where she could beg for privacy. Her chance came when they headed toward a small woodland at the base of another hill.

"You are not seriously thinking of dragging us through that terrain," Webb said.

"We'll go around." Lambert veered them slightly to the left. "It's longer, but the way'll be easier."

"Longer?" Webb said. "Are we not about there? These shoes will not last through much more of this."

I would rather your shoes than my bare feet.

"A mile, a mile and a half maybe," Lambert said.

"I hope this pampered weakling lasts that long."

"I am not the one groaning," Anne muttered. Webb pushed her.

Anne, with her hands still tied behind her back, stumbled forward over an extended tree root. This time, Lambert caught her before she fell.

"You will be the one groaning," Webb said. "Once we get to the lake."

Anne furrowed her brows. Why would she groan at a lake? Unless . . . She swallowed. Was drowning how they intended to kill her?

Anne tightened her muscles, searching the woodland as they moved closer to it. The grasses were so tall, the ground was so swollen with tree roots, and so many new trees grew between the larger ones that she could not see far inside it. Difficult to run through but otherwise perfect. *Be strong.* "I need a moment of privacy," she said.

"Tough it out," Webb said.

"I have been toughing it out for hours now."

Lambert turned back to them. "Go ahead and take her," he said to Webb.

"Have you forgotten I am in charge here?"

"Can't see how giving her a moment will change anything."

They stared at one another. At last Webb grabbed Anne's arm and yanked her through the jumble of weeds and shrubs toward a group of leafy wych elms. They moved behind one of them.

"Go ahead," Webb said.

Anne peered deep into the woodland. She quickly located a narrow, vacant corridor between dozens of thick trees. She would have to clamber over two fallen logs to get to it, but she would do it. She had to. "Please untie my hands."

"I will not."

"Then you will have to help me."

Webb rolled her eyes. "Surely this is a job you must take care of for yourself."

More for show than anything else, Anne shifted her stance and struggled against the netting that bound her wrists. She could not be certain, partly because she could not see it and partly because her fingertips were numb from scraping at the threads, but it seemed in the hours she had been working at the netting, she had managed to loosen one thread. At this rate she would not free herself in time. She scratched at it faster. "I cannot do this without my hands. Untie me, or help me."

"Something wrong out there?" Lambert hollered

Webb growled and reached for Anne's skirt.

"Not here," Anne said. "That log over there."

Webb shoved Anne over the first of the fallen logs. "Such a helpless little thing. It is a wonder you have survived your life this long. But then, I suppose everyone whose property has been given to them without even a thought of work or struggle has reason to live."

Anne searched the path ahead of her. The shadows were so thick, made thicker by the darkening sky, she could not see the end of the trail, but perhaps that was a good thing. If she could not see it, maybe her captors would not be able to see her either when they chased after her. "If that is what you think, why did you say all those things to me about asserting myself? Having my own mind? Developing my own strength?"

"I admit I was rather effective. But I knew even before I determined to get rid of Mrs. Jenkinson you would be easy to manipulate."

Anne's mouth tasted like ash. Webb was already a double murderer, and if Anne did not keep her wits about her, did not somehow escape the woman's clutches, she would be number three. If her mother had not already died. "She will suffer over her daughter's fate," Webb had said. Surely that meant Anne's mother still lived.

"All I needed," Webb continued, "was for you to gain enough of a backbone that you would step out of your mother's protection and into our hands, which you have done."

Anne clenched her jaw. Her mouth twisted with derision. Very well. She would agree she had stepped into their trap, but that did not mean she would not get out of it. Webb had helped her gain enough of a backbone for that too.

Anne lowered her head, mimicking submission, and focused even harder on the path. She walked forward. Perhaps Webb would help her over the next log too.

Webb yanked Anne backward. "That's far enough." She crouched and clutched Anne's skirt.

Now! Anne kicked backward. Her foot connected with Webb's shoulder. Webb fell backward over a bush, and Anne ran.

"Get back here!"

Anne clambered over the next log and charged through the brambles. She did not hear the rest of Webb's statement, but she was sure if Webb caught her, she would make certain Anne paid dearly for her attempted escape.

Run. Veer neither right nor left. Give them no chance to overtake you.

Behind her, Lambert's yells mixed with Webb's. Had he already caught up to Webb? Anne charged farther into the darkness. More yelling, but Lambert's voice rang closer. He had passed Webb.

Anne's skirt billowed round her legs. She stumbled over the ground's bumps and swells. Branches scratched her face and snagged her clothes as the footsteps pounded the earth closer and closer behind her. She had to hide. Now. But where?

Lambert's footsteps seemed yards behind her, but his voice rang through her ears as if he were only a few feet away. "Stop, or you will regret it."

I already regret ever meeting, ever trusting either of you.

Anne dove into a tangle of bushes. She lay flat on her back, held her breath to avoid sound, and did not move, even though thorns from wild blackberry brambles pierced her feet, chest, and throat.

Mr. Lambert raced past her. How soon would it be until he realized his mistake and came back looking for her? How close was Webb? Could Anne slip away from her hiding place before they returned? She looked over her shoulder. All she saw were more branches.

Anne pressed her body lower to the ground. Again she worked on the netting tied around her wrists. If she turned onto her side, the blackberry bush would swallow her and more thorns would stab her, but might those same thorns also cut through her binding?

Webb's voice shouted above her from one side of Anne's hiding place. "Any sign of her?"

Anne rolled slowly, quietly, into the bush. She rubbed the thorn pricks against her wrists. Moisture, likely her blood, wetted her hands, but still she rubbed.

"No sign yet," Lambert said. "But she can't have gone far. The last time I saw her, she was somewhere around here."

Grasses swished nearby. Anne, still scraping her bindings against the thorns, peered through the brambles and stiffened. Lambert stood next to her hiding place.

"We'd better find her soon," Webb said. "The exchange is in an hour."

"And darkness is before that." All at once the bushes spread open in front of Anne, and Lambert stared into her eyes. "Got her."

Anne's breath became ice, her blood stone.

Webb rushed in next to him. "Do not just stand there. Pull her out."

Anne backed away from his hand, but the blackberry bush blocked her escape. Lambert yanked her out of the bush and onto the pathway. Anne looked down at her bare and bloodied feet. While running and hiding, she had barely noticed the pain. Now it shouted at her with vengeance, never stopping, never succumbing to a numb throb, not even when they left the stickery woodland and again headed across the open, hilly countryside toward the exchange point—the place, Webb frequently told her, where Anne would breathe her last.

"I understand drowning is painful before one succumbs to death," Webb muttered from beside her. Since Anne's escape attempt, Webb had walked on one side of her and Lambert on the other. "When you're kicking and gasping for breath, think of the people—of my and Evans's parents—your father and mother forced into desperate circumstances. Think of their deaths."

So they do mean to drown me.

A short time later another woodland, vaster than the one they had recently crossed, grew in the distance with each forward step. Behind it a lake spread beyond either side of the woodland's edges.

Anne slowed her pace. She tugged harder on the netting around her wrists, scratched—wait! There was a tiny hole! She shoved her pinky finger into the opening and pulled down on it. The hole budged. It was only a thread and not enough to loosen her bindings, but it was something.

"Slowing down won't help you any." Lambert tugged her forward, but Anne dug her feet deeper into the ground. Both he and Webb, in front of her, scowled at her.

"I thought you two wanted to exchange me for a ransom," she said.

"We do," Lambert said. "We are."

"No one will give you a ransom if I am dead."

"They will if they see you tied to a tree and think you are alive," Webb said.

Anne pulled harder at the hole in the netting. Another thread broke. "They are not stupid. All they will have to do is take one look at my lifeless body, and they will know. And you will hang for my murder."

"They will not think you are dead." Webb pressed her hand against her chest and called out in a breathy, weak voice, "Mother? Someone? Please help me."

Anne cringed. Her senses shot out in every direction but found no place to land. "That is like my voice."

"It is." Webb grabbed her arm and tugged her forward again, faster than before. "A hidden talent, you might say."

Anne took in great gulps of air. She scraped harder at the binding. Her fingertips felt raw and sticky, but still she scraped. She yanked the netting. It ripped. Kept ripping. Hope leapt through her. Anne pulled harder, but the remaining netting still held her.

Webb said, "Fight all you want, but I must tell you it will not do you any good. There are some events in this life a body cannot run away from, no matter how strong that body is. And you are trapped in one of those events."

"On the outside or the inside?" Lambert muttered.

"What are you talking about?" Webb said to him.

Lambert, his stance rigid, glared ahead of them. "Something my daughter said."

They reached a pile of logs that lined the approaching woodland. Anne tried to pull away from her captors and run into the trees, but they gripped her arms tighter. They dragged her down the grassy, muddy slope to a rowboat tied to a large boulder at the edge of the lake. Low ripples swelled the water's surface and splashed on and away from the shore like a gentle, whooshing kiss. A Judas kiss.

Webb pulled Anne harder toward the water, but Lambert, his grip on Anne's arm still tight, stopped. Anne fought to get away, but no matter how much she squirmed or how many times she kicked their legs, neither captor released her.

"I told you I want no part of any killing," he said.

Webb and Lambert glared at one another.

"Running away always was your specialty," Webb said.

He stared at Anne. His gaze was furrowed, hard, like the jagged rocks that had cut her feet.

"Help me," Anne screamed.

"At least help me get her in the boat," Webb said.

Still he stared at Anne. He rubbed the back of his neck with one hand.

Anne yanked backward, slipped from his grip, charged back up the bank.

"You idiot!" Webb screamed at him.

Anne pushed her feet, her legs, harder through the wet soil. Webb grabbed her, pulled her backward, and dragged Anne into the water toward the boat. Reaching it, she grabbed it with one hand and, with strength Anne hadn't known the woman possessed, shoved Anne inside. Webb climbed in after her.

"Help!" Anne cried to Lambert, who still stood, motionless, on the shore.

Webb grabbed the oars and paddled to the middle of the lake. She stopped. "Goodbye, Miss de Bourgh." She pushed her. Anne, her hands still tied behind her back, fell forward. Cold water slapped her skin. Her body plunged below the lake's surface. She kicked. Her skirt tangled round her legs. *Air.*

Down.

She yanked at the netting around her wrists. *Please break.*

Down.

She hit the bottom and kicked upward toward the surface's blurred light. *Air.*

The light grew closer . . . closer . . . *I need air.*

Down.

She kicked, but she barely moved upward. The surface was too far away. *I am going to die here.*

No! She kicked again and yanked at the netting. Fight. Do not inhale.

A large shadow dove toward her. *Mr. Talbot.* He grabbed Anne's arm, tugged her with him to the surface, and pushed her head above the water. She gasped, gasped again, and clung to him as he came up behind her.

"Where did you come—" She coughed. "How did you . . . ?"

Mr. Talbot tore the binding from her hands and shoved Anne toward the shallows. "Swim!"

Anne winced. She did not know how to do much more than float. But there was no time to tell Mr. Talbot so, for Lambert was suddenly beside them. He grabbed Mr. Talbot around the shoulders from the side. Mr. Talbot, kicking, somehow staying afloat, elbowed him in the gut then swung around and punched him in the jaw.

Again Anne's shoulders sank beneath the waves. She gasped. *Do not panic.* She swished her hands back and forth in front of her the way Blanc and Mrs. Dramwell had taught her. Her body rose higher but not high enough she could easily fall forward and float. *Fall forward anyway.*

Lambert shoved Mr. Talbot's head under the water.

"No!" Anne screamed.

Mr. Talbot resurfaced.

Anne exhaled in relief.

Mr. Talbot pulled Lambert backward. Splashing, punching, pushing, they fought beneath and above the water. "Go!" Mr. Talbot yelled at her.

Anne took a deep breath, aimed her body toward the shore, and fell onto her stomach. She kicked even as water surged over her face. Was she sinking? She kicked harder. Sooner than she expected, she reached the shallows. She crawled onto the muddy bank, breathed, and looked up. Webb stormed toward her. Anne struggled to her feet and stumbled up the shore.

Webb grabbed her arm. Anne swung around, punched her with her free hand, and pushed her toward the water and away from the shore. Anne clambered up the bank, but before she reached dry land, Webb, yelling, grabbed Anne's skirt, pulled her off-balance, and yanked her back into the deeper water. Anne whirled. She slammed her fist into Webb's shoulders and kicked her in the shins. Webb slapped Anne across the face, but before Webb could lower her arm, Anne grabbed it with one hand and clawed the length of Webb's cheek with her free hand. Webb stomped on Anne's foot. She clutched Anne's neck with both hands and squeezed, choking her. Anne gasped, squirmed, and kicked backward, shoving Webb backward.

Anne scrambled up the lake bed.

Lambert sloshed toward them.

"Finally," Webb huffed. She caught up to Anne and grabbed her hair.

Anne, screaming, clutched the back of her head. She scanned behind Lambert to the middle of the lake. The empty lake. "Where is Mr. Talbot?"

"Take her," Webb said to Lambert, breathing hard. "Throw her back into the water. Make sure she stays there."

Lambert ran past them.

"Where are you going?" Webb yelled.

He glanced back over his shoulder, toward the middle of the lake. "After the waiting constables."

"What constables? Get back here, you coward!"

He kept running.

Webb stared after him; her grip on Anne's hair relaxed.

Sudden renewed strength surged through Anne. She shoved Webb away from her and charged up the bank. A step before she crossed the ridge, she tripped on an exposed root and dropped face-first into the grass. Webb grabbed both of Anne's feet and once again dragged her down the bank. Anne clawed at the grass. She tried to kick, but Webb held her fast.

"You will unhand Miss de Bourgh."

Relief, hope, so many emotions rushed through Anne. *Mr. Talbot. He is alive.*

"I will not take orders from a cripple," Webb said.

Mr. Talbot grabbed—vised—Webb's arm. She fought, but her struggles were no match for Mr. Talbot's strength. Finally, unable to get away, she released Anne's feet.

Anne, finally free, stood. She faced Mr. Talbot. Water dripped from his flat, dark hair, down his eyelashes, over his clenched jaw, and onto his moss-splattered tailcoat. His gaze locked with hers and held it. Her pulse stilled even as her thoughts leapt into the sky. Mr. Talbot had jumped fully dressed into the water to save her. He had not even removed his boots.

Anne glared at Webb, who still struggled against Mr. Talbot's grip. "Mr. Talbot may have a crippled foot, but he is the best person either of us will ever know."

"Come now," Mr. Talbot muttered beneath his breath.

Webb scowled between the two of them. "You are a fool, Miss de Bourgh."

"And you are blind." *To goodness.* There was no point in adding that last thought aloud, so Anne instead looked back to Mr. Talbot, who turned Webb toward the forest.

"You are also my prisoner," he added. "Come along."

Horses neighed. Webb cursed, and Anne grinned as the three constables who had been investigating Dr. Sinclair's murder, along with a fourth rider, approached them on horseback from around the south side of the forest. They rode single file. That seemed odd to Anne until she noticed Lambert, his wrists bound by a rope tied to Headborough Powell's saddle, trudging behind the second constable. The third and fourth man, she assumed, guarded their rear.

Webb kicked Mr. Talbot in the shins. "Let go of me, you crippled idiot."

"Gladly." As if Webb was little more than an unruly rag doll, he dragged her up the bank and limped toward the constables. Anne followed them, and Mr. Talbot handed Webb over to Headborough Powell.

"Traitor!" she yelled at Lambert.

Lambert, his expression stone, looked away from her. "I am not a killer."

"He did run right to us," the constable said. "But you are wrong in thinking he is the only reason you were caught. Lady Catherine sent us after you hours ago, and Mr. Talbot was watching for you long before you showed up. All that remained was for us to arrive and take you into custody."

"He could have killed me," Mr. Talbot said to Anne beneath his breath. "But he did not. He said he had changed his mind."

"You trusted him?"

"No, but at that point . . . without his decision, without his distracting Mrs. Webb, I could not have saved you, Miss de Bourgh."

Webb glowered at Anne, but the lake, the trees, even the sun danced around Anne's heart. Mr. Talbot was there.

CHAPTER THIRTY-FIVE

THE CONSTABLE BOUND WEBB'S HANDS with one end of a long rope, attached the other end to his saddle, and glanced down at Anne's bare and cut-up feet. At least they had stopped bleeding.

He removed a handkerchief from his pocket. "Perhaps this will help, miss."

The younger of the other two constables also climbed off his horse and likewise handed her his handkerchief for the other foot. "I know it is not the best of circumstances, but as I will be riding with Mr. Talbot and yourself while the others take the prisoners to London, I am afraid you will be obliged to ride with me."

"Actually," Mr. Talbot said, "my horse is just north of here. Since Miss de Bourgh and I are acquainted, perhaps she would feel more comfortable riding on my horse while I lead it?"

"Thank you, Mr. Talbot," Anne said. "I appreciate your thoughtfulness."

Mr. Talbot's gaze at her sparked. He turned back to the constable. "I will be only a few minutes. In the meantime, perhaps you could help Miss de Bourgh with her feet?"

He left Anne with the constable and hobbled off at a quicker pace than Anne had yet seen him move. The constable helped her walk to a nearby log where he then helped her wrap her feet on the few occasions she needed an extra hand. The men's handkerchiefs were by no means clean, but the fabric's soft pressure against her cut and swollen soles gave them a measure of comfort.

Soon after, Mr. Talbot rode toward them. Anne moved to get up from the log, but halfway upright, she collapsed back onto it. She smiled apologetically to the constable. "It appears my strength has exhausted itself."

Mr. Talbot reached them and dismounted.

"It is no wonder, miss," the constable said. "You have been through quite an ordeal."

"At least the worst is over."

She took the constable's offered hand and again tried to stand, but in the next moment, Mr. Talbot, instantly at her side, scooped her off the log, limped to his horse, and, leaning most of his weight on his good leg, lifted her onto the saddle. "Are you comfortable?"

She shifted herself, but as she clasped the reins, her ears began to ring, and she doubled over. *Hang on. Do not faint.*

"Miss de Bourgh!" Mr. Talbot leapt onto the horse behind her and wrapped his arms around her middle. "Forgive me, Miss de Bourgh, but I am afraid necessity requires I ride with you."

Anne's vision swirled even as surprised heat rose up her neck and spread through her cheeks. Her embarrassment at finding herself so close to him when she was drenched to the skin and covered in mud must have been stronger than her dizziness, however, for in the next moment she regained a bit of strength and sat up taller. Her vision cleared. She glanced down at Mr. Talbot's arms wrapped around her and his hands holding the reins in front of her. "Thank you, Mr. Talbot. I fear I would have fallen off if not for you."

"Thank you for letting me catch you."

Heat. All through her body. It both hid from and clung to Mr. Talbot's closeness. She could . . . not . . . breathe.

"You are settled, then?" the constable asked.

"We are," Mr. Talbot said.

"We'd best be on, then, before full darkness hits." The constable climbed onto his horse and motioned for Headborough Powell to move forward. He did so, and the group headed toward Brighton Road.

Mr. Talbot kept his horse at the rear of the group, so far behind the last rider, in fact, he and Anne could talk in relative privacy if they chose to. And Anne should choose to. The entire reason she was there was because she had run off to tell him her real feelings before he left England. *And now he's here. Right behind me. Tell him.*

"You are certain you are not hurt?" Mr. Talbot asked.

"I am a bit worse for the wear, as you see, but—thank you for coming when you did."

"I only wish I could have caught up with you sooner. What the devil were you doing out at night in the first place?"

Her hackles rose at the vehemence she heard in his voice, and she spat, "It was morning, not night, when I left, and Mrs. Webb, whom I thought was a trustworthy lady's companion, was with me." But as soon as the words left her—no, the moment he growled after her response—she realized he was not angry. He was worried. About her. "I am sorry. That was unkind of me. Especially after all you went through to help me."

"Thank you for the apology. Now, your answer, if you please?"

Anne bit the inside of her lower lip. Last night, with desperation racing through her blood and darkness veiling her impropriety, she had believed running after Mr. Talbot was her only recourse. Yet, now, decorum sat on her chest. She, a woman, should never approach a man who was not her husband and say the truth that was in her heart. She should never say, *Will you marry me?* And yet, if ever there was a moment to do so, it was now.

Mr. Talbot's arms tensed. He cleared his throat. "I—um . . ." He cleared his throat again. "I do not know what to say."

"Why would you need to say anything? I know I was foolish, but believe me when I say I did have good intentions. After speaking with your mother, she—what I mean to say is, we believed you had decided to leave for America for all the wrong reasons, and we did not want you to leave merely because you believed a lie. So I decided to go to London and find you. Your mother told me—no, *I* needed to tell you I was not engaged to Mr. Lambert, nor did I intend ever to be so."

"You could have asked Mother to send that message to me in a letter." His voice seemed to smile, which made it impossible for her not to smile, too, but at the same time, that dratted heat once again flamed down the back of her neck.

"You are right. I could have had her send a letter, but I had wanted . . ." *to tell you I love you.*

"Perhaps you had wanted to say something more?" His voice was so soft, so close to her, all she could hear, feel, think was his nearness pulsing in rhythm with her heart.

"Like what?" she asked.

"Like the question you asked me a moment ago. I admit, while I am honored and without question pleased, I am also a bit disappointed. Generally, when a man proposes to a woman, he is expected to confess feelings of love for his intended. I had thought, since you had taken that responsibility upon yourself, you would have done the same."

Propose? Anne's thoughts dropped. They shattered over her body, piercing her core like broken glass. Had she been so completely out of herself she had unknowingly spoken her thoughts aloud? His nearness . . . his words . . . That had to be exactly what she had done. She had proposed to him without realizing it. "I am sorry, sir. You must think me a complete degenerate. I had not realized I had spoken my wishes aloud."

If his arms had been tense before, they were metal rods now.

"I must be more ill than I realized," she continued. "You must know if I were in my right mind, I never would have said—"

"Please do not take back your proposal."

"I—" *He is too quiet.* Had she humiliated him as much as she had humiliated herself?

"The truth," he said, "is I feel more for you than I believed I would ever have the privilege of feeling for anyone. I love you, Miss de Bourgh. I have loved you from almost the first moment, and though you may not have wished to propose to me just now, I do wish to propose to you. Miss Anne de Bourgh, you know who I am and who I am not. I will never be perfect—"

"You are perfect to me." She rested her hands over the top of his.

Silence as taut as a stretched rope, as bright as the stars sparkling in the sky, as warm as his arms pressing closer against her arms and sides, filled the space between the pounding of her heart and the horses' clomping through the tall grass.

"Miss de Bourgh, will you marry me?"

"Yes."

"Are you certain? Perhaps it would be best if you were to take some time to think of whom you are promising your life to. We have not known each other long."

"I do not need time to think." She laughed softly. "I proposed to you first, remember? I love you, Mr. Talbot, and I have also loved you from almost the first moment."

He leaned closer to her and kissed the back of her hair. Her muddy, wet hair.

She swallowed. "Perhaps you are the one who needs time to think. Or perhaps you would prefer we have a long engagement, to be certain.

I do not expect it will be easy for you to be related to Lady Catherine de Bourgh."

He squeezed his arms tighter around her. "Not at all. Having you at my side will more than compensate for whatever inconveniences your mother may throw at us. As far as extending our engagement is concerned, I will leave that entirely in your hands, my dear."

"What about your trip to America?"

"I believe I will consult with Mrs. Talbot about that before I make any more arrangements."

"Your mother already says she does not want you to go."

"I was not speaking of Lady Talbot."

That was right. He had said *Mrs.*, not *Lady. He means me.*

Again Mr. Talbot pressed his lips against the back of her head. "And if or when I go to America, *Mrs.* Talbot will go with me."

Anne lifted his mud-caked hands to her lips and kissed them. Twice.

CHAPTER THIRTY-SIX

ANNE HELD MR. TALBOT'S HANDS until the front constables veered toward London with the prisoners and the fourth constable moved his horse in beside Mr. Talbot's. Two men riding side by side, he believed, would be more off-putting to any outlaws. Whether or not that was true, Anne could not say. All she knew was her chance to be relatively alone with Mr. Talbot had ended, and the sense of emptiness that truth brought with it would have to be satisfied by the feel of Mr. Talbot's arms around her waist and the memory of him telling her he loved her.

They did satisfy, a little, until Brighton loomed before them and nervousness set in. Soon they would reach Anne's residence on Marine Parade. Soon she would have to not only explain her actions to her mother but would also have to confess she was now betrothed to Mr. Talbot.

Mr. Talbot either noticed her concern or felt it himself because his arms once again tensed around her. "Do not worry, my love," he whispered. "I will be there with you."

The constable glanced at them, but Anne did not care. *My love.* Mr. Talbot had called her *my love.* No one had ever in her life called her *my love,* which made the words seem all the more hallowed, like they were something sacred she alone could treasure and replay whenever she so chose—which she chose to do then over and over again until they reached the de Bourgh townhouse.

Her mother must have seen their approach, for she, leaning on her walking cane, opened the door the moment Mr. Talbot climbed off his horse from behind Anne. He lifted her down and carried her toward her mother. The constable likewise dismounted his horse and joined them at the doorway.

Her mother's yellow-tinged face paled. "Oh, my dear Anne. Can you not walk?" So much terror flashed through her face that Anne instantly remembered those first moments when she had overheard Webb confess much of what she had done was because she had wanted Anne's mother to suffer.

"Please do not worry yourself, Mother. I am well. Yes, I can walk, but—"

Her mother ushered them inside. Moments later the constable closed the door behind them.

"Miss de Bourgh is relatively all right, your ladyship," Mr. Talbot said. "But as you can see, her feet are quite injured. Is there someplace you would like me to take her where she can be properly looked after?"

Her mother looked at Anne's wrapped and bloodied bare feet. Her face paled whiter. She called, "Mrs. Kelton!" She furrowed her brows. "Where is Mrs. Webb?"

Anne swallowed.

"I am sorry to tell you this, my lady," Mr. Talbot said. "But you will likely never see Mrs. Webb again."

"Is she dead?"

"Not yet," the constable said.

Her mother's face flashed from pale to fiery and back to pale.

"Mrs. Webb is in custody," the constable continued. "She is the one who orchestrated your daughter's kidnapping. She and Mr. Lambert."

Her mother stumbled backward. The constable caught her and steadied her until she regained her composure and brushed him away. "Is there anything else I should know about this incident?"

She also killed Mrs. Jenkinson. But that information could wait until later. "She took your broach," Anne said. "And sold it."

Her mother stared at Anne. Her chin trembled. She wrung her hands. At last she whirled toward the stairs. "Where is Mrs. Kelton?"

All at once Mrs. Kelton rushed out the parlor door and into the entry. She gaped between Anne, Mr. Talbot, the constable, Anne's mother, and back to Anne. "Shall I send for Dr. Fletcher?"

"Yes," her mother said. "Immediately."

Mrs. Kelton rushed out the door, and Lady Catherine turned back to the two men. Her voice was quiet at first, but the longer she spoke, the louder and stronger it became. "I am most grateful to you, sirs, for all you have done in bringing my daughter back to me, but I cannot in good conscience keep either of you here longer. Please, if you would be so kind, Mr. Talbot, set my daughter in this chair, and the two of you can think of yourself as fully relieved from your duties to us."

"On the contrary," Anne said. "Mr. Talbot is not—" Anne was about to tell her he was not going away at all, but Mr. Talbot's anxious glance and her mother's hinted scowl told her now would not be a good time to share such news.

"You are right, my lady," Mr. Talbot said. "I am happy to set Miss de Bourgh in this chair, but if I may be so bold, I believe she would be more comfortable in her bed."

She pressed her lips into a thin almost-smile. "Of course." She dismissed the constable and again faced the staircase. "Gale!" she called.

Moments later Gale hurried down the staircase. "Yes, ma'am?"

"See that Miss de Bourgh's room is ready for her." After Gale disappeared down the upstairs hallway, she turned back to Mr. Talbot. Tightness still filled her voice, but she had managed to wipe away her frown. Anne reached out and touched her mother's arm. Anne had always admired her mother's ability to control her emotions no matter the circumstance. Perhaps one day Anne would achieve that same prowess.

"Is something amiss?" her mother asked Anne.

"No. Only, thank you for your concern."

Lady Catherine pursed her lips, but otherwise, her expression remained still. "Follow me, Mr. Talbot." She led him up the stairs to Anne's room. Gale stood to attention at the foot of the bed. "Set Miss de Bourgh down," she said, nodding toward the bed. He obliged, and she added, "You may go."

Mr. Talbot headed for the door, but when he reached it, he stopped and looked back at Anne. "I hope to see you again soon, Miss de Bourgh."

"Yes," Anne said.

He left.

"Gale," her mother continued. "While I am collecting medical supplies from the staff, please help Anne out of her muddy dress."

"Yes, my lady."

Anne did not know her mother could move as quickly as she did, even when she was healthy, for Gale had barely accomplished her task when Anne's mother returned with a bucket of water and a small box.

"You may leave us," she said to Gale. "I will see to the rest of Miss de Bourgh's needs."

"You will?" Anne blurted.

Her mother arched an eyebrow at Gale.

"Yes, madam." She curtsied and left.

Her mother scrutinized Anne. "I daresay you need a bath, but caring for your feet is the higher priority."

"Truly, Mother, it is very kind of you to so concern yourself, but if you leave the water and a few bandages, I am sure I can manage on my own."

"I am sure you can, but as you see, you will not." Then her mother actually knelt on the floor next to Anne and carefully unwrapped the constables' kerchiefs from her feet.

"Mother! You have never—are you certain you should do this?"

"Hush. I can change, can I not? As you have done? More to the point, I am your mother, and I intend to meet the needs of my daughter." She did not look up at Anne, nor did anything in the sound of her voice indicate this was not a normal situation on a normal day, but so many emotions hugged Anne's core and filled her throat that if she had known what words to say, she could not have said them.

Her mother, too, remained silent as she dabbed the wet cloth to Anne's feet.

Finally, Anne found her voice. "Mother, there is something I need to tell you."

"Why you left. I know. You told me in your letter you needed to talk to Mr. Talbot." She carefully cleaned away the mud. "There is one thing I do not understand, however. Why did you leave in the middle of the night? Surely there was nothing you had to say that could not have waited until daylight." She spread balm over Anne's sores.

"If I had waited until daylight, you would have stopped me from going."

Her mother paused. "You are correct. And I would have been right in forbidding you—a young woman such as yourself chasing after a young man? The very thought of it is unseemly. Worst of all, look what happened to you."

"What happened to me had nothing to do with Mr. Talbot. What happened to me came because I—you and I—trusted the wrong people."

At last her mother looked up at her. Her eyes glistened with emotion, but her voice was calm. "What did happen to you?"

Anne briefly described her capture and barefooted travels, but when she reached the part about her fight at the lake, her mother started wiping so many beads of sweat from her own forehead that Anne shortened her account. To be sure, her mother was a strong woman, but some things, frightening things, were best left unsaid. Except, "I also learned Webb has been poisoning you. That is why you have been feeling so poorly."

Lady Catherine stared at her. "It seems Dr. Fletcher will have two patients instead of one." At length, she took a deep breath and dried Anne's feet. "I do not think I have ever told you of your birth, have I?"

"You told me I was frail and small but had a sweet smile."

Her mother removed several bandages from the box. "You had other problems too. With your lungs, the physician said. He said I should prepare myself for your passing."

"He thought I would die?"

"Everyone did, but I refused to believe it. The moment he said those words, I vowed I would prove him wrong. I would do everything in my power to see you had the best of care. I would see you became a woman, not only of means but also one to be reckoned with."

"A woman like yourself?"

"Someone better than me, I had hoped."

"Mother?"

She wrapped a bandage around Anne's other foot. "Yes, dear?"

"I have something on a slightly different subject I need to tell you, and I know you are not going to like it. I truly do not wish to disappoint you, but in this case, I do believe what I have done and the decisions I have made are for the best."

"Do not beat about the bush, Anne. What do you wish to tell me?"

Anne rested her hand on her mother's shoulder. "I am engaged to be married to Mr. Talbot."

"You are?" It was a question, but her voice did not lilt on the end. "Well, considering all that has happened and all he has done . . ." She shifted her position and frowned. At last she said, "I am surprised he summoned enough gumption to ask you. I will have to congratulate him."

"You are?" Anne shook her head. She touched her throat. Had she heard her mother right? "You will congratulate him?"

"I did wish for you to marry a man with what I believed was more substance than I believed he had, my dear. But if that young man, a man willing to sacrifice much for you, finally found the courage to ask you, then I believe there is hope for him yet."

"He did ask me, but I am afraid . . . with everything that happened, and I am sure you would have been proud of the way he rescued me . . . even so, I am afraid I proposed to him first."

Silence.

"I assure you it was an accident."

Still silence.

"Do you mind too much?"

Her mother's lips quivered with an almost smile. "On the contrary, my dear. I could not be more proud."

CHAPTER THIRTY-SEVEN

Aliston

ANNE'S BETROTHED, MR. TALBOT, STOPPED the carriage in front of the small cottage. It was about the same size as the one Webb and Mr. Lambert—rather Kenneth Bolton, as Anne now knew his real name to be—had confined Anne in after they had kidnapped her, and older too. It was perhaps even as much as two hundred years old, but immaculately trimmed hedgerows lined either side of the road that led to it and lush green shrubs and weeded flower beds—*daylilies!*—highlighted its perimeter.

Who cares for them? she wondered. Anne inhaled. The sweet-scented air reminded her so much of her garden back at Rosings that for a moment her eyes clouded with memories of Mr. Soulden before the woodland had caught fire. The fire, Webb had said, Dr. Sinclair, whomever he really was, had set.

"Do you think this is it?" Mr. Talbot asked.

"It is as Mr. Bolton described."

Mr. Talbot helped Anne out of the carriage, and they headed up the dirt pathway to the cottage. Yesterday Webb had faced the gallows, and in a few hours more Kenneth Bolton would set sail to Botany Bay on a sentence of fifteen years transportation. Anne had visited him last night, thanked him for helping Mr. Talbot save her life, and apologized that she had not been able to do more to lighten his sentence. While he had discounted much of her apology, he had taken her up on her offer to help him in another way. Anne once again felt the outline of the letter inside her reticule.

"Was there any point in any of it?" Anne asked Mr. Talbot.

"In speaking up for him? Or in paying off his debts?"

"Not the paying of his debts. I would hate to see a child or her aunt and uncle saddled with paying the doctor. But yes, in my speaking up for him. If even the testimony of Lady Catherine de Bourgh's daughter could not sway the court, why did I even try?"

"Because you are a good person. What is more, you did help him. You gave him life instead of the gallows. As long as there is life, there is hope. Your testimony simply could not wash away his other crimes."

"I am not certain Mr. Bolton would call it hope. He knows he will likely never see his daughter again. If only he had given up the name of their fourth accomplice. Perhaps then the judge would have been more lenient."

"It is not difficult to guess who it was."

"Evans? Webb did mention him."

"Or his wife. Or both of them. In either case, they have disappeared."

"And they go free while the others suffer."

Mr. Talbot said nothing—only pressed his hand against the small of Anne's back, but the movement comforted her as no words could.

Within moments they stood before the cottage door. Mr. Talbot rapped it with the tip of his cane. A woman with dark hair pulled back in a tight bun opened it. She had sad eyes, just as Kenneth had described his sister-in-law, Fanny, would have.

"May I help you?" She curtsied and stared between the two of them.

"We are sorry to bother you, ma'am," Mr. Talbot said, "but does Miss Grace Bolton live here?"

A slight nod.

"Her father, Kenneth Bolton, sent us."

Tears filled her eyes, and her cheeks flushed. Anne could not tell if her sudden emotion was from grief or anger.

Anne pulled the wax-sealed note from her reticule. "He bade me bring this letter to her." The woman's eyes narrowed. "I am Miss de Bourgh. I spoke with him this morning, and as his ship was soon to leave the harbor, he felt I was his only chance to send this message to his daughter."

The woman again looked between the two of them and stepped back. She opened the door wider. "Please, come in. I'll get Grace."

Although children's voices laughed and squealed from somewhere outside, Fanny went through the door that led to a back room.

Anne glanced about her—a wooden table and bench, a single cupboard, an empty kettle on the floor in front of the fireplace. Six people lived here.

Two adults and now, because of Grace, four children. How could anyone survive, much less prosper, under such circumstances? Would the couple, in the end, be forced to send Grace away? To an orphanage? Or the streets? Anne shivered. Surely she could do something to prevent that. Mr. Talbot clasped her arm.

The backroom door opened, and the woman, along with a thin blonde child with dark-brown eyes entered. Her gray dress hung over her like it was nothing more than a burlap bag tied at the waist with a frayed strip of cloth. Surely it was not a bag, yet it might have been.

Anne held her hand out to the child. "You must be Grace."

The child nodded. Her eyes were like the woman's, but the half-jovial, half-worried glint in them belonged to her father.

"Come here, child."

Grace looked up at Fanny, who nodded, and walked to Anne. Anne held out the note. "Your father bade me bring this to you. He also said because you could not read"—Anne glanced at Fanny. She had not considered it until then, but perhaps Fanny could not read either—"he wanted me to read it to you. Is that all right with you?"

Grace nodded, and Anne opened the letter.

> *My beloved Gracie,*
>
> *Your mother would say I should begin with the niceties, but I'm afraid my time to write is short, and I am unwilling to waste it on such things. First, I trust that under Dr. Lambert's care, your health has returned. I suppose I may never know for myself the truth of the matter, but as your aunt let me know it was so, I will believe her, and I will rejoice.*
>
> *Second, I am entirely to blame for my actions and the course my life has taken. I did commit the crimes I was accused of, and now I must pay the penalty. However, please know, my dearest Gracie, that in the end I did do as you bade me. I stood on the inside. I helped Mr. Talbot save the woman standing before you from being murdered.*
>
> *Miss de Bourgh is the woman's name. Please thank her for trying to save me from this fate. She did it because she believes I saved her, but the truth, my dearest Gracie, is you are the one who saved her. It was your words that made me do what I did.*

> *You stand on the inside, too, all right? No matter what this*
> *world hands you, though I pray it will be good things.*
> *All my love, forever,*
> *Pa*

Anne's lips trembled. She pressed them into a tight line and scanned once more over the letter.

"Is that all of it?" Grace said.

"Yes." Anne refolded the letter and handed it to her. She took it, ran her hand over the now-broken seal, and pressed the full of it against her chest.

Fanny cleared her throat. "I daresay it is not the happiest of endings, but I suppose it was the best he could do. 'Twas a fine letter though. Thank you for bringing it, Miss de Bourgh."

"I was happy to do so."

"And thank you for all you did for my poor brother-in-law."

Anne briefly clasped Fanny's offered hand. "I only wish I could have done—" Anne's thoughts raced forward. She glanced again at the empty kettle, at the too-small room, at the daylily-filled flower vase sitting in the middle of the table. "I do not wish to be impertinent," she said, "but can you tell me who cares for the grounds hereabout?"

"'Twould be my husband, Neil." She frowned as if suddenly embarrassed. "He lost his past position as an undergardener, but Mr. Frampton now pays him what he can for that bit o' work." She shrugged. "It's something in these hard times."

An undergardener! One of the undergardeners at Rosings had taken Mr. Soulden's position when he had died, leaving an undergardener's position open. *That is how I can help.* "I wonder," Anne said, "do you think your husband might be persuaded to come to Kent and work for my mother and me on our estate at Rosings Park? We have need of an undergardener."

She swallowed. "You'd have to ask Neil, but I believe—I'm certain he'd be pleased to do so."

"You do understand you and your family would be required to leave your home here and move into one of the cottages on our estate?"

"Oh, miss!" Fanny pressed her hand against her chest. "If you would please wait here, I'll go and find him. I'm sure he's not far away." She rushed to the door. "Grace, come along. We must find your uncle."

Grace kissed her father's letter, set it on the table, and raced out the door behind her aunt, leaving Anne and Mr. Talbot alone in the cottage.

Mr. Talbot's hand slipped around Anne's waist. "This is very generous of you. Do you think your mother will mind having the family of the man who kidnapped you on her estate?"

"I will explain the situation. In the end, I believe she will be relieved the problem of needing an undergardener is resolved."

"Yet something troubles you."

"I only hope I have chosen wisely. In truth, I have never even met the man. Neil, I mean."

"That may be, but you saw his work, and you have a keen eye. I trust your judgement."

"I wish I trusted it as much as you do."

He smiled and lowered his face to hers.

Anne wanted to throw her arms around his neck, but all she did was smile and lower her eyelids. "But I suppose that same judgement chose you, so it cannot be too bad."

He moved closer to her and cupped her face in his hands. He brushed his lips over hers. "Of that I am entirely certain, Miss Anne de Bourgh."

"Soon to be Mrs. Talbot," she whispered.

"Very soon, my love."

"In two weeks."

"Yes." He kissed one cheek and then the other.

Anne closed her eyes. Would it really matter if she kissed him? She did not answer that question. She simply did it. She kissed him. Because it was what she wanted to do.

Mr. Talbot did not seem to mind either.

AUTHOR'S NOTES

JANE AUSTEN ORIGINALLY WROTE *FIRST Impressions* between 1796 and 1797. She queried it soon after for possible publication, but it was rejected. Austen continued to write other books, and after the publication of Sense and Sensibility in 1811, she significantly revised *First Impressions*. *Pride and Prejudice*, as we know it today, was ultimately published on January 28, 1813. Because Austen made her final revisions between 1811 and 1812 and because the setting for *Pride and Prejudice* is only specified as sometime during the Napoleonic War (1799–1815), I imagined *Pride and Prejudice* as taking place between 1811 and 1812, allowing *Finding Anne de Bourgh* to begin in 1813.

I am not Jane Austen, nor do I wish to be compared to her. I am simply a fan of her work, and I have frequently found myself intrigued by Anne de Bourgh. In *Pride and Prejudice*, Austen positions Anne as a woman in the shadows of not only her mother but also her own life. Anne is the ultimate archetypal waif. However, there are three truths I fully believe, and they have influenced the creation of the lives and characters found in *Finding Anne de Bourgh*. They are:

1. Fictional characters, like living people, are frequently viewed differently by different people, so while many readers may consider Anne to be nothing more than a sickly, uninteresting woman, I see her as a young lady with a heart and soul of her own who has never been given the chance to let them shine.
2. Most mothers love their children, and though they make mistakes while raising them, they ultimately want the best for them.
3. People can change their lives and their characters for the better.

During the mid- to late Regency Era, manufacturers developed a popular emerald-green pigment, which was used in several products, including wall paper, glass, children's toys, and confectionary. Unfortunately, "emerald green" was made with copper arsenite, a highly toxic, deadly element. Scientists first discovered the pigment's toxic nature in 1822, but its use was not outlawed until 1960. Therefore, in *Finding Anne de Bourgh*, the fictional Rowes' death was never solved, because they died after eating sugar leaves colored with emerald green, and authorities at that time had not yet discovered emerald green's toxicity.[1]

Before and while writing *Finding Anne de Bourgh*, I researched numerous books and websites, which Regency-Era enthusiasts may enjoy. Three were especially helpful and enjoyable: *Georgette Heyer's Regency World* by Jennifer Kloester, *What Jane Austen Ate and Charles Dickens Knew* by DaNeil Pool, "Austenprose Sanditon Group Read: 'A Match for Every Disorder': Sea-Bathing in the early 19th century" at https://austenonly.com/2010/03/20/austenprose-sanditon-group-read-a-match-for-every-disorder-sea-bathing-in-the-early-19th-century/, and "Sea Bathing in the Regency Period" by Merryn Allingham at https://merrynallingham.com/regency-period/sea-bathing-in-the-regency-period/.

---

1 Vic. (2010, March 5). *Jane Austen's World*. Retrieved April 15, 2018, from Emerald Green or Paris Green, the Deadly Regency Pigment: https://janeaustensworld.word-press.com/2010/03/05/emerald-green-or-paris-green-the-deadly-regency-paint/

ABOUT THE AUTHOR

RONDA GIBB HINRICHSEN LIVES WITH her husband on a small farm in Northern Utah. They are the parents of three children, care for a few cows and goats, and own a thirty-seven-pound dog who thinks she should either be carried or sitting on her owners' laps. Ronda has a passion for reading, writing, and music, though not necessarily in that order, and she enjoys traveling the world with her husband. For more information about Ronda or to contact her, visit her website at rondahinrichsen.com.